I0594987

THE BEACH HOUSE

a novel

By Stephanie Pass

Copyright © 2025 by Stephanie Pass
All rights reserved.

No part of this publication may be reproduced, distributed, or transmitted in any form or by any means, including photocopying, recording, or other electronic or mechanical methods, without the prior written permission of the publisher, except as permitted by U.S. copyright law. For permission requests, contact stephanie@authorstephaniepass.com

The story, all names, characters, and incidents portrayed in this production are fictitious. No identification with actual persons (living or deceased), places, buildings, and products is intended or should be inferred.

Book Cover by Stephanie Pass
1st Edition 2025

To the believers in red strings and right
timing—
Love can be late and still be perfect.

***

BOOKS BY STEPHANIE PASS

THE ENCHANTED HEART SERIES

0.5 THE ALCHEMY OF US
Available Now

1 TROUBLE OF THE MOST
WONDERFUL KIND
Available Now

2 SOMETIME AROUND MIDNIGHT
Available Now

3 THE BEACH HOUSE
Available Now

HELL OF A TIME SERIES

1 THE FIRST SIN
Available Now

* * *

Content Warning

Every love story carries a little bit of heartbreak before it finds its way home. This one is no different.

The Beach House touches on themes of grief, loss, and second chances—alongside moments of joy, healing, and rediscovery. Within these pages, you'll find references to:

- The death of parents in a past accident

- A car crash and resulting injuries

- A secret teenage pregnancy and adoption

While the story centers on hope, love, and belonging, please take care of your heart as you read. If you've walked through any of these experiences yourself, know that Mallie and Jace's journey honors the messy, beautiful ways people find their way back to each other —and to themselves.

The Beach House Playlist

"*You and I Both*" - Jason Mraz
"*Love Story*" - Taylor Swift
"*August*" - Taylor Swift
"*You Belong with Me*" - Taylor Swift
"Black Coffee" - Nightly
"*seven*" - Taylor Swift
"*right where you left me*" - Taylor Swift
"*Jump Rope Gazers*" - The Beths
"*The Night We Met*" - Lord Huron
"*I Think I Really Love Her*" - Telehope
"*Kiss Me*" - Six Pence None the Richer
"*I Will Follow You into the Dark*" - Death Cab for Cutie
"*Ode to a Conversation Stuck in Your Throat*" - Del Water Gap
"*LA Lonely*" - Fly by Midnight
"*Close to You*" - Dayglow
"*All I Ever Dream About*" - daydreamers
"*Invisible*" - Knox

"*This Love*" - Taylor Swift
"*Feels Like*" - Gracie Abrams
"*Dress*" - Taylor Swift
"*Cigarettes & Wine*" - Del Water Gap
"*The Love You Want*" - Sleep Token
"*Atlantic*" - Sleep Token
"*Waterfalls*" - The Wldlfe
"*See Her Out*" - Francis and the Lights
"*Remember When*" - Wallows
"*Beach House*" - daydreamers
"*Clearest Blue*" - CHVRCHES
"*Medicine*" - The 1975
"*Fix You*" - Coldplay
"*Treacherous*" - Taylor Swift
"*Where's My Love*" - SYML
"*ILYSB*" - LANY
"*Mess It Up*" - Gracie Abrams
"*Good Intentions*" - daydreamers
"*Bloom*" - The Paper Kites
"*Light On*" - Maggie Rogers
"*I Would Do Anything for You*" - Foster the People
"*Miles Ahead*" - The Strike
"*Wanna Go Back*" - babyidondlikeyou
"*Always Been You*" - Shawn Mendes
"*Once in a Lifetime*" - John Michael Howell
"*First Day of My Life*" - Bright Eyes

CHAPTER ONE

Jace

Present Day

I hadn't been home to Dallas in months, maybe longer. Everything looked smaller now—my old room, the bed with its squeaky frame, the posters I'd half-ripped off the wall but never finished taking down. The air smelled like cinnamon and wood polish, like it always did when Mom cleaned before I came home. It was weird how a place could feel exactly the same while I felt like a completely different person.

We were leaving in a week—hitting the road as the opening band for one of the biggest tours we'd ever landed. The label was pushing for one more track to finish our sophomore album. We had good stuff, solid stuff, but nothing felt like *the song*. The one people wouldn't skip, that resonated. The one they'd sing along to, that stayed with them.

I dropped onto my bed, letting out a breath, and that's when I saw it—the notebook.

It was half-buried under an old shoebox on my nightstand, edges worn, the cover dull and peeling at the corners. My chest tightened the second I picked it up. I flipped through, past scribbled chord progressions and scraps of lyrics I'd long forgotten.

I knew exactly what I was looking for. I hadn't let myself think about it in a long time, but when I found it—buried in that notebook—I felt it hit like a punch to the chest. The melody. The scribbled lyrics. The weight of everything I never got to say. It was hers. It was always hers—*Mallie's song.*

I stared at the page, the words just as raw and desperate as the day I'd written them. That day was burned into me—how everything unraveled, how she disappeared like a door slammed shut. And still, reading those lines, I could feel it all like it had happened yesterday.

"You said always in a whisper, under stars and salty air..."

I didn't need to read the rest. I remembered every line.

I sat up, heart pounding, and pulled my guitar out of its case. The strings were a little stiff, but something clicked when I strummed the first chord. The melody came rushing back, simple and soft and full of an ache that still lived behind my ribs to this day.

I grabbed my phone, opened the voice memos app, and hit record.

"You were my truth in a world of noise, now I'm just a name, just one of those boys..."

The words fell out of me like they'd been waiting. My voice was lower now, rougher around the edges, but the song still fit.

I played through to the last chord and let it ring out before hitting stop. The room fell quiet again, but not in a hollow way. It felt full—like the past and the present had finally come together and shaken hands.

I named the file **Real You (demo)** and dropped it into the band group chat and lay back on the bed.

Me: Just found this. Might be the one we're missing.

A few moments passed before Dean replied.

Dean: Holy shit. Where'd you pull from? This is the one. Don't change a word.

I let the phone fall to my chest and stared up at the ceiling, the guitar still in my lap and the notebook open beside me.

My chest ached. All this time, yet she was rarely not in my thoughts and always somehow still in the music. Still in me. And the truth? The truth finally had somewhere to go.

I reached for the notebook again, meaning to tuck it back into the drawer—but something else caught my eye. Sitting on top of the nightstand, just beneath where the notebook had been half-buried, was a paperback. I hadn't noticed it before.

Every Summer After, the title read. I stared at it for a second. Was this… a romance novel?

I picked it up slowly, flipping it over like it might explain itself. I'd never read one before—not really my thing—but the name gave me a weird feeling I couldn't shake. *Every Summer After.*

I wondered if my mom had left it in here by mistake, maybe while cleaning. But something about that didn't quite track. She wasn't exactly the dog-ear type. She usually had an eReader tucked in her purse.

But this one? It was covered in margin notes. Tiny

writing in black ink, curved letters trailing through scenes, thoughts squeezed between paragraphs, underlined quotes, and loops around full sentences. It felt… private. A little haunting, honestly.

I thumbed through a few pages, half-curious now, half unsettled. Whoever had written in it hadn't just read the book—they felt it—reacted to it. Then my finger landed on a note scribbled on the corner of page 237.

But when I read it… I froze.

I didn't lie. I never would.
You were there. You know the truth.
I carry you with me now…

My breath caught. I stared at the words like they might rearrange themselves into something else. Anything else. But they didn't.

Those words. Mallie. All those years ago. The message I hadn't seen until days later. A message I had never been able to get out of my head, even now, years later. I sank back onto the bed, heart pounding, the book still in my hands.

What the hell was this?

It didn't make sense. How could her text—*her words*—be in a book that had been published years later? I flipped to the copyright page. Yeah, it had been published well after that year. So what was this? A coincidence? Some weird, poetic glitch in the matrix? Or… something else?

The room suddenly felt smaller. Colder. Like the past, or something, was watching me. I sat there for a long time, turning the book over in my hands, running my thumb across that one line in the margin over and over again. *I carry you with me now…*

I didn't know what it meant back then or now.

But suddenly, I couldn't stop thinking about her. Not just all those summers. But the girl who might've tried—against everything stacked between us—to still reach me.

Two days later, I was back in L.A., running on airport coffee and adrenaline. We had just a few days to make this song work before we hit the road on the biggest tour we'd ever been a part of. We were opening for The Fire Department, a band we'd all grown up blasting in our bedrooms, pretending our guitars were plugged into something bigger than heartbreak and garage amps.

We were holed up in our producer's studio by noon, crammed into a narrow space that smelled like old shag carpet and the kind of hope you can only hear through headphones. The booth was a little warm, the lights low, and the pressure high, but the second we started laying down tracks, everything clicked. The band fell into place like we'd been playing this song for years. It felt easy, and rare, and a little bit like... magic.

By the end of the third night, the work was done. We sprawled out on the ratty couch in the back room, passing around a box of cold pizza and listening to the playback on studio monitors that made every sound feel ten feet tall. It was amazing. Better than I expected.

Would anyone guess I wrote this as a fifteen-year-old kid with a broken heart and no clue how to handle it? Would they hear the truth behind the verses? The ache between the chords? I wasn't sure I could ever tell anyone, not even my bandmates, not the whole story. Not the part where I'd loved someone enough to etch her into my soul, then lost her to something I still didn't fully understand.

Dean leaned forward, nodding like he'd just heard gospel. "This is it," he said. "I can feel it. This is the song that puts us on the map."

The sound engineer turned around. "We need a title for the track."

I hesitated for a second, then said, "Real You."

Dean grinned. "We're playing it on tour. No way around it."

We stayed up all night getting it tight—reworking transitions, practicing harmonies, making sure it was show-ready. I was running on fumes, but the adrenaline kept me sharp and lit up from the inside.

And still, underneath all of it, I couldn't stop thinking about her. *Mallie.* The girl who wrecked me. The girl who, every summer, made me believe in always. Where was she now? Did she ever think about me? Had she ever heard one of our songs and wondered if it was about her?

Every time I hit the chorus, I felt like I was answering her last words—the ones I'd never forgotten. *I didn't lie. I never would. You were there. You know the truth. I carry you with me now.* And maybe, wherever she was, she'd hear this and know... I'd been carrying her, too. I'd never let go. I was still here—waiting, and hoping we'd find our way back to each other again.

By the time we rolled into Dallas, everything hurt. My throat was raw, my body ached, and the high I'd been living on for the last few nights was officially gone. The van smelled like old fries, wet socks, and something sickly sweet I didn't want to identify. We were down a set of cymbals, two guitar cables, and one very expensive pedalboard that had "mysteriously vanished" in Albuquerque.

The universe had been punching us in the face for

days. But somehow, *Real You* was climbing. Spotify had picked it up on some algorithmic whim, and now people were actually listening. Singing. Every night, the voices in the crowd got louder—lines I'd written with shaking hands now being shouted back at me like they belonged to everyone. It was... surreal.

And tonight? Tonight was my hometown—the only stop in Texas on the whole tour. I hadn't really been back in years—not counting the whirlwind two-day crash at my parents' place a little while ago. It felt strange seeing the skyline again, familiar and different all at once. I leaned against the window as we pulled into Deep Ellum, taking in the old streets, the glowing bars, the hum of a city that used to be home.

"Hey," Dean called from the front. "You good?"

I nodded, clearing my throat. "Yeah. Just... haven't been back here in a long time."

He didn't say anything, but I felt him watching me in the rearview.

Mallie's family had lived hours south, down in Austin. But still, something about being here stirred the feeling I thought I'd buried years ago. This ridiculous, impossible hope. Like maybe she'd hear one of our songs and show up.

I knew it was stupid. She was probably long gone, living some life that didn't include me somewhere far away. But I couldn't shake it. That quiet flicker that somewhere in this massive, humming city... she might be here, still think of me, and remember.

We pulled up to the venue, a mid-size club with exposed brick and weathered murals. I swallowed hard, stepping out into the humid Texas afternoon. Something about it just felt like nostalgia and second chances.

I couldn't shake the weird feeling, and I let myself lean into the hope that she just might be somewhere in the crowd tonight. Maybe listening. Maybe even singing the words. And maybe carrying me still. Just like I'd never stopped carrying her.

CHAPTER TWO

Jace

Age 5 - Rockport

The new people were late.

Mom said they were her college best friend's family and that I had to "make a good impression," whatever that means. She said the new family would be here any minute. Another summer, another family. Most times, there weren't any kids my age.

I was already on my second juice pouch and my fourth pirate battle against the porch swing with the most perfect sword stick I'd found in the yard when a red car finally pulled in. My stomach did a little flip as I ran out front, sword in one hand, a purple freezer pop in the other.

My mom stepped on the porch carrying my baby brother. She swore a little girl was coming this year. A little girl the same age as me. Not just boring grown-ups and teenagers who just sat around. I straightened up and squinted into the sun. The lady in the front seat opened her door first. She wore big sunglasses and smiled like a mom.

"Tessa, what a great location!" she said, all excited, like she'd never seen the ocean before.

My mom smiled back and waved. Grown-ups were always smiling and waving.

Then a teenage boy got out of the backseat, tall and skinny with headphones and messy blond hair. He didn't even look around—just shoved his hands in his pockets like he was thirty and allergic to fun. My stomach sank.

I stared at the driveway and sighed. Great. Another summer of digging holes by myself. I kicked the porch post, just a little.

But then... the other back door opened—and a little girl jumped out. She had dark, wavy hair in pigtails that bounced when she moved. Her shorts had stars on them, and her pink t-shirt had a sparkly unicorn across the front. She was wearing sneakers and had one of those Band-Aids with a mermaid on her knee.

She looked fast. And maybe fun. She didn't look like a kid who'd be scared of the ocean. I leaned forward a little, watching her. Please don't be one of those kids who never want to get dirty, like those girls at school who always wore dresses and would sit in a circle and talk about dumb things like kittens during recess.

She looked around and squinted at the house. She didn't smile. She stood behind the car door like she was ready to run back home. But my stomach felt funny. Maybe this summer wouldn't be boring after all. Or maybe I had eaten too many freezer pops.

But... maybe this year, I had someone to play pirates with. She could be a... princess or something. Or maybe, I thought, as I stood on the porch step, she'd wanna be a pirate, too. I'd be okay with that. I'd be... more than okay with that.

Mom nudged me. "Go say hi, Jameson."

I hopped down. "Hey!" I shouted, already halfway down the steps. "Wanna see a pirate ship?"

She blinked at me like I'd said something in Martian.

I walked right up to her. "So… you're the girl?" I asked.

She blinked. "What girl?"

"The one whose mom's Liz-buff."

She stared. "You mean Elizabeth?"

"Yeah, that's what I said."

She didn't say anything, so I tried something else. "I'm Jameson."

Still nothing.

"What's your name?"

She sighed. "Mallory."

I squinted. "Mallie?"

She opened her mouth like she was going to correct me, but then closed it again.

"So… wanna see it?" I asked, already walking toward the sand with my sword. I looked over my shoulder and said, "It's real, you know."

She followed. I knew she would. Girls always followed pirates.

"What's real?"

"The pirate ship." Then, I added quickly. "You can be the pirate queen."

Behind us, the screen door squeaked again. "Mallory! Do not get in the water!" Her mom called, voice big as a lighthouse. "Sand only! Sonny—keep an eye on them!"

"I got it," the teenager groaned, peeling off his headphones like it hurt, trudging after me with the slowest feet in Texas.

I handed Mallie a stick and pointed toward the shoreline. "We gotta find the treasure before the tide comes in."

She was quiet for a while, but she helped. Dug fast, too. When I said the sandcastle was our fort and that the plastic bucket was the royal treasure chest, she nodded like she already knew how this worked.

We were digging, looking for buried treasure, which was probably just a cool rock or a piece of sea glass, when she said it. "Jameson sounds like a dad's name."

I looked up, squinting at her through the sun. "It's my name."

She scrunched her nose like she didn't believe me. "But it's so… serious."

"It's a pirate name," I said. "Captain Jameson. That sounds cool."

She giggled and shook her head. "Nope. Still sounds like a dad. I'm gonna call you Jace."

I blinked. "What?"

"You'll be Jace," she said again, like it was obvious. "It's… better."

I thought about it for a second. No one had ever called me that before. Not even my mom. But when she said it, I liked it. It sounded like I could be a real pirate. Or a rock star. Or both.

I grinned. "Okay," I said, brushing sand off my hands. "But then we have to be pirates. Mallie and Jace, the Pirate Raiders."

When she grinned back at me, her face did a tiny crinkle-dot on one side, and I liked it. I didn't know the word for it—just that I wanted to make it show again.

"Deal," she said.

And just like that, I was Jace.

At one point, she asked, "Where's your dad?"

"Working," I said. "But he's coming in a few days.

My baby brother's here. He's named David. Mostly, he just drools."

David was in his bouncer in the living room when we got back, gnawing on a toy crab like it owed him money.

"See?" I said. "He's not very interesting yet."

She giggled again, and it made my belly feel funny in a good way. I didn't know why, but I wanted her to do it again. Maybe a hundred times. Maybe forever.

That night, we sat on the porch steps eating freezer pops while our moms talked and David made gurgling noises in his seat.

"You're kinda cool for a girl," I told her.

She rolled her eyes, but I could tell by the way her lips did this weird thing that she was trying not to smile. When she didn't make me stop calling her Mallie, I figured we were best friends now. And that meant someday I was probably gonna marry her.

CHAPTER THREE

Mallie

Present Day

The plane touched down with a jolt, dragging me out of the sleep I'd fallen into somewhere over the Pacific. My head throbbed from crying, and my back ached from sitting in the same position for nearly sixteen hours. I stood up, stretched, and then reached down to grab my bag from beneath the seat.

Thailand already felt like a different lifetime, even though it had only been a day since I walked out of the apartment and slammed the door on Devin and the girl he swore was "just a friend" in that stupid band he joined.

Six years together. Four years of bouncing around the world like we were the stars of some bohemian travel blog. And now I was back in Texas with nothing but a broken heart and a suitcase full of clothes that felt like they belonged to someone else.

I still couldn't believe I'd finally dumped him for good. It just took me finally calling Sonny, even if my fingers trembled as I dialed.

My big brother hadn't even hesitated. "Let me buy you a ticket home. Come stay with us."

Us. The word immediately brought Claire to mind, sending a flutter of nerves through my chest. It was funny since I'd been the one who helped Sonny find her again. But that didn't calm my anxiety now.

I'd only met her once, years ago, when they first met, that night he brought her to Pizza Verona. She'd seemed kind, warm even, but this would be different. This wasn't small talk and passing smiles. This was staying under her roof, probably becoming an emotional mess on her guest bed. Me, the girl showing up without much of a job, a plan, or even a clue.

I followed the slow-moving line of passengers off the plane, rolling my shoulders under my sweatshirt and popping my neck. The hum of the airport hit me all at once—conversations overlapping, carts beeping, the sharp scent of coffee and fried food in the air.

As I made my way toward baggage claim, my mind wandered the way it always did when I was this tired, this hollowed out, straight back to the past—to Rockport. To him. *Jace*—the boy I'd grown up with, the boy I loved with my whole heart before it all fell apart.

Our families rented the same beach house on the Texas coast every summer. It was one of those traditions that didn't seem all that special at the time, just something that happened, expected, and reliable. I didn't realize how much I'd come to cherish those summers until they were gone.

Every summer since I was five. Every year, without fail, he was there. Jameson. But I never called him that. To me, he was always Jace.

A soft smile tugged at my lips as I pictured the first time we met when we were five—me, quiet and wide-eyed, clinging to my mom's hand, and him, with sun-kissed skin, wild hair, bright green eyes, and a purple freezer pop in one hand. He came over, grinning, and asked if I wanted to play pirates. He even gave me a sword.

From that moment on, we were a pair. A summer duo. Peanut butter and jelly, sunburns, and pirates' treasure. We chased waves until our legs gave out, built sandcastles with seashell flags, and shared freezer pops on the porch until our tongues turned ridiculous shades of red and blue.

He called me Mallie from day one—mushed it up in his mouth like he wasn't quite sure how it was supposed to sound, then grinned and decided he liked it that way. I wrinkled my nose and told him to stop. I didn't mean it.

And when he told me his name was Jameson, I squinted at him and said, "That's a dad name."

He blinked, confused.

"So I'm gonna call you Jace."

But he didn't argue. In fact, he grinned and said I could be the pirate queen.

And that was it. Like those names themselves stitched a secret between us, something that was just for us. A version of me that only existed with him in the summer.

Looking back, those summers were some of the sweetest moments of my life. Simple. Golden. Untouched by the messiness that would come later. It was just me and Jace, and the kind of friendship that made everything else in the world feel like background noise.

When we were thirteen, he kissed me for the first time that summer, awkward and sweet. I still remember the feel of his lips. The summer we were fifteen was filled with secret kisses and whispered I love yous. There were so many quiet moments that summer that it felt like the entire world had narrowed to just the two of us.

And then… our first time. My first everything. It was beautiful. It should've stayed beautiful. Yet, it was the beginning of the end of everything in the worst possible way. We just didn't know it, and then… I never saw him again after that summer.

My breath hitched. It had been years, but the memories still hit like saltwater in a fresh wound. I pushed my hair back and kept walking, eyes fixed on the baggage claim signs ahead. But… my mind stayed stuck in the past. In Rockport. In that house by the sea. In the boy who once looked at me like I was the only girl in the world.

Where are you now, Jace?

Was he still in Texas? Did he ever do anything with his love of music? Had he gotten married? Built a life? Did he ever think about me? I bit my lip, chest tightening with questions I didn't dare speak aloud.

I'd made it through customs, picked up my bag, and wandered until the dull ache in my back reminded me I'd been sitting down for nearly twenty hours. My hair was a mess, my skin felt dry and gross from the recycled plane air, and I hadn't slept more than an hour at a time—but I was home. Or something like it.

The clink of ice in my glass and the low hum of chatter offered a strange kind of comfort as I sank into a barstool just past security. I pulled out my phone and dialed Sonny. He picked up on the second ring.

"Mal?" he asked, slightly breathless. "You back in Texas?"

"Yeah, just landed. I'm still at the airport. Thought I'd grab a drink before I try to figure out how to Uber all the way to you."

"Hang on a sec…" There was a rustle of papers and what sounded like furious typing. "I was just about to take a break. I'm knee-deep in a scene, a big plot twist, my detective's finally figuring out a suspect after 200 pages of being an idiot. Um… I hope it's okay… I sent Claire to get you. I checked your flight hours ago, and she's already on the way. She's not far."

"Um…," I hesitated, just for a second, but then guilt crept in. I was already imposing. The last thing I wanted was to make Sonny feel like he had to drop everything for me. "Yeah, uh, yeah, that's totally fine. Don't stop writing on my account."

"You're the best. Claire should be there in, like, thirty minutes. She's excited to see you."

"That's great," I said, injecting as much warmth into my voice as I could manage. "Can't wait to catch up with her."

Sonny didn't catch my hesitation. He launched into something about dinner plans and Thai food. I smiled through it, said all the right things, then hung up and immediately felt the nerves fluttering in my chest.

Of course, Sonny was busy. He was writing a book. He was getting married. Of course, this made the most sense. I was the one showing up with emotional baggage in addition to the literal kind. The least I could do was not make a fuss about the ride.

Truth was, I barely remembered what Claire looked like. We'd met once years ago. I remembered a nice smile, a soft voice, maybe red hair. But what if I didn't recognize her? What if she was waiting with a handmade sign and I walked right past her like a jerk?

I sat there sipping my watered-down vodka soda, watching travelers rush past, everyone headed somewhere with a purpose. Had I ever had a purpose? Or had I just been lost and treading water for years?

Twenty-five minutes later, Claire texted to let me know she was pulled up outside. I paid my bill and headed outside, spotting two women weaving through the crowd.

"Mallory! Welcome home!"

Claire hadn't changed much from when I met her years ago—still glowing with that effortless warmth and that smile I remembered. She did, in fact, have red hair. Her arms outstretched the moment she saw me. And next to her was someone I didn't know. She was petite, with bright eyes and dark brown short hair, wearing a black Murderino sweatshirt and balancing two iced coffees in one hand.

"You must be Mallory," she said. "I'm Darci. We brought you caffeine and zero judgment. We weren't sure what you liked, so we got an iced latte and an iced macchiato. Pick one or both." She smiled and shrugged.

"God bless you," I said, just randomly choosing a cup and chuckling, the tightness in my chest easing a little.

They talked a mile a minute as they helped me load my bags into Claire's trunk—Claire asking about the flight, Darci already telling me about the wild true crime documentary they were planning to watch that night.

"You have to watch it with us," Claire said, sliding into the driver's seat. "Murder Night is sacred. Cocktails, Thai food, and us yelling at the TV about bad life choices."

"Yeah, and if that's not therapy, I don't know what is," Darci added, twisting in her seat to grin at me. "You're officially adopted."

I laughed, really laughed, and for the first time in what felt like years, I didn't feel like I was intruding on something. I felt... included.

When we got to the house, Sonny opened the front door before we'd even made it up the walk. "There's my baby sister," he said with a grin, pulling me into a hug so tight my feet left the ground for half a second. He set me down, ruffled my hair, and then, of course, grabbed my suitcase before I could protest.

I stepped back, squinting at him. "Wait. What is that on your face? You've got a beard? When did that happen?"

He chuckled, hefting my bag onto his shoulder like it weighed nothing. "It's been... awhile."

Before I could poke at it, Darci breezed past us, smirking. "Claire's been swooning over it. Practically wrote a sonnet about his jawline."

Claire rolled her eyes, but there was a blush in her cheeks. "He can't shave it off until after the wedding. If ever."

I laughed, shaking my head. "Wow, I leave for a few years and suddenly my brother's a rugged romance hero."

Sonny just shook his head, smiling as he carried my bags inside.

Before I could say another word, Claire and Darci whisked me into the living room, handing me a plate of Thai food and a strawberry margarita, like I'd always been here.

Once we were settled on the couch, Sonny came

back for my last bag and said, "Don't let these two corrupt you."

I rolled my eyes, smiling. "Bro, I'm twenty-eight. If I'm corrupted, that ship sailed a long time ago."

He smirked and disappeared down the hall with my bags.

The next three hours flew by in a blur of laughter, green curry, and a truly disturbing documentary about a serial killer who'd evaded capture for over a decade by pretending to be a traveling handyman. I was curled up on the couch between them in leggings and mismatched socks, sipping cocktails and yelling at the screen every time someone ignored an obvious red flag.

"He literally said, 'I'm great with rope knots,'" Darci shouted, tossing popcorn at the TV. "How's that not a red flag?!"

"Honestly, how do people like this find dates so easily?" Claire added, sipping her drink.

I laughed so hard I almost choked on a spring roll.

Somewhere between my second cocktail and our deep dive into unsolved cases, I found myself really opening up. I told them about Thailand. About Devin. About the life I thought I wanted and the person I thought he was—and how it all came crashing down the moment I walked into our room and saw him with another woman in our bed.

Claire reached over and gently squeezed my hand. "I'm glad you're here now."

Darci gave me a sideways smile. "You've survived a manipulative man and international customs. That makes you basically unstoppable."

I smiled through the tightness in my throat, tears welling without warning. This may be right where I needed to be, like I'd landed in the right place, with the right people.

Over the next few weeks, I started piecing together a version of myself that wasn't built around someone else's choices. With Sonny and Claire's wedding coming up, I tried to stay out of the way. I didn't want to intrude any more than I already had.

But slowly I let my guard down, and she had become a true friend—the kind who never made me feel like a burden, but someone she rooted for, even when I wasn't sure which direction I was going. And her best friend, Darci? She reminded me how to laugh at dumb reality shows, how to sit cross-legged on the couch, eating dessert first, and forgetting the world for an hour or two.

I unpacked and started sleeping through the night again. As the weeks went by, I remembered how I liked my coffee and how silence doesn't always mean something's wrong. I finally just felt like I could breathe again.

So when I got a notice on my phone for one of my favorite bands coming to a club in Dallas, I didn't think twice. I bought a ticket—just one. I wasn't looking to date anytime soon. It wasn't that I didn't want to find someone new. I just wasn't sure I was in the right headspace for it. I was still learning to be on my own again, even if I was living with my big brother.

The night of the show, I put on jeans and a clingy top that had always made me feel pretty. I swiped on some mascara and red lipstick for no one but me. I just needed to feel like I was doing something new, pushing my boundaries, and moving forward, all on my own.

Traffic was a bitch, and I walked in halfway through the first opener's set. I was here just to see The Fire Department. That's what I told myself as I sipped on a lukewarm cider and pretended not to feel wildly out of place among the sea of glittering twenty-somethings, all pressed to the stage with their phones up.

I didn't even catch the name of the next band when it was announced over the speakers. They took the stage and opened in near darkness, just a haze of silhouettes and flashing red lights. I couldn't even make out their faces, but the crowd around me was buzzing, like maybe they already knew who these guys were.

Their sound was good, and it felt familiar. By the second song, the lights came up, blinding and bright, and I got a better look at the lead singer. He had a guitar strapped across his body, and a baseball hat hid his eyes. Dark, loose curls that touched his shoulders. He was in another band's t-shirt and faded jeans. He had the kind of presence that made you pay attention even before he opened his mouth.

By the third song, he was at the mic, staring up at the ceiling, and suddenly tossed his hat into the audience. He ran his hands through his hair, pulling it back from his face.

"Hey, Dallas," he said, voice rough around the edges but familiar. "We're The Midnight Run. Thanks for showing up early for us. We've been working on a new album," he said, voice warm and steady, "and we just recently cut this next song. It's called Real You."

Then he started to sing. And something in my chest broke. That voice. That tone. That song.

He was so familiar. The way he moved. The way he talked. The way he smiled. The way he sang, like every word still hurt. My breath caught in my throat. I stared at him, heart racing, trying to tell myself I was imagining it. But I wasn't.

Was that... *Jace?*

As the song continued, a sick, twisting feeling settled in my stomach. The lyrics hit too close. The words were raw, honest, aching in a specific way only the truth can. It wasn't just a lost love song. It was my story. Our story.

The way he sang about promises under the stars, about love that meant always, and then about losing someone, not because they left, but because they were taken. My mother's voice echoed in the back of my mind—sharp, unwavering, cruel—the lie that shattered everything.

And now, he was standing twenty feet away, singing our broken truth in front of hundreds of people. I felt frozen in place, my eyes locked on him, the noise of the crowd fading around me. He looked out over the crowd like performers do, scanning faces—until his gaze landed on me. Would he even recognize me?

But I swore something passed between us in that split second. His voice faltered—just slightly. His eyes widened. He did a double-take, eyebrows pulling together as his gaze stayed fixed on mine. Recognition. Confusion. Longing. Maybe even pain.

But he didn't stop playing. He didn't miss a word. He just closed his eyes and pushed through the rest of the song like it physically hurt to keep going. When it ended, the crowd erupted. He gave a tight smile, took a long drink on stage, and moved on to the next track without saying a word.

He sang three more songs after that—each one louder, more electric—but he never looked in my direction again. Not once. And I stood there, heart pounding, trying to keep my knees from buckling, while the girl next to me kept dancing like everything hadn't just shifted sideways.

He'd told the crowd they'd be at the merch table after the show. "Come say hi, grab a shirt, tell us what you thought," he said with a grin. The rest of the audience had eaten it up, cheering and clapping, but I was frozen in place, still reeling from the song, from the look in his eyes when he saw me.

The Midnight Run—the name hadn't registered because I hadn't followed his career. I just... had never been brave enough to look him up and see the life he built without me. So... I never did. Not when he never had the chance to know the truth.

I told myself he probably just thought I looked familiar. It'd been thirteen years. I'd grown up. My hair was shorter now, darker. The sunburned kid with a braid and bony knees was gone—traded for sharper lines, steadier posture, a smile that didn't give everything away. Freckles faded. The same eyes, just more careful about what they let out.

The lights pulsed and the crowd roared as The Fire Department took the stage, but I kept turning toward the merch table, hoping. It sat empty through every song—until the encore, when a mustached band member finally appeared with a couple of cardboard boxes, setting things out.

My heart twisted. Maybe Jace wasn't coming. Maybe he did recognize me and couldn't bear to see me again.

But when the show finally ended, I found myself drifting toward the merch tables anyway, pretending I just wanted a better look at the t-shirts. A small crowd had gathered, forming a loose line in front of The Midnight Run table, and I slipped in at the back, my heart pounding harder than it had during the entire concert.

I scanned the room, searching for him. And then —there he was. He stepped out from the side of the stage, weaving behind all the merch tables with that easy, confident walk I remembered all too well. His hair was damp, and he had on a different t-shirt than the one he'd worn on stage. He stopped along the way, animated with the fans, smiling, signing things, and taking pictures until he slipped behind the table.

When I finally reached the front of the line, he looked up from signing a t-shirt for the girl ahead of me—and froze. His eyes widened, just for a heartbeat—barely more than a blink—but I saw it. *Felt it.* Recognition. Surprise. And something that looked an awful lot like hope.

"Mallie?" he said more than asked. "I thought…" He let out a sigh as he shook his head, "I thought I'd never see you again." And then, that grin spread across his face, the one I used to fall in love with every summer, like it hadn't been years since I'd seen it.

And just like that, I was teenage Mallie. Only this time, I had a secret.

CHAPTER FOUR

Mallie

Age 5 – Rockport

I didn't want to go.

That's what I told Mom when she packed the suitcases and said we were spending the summer in Rockport, sharing a beach house with some other family.

"We're old friends," she said, like that made it better. "Tessa and I were roommates in college."

I didn't care. I was five, not stupid. I didn't want to meet some mystery kids. I wanted to stay home where my bed was soft and my stuffed animals knew exactly where to sleep.

I had plans—very important ones. I was going to finish building my pillow fort in the living room and teach my dolls how to have a tea party with real sweet tea and cookies this time. And I was supposed to go to Lucy's birthday party and ride the pony she promised would be there—a real pony.

The second we pulled up, my older brother Sonny, who was fifteen and too cool for everything, muttered, "Looks like we're staying in a sandbox."

The house was bright blue, but looked old. It definitely wasn't as nice as our house back home. Towels were drying on the porch railing, and a giant neon beach float shaped like a donut was in the yard. When I opened my door, everything smelled like salt and sand.

And then a boy ran off the porch. Fast. Barefoot. Loud. Dark brown curls, hair, and eyes as bright as green M&Ms. He skidded to a stop in front of me, holding a stick in one hand and a grape freezer pop in the other. His dark hair was sticking up.

"You're the girl?" he asked, squinting at me.

I blinked. "What girl?"

"The one staying here. Your mom's Liz-buff?"

"Nooo, it's *Elizabeth*, not Liz-buff."

"Yeah, that's what I said."

I rolled my eyes, "Okay, but I'm Mallory."

He frowned. "Mallie?"

My ears burned. "Mall-or-ee."

He nodded, completely ignoring me. "My name's Jameson." He said his name all proud and serious, like it was the fanciest name in the world.

I scrunched up my nose. "That's too long."

He blinked at me. "What?"

"It sounds like a dad name," I told him. "You got a shorter one?"

He screwed up his face like he'd never thought about it before. "No."

"Well, now you do," I said, shrugging. "I'm calling you Jace."

He didn't seem to mind. Just grinned wide, like I'd handed him a secret.

"Come on," he said, grabbing my arm and tugging. "The beach's this way."

"Wait—where are we going?"

"To the pirate ship!" he shouted over his shoulder

like it was the most obvious thing in the world.

I didn't remember agreeing to anything, but somehow we were already running toward the beach, and he was handing me a stick like it was a sword, and I was following him even though I wasn't sure I even liked him.

Behind us, the screen door squeaked. "Do not go near the water!" Mom called, all capital letters. "Sand only! Sonny—keep an eye on them!"

"I got it!" my brother yelled back, already trudging after us with a big sigh. He definitely looked like he didn't want to be here any more than I did.

I glanced back at the porch where our moms were still talking and bouncing the baby, then looked at the boy with messy dark curls and bare feet already kicking up sand. He talked a lot, like a whole lot. And he was bossy.

He said I could be the pirate queen, but only if he got to be the prince who defeated me and saved the whole beach.

"That's not how stories work," I told him.

"Yes, it is," he said. "It's how mine works."

"Do I have to be a prisoner?" I asked, trying to keep up.

He stopped, turned around fast. "What? No. I'm the one who has to fight you!"

I blinked. "Really?"

He nodded big, like this was a very serious deal. "Yeah. You get the gold crown I got from Burger King on the way here. And that sword—" He leaned close to my ear, and his breath smelled like fruit snacks. "It's made of lightning," he whispered.

I stared at him.

Then he smiled all funny and said, "You get to boss everyone around. Even me."

I liked the sound of that. So when he took off running, I ran after him.

When we got to the beach, he pulled the crown out of the sand bucket and plopped it on my head. Then, we built a crooked sandcastle together and stole one of Sonny's blue flip-flops and stuck it on top as a flag. Sonny rolled his eyes when he saw it, yanked it out, and walked off to the dock with his headphones on like he was allergic to fun.

Later, I saw Jace holding the chubby baby with big brown eyes. "This is David," he told me. "He drools, and he's boring. But he's my little brother."

David sneezed and grinned.

That night, after we both ate three freezer pops each on the porch, Jace leaned over with blue lips and said, "You're kind of okay for a girl."

I rolled my eyes, but I didn't say anything. And when he called me "Mallie" again, I didn't correct him.

CHAPTER FIVE

Jace

Present Day

My breath caught the second I saw her. *Mallie.*

It had been years, but how could I forget? Her name still hit me like an old song I didn't realize I'd been missing.

She stepped up to the table, nervous smile and all, and said, "Hey, Jace." Her voice quivered.

Neither of us moved. The crowd, the music, the chatter—they all faded into nothing. And then I laughed. That stupid, gut-deep laugh that used to get me in trouble. It just broke free.

"What the hell are you doing here?" I asked, leaning in, my grin widening like I couldn't help it.

She smiled again shyly, looking away. "I could ask you the same thing."

Our eyes met, and for a second, it was like no time had passed. Like those summers at the beach house were just yesterday.

I gave Dean a quick nod, and he stepped up to take over the table without a word. I pulled her to the side. I felt eyes from the women in line behind her, their stares sharp, but I didn't care. My attention was all hers.

"I can't believe you're here," I said, scanning the thinning crowd. "What... what are you doing after this?"

She shrugged, clearly trying to play it cool. "Just headed home, I guess."

"Can I take you to dinner? Catch up a little?" I asked, my voice a little rougher than I meant it to be.

She opened her mouth like she was about to answer, but before she could get a word out, I looked over at Dean. He caught it instantly and smirked, already knowing. Without missing a beat, he waved me off and called, "Go, Romeo. I've got this."

I didn't hesitate. I rounded the table like muscle memory had taken over, my hand finding hers as naturally as breathing. It felt the same—like it always had. Like Hollowbone and stolen hours and salt on our skin.

"C'mon," I said, gently tugging her toward the side door, heart thudding in that old, familiar rhythm—like the world might open up again just for us.

She laughed softly. "Okay, but... I kinda wanted to buy a t-shirt."

I stopped and gave her a once-over, slow and teasing. "Dean! Toss me a medium!"

The shirt landed in my hands, and I handed it to her with a grin. "There. Now let's go."

She reached for her bag. "Let me pay for it at least —"

I shook my head, already pulling her along. "Nope. On me. You showing up here? That's worth a hell of a lot more than a t-shirt."

As we stepped outside, I let my hand settle at the

small of her back, just instinct, and she didn't pull away. The night air was cool, grounding me. I looked over at her, barely able to believe she was real.

I looked around, trying to get my bearings on where we were, and said, "If I recall, there's a diner a few blocks from here. It's nothing fancy, but they have the best milkshakes in town. What do you think?"

She laughed softly. "You always did know how to woo a girl with a sweet treat."

"Some things never change, huh?" I said, shaking my head, remembering the freezer pops we shared the first day we met.

My hand brushed against hers as we walked, close but not quite touching. I wanted to reach for it again. God, I wanted to. But… I didn't know if I was allowed.

"So," I said, trying to sound casual, "you're in Dallas now?"

She laughed. "I'm up in Denton. Just moved here a few weeks ago. Long story. Let's just say… life has a funny way of keeping you on your toes."

I nodded, my grin softening as I let out a sigh. "You're the last person I expected to see tonight."

She looked at me like she wanted to say something, but all she managed was a small smile. Then, a moment later, she shrugged again and said, "It's crazy, right? I mean, you're here, playing in a band…"

"Yeah," I said, rubbing the back of my neck. "It's been a ride. Doing something I love." I paused, then looked straight at her. "But you…" I sighed, "Mallie… you're just as I remember… always."

That stopped her. She looked up at me with an expression I couldn't name, maybe disbelief?

"Jace, it's been thirteen years."

"I know," I said, hands sliding into my back pockets. "But seeing you tonight? I feel like I'm fifteen all over again."

Her cheeks turned red, and she gave me another shy smile before looking away just as we reached the diner. I held the door open for her. The smell of pancakes and strong coffee wrapped around us as we slid into a booth.

I leaned in, elbows on the table, looking at the menu. "What's your go-to? Sweet or salty?"

She shook her head, laughing. "Still sweet. Always sweet."

Of course. As long as I'd known her, she always had a raging sweet tooth. I hadn't forgotten.

We talked. Ate. Laughed. That smile and the dimple on her right cheek made their grand return. I teased her. She teased me back. God, it felt so easy. And with every minute, the space between us shrank until it felt like nothing had ever come between us.

"So," I asked eventually, letting the question hang between us, "what've you been up to all this time?"

She glanced away, her gaze landing on the window beside us. Outside, the streetlights flickered against the pavement, casting long shadows. It was late, and the crowds were thinning.

Her smile faltered, just for a second. She tensed— barely, but I saw it. The kind of stillness that says *there's more here.* Like one wrong word might shake it loose.

"Oh, you know… life," she said, too light, too rehearsed. She reached for her straw, turning it in slow circles. "Became a nomad and saw the world for a while. Doing freelance copywriting while I traveled. But now…" She looked up at me and sighed, "Now, I think I'm just trying to figure out what I want."

I narrowed my eyes, reading between the lines, my voice dropping. "And what do you want?"

That pulled another blush from her cheeks. And she shrugged.

God, I'd missed her. I wanted to say it, and the words almost slipped out. They were right there, aching to be said. But instead, I leaned in, resting my hand over hers, my voice low, "It's been way too long, Mallie."

She froze for half a second, just enough for me to catch the hitch in her breath, the flicker of heat in her eyes as she stared at our hands pressed together. But then she looked down and shook her head like it didn't mean anything. I didn't press further. I didn't need to. Her being here, just sitting across from me after all this time, was already more than I ever thought I'd get.

The waitress came by, asking if we wanted refills. I mumbled something about another coffee. Mallie ordered tea, I think. I barely heard a word. My eyes never left her. I was too busy soaking her in. The way she smiled without showing her teeth. The way her eyes flickered like flames and never stayed still for long, like maybe the past was still chasing her.

She tucked a strand of her raven hair behind her ear, and I watched her like she might vanish again if I looked away too long. Her presence still had the same effect on me, like everything else in the room blurred at the edges when she was in focus. I remembered this same feeling when I was just a kid.

Damn, it felt good to have her sitting across from me again.

"I thought about you. Over the years. A lot. I

didn't know if you'd still want to see me. After… everything."

She looked up, surprised by the honesty in my voice. "I…" She swallowed and said softly, "I've thought about you, too."

When we finished, we stepped outside again, the night air wrapping around us like a chilling reminder that time was running out. We didn't rush. Our feet found a slower rhythm, like we were both pretending there wasn't an ending waiting on the other side of this walk.

By the time we reached the edge of the parking lot, the venue was nearly empty. A few crew members from The Fire Department lingered loading the truck, their voices low, the thud of equipment echoing faintly in the background. But our van was gone. The guys had already taken off, probably back at the Airbnb by now.

I stopped. So did she.

My hands twitched at my sides before I shoved them into my pockets, fingers curling into fists. Touching her again felt like a need, but holding back felt like respect. I didn't know which one would win.

I asked, "Where'd you park?"

She pointed down the block at another lot and gave me a soft, uncertain smile—the kind that tugged at memories I didn't even know were still sharp—and said, "This was nice. I guess… I'll see you…" Her voice dropped off at the end.

When she turned and started walking away, my chest clenched at the thought of her slipping through my fingers again, and I didn't even think.

I followed her and blurted out, "Mallie… don't go."

She stopped mid-step, her shoulders stiffening as she looked back at me, confused. "What?"

No more pretending. I took a breath and stepped closer and pleaded, "Mallie..." My thumb brushed the back of her hand. "I've been dreading this... from the second I saw you tonight."

She was quiet, her eyebrows wrinkling as her eyes locked on mine like she was trying to read between the lines.

Then she asked so softly that the words barely reached me, "What are you...?"

All the what-ifs came rushing back, and I couldn't help but let the truth slip out. It had been sitting in my chest for years, just waiting for her to walk back into my life. "I didn't realize how much I'd missed you... even with..." I swallowed hard, "The thought of never seeing you again feels like it might undo me right here."

Mallie didn't speak. She sucked in a breath, pulling back like the truth hit harder than she expected. Her eyes found mine, wide and glassy with something raw. At first, I thought it might be guilt. But then I really looked at her. Was it... fear or shame? Whatever it was, whatever happened, I could see it was still tearing at her.

But she stepped closer, slow and careful, like she was afraid to let herself want this again. I felt the heat of her, and that was all I needed. I reached for her, one hand against the side of her face, the other curling around her waist. She leaned into me like she'd been waiting, like maybe she'd missed me, too. And then I kissed her.

God, I kissed her.

Her mouth met mine, soft and searching, and the moment it did, something inside me burst open. Not like it was the first time, but like it was the first time in forever, and I hungered for her. Like the world had hit pause just to let this happen.

Her hands found my chest, fingers curling into my shirt, and I pulled her closer, deepening the kiss. Space and time bent around us, the noises from the street fading until there was only the feel of her, the taste of something I thought I'd lost. She melted into me like she remembered the shape of us. And I kissed her like I never wanted to forget it again.

When we finally pulled apart, I didn't let go of her. I couldn't. My arms stayed around her like they knew something my brain hadn't caught up to yet. Her breath mingled with mine, and I leaned my forehead against hers, trying to slow the pounding in my chest.

"I've wanted to do that all night," I murmured, my voice raw around the edges.

She smiled—soft and real, and when that dimple reappeared, it undid me the way it used to. For the first time in a long time, it felt like everything was where it was supposed to be.

And then I said what I'd been holding back since the second I realized I wasn't ready to let her go again. "Come with me," I said, my voice steady even as my heart raced. "We have an Airbnb tonight. I've got my own room. We leave in the morning, but... I'd regret it if I didn't ask."

She didn't answer right away. I watched her take a deep breath, her eyes flickering like she was chasing something down inside her head. For a second, I thought she might pull away. Part of her looked ready to bolt, but the other part looked like it already belonged here, with me. She just stood there, staring at me like she was searching for something—an answer, a sign, maybe even a reason to trust me.

I breathed out, "Please? Come home with me tonight, Mallie?"

And then, her hands slid up my chest, slow and warm, and before I could say anything else, she rose onto her toes and pressed her lips to mine again and whispered, "Okay."

Relief hit me like gravity. I fumbled for my phone, fired off a quick text to the group chat with the band, then slid it back into my pocket and reached for her hand.

"Lead the way," I said, my voice quiet, but certain. We stepped into the night with her fingers wrapped in mine.

Twenty minutes later, the front door of the Airbnb clicked shut behind us. Two of my bandmates, Eddie and Jake, were sprawled across the couches, beers in hand, both shirtless in athletic shorts, watching some reality show, laughing.

"Jay!" They turned as one, their eyes flicking to Mallie.

Eddie grinned and said, "And you brought company…"

I didn't say a word. Just jerked my chin up in acknowledgment at them and walked Mallie straight to the bedroom, tugging her in behind me and locking the door with a soft click.

The laughter from the living room was a faint echo now, just a reminder that the rest of the world still existed. But I didn't care. It didn't matter. Not when she was here. Not when it was finally just the two of us… again.

CHAPTER SIX

Mallie

Age 11 - Rockport

I had a countdown going. I marked it on my wall calendar. Forty-seven days until the beach house. Then thirty. Then one. Until Jace and I were together again.

By the time Dad loaded the last bag in the car, I was already halfway through a bag of snacks, bouncing in the backseat like that could get us there faster.

The beach house wasn't just a vacation. It was the part of the year that made everything else worth it. Summer meant ocean air and sand castles and the rickety porch swing and sticky freezer pops —but mostly, it meant Jace—my best friend and my most favorite person in the whole world.

I'd imagined our reunion a hundred times. It was the same every summer. He'd see me, run up grinning, probably say something dumb but sweet. Maybe even hug me—he did that last year. We'd get a sunburn staying out on the beach the first few days and then stay inside the next few, gorging ourselves on popcorn and watermelon. I couldn't wait.

But... when we pulled into the driveway, he was sitting on the front steps with a boy I didn't know. The other kid was older—maybe thirteen—with sunburned shoulders, messy blond hair, and that smug look some boys get when they think they're the coolest person around and in charge of the world.

They were tossing a baseball back and forth like it was just another day. Jace didn't even wave. He didn't smile. He barely looked up when I scrambled out of the car.

"Hey, Mallie," he called as I started walking up the drive, like I was just some neighbor kid stopping by. My stomach dropped.

Before I could answer, Sonny climbed out of the car behind me and stretched like we'd just driven two days instead of three hours.

"Ah, yes," he said, glancing around. "Nothing like lukewarm showers and sand everywhere. Truly, the vacation of kings."

Dad snorted as he pulled the cooler out of the trunk. "You're lucky we still let you come, college boy."

Sonny grabbed some bags from the trunk as he said, "You just like having someone tall enough to fix the ceiling fan."

I almost laughed, but my eyes were still on Jace.

He looked taller. His hair was longer, falling into his eyes. But his face didn't light up. He glanced at me and just nodded like nothing had changed, then turned back to the other boy, tossing the baseball again.

Tyler. That's what I'd find out later—his name was Tyler, and his family was renting the light green beach house a few doors down. He was "cool," according to Jace. He played soccer. He could skimboard. He'd been to California.

The first week was the worst. Jace was constantly with Tyler. They were always laughing about something, and I was never in on the joke. I would hang around sometimes, hoping Jace would invite me to join in. But he never did. It was like I was invisible.

One afternoon, I drifted into the kitchen without really meaning to. Mom was at the counter, slicing strawberries, the window open beside her, letting the warm breeze in. I wasn't hungry. I was tired of being ignored and didn't want to sit outside pretending I didn't care.

She looked up as I grabbed a cutting board. "You volunteering for kitchen duty? Should I be worried?"

"I can help," I said, reaching for a knife.

She handed me a bowl full of strawberries. "Hull these."

We worked in silence for a while. I sliced the tops off strawberries, one by one, as the breeze lifted the corners of the recipe card on the counter.

"You okay?" she asked eventually, not looking directly at me.

I shrugged. "I guess."

She gave a quiet hum. "You guess?"

I kept my eyes on the berries. "I don't know what's going on with Jace."

Her hands slowed.

"He's always with that kid, Tyler," I said. "All week, it's been the two of them. They talk about stuff I don't get and laugh like nothing else matters. I try to hang around. I wait for him to ask me to go with them. But he never does."

Mom was quiet for a moment. Then she said, "That boy has always worshiped the sand you walk on."

I blinked. "Not anymore."

She shrugged as she worked. "Or maybe he's just expanding his horizons. Maybe you should, too."

I set another strawberry top in the compost bowl. "I don't know. What if Jace doesn't want to be around me anymore?"

Mom leaned back against the counter and looked at me like she was trying to see everything I wasn't saying.

"You don't have to make it a big deal," she said gently. "Just ask him to do something simple. Like looking for buried treasure along the tide line. Or building a seaweed trap for David's imaginary lizard army."

I smiled despite myself. "We were very serious about those traps."

"I remember," she said, grinning. "You used my salad tongs as 'capture claws.'"

She turned back to the strawberries, then said, like it was nothing, "Why don't you go hang out with that girl, Caitlyn? Her family's in the orange beach house, I think? She looks about your age. I've seen her reading on the porch. Doesn't look like she has many friends."

I made a face. "I tried once. She freaked out about all the sand."

Mom blinked. "But it's… the beach."

"I know. But she got some on her legs and screamed like she was being attacked."

Mom laughed. "Well, maybe not Caitlyn then."

"Yeah," I said. "Maybe not."

She smiled again. "If Jace keeps acting like you're invisible, I'll make sure he's stuck washing dishes after dinner all summer—and *you* won't even have to help. Deal?"

That pulled a laugh out of me.

"Deal," I said.

I finally asked him the next morning if he wanted to build a sand fort like old times or go exploring the dunes.

He shrugged. "I'm kind of doing stuff with Tyler today."

That was all he said. Like it wasn't a big deal, but it was. We were supposed to be best friends for life, always. We promised each other. And now he wanted nothing to do with me.

We made that promise two summers ago when we were nine, when Jace sliced his leg open on a jagged shell. It had bled so much, and I dragged him back to the house with his arm over my shoulders as he tried not to cry. His mom had to take him to the emergency room.

Ten stitches. No water. No sand. For the rest of the summer, while everyone else swam and played, I stayed with him. I brought him snacks. We drew pirate maps and made sand-free pillow forts in the living room. I didn't leave him once.

That was the summer we made the promise—best friends for life, always. Never let anything come between us. Ever. We even spit in our hands and shook.

But now something, or rather someone, had come between us. So I guess *always* didn't mean what I thought it did.

That afternoon, I sat on the porch swing next to David, who was five now and surprisingly opinionated. He had a plastic cup full of Goldfish crackers and was telling me a story about an imaginary sea monster.

"Jamie's being weird," he said through a mouthful of crackers. "Is he mad at you?"

"I don't know," I muttered. "But he's definitely acting weird."

David tilted his head. "Maybe his brain got cooked by the sun. That happens to people, you know."

I shrugged, "Yeah, but... I think it's something else."

"You want me to tell him he's a big dummy? I'll do it."

I smiled. "Thanks, but I've got it."

At twilight, the clouds were streaked in pinks and oranges when Jace and Tyler came walking up the beach toward the house, talking and laughing like everything was perfect. I was on the porch swing, and Jace glanced at me for just a second. That's when it sank in. He knew, he just didn't care. He chose not to, and that hurt so much more.

I stood up. I didn't plan what I was going to say—I just walked right down the steps and into his path.

"What is your problem?" I snapped.

Tyler stopped. Jace blinked. "What?"

"You've been ignoring me since I got here."

"I've been hanging out," Jace said defensively. "What's the big deal?"

"The big deal," I said, my voice rising, "is that we made a promise."

Jace rolled his eyes and shook his head as he smirked. "What're you talking about?"

"You really don't remember?" I tilted my head.

He shrugged. "I don't know, Mallie. We were little kids."

"We were nine! Your leg? I stayed with you the whole time. We made a promise—best friends for life. Always. Nothing comes between us." I huffed out a breath, "You meant it then."

He looked away. "Things are different now."

I poked him in the chest. "No, you're different. You think you're too cool now."

"I'm not trying to be cool." He glanced at Tyler.

"Yes, you are," I snapped. "You're trying to impress Tyler. And you're doing a great job, by the way. You're not just ignoring me, Jace—you're replacing me."

"That's not fair."

"No, what's not fair is how fast you forgot me." My voice cracked. "You don't even look at me. You act like I don't exist. We haven't done a single thing together since I got here. It's been almost two weeks. Do you know how that makes me feel?"

He threw his hands up in the air and started walking again. "God, Mallie! Maybe I don't want to spend every waking moment doing the same dumb baby stuff with you!"

It was like he'd just slapped me. My eyes burned, but I refused to cry.

"If I'm such a baby, then I guess we aren't friends anymore. Go be cool with Tyler and just forget that stupid promise we made. Seems like you already have anyway."

That got to him. He stopped and turned, and I saw it in the way his mouth dropped open—like he didn't expect me to hit back.

I didn't wait for Jace to say anything else. I couldn't, especially not with Tyler there. I turned and bolted down the worn path, through the drift of sand already cooling under the early evening sky.

"Mallory?" Sonny's voice called after me. "Hey, Mal!"

He must have been on the porch and saw what happened. I heard his footsteps on the stairs, quick and unsure, like he wasn't sure if he should follow. But I didn't look behind me or stop.

I couldn't bear to turn around and see the look on Sonny's face—pity, confusion, maybe even the beginning of understanding. I didn't want my big brother or anyone else to have seen that. To have witnessed what just happened between me and Jace. It felt like I'd just broken our friendship, maybe forever.

So I kept going, as fast as my legs could pump, toward the dunes—the ones we used to climb every afternoon, where the wind carved out hollows, and the sea grass bent. The wind picked up as I ran, whipping my braids across my face, stinging my cheeks. I didn't stop until the sounds of voices disappeared behind me, and the only thing I could hear was the surf and the heavy beat of my own heart.

I found one of those hollows between the dunes. The grass was blowing in the breeze, and the sand was still warm from the sun. The sky was darker now, soft and bruised, streaked with dark purples. I looked around, just to make sure no one was here, and dropped down in the dip, curled myself into a ball, and wrapped my arms around my knees.

I swallowed around the lump in my throat. I didn't want to cry. Not over him. Not over this. It was stupid. That promise we made was dumb. It had obviously never meant anything. Not to him. I don't know why I cared so much.

But the moment I tucked my head down and pressed my face to my arms, a sob broke loose. Loud. Raw. Ugly.

It wasn't just about Jace. It wasn't just the broken promise. It was this horrible feeling of being replaced, of being invisible. The way he looked at

Tyler was like he used to look at me. Like he wanted him there. But not me.

I cried until my chest ached and my throat burned. Like I was trying to empty myself. And I couldn't tell if the salt on my lips was from the sea air or my own tears. I cried as if I got it all out now, maybe I'd stop caring. But I didn't. I cared so much. Too much. Because I wanted him to come after me, come find me, but I wasn't sure if he would or if we'd ever come back from this.

CHAPTER SEVEN

Mallie

Present Day

As soon as the door shut behind us, Jace's hands found my waist, pulling me closer until the space between us disappeared entirely. I could feel the heat of his body as his lips traced down my neck. I let out a soft sigh and arched into him instinctively, wanting more. I had missed this, him, more than I realized.

And yet—beneath this need, the ache, the pulse between us—there it was again. The secret, my secret. Heavy in my chest, pressing against my ribs like it wanted to claw its way out. I could feel it crouched in the back of my mind, whispering warnings—*He doesn't know. He'll hate you when he does.*

But then his mouth brushed mine—soft, tentative, like he was relearning me, and I couldn't hold onto that fear anymore. Not now. One night. I could give myself grace for one night. One night, when I wasn't the girl with too much shame and not enough courage. One night where I could be his again—fully, wildly, completely—before the truth unraveled everything... again.

His touch became firmer and more insistent. His lips captured mine in a slow kiss that was almost hesitant, like he was asking permission, but it quickly deepened as I wrapped my fingers into his hair and the need between us grew.

I felt his fingers brush the hem of my shirt, his touch grazing the bare skin of my back. The sensation of his hands on me, gentle but urgent, gave me goosebumps and made me shiver. It had been years since I'd felt this kind of desire, this kind of pull. I let myself be swept up in it, my hands tugging at his t-shirt, eager to feel his skin beneath my fingertips.

He pulled his t-shirt over his head in one motion between kisses, and my hands splayed across his broad, muscular chest. His mouth moved down my neck, his breath hot against my skin. I leaned into him, my fingers tugging his hair, pulling him closer, feeling his hardness pressing against my stomach.

Jace's hand slid down my side, settling at the small of my back. His touch was both tender and possessive as he lifted my shirt over my head. The weight of his body pressed against mine, and I let out a breathless laugh.

"This is crazy," I whispered, barely able to catch my breath as he lifted me effortlessly, turning us until my back was pressed against the door.

His gaze locked onto mine, that familiar grin tugging at the corner of his mouth as his hand went to my jeans, unbuttoning them and pushing them down my thighs as I kicked off my boots.

When I was in nothing but my black pushup bra and panties, he murmured against my neck, "Crazy? Maybe. But *this* feels like coming home," his voice rough.

A curl of desire coursed through me, and I whimpered, "Jace..."

His lips found mine again, and this time there was no hesitation, no lingering doubt. Just the overwhelming rush of wanting, of needing. *Him.*

I unbuckled his belt, the metal clinking as I pulled it out of his jeans, and tossed it before I undid his pants, and they fell to the floor.

His bandmates were on the other side of these walls, but it felt like only the two of us were in the world. The only things that mattered were the way his body pressed against mine as he walked me back and lay me back gently on the bed, the desire between us, and the soft sounds of our kisses.

"Mallie..." With a dark grin, he sank down my body, his pupils blown as he growled, "I need to taste you."

Holy shit, this was no longer the fumbling boy I remembered. This was a man who knew what he was doing. Each touch, each movement, felt like an exploration, and I arched into him as he yanked off my underwear.

I felt the heat of his breath against my core as he parted me and licked from my clit down to my opening, swirling his tongue. I gasped, and he chuckled darkly as he used his tongue to play me like an instrument. He licked back up, flicking my clit, suckling it into his mouth, taking little nips with his teeth, and I moaned, running my fingers through his hair.

He flipped me over like a rag doll. His hands ran down my back, pulling my ass up in the air.

He breathed out, "Damn, you're fucking beautiful."

His mouth came down over me from behind, hot

and wet. He licked down from my clit to my opening, swirling his tongue again and again as I bucked my hips, convulsing with need.

"More... please," I begged.

"Fuck, Mallie, I like hearing you beg," He said, sitting up, and the sound of a condom wrapper ripping behind me.

I whimpered as he came up and over me, pulling my hips towards him. He pressed inside slowly and filled me completely. We both groaned when he bottomed out. It was like nothing I'd ever felt before. So many emotions flooded me, I felt worshiped, found, and loved.

My body was on fire for him. I pushed back, imploring him to move against me.

He wrapped one hand around my belly, draping himself over me as he started slow, pulling out all the way before plunging back in deep, and soon he began to stroke harder, faster, our skin slapping together as I met his strokes from behind.

I moaned, "Fuck, Jace... I love... love the way you...," I gasped, "feel inside me..."

I wasn't even thinking. It had just come out, but I think it surprised him. His strokes faltered, and it took him a second before righting himself and pounding me into oblivion.

My voice rose, "Oh god, oh god, oh god."

I couldn't hold it any longer as I clenched around him, and euphoria shot through me as I screamed his name. He followed me a moment later, groaning mine. Then, pressed his body over me, slick with sweat and heat, pulling me tight against him, both of us catching our breath before he rolled off me and tucked me against him.

He took a deep breath and confessed, his fingers running through my hair, "I've missed you so much."

I breathed in his leather and cedar scent as I snuggled into his neck. God, I still remember that masculine scent that was wholly Jace from when we were teens.

He kissed my forehead and played with my hair. His chest was warm against mine, a smattering of dark hair brushing my skin as I shifted against him. The silence between us had softened and wrapped around us, thick with something I didn't dare name yet. Without thought, I relaxed against him and felt like I could finally exhale after years.

His arm curled around me, bare and inked, and I found myself tracing the artwork that wound up his bicep. Lines and shadows swirled together—stars, a snake, and a faint compass tucked just above his elbow.

But it was the line drawing of a bone that stopped me on his upper arm—thin, elegant. Inked in gray, hidden between some red flowers, like a secret. It seemed quiet among the bolder images. And there, if you looked close enough, there were two rows of tiny dots and dashes through its center, that, if you didn't pay attention, looked like part of the shading.

Without asking, I was sure it had a hidden meaning for him, but I wasn't sure I was ready to hear the answer. Instead, I traced the tattoos up to his shoulder, my fingers making their way to his neck, and my eyes caught on something else—something older, familiar. The leather cord at his neck had darkened with time, but the little worn star at its center hadn't changed at all. A little scuffed, but still whole.

I reached out, fingers brushing the charm where it rested against his chest, the leather cord still worn smooth at the edges. The little star glinted in the low light, and for a second, I couldn't breathe.

"You… kept it?" I asked, my voice catching more from emotion than hesitation.

Jace's eyes locked on mine, steady and unflinching. "Always. Never take it off."

Something stirred low in my belly. Like the past had just reached forward and curled its fingers around the present—hot and aching and alive. I let my hand linger there, over his heart, before sliding it higher, behind his neck, and drawing him closer.

I kissed him like the question had already been answered. Like the answer was yes, don't stop, and… *always.* He rolled with me, his hand trailing down my spine. His touch was hot and sure. Our kiss deepened—no hesitation, just need and history and the electric pull of years that hadn't dimmed a goddamn thing between us.

We tangled together slowly, like neither of us wanted to miss a second of whatever this was. His lips dragged over my throat, my collarbone, lower. His name slipped from my mouth, unthinking. Everything about him felt maddeningly familiar and completely new.

And when he finally pushed inside me, this time it was with a sanctity that undid me. No rush. No frantic pace. Just this—us—written in the heat of skin and the ache of years apart. We moved together like we were remembering something our bodies never forgot, like coming home.

In sync, slow and deep, like the world had narrowed down to the pulse between us. His forehead against mine, our breaths catching in the same rhythm, our fingers twined like we were afraid of letting go. Every roll of his hips sent a new ripple of sensation through me, winding tighter and tighter, until I was trembling beneath him.

"Mallie," he rasped, voice rough and low, like it had been pulled from somewhere deep. "God... I... I'm right there."

"Me, too," I gasped, hips lifting to meet his. "Don't stop—please—"

He didn't. He held my gaze like it was the only thing keeping him grounded, like he needed to see everything I was feeling as much as he needed to feel it himself. The pressure coiled deep until it crested, sharp and blinding. I came first, a cry caught in my throat, legs locking around his waist as my whole body arched into his. He followed with a groan, burying his face in the crook of my neck, pulling me tight against him as he spilled into me, shaking with the force of it.

For a long moment, neither of us moved. Just the sound of our breathing—uneven, shattered, slowly settling. Then he leaned up and kissed me again, softer this time. A lingering thing, grateful. Maybe even a little awed. We didn't say anything. We didn't need to. I felt it, too.

Jace shifted onto his side, pulling me with him until I was tucked against his chest, one leg tangled over his, my arm draped across his stomach. His fingers skimmed lazy circles along my back, lulling me into a quiet warmth that settled in my bones.

The last thing I felt before I slipped under was the rise and fall of his chest against mine... and the quiet certainty that—for tonight, at least—I was no longer alone.

I hadn't meant to stay with him all night. I really hadn't.

Milkshakes turned into dinner, dinner into walking through the streets of Deep Ellum toward the venue's empty lot—just the two of us, trading memories—the night he kissed me for the first time, and the sea glowed, how the stars looked brighter when we snuck out at midnight. It felt so easy, too easy, like slipping back into summer.

And when he asked me to come home with him, I said yes before I let myself think. Before I could remind myself of all the reasons I shouldn't.

Sonny blew up my phone around midnight, like I knew he would. And I'd answered honestly, for once.

Me: I'm okay. I'm safe. I'll be home in the morning.

I couldn't tell him I was with Jace. He had no idea what I'd gone through when I was 15, when he was away at school. There was no lecture, no all-caps fury. Just a long pause and then a single word:

Sonny: Okay.

But I knew him. He was probably pacing the living room, Claire gently reminding him that I was a grown woman who could make my own decisions. He'd always been protective of me. Yet, Sonny always seemed to brace for fallout when it came to me, even though until I called him from Thailand, there'd never been one. It was like he was waiting for some mess he'd have to clean up or some mistake I'd try to outrun.

The strangest part was—he didn't even know the worst of it. Didn't know what happened when I was fifteen. Didn't know about the ache I still carried. I was almost certain our mother had never told him. And I sure hadn't. But still, he looked at me sometimes like he was waiting for the crash. And I couldn't decide if that made me feel more seen or more alone.

Now it was morning. Early. The sky was soft and gray, the air already thick with that sticky Texas humidity. We were standing outside a coffee shop with the rest of the band, waiting for a table, and I was trying to stay grounded, like I hadn't just completely undone every boundary I'd been carefully rebuilding over the last few weeks.

We lingered over breakfast, and I just sat next to him, quiet in the warmth of it all, still feeling the imprint of last night—his hands, his voice, the way we'd fit like we'd never been apart. But it was ending too soon.

As soon as everyone gobbled their food down, we stepped outside just as the sky started to brighten. And now, here I was, standing with Jace and his band, watching them joke and jostle around, their laughter curling into the morning like smoke, like the world hadn't shifted. Like we hadn't just shattered the last thirteen years of silence between us.

I wasn't sure what to do next. They were leaving straight after breakfast—Arkansas was next on the tour—and my stomach twisted around the question I couldn't stop asking myself. *Would I ever see him again?*

I tried to tell myself this didn't have to mean anything. That it could just be one unforgettable night. But deep down, I knew better. I knew if this had just been a one-night thing to him, it was going to kill me.

He stood a few steps ahead of me, talking to Dean, his hands in his back pockets in that nervous habit I remembered too well. Then he turned and caught my eye—and that look. That small crooked smile that was just for me. Like no time had passed. Like he'd been waiting this whole time for me to come back to him.

I was in so much trouble. How was I just going to say goodbye to him?

I hugged my arms to my chest, heart thudding. I didn't know what came next, but it felt like I was standing on the edge of something huge. Then Jace stepped back toward me, just enough to brush his hand against mine and lace our fingers, holding on tight. Like maybe he felt it, too.

He glanced toward the van, then back at me. "Look," he said, his voice rough, "the tour's another few weeks, but we can still see each other. I've got a few days off next week. I can come back to you. Or you could fly to me?"

He wasn't just saying it. *He meant it.* I could see it in his eyes. And suddenly, everything inside me was bursting. He wanted this. He wanted me. He was making plans. Real ones. He was standing in front of me, talking about flights, time zones, and showing up.

My throat tightened as something like disbelief and joy and panic collided all at once. I nodded, my breath catching. "Okay." It came out almost breathless, but it felt like saying yes to the universe.

He didn't let go of my hand. His eyes searched mine, brow furrowed, like he needed more. "Mallie..." He shook his head, "I don't care about what happened when we were kids. I don't want to lose you again." He swallowed hard, "I... I want this. Do you want this?"

"I do," I nodded again, the words stuck in my throat. "But Jace..."

He didn't wait. He tugged me across the parking

lot, pulling me toward my car, like he couldn't leave without knowing.

When we stopped beside the driver's side door, he turned to face me fully. "Okay. Long distance sucks, yeah. But it's not impossible. We've got phones, there's flights, and FaceTime. We'll figure it out." He was saying it like he was trying to convince himself.

I looked at him, and I saw the boy who used to kiss me in our secret place and whisper promises of *always* into the sea breeze, and I saw the man who still seemed to make my heart do the same stutter.

He leaned in, his breath warm against my cheek. "I can't let you go again," he murmured. "Don't make me."

My voice was small, but steady. "I'm scared… but I don't want to lose you again, either."

His face shifted—like every word he hadn't said, every feeling he'd buried, rose to the surface all at once. Not just relief, but longing. Reverence. The kind of look that could undo a person from the inside out.

He stepped in without a word, his hand sliding to the back of my neck, fingers sinking into my hair. And he kissed me. Not gently. But with everything he'd been holding onto—all the ache, the hope, the years we lost. His mouth moved over mine with a hunger that said this wasn't a goodbye. It was a homecoming. It was him saying, *You're mine.* And I wasn't going anywhere.

When he finally pulled back, he rested his forehead against mine, and his breath came in ragged. "God, Mallie, you still wreck me. Always."

Tears burned behind my eyes, and my voice was thick when I finally admitted, "Jace… I don't want you to go…"

He breathed out, "I know," before kissing me again, softer this time, like a promise. "I'll call you tonight after the show. We'll figure this out."

And somehow, standing there in the quiet hum of morning traffic, with their van engine rumbling on the other side of the parking lot and his thumb brushing against my cheek, I believed him.

The guys were rearranging gear in the back as they teased each other. They were about to get in the van like it was just another city, just another stop. But with his hand in mine and hope rising in my chest, I knew my world had shifted back into orbit around him.

CHAPTER EIGHT

Jace

Age 11 - Rockport

I didn't mean to hurt her. I swear I didn't. One second, we were standing there, and the next—she was saying all this stuff that made my chest feel tight and wrong, like I'd just breathed in a mouthful of seawater.

She looked at me like I was someone she didn't even know. And then she was gone. Just like that, she turned and ran.

"Mal?" Sonny's voice cut through the silence from the porch, sharp with confusion. I heard his foot hit the top step like he was about to go after her—but he stopped. Froze. His hands twitched uselessly at his sides. Maybe he thought she needed space. Maybe he didn't know what to do either.

Then his gaze snapped to me. His eyes narrowed. He didn't yell. Didn't even raise his voice. But the words hit just the same.

"What the hell did you do?"

I opened my mouth, but nothing came out. I just stood there like an idiot with my hands half-raised, like I could take it all back.

"She— I didn't —" I tried.

But Sonny just shook his head like that made it worse. Hearing me stammer was confirmation that whatever had happened had been bad enough to break her wide open.

"Go find her," he said, low and hard, pointing toward the beach across the street like it was a command. "Now."

And then he turned and walked back into the house, the screen door snapping shut behind him.

Tyler shifted next to me, blowing out a low breath. "Dude. That was intense." He nodded toward the dunes. "Is she always that dramatic?"

I didn't say anything. He said it as if Mallie were just some over-emotional girl, as if she weren't the only person I ever made a real promise to. As if she weren't everything. Like she wasn't *mine*.

I just stared in the direction she ran, toward the dunes.

He didn't get it. How could he? He wasn't here when I cut my leg open on that stupid shell and thought I was going to bleed out on the sand. He didn't see Mallie help me hobble all the way back to the beach house while I cried, scared of the blood. He wasn't the one trapped for almost two weeks straight in the living room while she did everything to make me laugh, playing dumb card games and watching movies together.

That promise was my idea. I was the one who said, "Nothing comes between us, ever. Always." And now look what I'd done.

I shoved the baseball into Tyler's chest. "I gotta go."

He blinked. "Wait, what?"

"I said I gotta go," I repeated, already on the

move. "You can hang out or head back to your place. Whatever."

I didn't wait for him to answer. I followed the way Mallie had run. The light was fading fast, but I knew where she'd gone. I didn't have to guess. When she was upset, she always went to the dunes.

We used to call it our kingdom. We'd climb to the top of the tallest one and pretend we were guarding something important. She liked how quiet it was there, how the grass whispered in the wind as if it knew all of our secrets.

It only took me a minute, and I found her tucked in a hollow between two of the dunes. She was curled into a ball so small she barely looked like a person—just a lump of hurt and freckles all because of me.

She was facing away from me and didn't see me walk up, and truthfully, I was relieved. Because I didn't know what to say. I stood at the edge of the dunes and watched her shoulders shake as she cried like everything inside was finally spilling out.

It hit me—this was all me. I did this. Not Tyler. Me. And that ripped something open in my chest. I didn't know what it was—shame, maybe. Guilt. Regret. All of it twisted together and knotted in my belly until I felt like I couldn't breathe.

I stepped down slowly, taking a shaky breath and letting the sand shift beneath my feet.

"Mallie?" I said quietly.

She didn't move. I sat a few feet away. Not too close. Not yet.

The backs of my eyes burned, and I let out a heavy breath. "I messed up."

Still nothing. But her sobs quieted as her breath turned into hiccups.

I looked out at the water. The tide was coming in,

smoothing out the shore like it was trying to erase the day. I wished it could erase everything from the past two weeks. Every time I didn't invite her to go with us. Every time I looked past her. Every second, I let her feel like she didn't matter.

"I didn't forget," I murmured.

That made her head twitch, just a little, like maybe she heard me.

"I just thought… maybe hanging out with Tyler would make me feel older. Like I wasn't just a kid who used to play pirates with a girl who always beat me in sword fights."

She sniffled, but didn't speak.

"I was scared," I said. "Scared that maybe I liked all that stuff more than I was supposed to, scared that I cared too much about you. So I tried to act like I didn't care at all. And that was the dumbest thing I've ever done."

She didn't uncurl, but her voice came, small and cracked. "You really hurt me."

"I know."

"You're my best friend. I meant it when I stayed with you that summer. Every day. I meant it when we made that promise."

"I know," I said again. "I did, too."

For a minute, there was only the wind and her trembling breath.

Then, she whispered, "You made me feel like I didn't matter anymore."

I felt like I couldn't breathe.

My voice shook as I whispered, "I'm so sorry, Mallie. I don't want to be the kind of guy who makes you feel that way."

I took in a breath and let it out slowly.

My voice steady now, I admitted, "I could never forget you. Ever."

Finally, she lifted her head and rolled over to look at me. Her face was blotchy, her eyes swollen and red as sand came off her braids. And still she was the prettiest girl I'd ever seen.

"I don't know if I forgive you, yet," she said.

"That's okay," I said. "I'll wait."

But it didn't happen all at once. Mallie didn't wake up the next morning and grin at me over pancakes like nothing had happened. She didn't sit next to me on the porch swing or grab my hand when we walked down to the beach. She didn't look at me the way she used to—not yet.

But she stopped flinching when I walked into the room. That was something.

The next day, Tyler came by again. He had a soccer ball tucked under one arm and a bag of chips in the other. I felt weird seeing him—like I wasn't sure if I should be friends with him anymore. But I waved him over.

Mallie was sitting in the sand near the porch steps, drawing something with a stick. I caught Tyler's eye, then turned and said, "Hey Mallie, want to come kick the ball with us?"

She blinked, surprised. "You want me to play?"

"Obviously," I said. "We need someone who can actually aim."

She rolled her eyes, but she stood up. When I introduced her to Tyler, I said, "This is Mallie—my favorite person on the planet."

She wrinkled her eyebrows like she wasn't sure she heard me right, but she didn't correct me. We weren't back to normal. But it was a start.

The next day, Tyler came over for one last skimboard run on the water. I went, and Mallie came, too. This time, I stayed close to her side, teaching her how Tyler taught me. Neither one of us was any good, and we spent most of the time wiping out and laughing. Tyler left early that night. His parents were packing up to go in the morning.

The next morning, the driveway for the green beach house was full of suitcases and plastic totes. I was on the front porch swing. Tyler waved at me once from the backseat of a black minivan, and I waved back. And then he was gone.

Then, it was just me and Mallie like it had always been. Like it was supposed to be. A little while later, my dad made me help him sweep the sand off the driveway. Afterwards, I found her crouched by a tide pool near the old jetty.

"Hey," I said, walking over.

She didn't look up. "There's a crab in here that looks like it's plotting something."

I sat down slowly beside her. Not too close.

"Maybe he's mad his best friend joined a different crab gang."

That got me a tiny chuckle. Barely there. But it was something.

Then, I found her down by the dunes that afternoon, lying on her back in the sand, watching clouds move across the sky. I dropped down next to her and picked up a stick.

She glanced over at me. "What're you doing?"

I started drawing a crooked little map in the sand —our beach kingdom, the castle, the dunes labeled with names we made up years ago, like Whale Tail Hill and Seagull Watchpost.

"You said all this was baby stuff," she said as she leaned sideways and watched.

I shrugged. "I was wrong."

She didn't say anything.

"I missed it," I added, quieter. "The dumb, made-up maps. Digging tunnels that we pretended led to pirate treasure. Guarding the dunes. But most of all, I missed you."

She sat up, cross-legged, brushing sand from her arms.

"Do you remember the password to the Castle of Summer Falls?" I asked.

She cracked the tiniest smile. "I might."

I handed her the stick. "Then help me build it again."

By the fifth day, we were both sitting on the porch swing again, this time watching David chase a lizard while having an entire conversation with it. She didn't say much, just bumped her shoulder into mine once when she sat down next to me and offered me a freezer pop. I didn't bump back, but I had to look away because I couldn't stop the stupid smile on my face.

On the sixth day, we went to the dunes again. We spent the better part of it guarding treasure. The silence wasn't heavy anymore. It was... comfortable again. When I found an earring poking out of the top of one of the dunes, we switched to digging for buried treasure.

At one point, she said quietly, "You know... you didn't lose me. But you got close."

I nodded. "I know and... I'm sorry. Really, Mallie."

Then she pulled out snacks from her backpack, and we lay back, sharing her beach towel, watching the clouds move. We didn't speak again until it was time to walk back to the beach house at sunset.

On the seventh day, she grabbed my hand after breakfast and said excitedly with a grin, "Come on!"

And that time, I didn't let go.

CHAPTER NINE

Mallie

Present Day

After all these years, he seemed just as happy to see me as I was him. That nearly undid me and made me wonder if I should have fought for him, for us, harder than I had back then with my mom. Would the outcome have been any different?

After the drive from Dallas, I went straight to the guest room—now my room—and stood in front of the bookshelf. The small wooden box sat on the top shelf, exactly where I'd left it. I hadn't opened it in over a decade. I used to keep it tucked in my suitcase, taking it with me all over the world like some anchor. My hands hovered above it like it might burn me.

Inside were hospital bracelets—the discharge papers. A photograph I printed off my phone that I wasn't supposed to take—her tiny fingers curled into fists, her face pink and scrunched and beautiful. Mine. His. Ours.

I sank onto the edge of the bed and let myself hold the memory, just for a minute. She was born in the middle of a rainstorm just after noon, one month before the end of my sophomore year of high school.

When my water broke early on a Tuesday morning, my mom drove me to the hospital without a word. She stayed for maybe thirty minutes—long enough to fill out paperwork, talk to the woman from the adoption agency, and check her phone twice—then told me she had a meeting she couldn't miss. And just like that, she walked out the door and left me there. Alone.

My dad was never home—too busy, too clueless, or both. So there I was—by myself, except for the doctor and nurses, a social worker, and the woman from the adoption agency.

After she was born, they cleaned her up a little and handed her to me. Swaddled in a pink-and-blue flannel blanket. A striped hospital cap with a tiny bow. Her face was all squishy and red. She slept in my arms. Peaceful. Weightless. She had a head full of dark hair. I named her Violet in my mind, but I never learned what her adoptive parents named her.

It felt like it hadn't even been five minutes. But then the social worker stepped forward—quiet, professional—and I knew. But she was my last connection to Jace. We had made her. And I clutched her tighter. My arms locked around her like they could keep her safe. Like maybe if I held her good enough, time would stop. But it didn't.

I didn't scream. I didn't fight. I just stared at the woman's hands as they reached for my baby. *My daughter.* I pressed my lips to her soft cheek one last time, breathing in the warm, powdery scent of her skin—and then she was gone.

The door clicked shut, and something inside me broke. I curled in on myself, knees to chest, arms wrapped around my stomach like I could still feel her there. The sheets felt too cold. The room was too quiet. The ache in my chest was brutal, clawing. I shook. The sobs came hard and fast. I thought I might choke on them.

No one came. Not right away. Hours passed—maybe more. Nurses peeked in once or twice, checked my vitals, and massaged my belly. They looked at me with soft eyes, full of pity, and tried to say things they probably thought were comforting—that I'd made a good choice, the right choice.

But I didn't reply. I just lay there. Silent. Wrecked.

When my mom finally came back, I was already dressed and sitting in a chair. Her face was unreadable. She didn't ask if I was okay. She didn't ask anything. She signed the papers and walked me out like we were checking out of a hotel.

After that, nothing ever felt right again. I hated myself for never telling Jace, but I never had the chance. My mother made sure of that. I still remember her voice on the phone—cold, righteous, calm like she was reading from a script.

A few weeks after I told her—early in the pregnancy, when my body still felt almost normal—I found where she'd hidden my phone and sent him one last message. I'd wanted to tell him in person. So my words were careful. Half-written. Hopeful.

He never responded. I didn't think he ever even read it. Because when I snuck my phone again and checked, days later, there was still nothing. That's when I gave up. She'd won and probably scared him off for good.

The whole pregnancy happened so fast. A private counselor. A new phone number. Homeschooling after Christmas. My friends at school just thought I had a bad illness.

After the baby, during my junior year, I couldn't stand being there anymore. I convinced my mom to send me to a boarding school near St. Jo's. So I could "start over." Then college, as far away as they'd let me go. Mom handled everything, and I let her because I was too ashamed to fight back—too afraid.

And when I finally found my voice, it was too late.

My mom was gone, both my parents, lost to a freak plane accident when I was a freshman in college. They left one morning from Austin to visit my brother up here and never came home. And all the things I'd never said were buried with them.

But now... I had another chance. Jace had walked back into my life, grinning, just like the boy I had once loved desperately. He didn't know the truth about what happened, *about her,* and I needed to tell him. I couldn't keep it hidden forever. Not now. Because deep down, I'd always known that one day, she'd come looking. And everything in me said—she already was.

CHAPTER TEN

Mallie

Age 13 - Rockport

We were back for another summer at the beach house, and I knew every inch of this place. The salty air always smelled like freedom, and the porch swing that creaked, and the mismatched rocking chairs. The floorboards were worn smooth from years of sandy footprints and late-night laughter. But nothing about this summer felt familiar.

Somewhere between last summer and this one, my body had hit fast-forward. My favorite shorts pinched in new places, my legs looked a mile longer, and even walking felt different—like I was relearning the controls. I kept forgetting what to do with my arms. And when someone stared too long, I didn't know where to look or how to hide the heat in my cheeks.

And Jace... He was taller now. Not by much, but enough that I noticed when we walked side by side and his shoulder brushed mine. His hair had grown out, more ringlets brushing his shoulders, which couldn't decide whether to be wild or tame. His face had angles I didn't remember—sharper cheekbones, a stronger jaw. His hands looked different, too—like they'd grown into something strong and capable.

But it wasn't just how he looked. It was how he looked at me like something had shifted. Like I wasn't just the girl he'd built sandcastles with or dared to eat handfuls of sour octopus gummies until we both puked. His eyes would land on me and linger—curious, nervous, warm. And when I caught him, he'd glance away fast, scratching the back of his neck like maybe it startled him, too.

But I felt it, too. Something stirring. Something reckless and terrifying in the way my heart reacted to his smile.

One morning, I'd been running down the beach with David, chasing him through the surf. I slipped trying to catch him and landed face-first in the water, soaked from head to toe, braid slapping me in the face like a soggy rope.

Jace sat on the second-to-last step on the walkway that led down to the beach, strumming an old, beat-up acoustic guitar like he had nothing better to do. When I looked up, he was already grinning.

"Nice wipeout," he called. "Your hair looks like it lost a fight with a fish."

I pushed to my feet, smoothing my hair down. "You're just mad I outran you this morning."

He laughed, but it faded quickly. The teasing dropped out of his smile. He shifted, suddenly shy.

"Nah," he murmured, gaze skittering away and returning. "Somewhere along the way you... changed."

I grinned, "What are you talking about?"

"You're—" his ears reddened as his voice softened "—beautiful, Mallie. I just... needed you to know."

My smile faltered as I looked away, and my stomach did a full cartwheel.

I'd had a crush on him since we were five—since that first summer our families started meeting at the beach house, and he'd let me bury his action figures in the sand like treasure. But I'd never told him. Never told anyone—not my mom, not Sonny, not my friends at school. No one. Every spring, I would count down the weeks until I saw him again, pretending not to care when he looked my way.

But this time, my cheeks flushed hot, and I glanced back at him, holding his gaze as I squeezed out the excess water from my braid before throwing it over my shoulder.

I tried to say it back, but it just sounded dumb. "So, um… same. You look… different, too. But… uh, good different."

He just nodded, not answering. One corner of his mouth hitched up, and he went right back to strumming his guitar again. But I knew something had just passed between us. Something big.

I hated how quiet I'd gotten around him. How nervous. How my face burned every time he touched my arm or passed me the sunscreen or looked at me too long—and I hated how badly I wanted him to.

Nothing about this summer felt normal. We didn't mention the last two summers. Not really. We were okay. Jace was still my best friend, but something just felt… different. There was a hush between us that hadn't been there before, the kind you get right before you tell the truth and change everything.

We were teenagers now, but we still built forts and played dumb games with David when no one was watching. We still ate freezer pops on the porch and watched the sunset from the dunes. But now, every time our fingers brushed, it felt like electricity. Every time he said my name, I forgot what I was doing. And sometimes, I'd catch him looking at me—not in the teasing, brotherly way he used to. Not even in the "you're my best friend" kind of way. It was different. It was as if he were seeing me for the first time.

One night, toward the end of the summer, everyone was inside, and it was almost dinnertime. But I was still outside, avoiding my mom, not wanting to be roped into a bunch of chores. I wandered over to the dock and sat down just as the sky started to turn gold. The water was calm, barely moving, and it looked like glass.

I heard footsteps behind me, but didn't turn. I knew it was him.

"You almost missed it," I said quietly.

He came up beside me and sat close. "Miss what?"

I didn't answer. I didn't need to. We watched the sun dip lower, the sky turning orange and soft pink, like it was trying to hold on to its last breath.

"You've been quiet lately," he said after a while.

I shrugged. "So have you."

He didn't argue. A breeze moved across the water, and I turned to look at him—and that's when I saw it.

"Mallie," he whispered.

And for a second, I held my breath. I thought he was going to do it. Kiss me—right there on the dock, with the sun slipping behind the trees. My first kiss ever. I felt it—every part of me braced for it. My heart, my hands, my breath. I was ready.

But then his eyes flicked away. His fingers twitched at his sides. His mouth opened slightly, like he might say something. But he didn't. He just gave this small, crooked smile—one I didn't totally understand—and sat back on his hands, looking out at the water like none of it had happened.

I pretended my heart hadn't just tried to leap out of my chest. I looked out at the water, too. The sun was almost gone now, and everything was bathed in orange. The quiet between us stretched thin just before Tessa, Jace's mom, called us in for dinner. And I tried not to wonder what would've happened if he hadn't changed his mind.

Late that night, after everyone had gone to bed, the house finally fell into a hush with everyone asleep. I was under my sheets, my damp hair pulled up into a messy topknot, a flashlight in one hand and a book in the other, when I heard the soft ping of something hitting the window. Then, another and another.

I climbed out of bed and peeked out the curtain. Jace stood below in the yard, moonlight catching in his hair as he looked up, another pebble in his hand, with that stupid, perfect smirk.

I opened the window just enough to whisper, "Are you crazy? What are you doing?"

He held up the pebble, closing one eye, and whispered back, "Practicing my aim."

I squinted at him. "It's midnight."

"Exactly," he said, motioning. "Come on. Climb down."

"I'm on the third floor."

"The trellis," he pointed. "Between our windows. I just came down it. You can, too."

I hesitated, looking over at the trellis and then the curtains blowing in his open window. He just waited, grinning like he already knew I'd say yes. I sighed and swung my legs out the window and climbed down. He held the trellis steady, whispering words of encouragement the whole way down.

Nearly to the ground, his hands found my hips to steady me the last few feet. I felt it again. That touch. A jolt. A current. Something. It was nothing. And also... everything.

Before I could say or do anything, he grabbed my hand. "Come on. You have to see this."

We ran barefoot down the winding path through the sea grass, breathless with laughter. Then, we stopped.

I stared. Because the waves—they glowed. Neon green rippled with every movement of the tide, lighting up the shore like the ocean had swallowed the stars and was letting them go again, one by one.

"Oh my god, it's beautiful. What is this?" I whispered.

"Bioluminescence," he said. "Plankton. They light up when the water moves."

"Can we... touch it?"

"Sure."

He took my hand again. My fingers fit into his like they'd always known how. He led me into the surf, our feet swirling with the glowing light.

"Isn't it amazing?" he asked.

I breathed out, looking all around us, "Yeah..."

We walked in the shallows for a while, quiet, the water painting our footsteps in light. Then he stopped. He turned toward me and brushed a piece of hair from my cheek, letting his fingers linger. The night held its breath around us as his eyes searched mine like there was something he'd been meaning to say for a long time, but never had the words.

"I've been, um, thinking about this," he said softly. "A lot."

I wrinkled my brow, not sure what he was

talking about, but then…

Then, he leaned in slowly and kissed me. Not like we were curious kids experimenting. He kissed me like he meant it. Like he'd thought about it a thousand times and finally couldn't hold it back. His lips were soft and sure, pressing against mine as his hand cupped my cheek. The moment went on—sweet and sharp. I felt warm and lit from the inside.

The world didn't spin. It glowed. And for the first time that summer or ever, I felt like maybe this crush, the one I'd had on a boy who'd been my best friend since I was five, wasn't something I'd have to get over. This was possibly something I could fall into.

That night, I was sure that this boy had been made for me, and he'd just kissed me like he'd finally realized it, too.

CHAPTER ELEVEN

Jace

Present Day

That moment I saw her, it was like no time had passed at all. Just bam, there she was—*my Mallie.* The girl I fell in love with when I was five. The one who inspired nearly every song I wrote in a journal I never showed anyone. The girl I thought I'd spend the rest of my life with. The girl who ripped my heart out 10 years later. And the girl I thought I'd never see again. And then she smiled at me across the merch table. One of those moments you remember forever.

It had been a week since that night. And now... Now I was three states away, but she was still everywhere—in my thoughts, in the silence between songs, in the way I kept reaching for her across unfamiliar sheets in a different roadside motel every night.

She looked the same, but not exactly—her hair was a touch darker, a little shorter, like maybe she'd needed a change but hadn't wanted to lose too much. Her laugh had the same rhythm, though it didn't linger as long. And her eyes... they still had that spark, but it flickered now, like a candle near the end of its wick. Like she wanted to let me in, but wasn't sure it was safe anymore.

I kept replaying it. All of it. The way she looked at me. And the way she looked through me, like I was part of some life she'd already let go and wasn't sure she could go back to. I wished, I ached, for just one more day —one more moment.

My bandmates thought I was zoning out because I was tired or coming down with something. And maybe I was. But it was more than that.

I kept replaying every second of our conversations from that night, looking for clues to what happened years ago. I wanted to ask her what happened. Why did she never call? Why did she vanish like I'd meant nothing to her?

But something in her eyes stopped me. There was something haunted there, and I wasn't about to rip it open when she'd just walked back into my life.

But yeah... I wanted answers.

I pulled out the leather-bound notebook I kept in the side pocket of the backseat of the van. No one touched it but me. It wasn't for songs and lyrics I planned to use with the band. It was for the ones I couldn't get out of my head but didn't have the guts to show anyone.

I flipped past pages of scribbled half-verses and melodic ideas until I found a blank space.

She was July and everything after,
    A spark in my chest, a burst of laughter.
    Salt in the air and a pull I couldn't name,
    A tide in my blood I couldn't quite tame.
    I found her once in the light, and again in the dark,

A whisper, a flame, a flickering spark.
And maybe that's what love really means—
Finding your way through forgotten dreams.
Over and over, no matter the cost,
Even when everything feels a little bit lost.

The words just poured out of me, but my hand paused. Some of these lines just hit too close. I tapped my pen against the edge of the page. Did she think about me all those years as much as I had thought of her?

Or did I just imagine it—make her a legend in my head because it was easier than accepting she just didn't want me anymore? I let out a heavy sigh, closing the notebook, and slipping it back into the pocket.

Dean was elbow-deep in a bag of spicy chips in the middle seat, Jake was strumming the same three sad notes on his travel guitar up front with Eddie driving, and I was doing my best impression of a ghost in the corner, staring out the van window like the rain might spell her name if I looked long enough.

They were talking about a stop for lunch, but I wasn't listening. I was still wrapped up with her in my bed that night, her leg thrown over mine under the sheets, her breath warm against my collarbone. Still watching her stir her straw in slow circles through her milkshake at the diner, eyes lowered, like the answer was written in the swirl of melted ice cream if she just looked hard enough.

Mostly, though, I was still remembering the taste of her lips beside her car, the air thick with everything we hadn't said. Still hearing my own voice crack when I told her I couldn't let her go again. And the way she looked at me then, with something flickering in her eyes, offering me a truth she couldn't say yet.

I'd always known something about the way we ended didn't make sense. Sure we were kids, but we had loved each other. Deeply. Truly. And people don't just disappear when they love you. Not like that. Something happened.

I had told her it didn't matter anymore. But the not knowing was eating at me.

"Alright, bro, you've officially hit main character mode," Dean said, flicking a chip at my head. "You've got that thousand-yard stare like your dog just died… or that girl from the other night stole your soul."

Jake didn't even look up. "He's in love. Guarantee it. Did you see that kiss he gave her? And… he's got the look. Bet he wrote a whole verse about her already and deleted it because it was 'too honest.'"

Eddie snorted from the front. "Probably doesn't even remember her name. Watch, it was something like Baylee with a silent Q."

"Real funny, assholes." I rolled my eyes. Softer, I said, "And her name's Mallie, uh… Mallory."

That earned me a pause.

"Oh shit," Jake said, eyes going wide. "We're using real names now?"

"Should we be sitting down for this?" Dean asked. "Is this going to be some kind of Nicholas Sparks flashback?"

I sighed. "Okay, look, you want the short version?"

Three sets of very interested faces turned toward me like I'd just said the word 'tour cancellation.'

"We met when we were five. Our moms were college roommates, and our families would rent this crappy beach house together every summer. We built sandcastles, played pirates, and had a secret hideout in the dunes."

Dean clutched his heart and sang out, "True... love..."

Jake asked, "Did you kiss her under a full moon or...?"

"Actually, yeah, something like that. First kiss when we were thirteen. We snuck out to see the bioluminescence in the tide, and I kissed her."

That shut them up for a second. A miracle, honestly.

Jake asked, "Okay... and ?"

"But then," I went on, voice a little quieter, "something happened. Her parents freaked over something. I was suddenly persona non grata. I still have no idea what happened, but we lost touch. I thought that was it."

"And then...?" Eddie prompted, looking back for a second like this was a soap opera, and I was the cliffhanger.

I dragged a hand down my face, trying to steady the flutter in my chest that always kicked up when I talked about her. "When we got to Dallas last week, I couldn't stop thinking about her. Out of nowhere. Just this feeling. And then—I swear—I saw her in the crowd when I started singing *Real You*. And it was like..."

I trailed off, the words catching before they turned too soft.

"Kismet?" Jake offered, tilting his head.

"Fate?" Dean said, mock-serious, but not unkind.

"Divine intervention?" Eddie added, grinning in the rearview.

I shrugged, looking down at my hands. "It felt like our whole story—every version of her I ever loved—hit me in a single breath, and then she was just...

standing there in front of me at the merch table. And it was like no time had passed."

Jake blinked. "Really?"

"Yeah."

Dean grinned, kicking back against his seat. "Did she know you were the opener?"

"I don't think so," I said, letting my head fall back. "Doubt she even knew I was in a band. She said she'd come to see The Fire Department."

Eddie breathed out, "Wow…"

The guys went quiet. Just long enough for me to breathe it in again—that moment, that flash of her smile under the stage lights like it had always been meant for me.

Then Dean nudged my boot with his. "So what I'm hearing is… this story's better than half our setlist."

Jake raised a brow and grinned. "Who's writing the ballad? Cause this one's gonna leave a scar."

I ignored their shit and just leaned back, heart thudding like I was still on stage. Mallie's face was burned into me now, and I had a feeling nothing could ever shake her loose. Not that I wanted it to.

Finally, they dropped it when a sign for Eddie's favorite Mexican restaurant said it was just a couple of miles away. But as we pulled into the parking lot, Dean leaned over suddenly and turned towards me. I flicked my eyes his way. His eyes narrowed like he was solving a murder mystery in his head.

"Wait a minute," he said, pointing a spicy-chip-dusted finger at me. "Is *Real You* about her?"

The van went dead quiet. Jake actually stopped strumming. Eddie turned off the ignition and turned around in his seat like we'd just entered a true crime podcast.

I bit my lip as I looked away. Didn't say anything. Didn't have to.

Dean let out a low whistle. "Holy shit. That's her song."

I just nodded, slow and tight, staring at the floor. Couldn't look at any of them. Because yeah—every lyric, every line, every heartbreak, that was Mallie. That was always Mallie.

Jake let out a long breath. "Dude."

Dean blinked like he was seeing the setlist in a whole new light. "I've played that song like a hundred times, and I just thought it was about... I don't know, a lost connection or some crap."

"Yeah, well," I muttered, "it is. Just... with her face on it."

Eddie said, "Wait... you wrote that song when you were just a teenager?"

I nodded.

Dean glanced down at the setlist on his phone. "You never really stopped writing about her, did you?"

I let out a long sigh.

Eddie broke the tension when he said, "Dude, when she figures out every song's about her..." He didn't bother finishing—just barked a laugh.

I chuckled, barely. Mostly because I didn't know what else to do with the ache in my chest. I was finally getting a second chance with the girl I'd always believed I would be with forever, and it was just too much to think about. Too much to hope.

Yeah, *Real You* was hers. It had always been. I wrote it when I was reeling after her mother said those things that broke my whole world into pieces —accusing me of something so vile. Something I would never do. I could never do.

I still vividly remember when my mom looked

me in the eye and asked me if it was true. She believed me. She knew I'd never do something like that, but I still felt something inside me tear in two. That was the last time I heard Mallie's name spoken in our house.

But even then—even when everything burned down around me—I knew in my heart it wasn't the whole story. I knew Mallie—the real Mallie. We had promised *Always* to each other—and meant it. And whatever had happened, whatever she'd been told to say or not say, there was something else beneath it. Something I could never figure out.

So I did what I always did when I needed to work through something—I wrote songs. Every lyric was a question she never got to answer. Every chord, a thread back to the girl I knew and loved with my whole heart—the one who kissed me under stars, who held my hand like it was forever.

Now she was back. And when she looked at me that night, I saw everything we were, all over again. That same fire she always had, only this time it was a little dulled and hidden by something. I honestly wasn't sure what had done that to her, and I desperately wanted to know.

I never asked, and she never brought it up, but I wondered if she recognized herself in the lyrics. Did she hear the heartbreak of a boy who never stopped waiting for the truth? Waiting for her? And if she did... Would she ever tell me what really happened? Or would she slip away like the summer again?

CHAPTER TWELVE

Jace

Age 14 - Rockport

Now that I was fourteen, my body had finally started to figure things out. My voice didn't crack every time I opened my mouth. I wasn't all elbows and knees anymore.

But my mom, god help me, kept saying I looked so... "rugged" now—whatever that meant. One day, Mallie overheard her, and she was never going to let me live it down.

She started calling me Paul Bunyan Junior in this over-the-top Southern accent, drawling it out like, "Paaawl BUN-yun June-yore," with her hand on her heart like she might faint from the drama—and then she'd burst into snorting giggles that always made me grin, even when I tried not to.

She did it so often that I rolled my eyes when she just looked at me with that stupid, certain grin on her face.

One morning, after the fifth or sixth "Well bless yer rugged little heart, Junior," I leaned in a little too close and said, "Careful there, darlin'. Keep that up, and I might have to start calling you something like... Mallie-boo Barbie."

She gave me the most dramatic eye roll a girl's ever pulled off and muttered, "That's the best you got?" before stealing the last bite of my Pop-Tart like it was revenge.

I stared, my mouth open. She laughed, flipping her braid over her shoulder like she hadn't just short-circuited my brain.

"Better watch yourself, Bunyan. This Barbie has sharp teeth."

"Yeah," I said, eyes lingering longer than I meant to. "I know."

But I didn't actually mind the stupid nickname. Because we were together again, back at the beach house—our beach house—even if it didn't belong to either of us. Same creaky screen door. Same old porch swing. Same stretch of sand that made everything else fade away.

We fell right back into being us. Best friends. Partners in crime. Like always. Only it wasn't exactly like always. Not since last summer, when I kissed her in the glowing surf, just once, soft and unsure. Both of us were breathing like the whole world had tilted, but we were the only ones who felt it.

But this summer... I never brought it up. She didn't either. I told myself it was because we didn't want to mess things up. It was better to keep things simple. But the truth was, I didn't know what to do or what to say. So I just pretended it hadn't happened.

We just went back to what we did best— exploring. That first week, we found a cave opening wedged in the rocks at low tide about a half mile away, one we swore hadn't been there before. It was tucked so deep you couldn't see it from the path, even if you were standing on top of it.

We were convinced it was a pirate hideaway full of secrets, and we named it Hollowbone. We made maps in our notebooks, drew symbols on the walls in charcoal, told each other it was cursed, or magic, or both. It became our secret place. But when we were there, I never held her hand or kissed her. And maybe I should have.

Because a few days later, Caitlyn showed up. She'd been here before, a couple of summers ago, but not enough to count as one of us. Still, by the second morning, she found us—strawberry lip gloss, sparkly tank top, and all—asking what we were doing and if she could come, too.

Mallie didn't say much. Just shrugged and went back to drawing spirals in the sand with a stick. But Caitlyn stayed right next to me.

She laughed too loudly at my jokes, kept bumping into me when we walked, and asked me to carry her stuff like her arms had suddenly stopped working. I didn't totally mind the attention, if I was being honest. Part of me wanted to prove I wasn't just a little kid anymore. But I felt Mallie's eyes on me like she was trying to burn a hole through me.

Every time I glanced over, Mallie looked away. Her jaw tightened, and her whole body stiffened like she was trying not to be completely annoyed with Caitlyn.

But then... Caitlyn "lost" her heart-shaped sunglasses in the dunes.

"I think I dropped them near the path," she said, brushing her hand down my arm like that would help me care. "Can you come help me look? I want to find them before the tide comes in."

Mallie was crouched near the entrance to

Hollowbone, sketching something in the dirt. She didn't look up.

I hesitated. But then I stupidly said, "Sure."

Caitlyn and I were gone for maybe fifteen minutes. When I came back, Mallie looked up and immediately packed up her notebook. She slung her backpack over her shoulder and started walking down the beach like I didn't exist. She spent the rest of the afternoon in the kitchen helping with dinner.

Afterwards, once it was dark, we went ghost crab hunting. Mom's idea—mostly for David, who, at eight years old, still thought anything that moved was a mystical creature sent to play with him. He ran ahead with our parents not far behind, shrieking about a crab the size of a dog.

Mallie and I had done this a hundred times before, but this time, she hung back, not saying a word. Her flashlight swung low in her hand, barely aimed at the sand, like she couldn't care less if she spotted anything. She didn't laugh. Didn't tease. Just slowed her steps like she didn't want to be there.

I aimed my flashlight at a cluster of rocks near the walkway, the beam catching on bits of wet shell and seaweed. I crouched down, nudging a stone with my toe like I was tracking something scuttling beneath it. But… I wasn't really paying attention to any of it. I was listening for her footsteps in the sand, closing the space between us.

When she finally caught up, I didn't look at her right away. Just let the silence stretch between us, tightening my grip on the flashlight.

"You mad or something?" I asked, keeping my tone light, even though my pulse had started to pick up.

She picked up her pace, brushing past me, her ponytail swinging, and tossed over her shoulder,

"Nope," popping the P like a door slamming shut.

I exhaled hard, the last thread of patience snapping. "Seriously, Mallie?" My voice rose as I threw my hands in the air. "What's wrong with you?"

She scoffed and said, "Didn't want to cramp your new fan club."

I frowned, jogging up and stepping in front of her, making her stop. "What's that supposed to mean?"

She huffed. "It means Caitlyn can find her own stupid sunglasses. And maybe stop hanging all over you every five seconds when we're trying to have *our* summer."

A flicker of something lit in my chest. I raised an eyebrow, "Wait... you're jealous?"

She scoffed and stepped around me, but I caught the wobble in her voice. "No. I'm—no. I just..." She huffed out a breath and put her hands on her hips. "She's annoying."

I grinned as I caught up. "You *are* jealous."

"Shut up, Jace."

I tried to keep the smile from my voice. "I didn't think..." I trailed off, rubbing the back of my neck. "After last summer... You never said anything. I thought maybe you didn't—"

"You never said anything either!" she snapped, stopping so fast I nearly ran into her. "I didn't know if you meant it or if..."

I cut her off, "I meant it, Mallie." I said softly, "We promised each other. *Always*, remember? And I meant it. All of it. Everything. "

The waves lapped nearby, the only sound filling the gap between us. David's laughter echoed farther down the beach, but it felt like we were in our own world, miles away from everyone.

I stalked towards her, putting my hand on her

waist. "You're the only girl I wanna chase crabs with."

Her laugh came out surprised, shaky. "That's the dumbest romantic thing I've ever heard."

"I can do better," I whispered as I came closer.

And then I kissed her. This time, I tilted her chin up gently, brushed my lips over hers once, then again—deeper, slower, until she opened for me. My tongue found hers, and the world just… vanished.

I didn't care if we got caught. She grabbed the front of my t-shirt with both hands, and I felt her melt into me, this soft, breathless sound slipping from her lips that I would remember for the rest of my life.

This was nothing like last summer. When we finally pulled apart, she was flushed, eyes wide, blinking like she'd just surfaced from underwater.

"You good?" I asked, my voice a little hoarse.

She nodded slowly, biting her lower lip. "Uh… yeah. Just… wow."

I reached down, found her hand, and laced my fingers through hers.

"Yeah," I said. "Me, too."

Hollowbone was supposed to be another one of our goofy adventures—like always. We brought snacks, a flashlight, a blanket to sit on, and her sketchbook. She wanted to draw some of the charcoal markings we'd added to the walls, and I told her I had an idea for a secret code we could hide in our maps.

But we never got to any of it. Because the second we ducked through the dunes and into that little hideout we'd claimed as ours, her hand found mine, and my stomach flipped so hard I forgot why we were there.

Mallie sat down on the blanket and tugged me

next to her. Her sun-kissed knees brushed mine. We started talking—easy, familiar—but our fingers stayed linked. Then she looked at me a little too long, like she was waiting for me to stop stalling.

I leaned in. Just a quick kiss. Then another. And another.

Before I knew it, I was lying beside her, one hand tangled in her dark hair while the other curled around her waist like it belonged there.

Her lips were soft and warm, and she tasted like watermelon gum. Her fingers caressed my shoulder, and she sighed into my mouth like I was something she'd been missing.

Every time we kissed, it lasted a little longer. Every time I pulled back, she tugged me closer. It wasn't urgent or desperate—it was just us, figuring out the edges of something new. Hollowbone had always felt like it belonged to us. But every afternoon, we ended up there, and it started to feel like we belonged to each other more and more.

We broke apart for breath, foreheads pressed together, both of us smiling like idiots.

"I think I forgot how to breathe," she whispered, her voice husky and low.

"Same," I said, laughing softly as I tucked a loose piece of hair behind her ear. "Pretty sure I'm ruined now."

She rolled her eyes, but her cheeks flushed. "Ruined, huh?"

"Yep," I said, leaning in again. "For anyone else..."

I wasn't ready to tell her I was in love with her, but I knew it deep down. I couldn't imagine kissing anyone else, wanting anyone else, loving... anyone else.

We didn't talk much after that. Just more kisses.

Slow. Sweet. A little bolder each time.

Outside, the tide crept up the shore, and the wind shifted through the dune grass like it was trying to warn us that summer was slipping through our fingers. But inside Hollowbone, time bent around us. Stretched. Softened. And I remember thinking— if she asked me to stay here forever, I would.

CHAPTER THIRTEEN

Mallie

Present Day

It started with a text.

Jace: Still thinking about that cinnamon roll you made disappear like a magician.

Also, can't stop writing lyrics that rhyme with "July." I blame you.

I stared at the screen before I even realized I was smiling. I was curled on the couch in my favorite threadbare sweatshirt, a mug of tea tucked in my lap, and the ghost of my fifteen-year-old self whispering, *Don't fall for him again.*

But it was too late.

Me: What rhymes with "July"? Pie? Sigh? Ill-advised?

His reply came fast.

* * *

Jace: Sigh. Definitely sigh. Also possibly "surprise."

It had been a week, just seven days since I'd seen him, kissed him, touched him. Wrapped myself around him. But we had talked, texted, or FaceTimed every day since he'd been here. Sometimes it was a good morning message or a late-night voice note when he couldn't sleep. Other times, we'd FaceTime after a show. He'd send me scraps of lyrics, little videos from the tour van or the stage during soundcheck with his bandmates, blurry snapshots of diner breakfasts and gas station coffee stops that made me laugh harder than I had in a long time.

We were older, but somehow still found the rhythm we used to have—the way we'd volley sarcasm and trade inside jokes only we could understand. We still reminisced about the beach house summers—the time David built a "seagull buffet" with chips on the porch and accidentally invited three birds into the kitchen. And when I slipped and fell on a dead jellyfish that still stung me, he carried me like I was made of glass.

Nostalgia was a dangerous thing. It was easy. Too easy.

Then he called late one night, his voice low and warm in my ear. "I've got three days off," he said. "I was thinking maybe I'd come see you."

I froze on the spot and didn't say anything back.

"Unless that's weird," he added quickly. "You don't have to say yes. I just… I want to see you. See where you live. What your world looks like now."

My heart beat too fast. I wanted him to come. Desperately. I craved his lips on mine again, his body intertwined with mine. But I also knew what he didn't—that if he came here, if he saw that box sitting on the bookshelf, if he started asking more questions—I might have to tell him everything. About why my mom made up that lie. About the baby. The adoption.

I wasn't sure I was ready. Or how he'd react.

"Can we wait?" I asked gently. "Just a little. Let me get used to this…" Whatever this was.

There was a pause. No breath. Just… nothing. I swallowed hard. His quiet hit harder than words ever could. My fingers gripped the phone tighter. I could almost picture the way he'd pull back, jaw clenched, eyes darting away like they always did when he was trying not to let something show when we were kids.

I'd hurt him. I didn't need to see his face to know that. And that gutted me because hurting him was the last thing I ever wanted.

Then finally—

"Yeah," he sighed before he said, "Of course. No rush. I'll just keep annoying you from a safe distance."

If he only knew, I'd been replaying his last voicemail all day. The way his voice dipped low when he said my name. The faint background noise of traffic and, just before he hung up, that quiet laugh he probably didn't mean for me to hear. It had filled my ears like sunlight, warm and dangerous.

"You're not annoying me," I murmured, tucking the phone closer like I could pull his voice through the line and keep it.

But after we hung up, I didn't sleep. I couldn't. I just stared at the ceiling, regretting that I told him to wait, wondering how long I could keep pretending this was simple. That reconnecting with the love of my life wouldn't unravel everything I'd spent the last thirteen years trying to hide and survive. Because the truth was coming, and when it did, I had no idea if he'd still look at me the same way.

The next day, I walked around the Square. The bell above the door let out a tired little chime as I pushed inside Recycled—cool air wrapped around me. The scent of aged paper, sunbaked wood, and the faintest trace of patchouli. The combination smelled like time itself had steeped into the walls. Dust floated in the late afternoon light, slicing through the high front windows, catching on the spines of books like memories caught mid-sentence.

I didn't have a title in mind—no purpose to even be there. I just needed to be somewhere else. Out of the house. Out from under Sonny's too-careful questions. Out from Claire's soft, knowing glances. Out from the truth that sat like a stone under my ribs—I'd stupidly told him not to come. And now I couldn't stop hearing his voice on the phone, hopeful and warm and a little unsteady. *I'll just keep annoying you from a safe distance.*

Dammit! Why had I said no?

The stairs to the fiction section creaked under my weight. My hand grazed the worn banister as I reached the top. I wandered between the stacks, fingers trailing spines without reading them, just breathing in someone else's stories for a while— because mine felt like too much.

I was halfway down the third aisle when I saw it —*Ever Summer After*, shoved between two crime thrillers like it didn't belong. The cover was creased. I reached for it, and something fluttered out.

A folded note drifted to the floor, soft as a feather, landing at my feet. I bent down, heart thudding, and picked it up. The paper was yellowed at the edges. I opened it, and it took less than a sentence.

My legs buckled, just a little. I gripped the shelf beside me. Because I knew this handwriting. I knew the words. It was mine. It was the letter. The one I wrote at fifteen, trembling in my room with a Sharpie and a tear-streaked face. The one I'd meant to send to Jace—my last attempt before giving up. A confession. A desperate cry. *I'm sorry. I'm scared. I think I'm pregnant.*

I remembered my mother had found it. How? I had no idea. I'd hidden in a book on my shelf. But her face was white-hot with rage, and I swore she'd ripped it into pieces in front of me and told me to forget him.

We lived in Austin then. So how the hell did it end up here? Whole.

My fingers trembled. My ears rang. The bookstore was silent except for the hum of the nearby window unit and my own uneven breathing.

I shoved the note into my purse. Put the book back where I found it and walked out. Fast. Not looking back. Not ready to ask the questions clawing their way up my throat. Not ready for what it meant—that something I thought was lost and destroyed was back again, and it found me.

By the time I got back to the house, the sun was low and buttery across the living room windows. I could hear feminine laughter before I even opened the door. Darci and Claire were curled up on the couch, a blanket twisted around their legs and a half-empty bag of popcorn between them. A dramatic narrator was describing blood spatter as if it were a bedtime story.

"Mallory!" Darci called, twisting around with a sly grin. "I texted you earlier. It's Murder Night, and we're judging the cops' facial hair in this documentary. Come. Join us."

"She already hates three of them," Claire added with a laugh, tucking her feet and patting the seat next to her.

Darci tossed a piece of popcorn in her mouth. "And I stand by it. If your mustache looks like it moonlights as a taxidermy intern's first project, I have concerns, and I'm gonna assume you're guilty of something."

I laughed—genuinely—and dropped my keys onto the entryway table. "You're both unwell."

Claire patted the couch cushion beside her again. "Come sit."

I wanted to. It would've been so easy to fall into that warmth, the bubble of their affection. And I knew it was what I needed, but… the note in my bag felt like a stone dragging me under.

"I'd love to," I said, trying to sound casual. "But I've got a deadline. A client expecting a pitch first thing tomorrow."

Darci gave me a mock pout. "Boo, capitalism."

"Rain check," I promised, already turning for the hallway.

Once I reached my room, I shut the door behind me and leaned back against it. I could still hear their laughter and the muffled hum of the TV down the hall, and I felt a pang of regret.

I sat on the edge of the bed and pulled the note from my purse with careful fingers, like it might crumble if I moved too fast. I unfolded it and reread the words. My own voice, younger and aching, echoed back at me from the past.

I'm sorry. I'm scared. I don't know what to do. I think I'm pregnant.

I miss you. I love you.

* * *

I traced the edges of the paper, letting the silence press in. And then—on instinct—I flipped it over. At first, it looked blank. But then, there was... something. Faint. Scrawled in unfamiliar handwriting. Not mine.

Tell him. Or lose him again.

And below that, almost like a signature...

It was always meant to be.

The hairs on the back of my neck stood up. The air felt different all of a sudden, electric and thin. I ran my finger over the writing, my skin tingling.

I didn't know how it got there. I didn't know who wrote it. But somehow, deep down, I felt the truth of it settle into my bones like something ancient and real. Maybe I hadn't just stumbled across that note. Maybe it had been waiting.

I took a breath and folded the note along the old seams—half, then half again—pressing each crease until it held. When it was small enough to disappear inside my fist, I walked over to the box on the shelf. I pulled it down and sat cross-legged on the rug.

Inside, time waited. I ran my fingers over the hospital bracelets, the folded discharge papers, and the photo I wasn't supposed to have. My throat stung. I rested my fingertips on the picture, not daring to lift it.

"Hi," I whispered, but it wasn't to the box.

I set the note on top of the bracelets and paused. For a heartbeat, I hovered, then changed my mind and slid it beneath them, tucking it farther down like it belonged with the rest of the truths I hadn't known where to put.

I closed the box and stood up, sliding it back into place on the shelf. When I turned around, everything else still looked exactly the same. Same bed. Same lamp glow on the wall. Same shadows in the corners.

But I didn't feel any better. I just felt weird... like maybe the past wasn't done with me. And what that even meant.

Then, I got ready for bed, turned off the light, and lay down, facing the shelf, wondering what it meant. And I didn't try to forget. I let it be there. I let her be there.

CHAPTER FOURTEEN

Mallie

Age 14 - Rockport

It was nearly the end of summer, the way it always crept up too fast. The air felt a little cooler, the days a little shorter, and our parents had gone all-in on one last cookout on the beach behind the house.

They invited everybody—the families from the other beach houses, even the old couple who owned the tiny souvenir shop down the road. Our moms headed into town for groceries, while both our dads dragged out the folding tables and the big, rusted grill, as if it were some kind of ceremony.

Somewhere in the mix, Jace's dad, Fred, sent Sonny and Jace down the beach to gather up as many beach umbrellas as they could find from the neighbors. It took them the better part of the morning knocking on doors and calling out to people we barely knew.

I was stuck in the kitchen. My mom had me make the strawberry salad first thing so that it could chill in the fridge before the party. I finished way before they got back, wiping my hands on a dish towel and slipping out to the sand with an old magazine while my dad cleaned up the grill.

But really, I was watching for Jace and Sonny. They hauled in what had to be at least a dozen umbrellas, Jace dragging his half across the sand like a pack mule. I lay back on a beach towel, flipping pages, pretending not to watch him through my sunglasses, but I was. I felt his eyes find me more times than I could count.

By the time they were done, the beach behind the house looked twice as big as it had this morning. People were already arriving to stake their claim, bringing folding chairs and coolers. Fred came around the side of the house, a bag of ice in each hand, before sending Sonny and Jace back to the car for cases of sodas and beer, shouting something over his shoulder that made the grownups laugh. The party hadn't even started yet, but it already felt like the whole world was showing up.

David had been complaining that he was bored since breakfast, so when Fred asked if we could keep him busy until the party started, I grabbed some shovels and the old red pail, and Jace, David, and I headed further down the beach. We found a spot near the tide line, where the sand was damp and easy to dig, and set to work. David dug like his life depended on it. Jace started packing wet sand into the bucket, flipping it over to build the first tower of what he called the Super Duper Amazing Sandcastle —his words, not mine.

David was the one who found something first—a smooth, pale sand dollar, completely intact. He held it up like it was solid gold before shrieking and nearly jumping out of his skin when a tiny school of fish darted around his ankles.

I sat down beside him in the shallow water, showing him how to dig wider and slower, letting the tide help us. After a little while, he stood up and started running through the surf and diving into the water before deciding to help Jace pack the pail with sand for more towers.

They kept building towers, Jace humming some song I couldn't quite place. But I kept on digging, and that's when I hit something. It felt solid under my shovel, not like the usual shells or bits of driftwood. I dug my fingers in, pulling it loose from the packed sand.

It was a chest of some kind—small, maybe the size of a jewelry box, with little brass hinges half-rusted shut.

I glanced at the boys—they hadn't noticed. My heart thudded a little harder as I popped it open. Inside was a small pendant, shaped like a tiny star. It was tarnished with streaks of black and worn smooth like it had been buried for a long time, but I swear it flared in the sunlight for just a second. It didn't look like it was worth much, but somehow it felt... special, like it had been waiting for someone to find it.

I slipped it into my pocket before they could notice. I didn't know why. I just wanted to hold on to it for a minute. I had this stupid thought about stringing it on something and giving it to Jace before the summer ended.

But I did hold up the empty box. "Look what I found!" I called out.

David and Jace scrambled over, forgetting all about the castle.

"Cool!" David shouted as he grabbed it from my hands. "It's like a real treasure chest!"

Jace leaned in, taking it from David and brushing the sand off the old wooden lid, his finger tracing the edge like it might reveal something to him.

"Where'd you find it?" he asked, his voice low, like maybe he thought it could actually be real treasure.

I swallowed and shifted back on my heels, wiping my sandy palms on my shorts.

"Buried about a foot deep right here while I was digging," I said, nodding toward the huge hole filled with water in front of me. "My shovel hit something hard. Thought it was driftwood or a big rock at first."

I tried to sound casual, like it wasn't a big deal. Like my heart hadn't skipped when I opened it and found the little star.

Jace looked up at me then, grinning like I'd just handed him a map to something huge. I forced myself to smile, hoping he couldn't tell I was holding something back. He popped the lid all the way open and let out a low whistle, even though there was nothing in it but damp sand and a few pieces of seaweed.

"Well," he said, brushing it out with his hand, "guess it's up to us to fill it."

David perked up at that, already digging through the sand like he expected pirate gold to just appear. "What do we put in it?"

Jace looked at me with that crooked grin that always made my stomach do something weird. "Only the best stuff," he said, like it was obvious.

So that's what we did. They forgot all about building the castle. Instead, the three of us started digging and collecting, like we were pirates and this was our real treasure chest. We found a piece of green sea glass, smooth as marble. A bent gold earring with no match. Tiny white shells shaped like little trumpets. A metal bead from someone's broken bracelet.

By the time we finished, the box was full of junk that only we could've thought was priceless. The sun was setting, and we knew it was time to get back to the beach house. The party would start soon.

We snapped it shut, and I carried it back with us like we had something worth everything. And even though they didn't know it, I was proud of the real treasure tucked safely in my pocket.

As we walked back, David said, "I bet pirates really left it here, like… a long, long time ago."

Jace smirked, ruffling David's hair. "Yeah? What if it's cursed? Maybe whoever touches it gets turned into a crab."

David gasped so loudly that I almost laughed. "Like… forever?"

I shook my head, rolling my eyes, but I couldn't stop the smile tugging at my mouth. "Please. If it were real pirate treasure, they wouldn't leave seaweed in it."

I leaned over to David, dropping my voice like I was telling the world's biggest secret. "I think it was left here by a shipwrecked prince. He had to bury his greatest treasures before the sea witches could steal them."

David glanced at the chest, his mouth dropped open like I'd just changed his whole life. "What kind of treasures?"

Jace picked up an old bottle cap with the word Lucky stamped across the top, turning it between his fingers. "The Lucky coin," he said, real serious now. "Legend says if you flip it three times under a full moon, you can wish for anything you want."

David scrambled to grab it, almost dropping it again.

I blurted out, "What would you wish for?"

Jace looked at me for just a second, but long enough to see the mirth in his eyes. "I'm not telling," he said, grinning. "If you say it out loud, it won't come true."

David nodded, like that sealed it.

I slipped my fingers into my pocket, brushing over the little star, wondering what I'd wish for if I ever got the chance.

All night, throughout the party, I couldn't stop thinking about the little star-shaped charm I'd tucked in my pocket like it was waiting to be found and waiting for me.

Back in my room, I rummaged through the pockets of my duffel and pulled out the shark tooth necklace I'd embarrassingly begged my mom to buy me from the souvenir shop when I was seven. I'd worn it everywhere that summer—thought it made me look brave, cool, maybe even a little dangerous.

The shark tooth was long gone now, probably lost to a rogue wave or one of our adventures, but the leather cord was still intact. I slid the star onto it and tied it off again. It was nothing fancy. But the second I saw it, something in my bones whispered it was his, like it had been waiting there all along—for me to find, for him to keep.

The next afternoon, Jace and I walked into town for ice cream. It was one of those slow, hot days when even the beach and the water felt like too much effort. He got mint chip. I got black cherry. We took the corner booth by the window, the one where we'd sat a hundred times before. I couldn't stop fidgeting. The necklace was in my pocket, the star warm from my hand. I didn't even know why I brought it—except I did.

"I made you something," I said, suddenly nervous, unable to meet his eyes.

He raised an eyebrow, curious, as I set it gently on the table.

"This cord used to be my shark tooth necklace," I said, trying not to cringe. "Remember the one I begged my mom for when I was little?"

He grinned and nodded like he remembered it, like he remembered everything.

"And then... I found this star in the treasure box yesterday. I thought maybe... if you wanted... it could be yours now."

He didn't tease. Didn't make it weird. He just looked at me with something quiet and warm in his eyes, then slipped the cord over his head. It landed just under his Adam's apple, lifting when he swallowed.

"I love it," he said, voice low. "Thanks, Mallie."

And under the table, without looking, he found my pinky with his—and didn't let go.

CHAPTER FIFTEEN

Jace

Present Day

She didn't want me to come. She'd said to wait. But I booked a flight the day after our last show that week. The morning after the show, I tossed a duffel over my shoulder and told the guys I'd be off the grid for a few days. Eddie gave me a look like he knew it was about her. I didn't confirm or deny it. Some things don't need to be said out loud.

I'd texted her my flight info right before I boarded the plane.

Me: Wheels up soon. Claim me at baggage. I'll be the guy who needs you more than sleep.

And when I spotted her just outside baggage claim, standing with her arms crossed, sunglasses perched in her hair with one brow up and a smirk that knew me, my chest did that dumb stutter it only did for her.

She looked like a version of summer I used to dream about. She still had that restless, sun-warmed glow, and she still made my stomach do that stupid, traitorous flip.

She spotted me and offered a small smile. "Hey."

I couldn't help my grin when I said, "Hey, Mallie."

Her smile widened just a fraction. No one else ever called her that. I used to tell myself it was because she made everything feel a little softer—a little more mine.

"You came," she said, like she still didn't quite believe it.

I tilted my head when I said, "I know you said wait, but you sounded like you wanted me to come."

Her smirk flickered. Heat climbed her cheeks as she glanced away, the keys in her fist giving a tiny jingle. "I did," she said, soft, then steadier as she met my eyes.

I slung the strap of my duffel higher on my shoulder and leaned over to kiss her cheek. Then, I grinned and said, "Called it."

She drove us to a cozy little bungalow surrounded by big trees in a quiet neighborhood with a wide porch and mismatched patio furniture. It was Sonny's, she explained. I remembered Sonny. Barely. He was like ten years older than us, but he came every summer with his family to the beach house. Always seemed like he was trying too hard to be the adult.

His fiancée, Claire met us at the door with a warm smile and a tea towel slung over her shoulder.

"You must be Jameson," she said. "Or do I call you Jay?"

"Dealer's choice," I said.

She laughed. There was something easy about her—a calm presence that instantly made you like her.

Mallie had told me on the drive over that she didn't know Claire all that well before moving in, but you'd never know it. I watched the way Claire talked to her, folded her in like she belonged, and I could tell that meant more to Mallie than she ever said out loud.

The screen door to the back porch banged open, and a blur of brown fur came skidding across the floor. A Boxer dog galloped straight for me like I was his long-lost person, tail helicoptering a mile a minute. He nudged my hand with his nose, then did a few tight, joyful loops in front of me—absolutely losing it with excitement like I was Santa and steak combined.

I crouched, scratching behind his ears as he wiggled and whined, soaking up every second of affection.

Mallie crouched down next to me, "Meet Bandit, my brother's pride and joy."

Sonny followed him in, carrying the sun with him like he always had, tall and tan, still somehow looking exactly like the guy who used to glare at me across the bonfires when Mallie and I sat too close. But now, he sported a full beard and a grin.

"He likes you," Sonny said, handing me a beer. "Which is weird, considering you've never met. But hey—he's got good instincts."

I smirked as I stood up, glancing down at the dog who'd leaned against my leg and basically declared me his favorite person.

"Smart dog," I said.

Sonny chuckled. "Or knows an easy target."

After dinner—lemon pasta and homemade bread with soft music and laughter in the kitchen, Mallie and I slipped outside onto the back porch. Bandit insisted on coming, chasing bunnies through the yard.

The evening air was thick with that warm, humid Texas heat, crickets humming, stars peeking out. She leaned over the railing. Her hair was pulled up, and one foot crossed over the other like she was trying to seem more relaxed than she was.

"I know it's kind of weird," she said. "I'm almost 30 and living with my brother like I'm some kind of failure to launch. I'm constantly being bombarded with their perfect fairytale world. Bridesmaid duties, group chats I didn't ask for…"

I smiled. "You like it."

She shot me a look. "I didn't say that."

"But you do," I said softly. "It shows. You're standing still for once."

She sighed, then shrugged one shoulder. "Claire's… perfect for Sonny. So perfect and nice. Too nice. I keep waiting for the catch."

I stepped a little closer. "Maybe there isn't one."

She didn't answer.

"I've missed this," I said after a beat. "Just… talking to you. Our friendship."

She looked up at me. "We've barely said anything."

I smiled. "Doesn't matter. Still feels like… home."

Her cheeks turned red as she turned away, like she didn't know what to do with that.

"I want to ask you something," I said. "But I'll back off if it's too much."

She glanced back at me for just a second before staring off into the trees. Her jaw tensed. "What?"

"I know I said it didn't matter, but… will you tell me what really happened, Mallie? Back then. Why your mom… Why you disappeared?" I sighed, "I feel like there's something missing, and I think I deserve to know."

She didn't speak for a long time. Her hands gripped the porch railing, her knuckles turning white before she walked towards the screen door and let Bandit back in the house. I thought maybe she was going to shut down. Walk inside.

"You deserve to know," she said softly, "And I want to tell you. But… It's not something I can say out loud. Not yet."

I walked over next to her. "Okay, when you're ready…"

She turned to me then. Her eyes were shadowed, full of things she wasn't ready to say. But she didn't ask me to leave. And when my fingers brushed her waist, she didn't pull away.

We stayed on the back porch longer than we probably should've. My arms wrapped around her as she leaned against me, watching the stars blink to life. Mallie burrowed into my chest, like she was cold, but I knew it wasn't the breeze.

I tried to tell myself this was enough—just being near her again, just holding her again. But it wasn't. So I tried one more time. I tightened my hold, like I could make a promise with muscle alone. Land here, I thought. I'll be your soft landing—every time. Let the world swing, and I'll be the place that doesn't.

I didn't think I said it out loud, but against my chest, I felt her relax, letting out the kind of breath that sounded like she'd been holding it for years.

"I know you want me to tell you everything," she whispered. "I just… I want to. I'm just… not ready. I worry you won't be ready either. And I don't want to lose you. Not again."

"You won't lose me, Mallie. Remember we said… Always."

I rested my chin on her head, the scent of her strawberry shampoo hitting me like a memory I didn't know I'd kept.

"I got your last text," I said.

She shifted slightly in my arms, looked up at me, confused. "From this morning?"

I shook my head.

"No. I mean the last one. Back then. When you said, 'I carry you with me now.'"

Her breath caught. "You did?" she asked, voice soft, disbelieving.

I nodded. "But I never knew what you meant by it."

She looked away, toward the yard, lips parting like she might explain. "I..."

But the words never came. She looked back at me instead, eyes searching mine, like she was trying to decide if it was safe.

And then she leaned forward—slow, quiet—and rested her forehead against my chest.

"I want to tell you..." she murmured. "I just... can't, yet. I've never told... anyone." The last words she barely spoke, just breathing them out.

"I'll be here. I'm not going anywhere. You can tell me... when you're ready."

I held her there, my arms circling her like I could keep the rest of the world out if I just stood still enough. The crickets hummed. A breeze shifted the wind chimes.

She didn't say anything else. And I didn't ask again. Instead, I slid my hand down her arm, fingers curling gently around hers. She didn't pull away. Just followed—barefoot, silent—as I led her inside. The house had gone still, humming only with the quiet sounds of the night.

Claire and Sonny had already gone to bed, taking the dog with them. Their door was closed down the hall. They'd left a hallway lamp on, casting a warm amber glow. It made everything feel gentler and quieter, as if the house itself was giving us space.

Mallie didn't say much as we stepped into her room. She closed the door behind us with a soft click, and I turned to face her, both of us standing at the foot of her bed. For a second, neither of us moved. Her eyes flicked up to mine, wide and unsure and wanting.

I reached for her hand and brought it to my chest. "We don't have to do anything tonight. No expectations," I said gently, brushing my thumb across her knuckles. "I just… I can just hold you all night, if you'd like."

Her breath hitched. She didn't answer right away. Just looked at me like I was something fragile she hadn't let herself touch in years.

But then she stepped closer. Her fingers caught the hem of my shirt, and she whispered, "I need this. I need you."

There wasn't anything rushed or wild about it. No desperation, no frenzy. Just the weight of everything pressing down on us—the years, the silence, the ache of what could've been—and now finally was.

My hands found her waist, and I leaned down, brushing my mouth over hers. Once. Twice. Like a vow.

Then I swiped my tongue against her lips. She opened for me, and our kiss deepened, slow and full of every "I missed you" I didn't know how to say. Her hands found my chest, then curled around my back, pulling me closer like she needed to feel every inch of me.

We undressed in silence. I pulled her shirt over her head. My fingertips were grazing the line of her spine before sliding my hands down into the waistband of her pants and underwear, and pushing them down her legs. She lifted my shirt, pulling it over my head and tossing it aside, and I unhooked her bra and pulled it off her. Her mouth was against mine again and again as she unbuckled my belt and popped the button on my jeans before I kicked them and my boxers off.

I didn't know what happened. Not yet. But I knew whatever took her away had left marks. I could feel them in the way she held so much tension in her body, the way she let it go only when I held her in my arms. And if this were how I could ease it —if this was how I could remind her who she used to be, who we still were underneath it all—I'd give her that. Over and over again.

I held her first. Just held her. Her back to my chest, my hand caressing her body, my nose tucked into her hair. She was warm and soft, and it was all I had ever begged for in my prayers, in my dreams. She turned after a moment, eyes on mine, and pulled me into a kiss that made me feel molten. And that... told me exactly what she needed without a single word.

I trailed my lips down her neck to her chest and sucked one of her nipples in my mouth as she arched into me, closing her eyes. I let my fingers play with her other breast, palming it, rubbing my thumb over her hardened nipple as she moaned, pulling me even tighter against her. I let go with a pop and came back, licking the corner of her lip before taking her mouth completely.

My hand migrated to her heat, feeling the wetness through her dark curls. I pressed a finger into her, curling it just the right way. She gasped and breathed out my name as I slowly worked a second finger in while pressing my thumb into her clit. Her legs widened as my strokes grew steady.

I licked up her neck and whispered against her ear, "Is this what you needed, baby?"

"God, yes…"

She was riding my hand like she would shatter soon.

"Fuck… Jace… don't stop. Please…"

I grinned at her, one hand wrapped around her body, the other fucking her like it was my only job.

"Come for me. All over my hand."

"Oh fuck… I'm going to…"

Before she could finish her thought, she let out a low moan. "Oh… my…. God… Jace…"

I kept pumping in and out until she started to come down. Then, I pulled my fingers from her, bringing them to my mouth. Her eyes darkened and dazed as she watched, breathless, still trembling from her release as I sucked each one.

Her hands reached out to my abs and slid down, finding my rock-hard cock, and she began to stroke me.

She whimpered, "I need you… Now. Please…"

I leaned closer, sucking her bottom lip into my mouth before kissing her again.

I growled and said, "I love it when you beg."

I leaned over the bed, found my jeans, and pulled out a condom. I tossed it to her, and she slowly unrolled it over my pulsing cock. Then I rolled her to her back and crawled between her legs, lining up with her entrance. I pushed in all the way, bottoming out in one smooth stroke, and we both groaned. Nothing, and I mean absolutely nothing, could ever top that feeling.

And then we moved together like nothing had ever come between us. No questions. No past. Just the hush of the room and the weight of my body over hers, skin to skin. Her lips were on my neck.

My hands were in her hair.

Her breath stuttered when I whispered, "*Mallie.*"

I desperately wanted to tell her I still loved her, but something told me that might be the thing that undid all of this when it was still so new. So I stuffed those three little words down, and instead told her with my body, slowly making love to her, until we both shattered together, twice more.

I didn't want to break her open—I just wanted to be the place she could rest. I wanted her to remember how it felt to be loved and cherished and adored. And in these moments together—quiet, hushed, real—I think she did.

CHAPTER SIXTEEN

Mallie

Age 15 - Rockport

Jace's family pulled up just before noon, the familiar crunch of tires on gravel echoing down the drive. I was already on the porch swing, pretending to read a mystery novel my mom had brought, but mostly I was waiting. I'd been there since just after breakfast, unsure when they'd be showing up.

Sonny stepped out onto the porch behind me, sipping something golden from a fancy bar glass.

He smirked and asked, "You waiting for your boyfriend like he's returning from war?"

I rolled my eyes. "He's not my boyfriend."

Sonny gave me a crooked smile and raised an eyebrow. "Could've fooled me with the way you two sneak off for hours."

"Why are you even here? You're a grown man. Shouldn't you be, I don't know, going on vacations with friends or to 'find yourself' at this point?"

He smirked and lifted his glass to take a sip. "Hard to pass up a free vacation with meals included."

I snorted. "And what's with that fancy drink of yours? It's not even lunchtime. You trying to manifest a yacht or just hoping someone thinks you're a rich divorcee?"

He took another sip, totally unfazed. "This is what writers do. We brood and sip things dramatically."

Sonny was nearly finished with his master's degree and thought he was already some New York Times Bestselling Author.

I shook my head and muttered, "Whatever, Edgar Allen Bro."

A moment later, Jace's family pulled into the driveway. Sonny raised his glass in a lazy salute and headed out to greet them.

Their car doors swung open, and Jace stepped out. He'd cut his hair, but it still curled like it always did. I stayed where I was, holding onto the porch rail, my heart doing that stupid skip it did every summer when I saw *him.*

He headed right for the porch steps as his hair ruffled from the wind, a grin tugging at the corners of his mouth like he couldn't hold it in. His t-shirt clung to him like it was a size too small, but he looked like summer, like every memory I ever had. And I had no idea what we were supposed to be to each other now.

Maybe he had a girlfriend back home. Maybe last summer had been a fluke. Maybe he'd forgotten all about what we'd been in Hollowbone.

As soon as he hit the porch, he reached for me like he wanted to wrap me in his arms, but stopped short when he remembered we weren't alone. His hand brushed mine instead, and he leaned in just close enough for me to hear.

"Come on," he murmured. "Let's go dump my

stuff in my room and go explore."

Something warm bloomed in my belly. That sure didn't feel like he'd forgotten.

"Go explore" had been our secret code since last summer, for slipping away alone to Hollowbone and spending the afternoon stretched out side by side, kissing like we'd invented it.

As we walked toward the dunes, everything felt golden, like the world knew that this summer was going to be special. When we were out of view of the beach house, Jace reached for my hand, casually, as if it were no big deal. But the second our fingers touched, something sparked down my spine. I followed him off the path and through the tall grass, our steps soft against the sand.

My heart raced as we headed toward the entrance to Hollowbone. We hadn't been here in a year. What if someone else had found it? What if the wind had shifted the dunes, or a storm had knocked it down, or maybe some other kids had stumbled on it and turned it into something else? What if it wasn't ours anymore?

But when we reached the dunes, Jace parted the tall sea grass and... it was still there. Still hidden. Still ours. Untouched, like it had been holding its breath all year, waiting for us to come back.

I let out a shaky breath I hadn't realized I was holding as I stepped inside. The air was cool and still, and the sunlight filtering through the grass above painted shadows on the sand.

"It's still here," I whispered, my voice barely carrying as I touched the charcoal drawings we had made, finding the one where Jace had written our initials "JS + MW" in a heart.

He didn't answer. He ran his fingers along our initials before turning to look at me—searching my face and then… Then, he kissed me.

Everything in me surged at once. My chest, my stomach, my whole heart. I kissed him back like I was trying to memorize the shape of his mouth all over again, as if nothing else mattered except this moment and the fact that we were finally here, again—just us.

And Hollowbone was still ours. After that first day, we spent nearly every afternoon there, our secret tucked between the dunes, where the world slowed down and the only thing that mattered was his breath mixing with mine.

Jace brought a blanket, and I'd bring snacks— even if we rarely remembered to eat them. We'd lie on our backs, side by side, our fingers tangled together like we couldn't not touch. Sometimes we kissed and touched for what felt like hours. Other times, we just talked about everything and nothing.

"You think we'll ever find another place like this?" I asked one afternoon, my head resting on his chest.

"Not a chance," he said, his fingers combing absently through my hair. "There's only one Hollowbone."

I smiled against his shirt, just breathing in his comforting scent, letting my eyes flutter closed.

One evening, after homemade pizza and s'mores, it was game night. We'd played card games with our families until they broke out the poker chips. David had already been put to bed, and Sonny… he was somewhere, probably mentoring himself.

Jace and I found ourselves in the dark on the porch swing. It creaked beneath us, swaying gently with the warm night breeze as we listened to the sounds of the ocean. I curled into him, my legs draped over his, and his arm settled naturally around my shoulders. We didn't say much. Just listened to the waves and let the quiet stretch.

His warmth, his scent, just... him—it was so comforting. I must've drifted off because the next thing I knew, someone was gently shaking my shoulder.

"Mallie?"

I blinked awake to find my dad standing at the screen door, smiling in that knowing way parents do when they've seen more than you want them to.

"She's out," he said softly to Jace. "Can you help her to bed?"

Jace nodded, sliding out from under me and steadying me as I stood, still half-asleep. He walked me inside and up the stairs, his arm tucked around my waist.

In my room, I flopped down onto the bed and rolled to my side.

"Thanks," I mumbled, eyes already fluttering shut.

He pulled the blanket over me, brushing a strand of hair away from my face. His touch lingered, gentle.

"Goodnight, Mallie," he whispered, and pressed the softest kiss to my temple.

Something stirred in my chest, something warm and steady and too big for words.

The next morning, we went with Sonny and David to the pier to fish. But that afternoon, we were back in Hollowbone—just the two of us.

The sun hung low, golden light filtering through the dune grass. We kissed slowly. His hand was on my waist, mine curled behind his neck, our breath shared in the small space between us.

His hands slid into my hair, and when his lips found mine again—hungrier—it was like the rest of the world blinked out.

My heart was pounding so loud I was sure he could hear it. I let my hand fall, slipping beneath the edge of his shirt. My fingers brushed the warm skin of his stomach, and he tensed under my touch—just for a second—but it sent a rush straight through me.

I swallowed hard as my fingertips skimmed over the curve of his chest. He shivered, and something about that made me brave and shaky all at once.

We kissed again—deeper this time, like we were both trying to hold onto something—and before I could second-guess myself, my hand moved lower, hovering at his waistband. My breath caught. I didn't know exactly what I was doing. I just knew I didn't want it to stop.

He stilled, pulling back just a little. "Mallie... wait."

I searched his face, not sure what I'd done wrong.

"I just—" He swallowed. "Are you sure?"

I didn't answer right away. But he waited. The ocean murmured outside like it knew the conversation hanging between us, tiptoeing closer.

When I finally spoke, I nearly whispered, and Jace had to duck his head to hear me. "Have you ever...?" I asked.

He flinched, like my question had thrown him for a loop. He sat up as his brows drew together, and something flickered across his face. A knot twisted in my belly when I realized it was probably hurt, but I didn't know why.

"No. Of course not," he said, voice rougher than before. "What—do you really think I forget about you the second I go home?"

I sat up. "No," I said a little more forcefully than I meant. "I just thought you'd already... y'know."

He shrugged, trying to sound casual, but I could

see right through it. "I mean, I think about it, obviously, but I... I don't know. I guess I always kind of thought..."

He stopped, and something shifted between us. My gaze locked on his. I could feel the weight of whatever he wasn't saying.

"Thought what?" I asked, as nonchalantly as I could.

He stared at me. The silence stretched, thick and tight, and I could see it—his chest rising and falling like he was working up to something. And then, like the tide finally pulling loose a buried shell, he said, "I always kind of thought... it would be with you."

Everything went quiet. Not just around us—but inside me, too. I could feel my heart beating like a drum in my ears.

"Jace..." I breathed out.

He looked down, his fingers curling in the sand like he needed a distraction. "Not just this. I mean, everything. Every time I think about what it'd be like—the first time, the falling-in-love stuff—it's always you. It's only ever been you."

He finally looked back up at me.

"There's never been anyone else," he swallowed hard, "since we were five." His voice was gaining momentum, like once he started, he couldn't stop. "That first summer. The tide knocked down our sandcastle, and I was trying not to cry, and then you sat down next to me and just started rebuilding it. No questions, no 'it's okay'—just... helped me make it even better."

I looked away, a shy smile pulling at my lips as my cheeks flushed. I tucked my hair behind my ears, heart still pounding. And then... he said what I think I'd been waiting to hear for years.

"I've been in love with you for as long as I can

remember," He murmured.

My mouth parted, but I couldn't find the words. My cheeks were burning. But I didn't laugh. I didn't pull away. I just looked at him like he'd handed me something fragile and perfect—and he had.

"I know it sounds stupid," he said quickly.

"No," I whispered as I shook my head.

I'm not sure he even heard me because he went on. "I mean, we were literally five. But every summer, it just—it got worse. Or better. I don't even know."

And then, soft and breathless, I put my hand over his and whispered, "Me, too."

Those two words felt like a spark catching flame. I saw it in his eyes—he felt it, too. I just stared at him, my chest so full I wasn't sure it could hold it all. His voice was rough and real. "And now you're looking at me like this, and I just... I want it to be you. So badly. But only if you're sure, Mallie. Because if you ever regret it, I swear it'll break something in me."

My eyes burned, but I didn't cry. I just felt... everything—brave and wild, and like I finally knew where I belonged. And that was next to him.

"I'm sure," I whispered, brushing my lips against his. "No one has ever made me feel like you do. I want to share this with you. Only you."

He closed his eyes for a second and let out a breath. We lay back down, forehead to forehead, his fingertips brushing gently over my collarbone. A shiver ran through me, and I leaned up to kiss him again, softer this time.

"But... not here," I whispered against his lips. "Not in Hollowbone."

He looked at me, voice hushed. "Where? The beach house?"

I nodded. "Yeah."

"My room?" he asked, his breath warm on my cheek. He grinned, "I do have the bigger bed."

I let out a breathy laugh, "Oh, I'm fully aware," I said quietly.

Jace's bedroom at the beach house had been a point of contention for years between all of us kids. He had a queen-size bed, and Sonny, David, and I all got twins. What was up with that? It was totally not fair.

He kissed me again, languid and sweet. "The night before the big dinner, come to my room after everyone's asleep. I'll leave it unlocked."

My heart thudded. "Okay."

We were really doing this. It was happening—the thing I'd dreamed about a hundred different ways. And it was what I wanted. I knew that. But… was I really sure? It had all come out in the heat of the moment, but that didn't make it any less true. Deep down, I wanted this. I just never thought he'd want it, too.

Everything changed when we were 13 years old, more serious, more real. The past couple of summers, we kissed and touched and wandered back to each other like it was inevitable. But still, I thought maybe he was just… indulging me. Letting me play out my silly, hopeless crush. I never imagined he actually felt the same way—loved me. Not the way I loved him.

But we didn't say anything else. We just held each other tighter—my head resting on his chest, his slow, steady breaths coaxing mine to match. One of my legs tangled with his, and outside, the wind rustled through the dune grass. Our hearts beat in time, quiet and sure, like they'd known everything all along.

CHAPTER SEVENTEEN

Jace

Age 15 - Rockport

The house was in chaos. Laundry baskets full of freshly washed clothes, my mom and Elizabeth yelling at all of us to clean. All day, I'd been doing what I was told—folding my laundry and packing my suitcase, cleaning the cooler, hauling beach chairs out of the shed.

But my mind hadn't been on any of it. It was on her. Mallie. On how I hadn't had more than a minute alone with her since yesterday. On the way her hand had found mine under the table at breakfast. On how she looked when she smiled at me, even when her cheeks turned pink from trying not to. And on tonight.

I wasn't ready for it. I wanted it—God, I wanted her—but my whole chest felt like a knotted-up rope. I couldn't sit still. Couldn't breathe right. Every time we brushed past each other, it felt like the ground shifted under me. So when I finally got a break from all the chores, I snuck out and did what I always did when I didn't know what to do. I slipped out the back door, barefoot and restless, and followed the path I always did when my head got too loud.

The beach was nearly empty—just wind and waves and space to think. I dropped onto the sand, pulled my guitar into my lap, and let my fingers find the chords on their own. Not a song. Not yet. Just something to keep my hands busy while I waited for my heart to catch up.

I didn't hear her at first—just my music and the steady rush of the waves.

Then, soft and certain, "Hey."

I turned. And there she was. Barefoot, hair windblown from the walk down. Her smile hit me like the sun.

I couldn't help my grin when I set my guitar down and said, "Took you long enough," trying for casual but already feeling lighter.

"Got cornered by your mom. She made me vacuum the living room."

I winced. "She's ruthless."

She laughed and closed the gap. I tipped the guitar aside and caught her hand, guiding her down. My hands found her waist, and I felt steady for the first time all day.

"What're you doing out here?" she asked.

"Trying not to freak out about tonight." I shrugged. "And maybe hoping you'd find me."

And then I kissed her. No hesitation. No overthinking. She melted into me like she'd been waiting all day, too.

It wasn't slow or frantic—just the kind of kiss that made the whole world quiet. The kind that said I know we don't have forever, but we have now. And now is everything.

She leaned into me, her fingers curling in my shirt. I could've kissed her for hours. I wanted to kiss her for hours. But of course, "Ewww!"

We jumped apart, and I turned, already bracing for Sonny or—God forbid—my mom. But it was David, standing a few yards away, clutching a blue plastic bucket and grinning like he'd just discovered Santa Claus mid-smooch.

"Are you kissing?" he shouted, glee in every syllable.

I dropped my forehead against Mallie's shoulder with a groan. "We are never living this down."

David marched over and plopped into the sand next to us like he owned the place.

"Can I have a turn next?"

Mallie snorted, and I nearly choked.

"Dude, no!" I sputtered.

He made a gagging noise and rolled his eyes so hard I thought he might fall over. "With the guitar," he said, like we were the idiots. "Not the kissing. Gross."

"Oh." I cleared my throat, my ears burning. "Right. Obviously."

Mallie just giggled beside me, and I glared at her, but it only made her laugh harder.

David pointed. "So can I?"

"No," I said, hugging it closer. "It's my guitar."

He shrugged like he didn't care that much anyway. "Whatever. I got rocks in my bucket."

He pulled out a smooth flat one and whipped it across the water. It skipped three times. Maybe four.

Mallie ruffled his hair and peered into the bucket before reaching for her own rock. "You're gonna show us up, huh?"

He grinned. "Probably."

Then, we were all skipping rocks.

Even though the moment had been broken, she was still beside me—close enough to touch, to breathe in her scent, and having her next to me was enough to quiet the noise inside me, for now.

I glanced at her from the corner of my eye. She was helping David sort through the bucket of damp, sandy rocks like it was the most important task on earth. Her hair was lit up by the late sun, the dark strands glowing red, her knees dusted with sand. And I thought—like I had a thousand times before—*how is she real?*

I was so nervous about tonight, I thought I might puke. Not because I didn't want it. I wanted it more than I'd ever wanted anything. I just wanted it to be right. Special. Unforgettable. I wanted her to wake up years from now and still remember how it felt when I touched her, like she mattered more than anything because she did.

But then I caught myself. I was freaking out and overthinking like I was about to meet her for the first time, not the girl who knew all my stories, who'd seen me cry when the tide ruined my perfect sandcastle, who'd helped me bury a dead jellyfish because I couldn't stand to leave it on the beach to rot.

This was Mallie. The girl I'd loved since... forever. The only girl I'd ever wanted. The only one I ever would.

So yeah, I was scared—but not of her, not of us. Not really. I was scared because I knew the truth—deep in my bones, past the fluttering nerves and pounding heart. She was it.

One day, I would marry her. I didn't know when or how, or if we'd live by the ocean or in some town we'd never even heard of yet, but I knew this much—*she was mine.* She always had been. And tonight wasn't the end of our story. It was just the next chapter. One we'd write together, slow and soft, in a language only we knew.

It was nearly midnight. And as I sat up in my bed, I'd never paid more attention to the creaks and clicks of this old house in my life. Every shift of the floorboards, every hush of voices from the hallway had me sitting up, breath held, heart ready to sprint.

I was pretty sure Mallie's parents had gone to bed. Her mom had hollered a goodnight up the stairs a while ago. Her dad grumbled something about how they were completely out of aloe—like it was the ultimate betrayal after weeks of beach days and sunburned noses.

My mom had tucked David in around nine, and I hadn't heard a peep from him since. I was pretty sure I heard my Dad climb the stairs heading to bed not long after. Sonny was probably still downstairs with his headphones on, zoned out in front of his laptop at the kitchen table. His bedroom was on the first floor anyway, which was as good as locked away for the night. We were pretty much in the clear.

We'd planned this. Not just some heat-of-the-moment promises. It was real. I'd told her to come to my room once everyone was asleep, once the house was quiet, and we wouldn't be interrupted. She'd kissed me when we'd made our plan—her cheeks pink, eyes bright and serious.

Still, now that it was actually here, I couldn't stop second-guessing. What if she changed her mind? What if I'd misread everything?

I lay back, staring at the ceiling. My palms were sweaty. My heart had been thudding steadily and stupidly for the past hour. Should I pretend to be asleep? Sit on the floor like I wasn't waiting for her?

Pick up a book and act casual?

The clock read 11:58. My fingers curled on the edge of the blanket. Part of me wanted to go knock on her door. Just once. Just to be sure. But before I could sit up, I heard it—the soft twist of my doorknob. I froze. My bedroom door opened just a crack, then slowly, carefully, she stepped inside wearing my hoodie.

It hung loose on her, the sleeves hiding her hands, the hem brushing the tops of her bare thighs. I didn't even remember when she'd taken it, or why —but the sight of her in it made something warm and dizzy rush through me. Like seeing her wrapped in something that was mine made it real. Made her *mine.*

She shut the door behind her, quiet as a secret, and crossed the room.

"Hey," I whispered.

"Hey," she whispered back, her voice barely carrying through the quiet.

She sat down on the edge of the bed like it was nothing. Like it was everything, and then I lifted the blanket without thinking. She crawled towards me. Her leg brushed mine under the sheets, and I felt that jolt in my chest, sharp and soft all at once. I couldn't breathe.

For a second, we didn't speak. She just slid her hand into mine, our fingers twining like they'd always belonged together.

"You okay?" I asked.

She nodded. "Yeah. You?"

"Yeah," I said, and meant it. "I worried you changed your mind..."

"We said we would," she whispered. "We promised."

I looked at her and said, "I know. We did."

She kissed me then, slow and sure, like we'd both known this was inevitable.

When we pulled apart, I whispered, "You still want to?"

She nodded as she nestled against me, and I inhaled her shampoo.

"I do. Do you?"

"Yes, but... can we stay like this? Just for a little while?"

She nodded against my shoulder. And so we did. Her head on my chest. My arm wrapped around her. The feel of her against me sparked something just beneath my skin.

The wind rustled the trees outside, and the old beach house breathed slowly and quietly around us. The sound of the ocean drifted through the open window, soft and steady, like it had seen moments like this play out for centuries. Like it already knew how this night would go.

She leaned back, her head against the pillow, and stared up at the ceiling. "There's really never been..." she began, then paused. Her voice was quieter than the waves. "...anyone else?"

"You think I could forget about you for a whole year?" I chuckled, but it came out cracked. "You've ruined me for every other girl, Mallie. I'm half-alive waiting for June since the second I leave every August."

Her eyes flicked towards me, and something shifted in her—relief, maybe. Or something bigger. Like hope.

"I thought," she whispered, "if it were with you, it wouldn't feel scary."

God, my chest. It ached with how much I wanted to be the safe place for her. The only place. Forever.

"I'm scared, too," I admitted, the truth of it raw in

my throat.

She let out a small, breathy laugh. "You're not supposed to say that."

"Why not?"

"Because you're... you," she said, like that explained everything. Her voice dropped off as she added, "And I'm just me."

"Mallie..." I turned toward her fully, heart wide open. "You're the only 'you' I've ever wanted."

Her eyes went glassy. "I love you, Jace."

I reached up, holding her chin. "I love you, too. I've loved you forever."

We lay together for a long, quiet moment—the weight of what we'd said pressed around us like the warm night air. I reached for her hand, fingers hesitant at first, then sure as I laced our fingers together. She didn't let go.

"Okay," she said, her voice shaking. "So we're scared. But we're together."

"Always," I said. And then, softer, "Even if it's just summers."

She turned her face toward me, that wild, brave look shining in her eyes—the same one she'd worn the first time I kissed her two years ago. Then she whispered, "I don't want this just to be summers."

My heart beat wildly. The ocean kept rolling in the background, steady, but everything else felt still, like even the world was waiting. I leaned over and kissed her—slow, careful. Not rushing it, just... meaning it. Telling her without words, *I'm yours. I mean it, for real.*

She sat up, letting the covers fall as she came over and straddled me. Our eyes locked as she quietly pulled my hoodie off. Letting me see her—not just her body, but all of her.

My hands were shaking, my heart thundering,

and I felt completely undone as I lifted up and reached to touch her.

She leaned down, meeting me halfway, and I kissed her again. Tender. Reverent. Then, she laced our fingers together, and the world tilted, but she steadied me. And outside, the tide rolled in as I made love to her for the first time.

CHAPTER EIGHTEEN

Mallie

Present Day

We spent the next day in bed like it was Hollowbone all over again—just the two of us, wrapped up in the kind of quiet closeness I didn't realize I'd been starving for. During that last summer, it had been stolen afternoons in our secret sea cave, whispering dreams into the salt-heavy air. Now, it was warmth and skin and low conversation, the press of his mouth on my shoulder, the weight of him beside me anchoring me in a way nothing else had in years.

I had no idea why I'd told him not to come. My stupid fears, probably. Or the foolish belief that I could handle seeing him again without needing him. But now, with the soft light spilling across my sheets and his fingers trailing lazy circles on my hip. I was so glad he hadn't listened, and he came anyway.

As I curled against his chest, he told me the whole story of how the band started sophomore year of college, a half-serious thing with his roommates in someone's basement. By junior year, it was all he cared about. He skipped class for rehearsals to play shows and stayed up all night writing songs. He dropped out without a plan, just the certainty that he had to try. The early years were rough—crappy motels, cheap takeout, empty bars—but they stuck it out. And now they toured twice a year and made a solid living. He still got emotional when people sang his lyrics back to him.

We were both starving by late afternoon, and nothing in the kitchen looked good. So I took him to Morning Glory's for waffles. I'd been obsessed since Darci and Claire took me there one weekend—crispy edges, real butter, magic. He took one bite and groaned like it was a religious experience.

"I'm not saying this is better than sex," he said, pointing his fork at me, "but I am saying this is dangerously close."

We wandered the Square after breakfast. I wanted to show him Denton—my version of it. We hit Atomic Candy and ate so many sour belts our tongues were raw. At the record store, he flipped through vinyl and rolled his eyes at my love of cheesy yacht rock. Then we wandered into the vintage shop, where I made him try on a rhinestone-covered western shirt that looked like it belonged on a Vegas magician.

But the best part—easily—was Replay.

We found our way to an old Galaga machine, and I absolutely destroyed him. Twice.

He threw his hands up in surrender. "Joystick drift. It has to be."

I grinned and leaned in close. "Pilot error. Some of us peak at thirteen, Jace."

He squinted at me, trying to hide a smile. "Wow. First you steal my heart, now you steal my high score?"

I grinned, nudging him with my shoulder and trying to ignore my heart beating out of my chest. "Please. You never owned the high score. I am the high score."

Later, we ended up on a bench outside, sipping the weird soda flavors we bought at the candy store like we were teenagers again. His leg brushed mine. My shoulder leaned into his. It felt… inevitable.

I looked over at him, trying to find the right words. "I'm really glad you came," I said finally. "Even though I told you not to."

He glanced sideways, eyes soft, lips tilted into a half-smirk. "Yeah, well. You never were great at knowing what you wanted."

"I know now," I whispered.

He didn't reply, but his hand found mine on the bench between us, fingers slipping between mine like they were always meant to be. And that made something settle inside me. This wasn't just nostalgia or some old story we were trying to rewrite. It was a new chapter, and I was ready to live it.

He left the next day. I'd dropped him off at the airport in the morning. He'd given me just a quick kiss on the cheek before slipping out of the car door with his duffel. Just a warm "Talk soon, Mallie," like it didn't completely wreck me. Like we hadn't reconnected into something deeper these past few days. I felt like I was unraveling.

For the first time in days, I was alone. Claire had gone to a dress fitting before work. Sonny had some papers to grade, so he went in early before his late class tonight. I should have felt relieved to have the house to myself. Instead, I felt like I couldn't breathe.

I'd fallen back into Jace's rhythm so easily—too easily. The way we used to talk, the quiet looks, and the stupid inside jokes that I loved. I kept catching myself smiling without realizing it. And every time I did, guilt snapped right back at my heels like a whip.

He had no idea what I'd done. No idea that I dragged this heavy shadow with me everywhere I went. That I woke up nearly every day thinking of the child I gave away. *Our child.*

When he said he hoped to be a dad someday, just tossed it out there with a dreamy grin, I nearly fell apart. Because he already was. He just didn't know it yet, and I had no idea how to tell him.

Then the email came. At first, I thought it was spam. I was scrolling absentmindedly, killing time before a client call, sipping lukewarm coffee, not even really seeing the screen. But then I saw the subject line. I froze. For a second, I wasn't even sure I was reading it right.

Subject: Inquiry From Adoptive Family – Openness Request
From: Marigold Family Services
Forwarded by: *G. Beasley, Esq.*

I hadn't heard from him in ages. Seeing Mr. Beasley's name made everything feel suddenly, frighteningly real. He had been my parents' attorney for years—the one who quietly facilitated the adoption. The same man who'd helped Sonny and me sort through the wreckage after the accident.

But it was real. Violet—her name wasn't Violet anymore, I reminded myself, though I'd never stopped thinking of her that way—was almost thirteen.

My hands shook as I clicked the message. It was

polite. Careful. Hopeful.

"Abigail just wants to know you're out there," the adoptive mom had written. "We're open to a letter — a photo. No pressure. Just… a beginning, if you're open to it."

Her name was *Abigail*… I closed my laptop as my pulse roared in my ears. *A beginning*. I hadn't let myself hope for one. Not really. And now here it was. And Jace was back. And he didn't know.

I folded my arms on the table and lowered my head onto them, letting out a breath that felt like it'd been trapped for over a decade. I couldn't keep this to myself anymore. I had to tell him. I had to. The sooner the better.

But telling him meant whatever was building between us might end, and it was the one thing that was finally letting me feel like I was beginning to heal. How would I deal with that?

It was almost eleven when I heard the front door click open.

Claire had already gone to bed hours ago, and I'd been sitting on the couch in the soft glow of the TV for… I didn't even know how long. I wasn't watching any of it. The voices were just noise, filling the silence so I didn't have to listen to my own thoughts.

Sonny walked in, the strap of his leather messenger bag slung across his chest, and a takeout bag in his hand.

"Hey," he said, dropping his keys in the bowl near the door. "You're still up?"

I shrugged, curling my legs under me. "Didn't feel like going to bed yet."

He collapsed onto the other end of the couch with a tired sigh. "Class ran over. My students are convinced finals are optional, and I'm trying not to lose faith in the youth of America."

I smiled faintly, but it didn't stick.

We sat in silence for a few minutes, both of us pretending to pay attention to whatever cooking competition was flashing on the screen.

"You okay?" he finally asked.

I hesitated. Then I muted the TV and turned to face him. "Can I tell you something?"

His eyebrows rose as he leaned forward, elbows on his knees. "Yeah. Of course."

I took a breath, twisting my fingers in my lap. "Do you remember my sophomore year when Mom pulled me out of school and I just kind of... disappeared?"

"Yeah," he said slowly, frowning. "She just said you needed a break. That high school had been rough on you. That homeschooling was what you needed." He glanced at me, "I tried calling a couple of times, but she said you didn't want to talk."

I looked down. "It wasn't true."

His voice softened. "What do you mean?"

"I was... pregnant."

Silence.

I glanced up. His face was frozen—like I'd dropped a bomb he couldn't quite process.

"When I found out, I went to her, and she shut me down before I could even tell the father. She gave me two choices—an abortion or adoption. Then, she told me not to contact him, told me I'd ruin his life. She made up this horrible lie and told his family..." My voice cracked. "At first, I was so ashamed. I felt so stupid. I wasn't sure I wanted you to know. But then she said you were busy with school, and it would be 'too much stress.' So she made me keep it from you."

Sonny sat back, stunned. His eyes searched mine like he couldn't believe what he was hearing. "Jesus, Mal..."

"I gave the baby up for adoption," I whispered. "A girl. I just found out her name is Abigail."

He ran a hand over his face, overwhelmed. "I had no idea. I thought—God, I thought you just changed. You were different the next summer when I came home. Quieter. You seemed... sad. But Mom made it sound like you were just going through something."

"I was," I said bitterly. "And she made sure I went through it alone."

He was quiet for a long moment. Then, softly, "I would've come home. I would've fought for you. You know that, right?"

Tears burned in my eyes. "I know, but... I didn't know anything back then. I was just a scared fifteen-year-old kid who felt terribly alone."

Sonny's voice was raw now, threaded with rage. "I just can't believe she let you go through that alone. What the hell was wrong with her?"

I didn't have an answer.

He stood up suddenly, pacing the room, then stopped and turned to me. "The guy... the father? It's... Jace, isn't it?"

I nodded.

His eyes filled with understanding. "That's why this is all coming back."

"He doesn't know. I wanted to tell him. I was going to... but I just..." I swallowed, "You're the first person I've told in years."

Sonny fell back into the chair across from me, eyes full of pain. "You've been carrying this all alone."

I nodded again as I took in a breath. "And now the adoptive family has reached out. She wants to know me. And Jace—now that he's back in my life... I have to tell him..." My voice dropped off at those last words as I wiped the tears from my eyes.

His voice was gentle as he scooted closer on the couch, moving beside me. He pulled me against him, "You're not alone anymore, Mal. I've got you. I always did. I just didn't know you needed me."

My face crumpled. I let the tears fall and leaned into him.

He rested his cheek on the top of my head and whispered, "What can I do?"

"I don't know," I whispered into his shirt. "I think I need to tell him face-to-face."

"Is he still on tour?"

I pulled back and nodded. "Yeah. Denver tonight, then a couple more before L.A."

"You want me to get you a plane ticket?"

My voice was shaky. "I think I do. I should have told him while he was here, but I couldn't get the words out. But I need to. Soon. He's supposed to call when he gets back to the hotel room tonight."

"Just say the word," Sonny said. "I'll handle the rest."

I nodded, guilt tugging at me. His wedding was weeks away. This wasn't supposed to be about me.

"I will," I said, rising to my feet and stretching. My body felt like it had aged ten years in an hour. "I'm going to bed."

Though as soon as I closed my door, I felt a surge of energy. I sat down on the bed, opened my laptop, and stared at the blank page for nearly an hour before I typed the first word.

Dear—

Not Hi, not To whom it may concern. Just Dear.

Because how do you start a letter to someone who changed your life before she could even speak?

I backspaced and started again.

Dear sweet girl,

My fingers hovered over the keys. I wasn't supposed to call her that. The agency had rules. Guidelines. Encouragement to "keep the tone neutral, to avoid possessive language." But she wasn't neutral. She was never neutral.

She was the hardest and bravest choice I ever made.

I glanced toward the box on my bookshelf—the one no one knew about. Inside, under hospital bracelets and folded papers, was the photo I wasn't supposed to have: a tiny, wrinkled, squishy newborn wrapped in a pink-and-blue blanket. They told me not to take a picture. I did anyway. I needed proof she was real, that I hadn't imagined her heartbeat against mine.

I started typing again.

Dear sweet girl,

You don't know me, but I've thought of you every single day since the day you were born...

The words didn't quite flow, but they started to come slowly and steadily. I told her the truth about my love for her. I told her the way I used to imagine her growing up with sunshine in her hair and wildness in her spirit. I told her that she would never be forgotten. That giving her up wasn't about not wanting her—it was about wanting more for her than I could give.

As I typed, my hands trembled, but something about it didn't feel quite finished. I saved the letter but didn't send it yet. Not until I did the other thing I'd been putting off. The harder thing—telling Jace.

147

CHAPTER NINETEEN

Mallie

Age 15 - Rockport

The room was wrapped in that quiet kind of light that only came just after dawn, soft pale pinks and blues. The ocean was the only sound, a gentle hush through the open window, like the world was still sleeping.

When I woke, my body was tucked into his like a puzzle piece that had finally found its perfect fit. I hadn't meant to fall asleep. That hadn't been the plan.

The plan was to sneak back to my own bed while the stars were still out, before anyone woke up and started asking questions. But somewhere between the sound of his heartbeat and the feel of his arms around me, I'd stopped caring. I didn't want to be alone, without him. Not after last night. Not ever, if I could help it.

His arm was draped around my waist, our legs tangled beneath the sheet. He was warm and still asleep, his breath slow and steady against the back of my neck. When I shifted, he tightened his hold for a second, like his body wasn't ready to let go either.

But I panicked. I had to go. The sky outside his window was brightening. And the last thing I needed was to be out of my bed when someone tried to wake me. Or worse, in Jace's bed when someone tried to wake him.

Carefully, I slid from his arms, moving slowly so I wouldn't wake him. My bare feet hit the floor, and I crouched low, scanning for my clothes in the soft blur of morning light. My underwear was halfway under the bed, and his hoodie was on the side of the bed. I wasn't even sure when I'd taken it off.

I put them on as my heart still hummed from everything we'd shared, like last night had set something in motion inside me. Something permanent.

I tiptoed to the door, paused, and peeked out. All was quiet. It was too early for my mom—too early for breakfast.

I slipped down the hall and back into my room, climbing under the cool sheets and wishing I was still wrapped up in the warmth I'd just left. I buried my face in my pillow to muffle the giddy little smile stretching across my cheeks. My whole body felt golden and fizzy, like I was made of something new.

I stared at the ceiling, and all I could think, over and over, like a secret I couldn't hold onto anymore, was *when can we do that again*? Because nothing had ever felt that right, and I didn't want to wait a whole year to feel it again.

I couldn't sleep and just lay there replaying everything in my head until I finally drifted off. Sometime later, the smell of bacon hit me. I had no idea what time it was, but the sun was bright and shining through my window right in my face.

I groaned and stretched, feeling a little sore before

changing clothes. I put on a pink tank top and my favorite cutoffs before glancing at Jace's hoodie on the floor. I scooped it up and slid it back on. There was no way he was ever getting it back.

My mom yelled, "Mallory, breakfast!" before I even made it downstairs, and my stomach did a weird little flip, not from hunger, but from remembering again.

Last night. Jace. Us.

By the time I walked into the kitchen, my cheeks were heating. Not that it mattered. They only got redder when I saw him sitting at the table like nothing had changed. Like the whole world hadn't rewired itself in the quiet hush of his bedroom.

His hair was still messy from sleep. His eyes flicked to mine and held. And my knees nearly gave out because I forgot how to walk like a normal person.

"Mallory, sit down," Tessa said, cheerful and already juggling three platters. "We're doing a big breakfast this morning. All the fixings! One last hurrah."

My mom was setting a plate of pancakes on the table, her "we're celebrating summer smile" firmly in place—but her eyes caught on me just a little too long.

Jace looked away first, but not before his mouth twitched like he was fighting a grin. I sat down right across from him. I felt his eyes caressing me, and I couldn't stop remembering the way he'd looked at me in the dark like I was magic. Like I was his.

My legs ached. My cheeks were already warm. And I suddenly couldn't remember if I'd brushed my hair or just hoped for the best.

"Sleep okay?" my mom asked, cheerful and casual

as she set the syrup down in front of me—way too deliberately.

"Yeah," I said quickly. "Fine."

She didn't say anything, but I could feel her watching me. She only got this observant at the beach house, when we played at being a normal family—matching towels, board games, my mom remembering how to ask about our lives. The rest of the year, she stayed busy and distant. But here? She noticed things. And this morning, she definitely noticed something.

The hallway creaked, and then Sonny came in, yawning and scratching his head like he hadn't slept in a decade. He flopped into the chair next to me and grabbed a pancake straight off the plate.

"I had a dream I was teaching Intro to Philosophy but forgot to assign any readings, so I just made the whole class watch The Matrix and told them to interpret their feelings."

My mom blinked. "Was that the nightmare part?"

Sonny shrugged, chewing. "The nightmare part was I had a ponytail."

That got a laugh out of Jace, low and quiet.

I finally looked back over at him. He didn't say anything. Just smiled, that soft, crooked kind of smile that made my stomach flip like he didn't regret a thing. Like, we were still okay.

"So," Tessa said as she buttered a biscuit, "I was thinking—Mallory, would you and Jameson mind watching David this afternoon? We want to run into town for souvenirs and pick up everything for the goodbye dinner tonight."

I opened my mouth to say "sure" because I always said yes to watching David. But—

"We actually have plans," Jace cut in, too quick and obvious. "Important ones. David can't come."

I nearly choked on my eggs.

Mom paused mid-pour of syrup, her eyebrows wrinkling. "You have... plans?"

Sonny narrowed his eyes like he was trying to solve a riddle. "What kind of plans could you two possibly have that can't include a nine-year-old sidekick?"

Jace opened his mouth. Then shut it. Then looked at me like *Help?*

Luckily, Sonny didn't wait for an answer. "You know what? I'll take David down to the pier. We'll fish. Eat snacks. Be better company anyway."

Tessa smiled. "Sonny, that's so thoughtful of you."

He grinned, all smug and knowing, and shot me a look like *I see you, little sister.* I stuck my tongue out at him before anyone could notice. And that's when Dad decided to pile on.

"So what are these mystery plans you two have?"

My face went full nuclear.

Jace didn't skip a beat. "We're... going to the dunes," he said, shrugging a little too casually. "Mallie wanted to go one more time. Said she had something to show me."

I blinked. I *what?*

But then he met my eyes again—warm and secret and a little smug in his own way—and I just nodded, heart thudding.

"Yeah," I said. "I do."

Dad looked between us, eyes narrowed like he was deciding whether to press or not. "Hmm," he said. "Just don't be late for dinner." Then he went back to his coffee.

And I swore I could feel Jace's hand brush mine under the table.

After breakfast, we walked down the beach with the sun on our shoulders and sand between our toes, pretending like we weren't glowing with the kind of secret that could set the whole world on fire if anyone ever found out.

Behind us, the house was a blur of voices as our moms and dads piled into Jace's family SUV to head into town. But out here, it was just the two of us, wind and waves and the dunes waiting. We were almost past the bend where the beach curves and the house disappears from sight when Jace suddenly reached for my hand and stopped walking.

"Are you okay?" he asked, his voice low and serious.

I looked up at him, surprised, and gave a small, shy smile. "I'm fine. In fact..." I laughed under my breath, shaking my head a little. "I'm better than fine. I feel... amazing. Like the entire world changed overnight, and we're the only two people who know it."

His face lit up with that grin—god, that grin—and then he leaned in and kissed me, slow and full of relief.

"I woke up," he said quietly when we parted, "and you were just... gone." He swallowed hard. "I worried."

"No," I said quickly, reaching for his hand, "everything's fine. I just—I wanted to get back to my room before anyone, you know..."

"Yeah," he nodded, exhaling. "Yeah, I get it."

I stepped closer and placed my palm gently on his cheek. He leaned into it without hesitation.

"I hated having to leave you," I whispered. "If I could've stayed tangled up with you all day, I would have."

He kissed me again, wrapping his arms around my waist and pulling me against him, warm and certain.

"I know," he murmured into the space between us. "Me, too."

The breeze moved around us, soft and slow, and for a moment, I forgot about everything else. The packing. The goodbyes. The ticking clock counting down to morning. We still had time. And right now, it was ours.

When we got to Hollowbone, the world felt quieter. The wind softened as we ducked beneath the curve of rock, and the sun spilled in low and gold through the opening, painting everything in light.

Jace laid out the old blanket we kept stashed there, smoothing it over the packed sand floor like it was something sacred. We'd claimed this place when we found it last year, sworn ourselves to its silence and shadows, and now it felt like the only spot in the universe big enough to hold what we were becoming.

I looked over at him, my chest tightening the way it always did when the future crept in. "How am I going to survive without you until next June?"

He exhaled, glancing down at his hands for a beat. Then he looked at me, something new flickering behind his eyes.

"I don't know," he said. "But I was thinking... I turn sixteen in November."

I blinked. "Okay..."

"I already have my permit, and if I can get my license right away," he continued, "I could drive down to you. To Austin. It's only three hours."

I stared at him. "You're serious."

He nodded, not even smiling. Just serious. "I can't

imagine going that long without seeing you again. Not after… everything."

A breath caught in my throat. "You think your parents would let you?"

He shrugged, looking suddenly younger and braver all at once. "Maybe not at first. But I'll figure it out. I'll come up with something. I just—" His voice faltered, and then steadied again. "I don't want us to be a once-a-year thing anymore."

I didn't realize I was holding his hand until I squeezed it. "Me either…"

He looked at me then like I was the only girl in the world, in the universe. His thumb brushed across my knuckles, and I just couldn't hold it in any longer.

"I love you," I whispered.

"I know," he said softly. "I've loved you since before I even knew what it meant. Since you helped me name every single seashell we found and told me your favorite color changed every week."

I laughed, watery and stunned. "You remember that?"

"I remember everything," he said.

And when he leaned in to kiss me, the rest of the world disappeared again.

CHAPTER TWENTY

Jace

Age 15 - Rockport

The fire crackled low behind the beach house, casting flickering light across the sand and the backs of the beach chairs we had dragged out from the shed yesterday. Someone brought marshmallows. Someone else passed around plastic cups filled with warm lemonade and maybe something a little stronger for the adults.

The neighbors were out. Kids running wild near the water. Parents laughing too loudly. Someone had a Bluetooth speaker playing a playlist that kept skipping between classic rock and country.

But none of it touched me. Not really. Because Mallie was next to me.

We were sitting on an old piece of driftwood just outside the main circle of chairs, close enough to be seen, far enough to be forgotten. The air was cooler now, breezy in that way it only ever got on the last night—like the whole beach knew we were about to leave it behind.

She had her chin resting on her knees, eyes

reflecting the firelight, that soft smile she got when she was quiet and thinking.

And I had my guitar.

I didn't even remember bringing it out. I just knew I'd grabbed it before we left the house, like some part of me had decided this was how it needed to go.

I plucked at the strings—easy, quiet, something low and aimless.

She turned toward me, her voice soft. "Play something."

"I don't really know how this one ends," I admitted, still not looking at her. "It's... not finished."

"That's okay," she said.

I glanced at her then, and it knocked the air out of me for a second because she was looking at me like I was it. Like I was enough.

I didn't think. Didn't worry about the notes or the people or if anyone else was listening. I just sang— quietly, the way I always did when it was only for her.

It was a nothing song. Just a few verses strung together. Half-written lines about late nights and secret caves and the feeling of holding on too tight because you're scared to let go. It was about the dunes. About her. About everything I didn't know how to say out loud. Her eyes didn't leave me once.

Even after the last chord faded into the sound of the ocean, she was still watching me.

She reached over and rested her hand on mine. "That was beautiful," she whispered.

I shrugged. "It's not done."

"I already love it."

Something inside me tightened. I wanted to tell her I'd write a hundred more songs if it meant she'd look at me like this.

But all I said was, "One day, when I finish it... I'll play it for you again. Wherever you are."

She nodded, and I could see it in her face—that she believed me.

"Just promise me you'll never stop writing," she said.

Only Mallie could make something sound like a vow just by whispering it.

"Only if you promise never to stop being the girl I write about."

And then I kissed her. Soft and slow. Our parents were sitting right in front of us with the firelight— the smell of smoke and sugar and sea salt in the air.

Somewhere, someone was yelling about burning their marshmallow. A kid was crying. The playlist skipped again. But none of it mattered. It was just me and Mallie.

The fire crackled, and Mallie leaned into my side, her head resting lightly on my shoulder. The conversation around the circle had gotten louder, looser—everyone drifting into that warm, sugar-slow daze that only happened on the last night of vacation.

But I couldn't stop thinking about her. The way she'd looked at me, like I was more than just the kid she saw every summer. Like I wasn't just Jace at the beach house. Like I meant more to her than anything else.

She tugged gently on the hem of my sleeve. "Let's go," she whispered, soft and secret.

I didn't ask where.

We stood up without a word, brushing sand from our legs. The grown-ups were all deep in conversation about something, laughing and joking among themselves. No one said anything, no one called after us.

But just as we turned away from the fire, I caught movement out of the corner of my eye—my mom, watching us from her chair with a mug in her hands. And she smiled. Not surprised. Not suspicious. Just… knowing.

I blinked and looked away quickly, heart thudding for a whole new reason.

Mallie was already tugging me toward the dunes, her hand cold from the breeze but locked tight around mine.

We ducked into the cave a few minutes later, our own little universe waiting for us. She sat on the blanket like she belonged there, like we belonged there, and I sank down beside her, close enough that our legs brushed.

"Do you think anyone saw us leave?" she asked.

I hesitated. Then said, "My mom did."

Mallie froze for a second. "Wait—what?"

"She smiled," I said, bumping her knee with mine. "Like, really smiled. Not like 'aw, they're being cute'—more like, 'finally.'"

Her face flushed instantly. "Oh God."

"You're fine. We're fine." I laughed. "I'm telling you, they know. They've known how we felt about each other for years."

She buried her face in her hands with a groan. "Nooo."

"Come on, Mallie. You think my mom hasn't noticed the way I look at you? Or the way you follow me around like you're trying to memorize my shadow?"

She peeked at me through her fingers. "I do not."

"You do," I said, grinning. "But don't worry. I follow you around, too."

She rolled her eyes, but she was smiling now, her

embarrassment melting into something softer.

"You're not helping," she muttered.

I leaned in. "I wasn't trying to."

And then I kissed her.

She shifted closer, one hand curling into my hoodie, and I thought—I'll remember this for the rest of my life. This cave. This night. Her.

We didn't say the big things. But we said enough. And in that quiet, starlit place, we made a promise we didn't need words for—for always. That summer wasn't the only place where we existed. That even if our parents did know… It didn't make it any less ours.

The next morning, the sun hadn't even fully risen when I woke up—the familiar chaos of departure. I could hear voices and the rustle of suitcases and totes being shuffled around in the other rooms, the low thud of footsteps on the stairs, and drawers opening and closing.

It was… the last morning. I sat up in my bed, still dressed from the night before. My first thought was Mallie. My chest ached with it.

We'd stayed at Hollowbone longer than we should have, curled together on that blanket, kissing and whispering and pretending like time wasn't something that could steal us away. We hadn't gone back to the fire. To the party.

Eventually, we walked back to the beach house. Neither of us said goodnight—we just looked at each other. Like if we stared long enough, it would hold us over until next time.

But now, the sun was creeping up, and our time was nearly gone.

I pulled on a fresh t-shirt and slipped downstairs. The front door was already propped open, letting the breeze in. I saw her before I even stepped outside. Mallie was standing on the porch in my hoodie and her favorite cutoffs, her raven hair piled in a messy bun on her head, arms wrapped around herself like she wasn't quite ready for the day to begin.

She looked up the second I stepped outside.

Her face broke into a small, sad smile. "Hey."

"Hey," I said, my voice rough.

Their car was already packed. I saw Sonny in the front seat, reclined back with his sunglasses on like he was already halfway home. Her dad stood near the trunk, chatting with my mom. Her mom was making the goodbye rounds with the neighbors, offering tight hugs and promises to email vacation photos.

Mallie already had her backpack slung over one shoulder. She was trying to look casual. She didn't.

I didn't say anything. Just reached for her hand. She didn't hesitate. I tugged her around the side of the beach house, away from the porch, away from the others—until we were tucked in the narrow space between the weathered siding and patches of dune grass.

We just stood there for a second, the seagulls already screaming overhead like they, too, thought the world was ending. I stepped closer, and she met me halfway. Her arms wrapped around my waist, mine around her shoulders. We fit together like we always had. But it felt different now. Heavier. Realer.

"Do you know when y'all are leaving?" she whispered.

"No," I said. "But probably soon."

Her forehead went to my chest, and she buried her nose in my shirt as she nodded against me.

I pulled back just enough to see her face. Her eyes

were glassy, but she wasn't crying. It was like we'd both let everything out we needed to last night—in the cave, in the way we held each other, in that last, aching kiss.

"I meant what I said," I told her. "About November. About driving to you."

"I know," she whispered. "And I'll find a way, too. We'll figure it out."

"Promise?"

She looked up at me, full of that brave, heartbreaking smile. "Always."

I leaned down and kissed her—soft, slow, final, but not. Just enough to say what I couldn't. That I loved her. That she was mine. That no matter how far apart we were, I'd still carry her with me.

When we broke apart, I could hear her mom calling her name now, casual but getting closer. I took a step back. Then another.

She didn't say goodbye. Neither did I. We never had to. Because we already knew—This wasn't the end. It was just until… next time.

CHAPTER TWENTY-ONE

Jace

Present Day

I'd texted her when I landed in Denver.

Me: Made it. Running on fumes but still flying from seeing you. I'll call you after the show tonight.

She sent back a heart—just that. But I knew her well enough to read between the lines.

After the show, I pulled my phone out of my pocket as the green room emptied and hit call before I could talk myself into a text.

"Hey, how was it?" she asked, voice soft, sleep-warm.

"Hey." I leaned against a road case, still half-wired from the show. "Crowd was loud. My head's louder." I swallowed. "I miss you. Wish I was still there—your mouth, your bed, the way you throw your leg over mine when you're about to fall asleep."

I walked down the hall, The Fire Department's bus generator humming loudly through the open side door. "Tell me something," I said. "Make me feel like I'm there."

I heard her smile. "Hall light's still on," she murmured. "I'm in your hoodie, I can still smell you on my pillow, and I keep rolling to your side like you might be there."

"Save me that side," I said. "I'm coming back for it."

"It's waiting. So am I."

My grip tightened on the phone as heat climbed up my spine, steady as a fuse.

"We're gonna push tonight—drive straight through," I went on. "Next city by morning, then hotel. I'll call you as soon as I get to my room."

"Promise?"

"Scout's honor," I said, even if I'd never been one. "Text me if you can't sleep."

"Only if you answer."

"I will."

A beat of breathing between us.

"Drive safe, rockstar," she whispered.

"I will. Goodnight, Mallie."

"Goodnight."

It was three o'clock in the morning. The post-show buzz had already faded, leaving only the crash. Muscles sore, throat raw, and a familiar ache settling in my chest—the kind that had nothing to do with singing. We were driving through the dark somewhere between Colorado and Utah, and I had no idea what time it was. The van was humming like a lullaby. Eddie was driving, and the others were asleep or at least close to it. I was stretched out across the back bench, staring up at the ceiling with my hoodie pulled over my head. My body may have been wrecked, but my mind was wide awake.

I wish we could have talked longer. I couldn't

help myself when I pulled out my phone and sent a text, knowing she was probably sleeping.

Me: Van update: the air freshener is Leftover Burrito mixed with Regret. Miss you and desperately need your lips on mine.

Two days. That's all we'd had before the tour pulled me away again—two perfect, reckless, heart-punching days. We barely slept, and I couldn't wait until we were together again. I could still feel the ghost of her laugh in my chest, still smell her shampoo on my jacket. I'd seen her just this morning, yet I was counting the days until we could be together again.

My phone buzzed.

Mallie: Can I call you?

Me: I'm in the van.

Mallie: I need to tell you something.

I sucked in a breath. I knew what this was. It had to be the thing I'd asked about. The thing she'd deflected. I remember the look in her eyes when I pressed, like she wanted to say it but couldn't. My fingers hovered over the keyboard.

Don't push. Don't scare her off.

I forced myself to breathe, then typed:

Me: Okay... You okay?

The dots bounced. Stopped. Started again.

Mallie: I don't know. But I think I will be. I'm

going to book a flight to Salt Lake for later today. I think we need to talk face-to-face.

I sat up, heart hammering now. She was coming.

Me: Yes. God, yes. We're playing the Avalon Theater. I'll leave a pass for you at will-call.

She replied almost instantly.

Mallie: I'll be there. I can't wait to see you.

I stared at the screen, the glow lighting up the van. Everything inside me was buzzing—hope, fear, love. I let the phone fall to my lap and dragged a hand through my hair. The air in the bus suddenly felt too thin.

Whatever this was—whatever she'd been holding back—she was ready to hand it to me. All I could think about was the way she'd looked when I was leaving this morning—like she wanted to say more but was too afraid to let it spill. She was coming to me. And no matter what it was—I wanted her to.

I couldn't sleep, not after her cryptic texts. Instead, I watched the slow rise of the sun over the Red Desert, sage going gold, as I checked my phone for the millionth time—still nothing.

We arrived at our hotel a little after nine in the morning, and luckily, they had rooms already available. I crashed until the afternoon. I felt terrible that I'd slept through her texts letting me know her flight landed at five o'clock tonight.

Now, it was after six, and we were doing soundcheck with the tech crew buzzing around the stage like bees on caffeine, but I couldn't focus on anything except the fizz of nerves I couldn't shake.

I still couldn't quite believe she was flying all the way up here. After all these years of silence between us, and after all the questions I hadn't dared ask, she was coming. And she had something to tell me—that part haunted me.

I didn't know what it would be. But I knew it was big. Her voice in that text had carried weight and fear.

Mallie: I'm here. Parked behind the venue next to your van.

My heart kicked.

Me: On my way.

I didn't wait. Just slipped through the side door without a word. Someone—maybe the stage manager—called after me, but I didn't look back. I was already gone.

Outside, the sun hung low and angry, heat rising off the pavement in shimmering waves. Gear cases and busted pallets lined the loading zone. And there she was.

Climbing out of a white rental car, sunglasses in her hair. Her bun was falling loose, like she'd done it in a rush. She'd just closed the driver's side door, but when she saw me, she straightened.

And then she gave a little wave and smiled. Tentative. Shaky. The kind of smile that said she wasn't sure if she had permission to stay, and it made my heart ache.

I didn't say a word. Just crossed the lot in three strides and pulled her into me.

She came easily, her body folding into mine with

the aching relief of something lost and finally found. Her fingers twisted in the back of my shirt as I tucked my nose into the curve of her neck.

"You made it," I said as I breathed in her scent, my voice catching.

"Barely," she murmured against my collarbone. "My flight was almost canceled."

I eased back, hands still on her waist. Looked at her like I was trying to memorize every freckle, every unspoken sentence behind her eyes.

"You okay?"

Her lips parted, then pressed together. She gave a slight nod. That twist in my chest just kept gnawing and didn't ease.

"Come on," I said gently, threading my fingers through hers. "Let's go somewhere quiet."

We slipped inside through the side entrance, past towers of speaker cases and coils of cable. The hallway buzzed with noise—distant chatter, the faint hum of an amp still plugged in somewhere. The walls were plastered with fading posters and old tape marks, and the smell of sawdust hung thick in the air.

Someone bumped my shoulder and muttered an apology, but I barely acknowledged it. Mallie stayed close, her fingers laced through mine like I was the only steady thing she could hold onto. She didn't say anything, and neither did I. We made it to the green room. The door clicked shut behind us. And still, she didn't let go of my hand.

I'd barely looked around the green room earlier— just dropped my stuff and left. Now, with Mallie standing in front of me, everything came into focus. Muted lighting. A worn leather couch. Some unopened water bottles and energy bars were on a folding table. Posters from old shows lined the walls. Lyrics scribbled on the mirror in black marker.

But none of that mattered because there was something in her silence, and whatever it was, it sat between us, heavy in the air. But underneath it was something fragile and delicate. Maybe hope?

I watched her like a storm I knew was coming—one I didn't want to run from, no matter how hard it hit. So I just kept still and let her find the words.

I led us over to the couch, and she sat down slowly, like she was bracing for an earthquake. She pressed her hands to her knees, trying to keep them still, but I could see the way they shook. I dropped down across from her on the coffee table and covered her hands with mine, rubbing my thumbs gently over her knuckles until the tremor eased.

She looked up at me. "I... I don't know where to start," she said, her voice so soft it barely crossed the space between us.

I leaned back, just a little, to give her space, resting my elbows on my knees. Then, gave her the slightest nod.

"Anywhere," I said quietly. "Just talk to me."

Her eyes dropped to her lap. She rubbed her hands against her jeans like they were damp, then clenched them into fists. I remembered all that fire in her—sharp edges and spark—but now it was like watching a match burn low, unsure if it had enough left to light anything.

She glanced back up at me. "You remember our last summer at the beach house?" she asked.

I grinned and took her hands again, "Like it was yesterday."

She nodded once, then took in a breath and let it out slowly before giving me the truth that rewrote everything I thought I knew, "After our night...

together. I, um… I found out I was pregnant a couple of months later."

My thumbs went still on her knuckles. The breath I was taking caught halfway and burned. The coffee-table edge bit into my knees, and the room shrank to the word she'd just said. She kept talking as her eyes stayed on her hands, anywhere but me.

"I wanted to tell you. I swear. I didn't know what to do. I was terrified, so I went to my mom. And she… shut everything down." A tear slipped down her cheek, "I begged her to let me tell you. I begged. But she said I couldn't. She said…" Her breath shuddered. "She said this could ruin my dad's chance at being mayor, my life, your life…"

She pressed her palms hard into her thighs and peeked up at me again.

"The day she took me to the doctor," she whispered, "she called your mom. Made up that stupid lie that you'd hurt me. I didn't even know she was going to do that shit until she already did it. I was… horrified."

Pregnant? She'd been… pregnant.

I sat back, slowly nodding, like the wind had been knocked out of me in a single, brutal punch. There'd been times I'd wondered, even considered it, but I'd quickly discounted it and thought that couldn't have been it. Even in the van this morning, the thought crept in again the second she said she needed to talk to me, but still, it was the last thing I thought could have been it.

Everything around me blurred under the weight of the memories. I was fifteen again. Pacing my bedroom, my mom standing in the doorway with that look on her face—the one that said she didn't know how to make sense of what she'd just heard. She'd already told me what Elizabeth had said when she'd gotten home from work that day.

But she'd walked in, closed the door behind her with her voice low so my little brother wouldn't catch it. She told me to delete Mallie's number and block her.

When I asked why, when I demanded why Mallie would do this, she'd just shaken her head and said, "I don't think it's Mallory. I think... it's her mother."

My voice cracked when I asked, "But why, Mom? Why would she do this?"

She shook her head and didn't have an answer.

And just like that... Mallie was gone. No goodbye. Just a sudden, gaping silence where she used to be. I spent weeks walking around like a bomb had gone off inside me, wondering if I'd messed things up. If it had all meant more to me than it did to her. If I'd imagined everything.

But I hadn't imagined it. I hadn't misread it. She didn't walk away. She'd been cut off. Hidden. Erased. And so had our... baby.

Now she was here, sitting in front of me, telling me the truth I'd waited so long to hear. And I didn't know which version of me hurt more—the boy who was left behind, or the man finally seeing what had been stolen from him.

"What... what happened?" I choked out.

"She gave me two choices," Mallie said, swiping at her tears as she quickly glanced up at me and then looked away again. "End the pregnancy or adoption." She swallowed hard. "I couldn't—I couldn't do it. I thought I might. But when I knew for sure... I couldn't."

Her eyes flicked to mine, and for a moment, she looked like she might shatter.

"So I gave her up. For adoption." She let out a breath. Not relief. Just release.

"I stayed in school until the holidays. But come spring, she pulled me out. Said I'd be homeschooled. God, she was so afraid it would get out, ruin my dad, that she hid me. " She gave a hollow laugh. "Then after I had the baby, she decided I wouldn't go back to school, just in case people might talk. But... by my junior year, I couldn't take it anymore, the way she could barely look at me, and she basically acted like it never happened. So... I convinced her to send me to a boarding school up in Saint Jo."

I dragged a hand down my face, and when I asked, my voice didn't feel like mine—soft, shaky. "Can I ask...?"

"What?" She asked softly, searching my eyes.

I wet my lips, the crease between my brows tightening as heat crept into my cheeks. "Was it... a boy or a girl?"

"It was a girl," she whispered with a small smile. "I knew it before the scans. I called her Violet in my head. But her name is Abigail."

She paused, eyes distant now and somewhere far from this green room.

"I got to hold her for a couple of minutes." She looked up at me. "But she was mine. Ours. She had a head full of dark hair. I have a picture I took at home. I can show you sometime."

"I'd like that," I said quietly.

When I looked at her, my chest ached with all the years between then and now. I wasn't angry. Or even shocked anymore. I just felt like I'd been broken wide open.

"You really thought this would make me run?" My voice came out low, rough.

"No... I—" she said. Her hands twisted in her lap. "For years, I tried to bury it. Run from it. All of it.

You. The baby. Everything. And then... Then, we found each other again, and it all came rushing back, and I have been so scared. Terrified, this whole time. I was so worried that this would ruin us all over again. That you'd look at me differently. That it would make you hate me. That this would make you..." She didn't finish, just let out a shaky sigh.

I stood up, crossing the small space between us like it was delicate, then knelt in front of her, between her legs, my hands on her thighs. I met her eyes and let her see all the versions of me that loved her. The boy who kissed her on the beach. The boy who never stopped waiting for her to come back. The man who would've given anything to have been there for all of it.

"It breaks me," I said. "What you went through."

A tear slid down her cheek. I reached up. Wiped it away with my thumb.

"I wish I could've protected you. Both of you."

She blinked too fast, then stopped as her shoulders dropped just a fraction as she said, "I wish you'd been there. For everything."

I leaned forward and rested my forehead against hers. My hands cupped her face like it was the only thing steady in the room.

"I want to know her, too," I whispered.

Mallie nodded, a sob catching in her throat.

"Well... um," she said, her voice thin, "a couple of days ago, she reached out through the agency. She wants to know who I am. And I think she should know you, too."

I nodded. "I'm here for all of it—whatever comes next."

"Okay."

I pulled her into me, her head tucking beneath my chin as I ran my hand through her hair—slow, steady—like I could calm the ache out of her.

"Jace..." she whispered, my name breaking like a breath. "I'm sorry."

I leaned back to look her in the eyes. "It's not your fault, Mallie. It's not. I don't blame you for any of it."

Her breath hitched once as I pulled her back into me and another sob broke loose. She tried to swallow it, but more came shaking through her into me. I held on. The tension went first, then the fear, then whatever shame she'd been carrying. She melted into me as my shirt turned damp, like she'd found her way back home. And I was never going to let go.

CHAPTER TWENTY-TWO

Mallie

Age 15 - Austin

Three minutes. That's all it took to change everything.

My breasts had started aching weeks ago. Then my period was late, which had never happened before. Then, when the nausea didn't go away, I blamed the school cafeteria. Then a virus going around. Then the stress of the new school year.

But deep down, I already knew. My mind had been whispering the possibility for weeks before I finally gave in after school today, walking into the pharmacy with my hood pulled up and my heart pounding in my throat.

Back at home, I sat on the closed toilet seat with my legs pulled up tight, arms wrapped around them like that could hold me together. The pregnancy test sat face down on the sink. I couldn't look at it. Not yet. It felt like it was watching me anyway, daring me.

I pressed my forehead to my knees and tried to breathe slowly, but my chest was too tight. My heart had been pounding since that second bright pink line started to show up on the first test, *two tests ago*. This was the third. I kept hoping maybe the others were wrong. Maybe this one would be different.

I closed my eyes and thought of Jace. I thought of that night—his hand on my cheek, the way he looked at me like I was the only person in the universe. The way he whispered "I've always loved you" like it was something sacred. That night had been perfect. Scary, new, overwhelming—but perfect. I didn't regret it. Not that part.

But this? *This* could ruin everything.

I bit the inside of my cheek, hard. It didn't stop the tears that prickled behind my eyes. I couldn't be pregnant. I was only fifteen. I had a plan. I was one of the smart ones, college applications already sketched out in my head. I was the good girl, the people pleaser. The one teachers trusted and friends secretly measured themselves against. This wasn't supposed to happen to girls like me.

I couldn't even tell my friends. Especially Chelsea. She had the biggest mouth this side of the Mississippi. If she knew, everyone would know by lunchtime. This was something I had to deal with entirely on my own.

I looked around the bathroom, like something in here could help. My toothbrush. The cracked tile near the tub. The towel I hadn't bothered to hang up. Everything looked exactly the same, but it all felt different now. Like the world had shifted under my feet and I was falling through a crack I hadn't seen coming.

I glanced at the phone in my hand. Two minutes and forty-three seconds. Seventeen seconds left. I shut my eyes again and started praying—*Please,*

please be wrong. Please let this be a scare. Let it be the flu or stress or anything else. I'll never have sex again, I swear. Just don't let this be real.

I didn't want to think about school. What people would say. The whispers. The stares. The way even the teachers would look at me differently.

"Not Mallory. No way."

But they'd know. They always did. And once they did, I wouldn't be the smart one or the good girl anymore. I'd be *that girl*. Just another story people tell each other when they think you can't hear.

The phone buzzed softly in my palm. Three minutes. My fingers hovered just above the plastic stick, trembling. I held my breath, like maybe if I didn't inhale, the truth wouldn't exist yet. Like maybe time could still freeze and save me from this. But it didn't. And the answer was already there, waiting for me. With a sharp breath, I flipped it over.

Two pink lines. Clear. Bold. Undeniable.

The air rushed out of my lungs in a single, jagged exhale. The room tilted a little. I blinked, hoping it might change if I looked again. But it didn't. The second line didn't fade. Didn't blur. It was just there —bright pink and terrifying.

I stared at it for what felt like forever, my pulse roaring in my ears. The test wobbled in my grip, and I set it down as delicately as I could, my fingers suddenly numb.

This was real. The words echoed in my head. Not a scare. Not a virus. Not just the stress of school. This was a baby. *A baby.*

Tears burned the backs of my eyes, but I didn't cry. I couldn't. I just sat there, frozen, as the weight of it pressed down like something invisible and crushing. I tried to picture telling Jace.

I could still see his smile in the moonlight that night. The way he kissed me like he meant it. Like we were forever. We said always. But always wasn't supposed to look like this. Not yet.

Would he still love me when he found out? Or would he disappear, like everyone said teenage boys always did? Would he even believe me? Would my mom?

A sob clawed its way up my throat, and I slapped a hand over my mouth to keep it in. I wasn't ready. I didn't know what to do, but it didn't matter now.

Ready or not... Everything had changed, and there was no going back.

It took me two weeks to get up the nerve—*two weeks*. I'd carried the truth around like a splinter I couldn't dig out, catching every time I moved. I counted days on the calendar, blamed my nausea on something I ate, and hid the test under coffee grounds in the trash. But I realized I couldn't keep it to myself anymore. I had to tell her.

I found my mom exactly where she always was after dinner, propped up against the headboard, her reading glasses perched on her nose, and a novel cracked open in her hands. The lamp beside her glowed softly, casting a golden warmth across the room. I stood frozen in the doorway for a moment, silently wishing I could turn around and pretend none of this had happened.

But my feet moved on their own.

I crossed the room, climbed onto the bed, and curled up beside her like I had so many times when I was little, when scraped knees or bad dreams or middle-school drama felt like the worst things imaginable. Without a word, she set her book aside and wrapped an arm around me, gently smoothing her hand over my hair. That nearly undid me.

"Everything okay?" she asked.

I squeezed my eyes shut, willing back the tears. I didn't want to cry, not yet. I wanted to be strong, to speak clearly. To finally let the truth out of my chest, where it had been clawing to escape for weeks.

"I need to tell you something," I whispered.

Mom stiffened just a fraction, but she didn't let go. "Okay," she said softly. "What is it?"

I took a breath so deep it rattled my shoulders. "I... um, I think... I'm pregnant."

The silence that followed was deafening. I felt her hand go still against my back, heard the slight hitch in her breathing. When I pulled away just enough to look up at her face, her expression was carefully composed—but just barely. Her lips pressed tight, eyes wide.

"Are you sure?" she asked, her voice thin.

I nodded. "Pretty sure."

"How long?"

"About two months."

Mom blinked, stunned.

She shut her book with her thumb still marking the page. Her gaze flicked to the little calendar by the lamp, then to the beach photo on the dresser—two kids in towels, his grin tipped toward me—and back again. Her jaw tightened, just a notch. She didn't ask who. She didn't need to.

"Does he know?"

I shook my head. "Not yet."

"Good." She set the book on the nightstand, thumb still marking her place. The little calendar got another glance.

"We'll handle this," she said. "Quietly." Her voice went soft in that careful way that meant rules were coming. "You will not call him. You will not text him. And you will not see him. Do you understand?"

"Mom—" His name was right there, but it stuck.

"How did this even happen?"

"It was… at the beach house," I added quickly, my voice small and raw.

She cut in. "Did he push…? Did he pressure you?"

"No." My voice cracked. "I wanted— I mean, we both—"

"You're only fifteen." She said it like a verdict. "He should have known better."

"He's fifteen, too—" I tried again.

"We are not discussing him," she said.

My mouth trembled once, then steadied. "It wasn't some stupid mistake. We love each other."

The shift was immediate. She sat up straighter, jaw tightening. She stared straight ahead, already plotting her next move. "Okay," she said evenly, nodding to herself. "It's October. We still have time. Nobody at school needs to know."

My stomach turned. "What do you mean?"

She reached for the pad she kept by the lamp. "Tomorrow I'll make some calls. There are people who help girls in your situation. Good people."

I nodded because it was easier than arguing. The room felt smaller. My hands wouldn't stop twisting the hem of my shirt.

She looked at me squarely. "We need to be smart about this. With your father on the city council and running for mayor, we have to think about the bigger picture. This isn't just about you, Mallory. It's about this family."

I pulled back, suddenly cold. "But it is about me."

"Yes," she said gently, "but it's also about your future. You can't keep it. It would make things so much harder on you. It would destroy everything you've worked so hard for. College. Your reputation.

It would label you forever."

My throat tightened.

She pressed on, her voice growing firmer. "You have two choices. You can have the baby and give it up for adoption, or—if there's still time—you can end it."

I stared at her. But she just kept talking. "I know it's a hard decision, but you can't keep it. You're too young. It will ruin your life."

Tears spilled down my cheeks. "I want to call Jace. He deserves to know."

Her expression hardened like stone. "Absolutely not."

"But—"

"No. You're not speaking to that boy again. Do you hear me? That little... dalliance is over."

"What?" I blinked at her, disbelief tightening around my chest. "You can't just make that decision for me."

"I can, and I am," she snapped. "You've made a huge mistake. I won't let you make another one."

I snapped back instantly, desperation thickening my voice. "I love him, and he loves me. That's not..." My throat tightened, strangling the rest of the words. My voice dropped, going small and unsteady. "...a mistake."

My mother's expression shifted, her eyes flickering with impatience like she was about to roll them. "Mallory, you're too young even to know what love is. In a few years, you'll forget about this whole thing and move on with your life."

I was never going to forget about this, ever. But I didn't say another word. I just lay there, staring at the ceiling, wishing desperately I could rewind time, back to the beach house. Back to when Jace and I whispered I love yous and meant every word.

I wanted her to ask if I was scared. I wanted her to say my name the way she does when I'm sick. I wanted her to hold me and tell me it was going to be okay. Instead, she clicked her pen and wrote something on her pad, and I just curled into myself. Now all I felt was cold, as if something were being torn from me before I even had the chance to hold it.

I went back to my room and cried until there was nothing left—no tears, no breath, just an overwhelming ache settling in my chest like a bruise. My pillow was damp and mascara smudged beneath my eyes, but I didn't care. I folded inward, beneath the covers, wishing I could sink into the mattress and just vanish.

Thank god Sonny was already back at school. I couldn't imagine facing him right now—not with this, not with this crushing weight pressing down on every part of me. My perfect older brother, always so sure, so steady. He'd be disappointed. Or worse—he'd pity me. And that might just break me.

Would Mom tell him? The thought made my stomach turn. I pictured Sonny picking up his phone, hearing those words, my name spoken as if I were a problem that needed fixing. I hoped—prayed—that Mom would keep this to herself. That she wouldn't let Sonny look at me like I was someone else.

I rolled onto my side, staring up at the thin crack that ran across my ceiling—the one I'd traced with my finger a thousand times when I was little and couldn't sleep. Back then, it had felt comforting, like following the winding path of a tiny river. Now it just looked broken, a harsh reminder of how quickly everything could change. And nothing I did could put it back together again.

* * *

I sat at the kitchen counter, slowly chewing a slice of apple, though I couldn't really taste it. My stomach still felt strange—part nerves, part lingering nausea from the morning sickness that seemed like it was never going to end.

It had been a week since I'd told my mom, and today's appointment had been... a lot. She'd picked me up early from school, barely speaking as we drove across town to Dr. Bennett's office. I hadn't known what to expect, but it definitely wasn't the ultrasound wand or the sterile paper gown or the flicker on the screen that made my breath catch.

Eight weeks, the doctor had said. Based on the measurements. It was too soon to tell if it was a boy or a girl, but somehow, I just knew—she was a girl. I'd felt it deep in my chest the second I saw that tiny flutter of a heartbeat.

I wished Jace had been there. He should've been right next to me, holding my hand, whispering something sweet into my ear like he used to during those stolen afternoons at Hollowbone. This was the most important thing that had ever happened to him, too—and he had no idea. I couldn't even tell him. The thought ripped at my chest, leaving me raw, hollow, desperate.

The door creaked open, and Mom stepped into the kitchen, phone already in her hand, her expression tight and unreadable. She didn't even glance my way, just moved swiftly across the room and began tapping sharply on the screen. My pulse sped up, pounding loudly in my ears.

My breath caught when she set it down on the island. My stomach sank, dread pooling deep and heavy. The phone began ringing. Once. Twice.

"Hello?" Tessa's voice came through—Jace's mom.

"Tessa, how are you?" my mom said, her voice

cold, clipped. Terse.

I froze, apple slice still in my hand, forgotten. I had no idea what she was doing, but my gut already knew it wasn't good.

"Elizabeth? I'm... fine. Is... everything alright?" Tessa asked.

Mom's voice was ice. "No, it's not. I'm calling to make something very clear regarding your son. Jameson is to have no further contact with Mallory. None—no calls, no texts, no messages. If he reaches out in any way, I will pursue legal action."

I sat up straight, the blood draining from my face.

"What?!" I choked out, barely able to get the word past my lips.

Mom didn't even glance at me. She kept her eyes forward, like she wasn't blowing up my entire world with every word.

"I... I don't understand what's going on?" Tessa sounded confused, alarmed.

Mom took a breath, steady and sharp. "Mallory told me everything. She said no, and he... He didn't stop."

My heart dropped into my stomach. I felt like I'd been slapped.

"That's not true!" I blurted out, standing so fast my chair screeched against the tile. "Mom, that's not what happened!"

She turned to me then, her eyes hard. "Enough, Mallory."

Tessa was still on the line. "That doesn't sound like Jameson. They care about each other. He would never—"

"We all like to pretend our children are blameless," she interrupted, her eyes cutting to me. "What matters is that he stays away from my daughter. Or we will go to the police."

My hands were shaking. I couldn't breathe. I reached for the phone, but she ended the call before I could even get close.

"You lied," I whispered.

She turned her back on me and calmly set the phone in her purse. "I protected you."

"No," I said, my voice cracking. "It wasn't me you were protecting. You ruined everything."

She picked up a dish towel as if this were just another normal evening, like she hadn't just ripped my life apart. I stood there, shaking, the image of that flickering heartbeat still burned into the back of my mind—fragile, real, and now completely alone.

CHAPTER TWENTY-THREE

Jace

Age 15 - Dallas

I was sprawled on the couch, flipping channels without really watching anything, when I heard the front door close and Mom's heels clicking against the floor. Something about the rhythm made me look up. Too fast. Too sharp.

She came around the corner clutching her phone like it had personally betrayed her, her face pale and tight.

"Jameson," she said. "Where's your brother?"

I flicked a glance at her, "Playing a video game in his room. Why?"

She looked up towards the stairs and pressed her lips together. "We need to talk."

I sat up slowly, the remote slipping from my hand. "What's going on?"

She just stood there, as if the weight of whatever she was holding would crush her if she sat down.

"I just got off the phone with Elizabeth," she said. Her voice wobbled a little, but she held it steady.

My stomach dropped. "Is Mallie okay?"

She really looked at me then, and I knew this wasn't about anything normal. "Did you... did you force yourself on her?" She asked in a hushed whisper, like she couldn't quite say it.

The words landed like a punch to the chest. I flinched, like maybe I'd misheard.

"What? No. I would never —" The words tore out of me before I could even breathe. For a second I didn't get it. Then her meaning dropped in, heavy and sick, and I felt my insides twist. Mallie's mom thought I'd —

"God, no, that's not —" Heat scorched up my neck, shame and fury colliding until I had to stand. My hands shook. "Mom, that's not what happened. You know I would never —"

She let out a sigh, "Then, what happened?"

"We—we were together because we wanted to be. She said she loved me. We both did."

She held up a hand. "That's not what her mother is saying. She said if you try to contact Mallory again, they'll go to the police."

"But I... I didn't do anything wrong!" My voice cracked. Panic crawled under my skin. "It wasn't like that. We... I... why would she say that?"

"Breathe, son. I believe you," she said quickly. "I saw how... you two were together. But it's not about what I believe. It's what they can make others believe."

I just stood there, frozen. My heart was pounding, but everything else felt numb.

"They could twist this," she went on, more gently now. "They could make this look like something it wasn't. If this goes public... I don't know if we can protect you from that."

I backed up a step, my throat thick. "But she wouldn't... She knows—" My voice broke. "We said we loved each other."

Mom looked down. "Maybe she doesn't have a choice. Or maybe her mom is now controlling everything. Either way, you can't talk to her. Not a text. Not a call. Nothing."

I didn't say anything. I couldn't. The truth was beating like a drum in my chest, but no one could hear it. No one wanted to.

I turned and walked past her, up the stairs, each step heavier than the last. My phone was in my pocket, warm against my leg. I pulled it out when I got to my room, staring at her name on the screen like it might disappear on its own.

I pressed it. Hovered over the message window. My thumb trembled. I could send one last text. Just one. But Mom's voice echoed in my head. *They could make this look like something it wasn't.* I swallowed hard, pressed my lips together, and hit Block Contact. The screen went blank and so did I.

I dropped the phone on my bed like it was burning me. My hands were still shaking. It was too quiet, too still. I paced once, twice, then crossed to the corner and picked up my guitar off its stand. It had always been the thing I went to when things didn't make sense. And right now, nothing made sense at all.

I sat on the edge of my bed and let my fingers fall into familiar positions, the strings humming beneath them. I didn't even think, just let the ache in my chest guide me. A few soft chords. Minor, raw. A slow rhythm that felt like breathing underwater.

Then the words came, low and rough at first.

"You said forever in a whisper, under stars and salty air...
Now I'm a stranger in your silence, like we were never
there..."

* * *

The backs of my eyes burned, and I blinked. But the tears came anyway. I let them fall. Didn't bother wiping them away.

"They say I hurt you, say I lied, but I was there, and I know why—
It was love, it was real, now it's lost in what they feel..."

I kept playing—verse after verse. My voice cracked once, but I didn't stop.

I thought of her face when she laughed, the way she'd tucked her hand into mine like it had always belonged there. I thought of that night in my bed— how she looked at me like I was something sacred.

And now... I couldn't even call her. Couldn't defend myself. Couldn't hold her hand while the world turned upside down.

"You were my truth in a world of noise, now I'm just a
name, just one of those boys.
They built a wall I can't break through, but I still see the
real you..."

I sat there for a long minute, letting the last chord fade, the weight of the song still thick in the air. My fingers hovered over the strings, aching like the rest of me. This wasn't just a song—it was her. Us. Everything that had been ripped away from me without warning.

I reached for the notebook on my nightstand, the one I used when I didn't know what else to do with how I felt. I flipped past half-written lyrics and chord sketches until I found a blank page.

My pen moved fast. I wrote it all down—every line, every verse, every quiet truth I couldn't say out loud. I pressed harder than I needed to, the ink digging into the paper. The chorus spilled out like a wound, "You were my truth in a world of noise, now I'm just a name, just one of those boys. They built a wall I can't break through, but I still see the real you..."

I paused once, the pen hovering over the page, then finished the bridge. It hurt, writing it. But it felt honest. It felt like the only thing I still had that belonged to me. When I was done, I closed the notebook gently, like the song inside was something fragile. I didn't know when, or if, I'd ever play it for anyone. But I'd saved it. For her. For me. For a time when the truth could finally be heard.

Two days. That's how long it had been since I blocked her. Two days of trying to convince myself I did the right thing. That I was protecting her. Protecting myself. That this would blow over, and we'd find our way back to each other. But none of it felt true.

I sat on the edge of my bed, staring at my phone for what had to be the hundredth time. My thumb hovered over her contact, like maybe this time I'd have the nerve to unblock her. Just to see.

I didn't expect a message. I didn't expect anything. But the second I hit "Unblock," it came in. One text. Sent that same night when everything fell apart.

Mallie: I didn't lie. I never would. You were there. You know the truth. I carry you with me now...

The breath left my body in one sharp exhale. I read it again. And again. Each line was heavier than the last. Her words echoed in my head, louder than the silence that had been there for days.

I carry you with me now. What did that mean?

My heart pounded as I stood up, pacing, the phone still clutched in my hand. It didn't say what she meant outright. But something was there. Something big. Bigger than the lie her mom had told. Bigger than even I could understand.

Why would she say I hurt her? Why would she lie? What had happened after we left the beach house—what had changed?

She'd said she loved me. She meant it. I know she meant it. And I loved her, too. That night wasn't a mistake. It wasn't something shameful. It was the most real thing I'd ever felt.

So why this? Why now?

I stopped pacing and dropped onto the floor, leaning back against the wall as my brain spun. *I carry you with me now...* Was she saying she missed me? She loved me? That she was trying to hold on? Or was it something else?

The more I thought about it, the more that last line rattled in my chest. Not just emotionally. Literally. Was she...? *No.* There was no way.

I sat forward, hands running through my hair. My heart kicked against my ribs like it wanted to escape. I couldn't say it. Couldn't think it. But suddenly her mom's rage, the threat of police, the desperation to sever us—none of it felt random anymore. It felt calculated. It felt scared. And it made me sick.

I buried my face in my hands, wishing I hadn't blocked her. Wishing I could call her right now. Ask her what she meant. But I couldn't. Her message sat there, burning a hole in my chest. And I was too late.

CHAPTER TWENTY-FOUR

Mallie

Present Day

A knock at the door made me flinch. Jace's arms tensed around me, but neither of us moved. The door cracked open a second later, and a man, about mid-40s maybe, with a goatee, headset askew, a tablet in one hand, poked his head in.

"Soundcheck's in two," he said, his voice too casual to be anything but carefully measured. His eyes flicked to me, then back to Jace. "You good?"

Jace didn't answer right away. I felt it, in his pulse thudding against my ear and the way he tensed, like he was biting back words.

"Just... give me a minute," he said.

The guy, his manager, probably, gave a quick nod and stepped back, the door clicking softly shut behind him.

I scooted over and stood up, taking a step to the side, already brushing at my face, trying to wipe away the tears, the mascara, the mess. "You should go. I'll get out of your way."

"Mallie—"

"You need to get your head on straight. You've got a show. I'll be back before it starts."

I tried to smile, but it was shaky before I turned and headed towards the door. I still felt so exposed, like my seams had come apart.

"I don't want you to go, but if you need to..." he said as his voice dropped off at the end, and the way he said it made me stop.

When I glanced back, he was already walking towards me and reaching into his back pocket. He pulled out a hotel key in a folded sleeve and looked at it like he wasn't sure if he was being too much—but held it out to me anyway.

"Here—I got my own room this time," he said. "After our texts, I couldn't imagine going back to a room full of guys if you were coming. I wanted—"

He swallowed hard.

"I wanted somewhere we could be alone. Just us."

His thumb brushed my cheek.

"Room 214," he added. "At the Harborview Inn. Take a shower. Eat something. Sleep if you can."

He paused.

"You don't have to come to the show if you're not up for it. I can meet you there after."

I looked down at the key in his hand and felt that same ache I'd felt when we were kids—when he gave me his sweatshirt without saying a word, just because I looked cold. This was one of those times he saw what I needed before I did.

When I took it, his hand closed gently over mine before I could pull away. And he pulled me back into him. His arms wrapped around me, tight and warm, and for a second, I just let myself lean into him. Let my forehead fall against his shoulder and breathe him in. Everything in me felt like it was trying to remember what it felt like to be loved.

He kissed me again—soft and unhurried, like he wasn't asking for anything but time. When he pulled back, his voice was rough. "When I told Tom I needed a minute, that didn't mean from you. All I want is more time with you."

He stepped back, just enough to let me go. I smiled at him, but I could feel it wobble at the edges even though I meant it. And then I slipped out of the room and closed the door behind me.

But as I walked back to my rental car, the hotel key clenched tight in my hand, for the first time since I was 15 years old, I wasn't trying to get away. I was headed toward something. Toward him. Toward us.

It only took 10 minutes to get to the hotel. The room was quiet when I stepped inside. The afternoon light spilled through the space between the curtains, casting soft gold across the hotel carpet. It smelled faintly of lemon-scented cleaner. The sheets were rumpled, the pillows piled together, like he'd taken a nap earlier.

Jace's duffel was half-unzipped on the chair, a hoodie tossed on top like he'd pulled it out earlier and forgotten about it. I dropped my bag by the foot of the bed and walked over, my fingers brushing the worn cotton fleece without thinking. I picked it up. Navy blue, the neckline frayed, sleeves slightly stretched—like it had been lived in.

I held it to my face. The scent hit me instantly. Warm. Clean. A little bit of his cedar and leather and something deeper—maybe his shampoo, maybe just him. My chest tightened at the scent, the memory it evoked.

I slipped it over my head without even thinking. It was too big. The hem hit halfway down my thighs, and the sleeves swallowed my hands. But it was warm and his. And right now, that felt like safety.

The bed creaked softly as I lay down, one sleeve tucked beneath my cheek. I didn't mean to fall asleep. I told myself I'd rest for just a minute—just until the ache in my chest settled. But his scent wrapped around me, comforting and grounding, and I drifted off.

I woke up lying in a field. The grass was lush and cold beneath my bare feet—damp with dew and soft like velvet. I looked down, breath catching at the sight of my bare legs, my toes sinking into the earth.

The air was eerily still. The world was dark and endless. And above me, lanterns floated—hundreds of them. Thousands. They drifted like fireflies, made of silk paper, and glowed a warm gold. Each one moved so slowly, pulsing faintly, with a heartbeat of its own.

I turned in place, the grass tickling my ankles as I walked. There was no wind. No sun. Just darkness and this sea of lanterns that moved like a murmuration in this strange fluid movement, like a thousand birds turning in silent rhythm.

One lantern lowered, hovering in front of me like it had chosen me. I reached out and held my breath, and the moment my fingers brushed the light, it opened in a flash of brilliant light. There was a memory, almost like a movie, and I was in it. I was fifteen, sitting on the cold bathroom tile, holding a pregnancy test with both hands like it might bite. My knee had a bruise I didn't remember. I was shaking my head as my lips whispered, "No, no, no..."

The lantern closed, and the light faded. But then another came down. And another.

One showed me lying on an examining table, wearing a paper gown, the screen showing a flickering heartbeat. Another showed the hospital, sterile and white. I was in a pink hospital gown, lying in bed and holding a bundle as tears dripped down my face.

Another lantern opened to our kiss on the shore. His whispered promise in the dark. "You're the only girl I wanna chase crabs with."

More floated down. I opened them one by one. Each memory landed like a letter in a long-forgotten shoe box. And then, one wouldn't open. It hovered lower than the others, brighter—a deeper gold, like sunset. I wrapped my hands around the edges and pulled, but it stayed sealed.

Before I could try again, someone stepped beside me. I didn't have to look. I knew it was Jace. The same version of him I'd seen earlier today, with worry lines around his eyes. He was barefoot, his jeans damp at the hem, like he'd been walking through this place for hours.

He met my eyes, then reached forward. The lantern opened for him, and inside was a girl. A teenager, cross-legged on a wooden floor, surrounded by books, with a half-eaten granola bar in her hand. She had his eyes and my heart-shaped mouth. Her face was tilted toward a window, the light catching her in a way that made my chest ache.

She smiled. Not shy or startled, but like she knew me. Then, the lantern shut softly and rose, drifting out of reach. I turned to Jace, and he reached for my hand. When our fingers touched, the whole dream dissolved—like fog under the sun.

I woke with a gasp, still curled up in bed, still wearing his hoodie. The room was quiet, now dark, but the girl in the lantern—she stayed with me.

I grabbed my phone and checked the time. 7:30. I'd somehow slept through my alarm. The show was starting in thirty minutes. If I hurried, I might make Jace's set, but I'd probably be late.

I sat there for a second longer, clutching the phone in both hands. The dream clung to me like mist. That girl in the lantern still hovered behind my eyes. She'd looked straight at me, like she knew who I was. Like she'd been waiting.

I stood, legs unsteady. The room was darker now, shadows stretching long across the floor. Jace's scent still lingered in the hoodie wrapped around me. I pulled the fabric tighter around myself.

For a moment, I thought about staying here, trying to return to that dream. I could've curled back up and waited for him to find me again. But the thought of him walking onto that stage, scanning the crowd and not seeing me made something catch in my chest. I wasn't going to miss this. I'd already missed so much from our years apart. Not again.

I shoved my feet into my shoes, pulled my hair back up into a messy bun, and grabbed my keys and my phone. I headed out, my pulse quickening with every step, down the hallway and into the elevator, through the lobby.

The bass thumped through the pavement before I even reached the doors.

I slipped past the line of latecomers and ducked around the side entrance, showing my pass to the security guard. He barely looked at me when I gave my name—just handed me a wristband and nodded toward the hallway beyond.

The sound swallowed me whole. Pounding drums. The high shimmer of a guitar. The whistles and screams of the fans. All of it vibrated through my ribs, my throat, my spine. The crowd was a sea of bodies packed shoulder to shoulder under pulsing lights, arms raised, phones glowing like tiny stars.

I hovered near the back, heart hammering. My breath caught at the sight of the stage. And there he was—*Jace.*

He stood just off-center, mic in one hand, guitar slung low. He was lit from behind, haloed in amber light, sweat darkening the collar of his shirt. His hair curled damp against his temple, and his lips moved around the lyrics.

I didn't recognize the song at first. But then I heard the chorus, and my knees nearly buckled. It was raw, quietly aching. About someone who slipped through the cracks and came back anyway. About finding pieces of yourself in the wreckage of what you lost. I pressed a hand to my chest.

He hadn't seen me yet. But somehow… I think he felt me. He closed his eyes on the last line. And when he opened them, he looked right at me. Straight through the crowd. Straight to where I stood in the back, tears on my lashes, barely able to breathe. And then he locked eyes with me and grinned. Like he'd been playing every note just to bring me here, and in that look, I swear I heard—*There you are.*

CHAPTER TWENTY-FIVE

Jace

Present Day

We'd barely cleared the last note when I handed off my guitar and jogged straight offstage. I didn't stop to catch my breath. Didn't look for a towel or water or even check to see if the house lights had come up. I just needed to find her.

I couldn't shake the moment our eyes met during the set. She'd been standing at the back of the crowd, and for a second, it felt like the world had stopped. And it was just us.

I cut through the backstage hallway, heart pounding harder than it had on stage, and turned the corner, and there she was. Leaning against the wall like she'd always been there.

"Hey," I said, still catching my breath. "I missed you."

She smiled, small, a little shy. "I'm here."

I reached for her hand without thinking. "Come on. Let's get out of the noise."

She let me lead her through a side door. The night air hit us like a wave, cool and calm. I didn't stop until we were tucked beneath a flickering security light, just the two of us.

I turned to face her, rubbing the back of my neck. "This is gonna sound completely insane, but... I took a nap in the green room before the show, and I had this dream."

Her head tilted, eyes narrowing slightly.

"I was in a field," I said. "Dark. Totally black sky. And there were all these floating lanterns—like a thousand of them. Just hanging there in the air, glowing like stars hung low."

Her lips parted. She didn't move. Didn't blink.

"I think... I think I had the same dream," she said, breathless.

My pulse skipped. "What?"

She nodded, slower now, eyes locked on mine like she was afraid saying it out loud might make it too real.

"In my dream, I was barefoot in a field. It was dark—really dark—and cold. The grass was wet. And I saw lanterns, too. They would float down to me, and I kept opening them and seeing things—our memories. The cave. The beach. *That night.*" Her voice cracked. "But there was one I couldn't open. No matter how hard I tried."

A chill crept up my spine.

"I saw you," I said quietly. "...standing there, struggling with that lantern. I walked over. Put my hand on it—and it... just opened."

Mallie sucked in a sharp breath and stumbled back a step. One hand flew to her mouth.

She looked at me, eyes wide, shimmering. "And inside... was there a girl?"

My heart stopped. "Yeah."

She shook her head, whispering. "God, Jace... what if that was her? Abigail?"

For a second, all I could do was stare at her. Because somehow —I knew, not just in a dream-logic kind of way, but in that deep-down place you don't question. The one where my music lived. Where I knew Mallie was it for me when I was just a kid.

I reached for her hand.

"Mallie," I said, my voice low. "We were in the same dream. I don't know how. I don't know what it means. But I felt you there. Just as real as right now. And that girl… I feel it in my bones, that was her."

The wind came through like a breath, too warm and almost alive, and it felt like the beginning of something. The space between us felt charged like the dream had followed us into the real world and was waiting to see what we'd do next.

Mallie looked down at our hands, then back up at me.

"Remember earlier," she said, her voice barely above the hum of the street behind us, "when I told you she contacted me? Well, I started writing her a letter, but I never sent it."

I nodded, heart thudding.

"Why don't we finish it together?" she asked. "Back at the hotel. You can read what her mom sent, and then we'll write back. Together."

My throat tightened. I wrapped my hand around hers a little tighter.

"Yeah," I said softly. "I'd like that."

By the time we made it back to the hotel, it was nearly one in the morning. We sat cross-legged on the floor of my hotel room, Mallie's laptop balanced between us. I'd lit the sandalwood travel candle I always kept stashed in my bag—some habit I picked up on tour, trying to make impersonal places feel a little more like mine. The flame flickered low, warm and steady, and I hoped it helped.

Mallie let out a sigh and then clicked something, then turned the screen toward me.

"This is the letter I wrote her," she said quietly.

Her hands were folded in her lap, fingers woven so tightly it looked like she might be holding herself together by force alone. I didn't reach for them. Just leaned in and started to read.

Hi Abigail,

My name is Mallory. I gave birth to you. I'm not sure what you might want to call me. Maybe birth mom, maybe something else, or just Mallory. That's okay. You get to decide. I just hope, from this point on, I can be someone you can trust.

*There's a lot I want to tell you, but the most important thing is this—***You were never unwanted. Not for a single second.***

When I found out I was going to have you, I was only 15 years old. I was scared and didn't know what to do. A lot of grown-ups around me made decisions I didn't agree with, even when I asked them not to. One of those decisions was placing you for adoption.

It all happened really fast. Too fast. And it broke my heart.

I got to hold you once—just for a few minutes—but I've remembered it forever. I never knew your name. Abigail is a beautiful name, and I hope you love it. I hope it makes you feel strong and special.

I've missed you every single day. I've wondered what you're like. If you love reading, or if you're the kind of kid who climbs trees or tells stories in your head. I've always carried you in my heart.

I don't know what you're thinking or feeling right now, and that's okay. This kind of thing can feel really big and weird and maybe even scary. You don't have to have any answers yet. You get to go at your own pace.

If and when you ever want to talk more, I'd really love that. I'd love to hear about your world. And if you have questions about me, I'd be happy to answer them.

With love,
  Mallory

It was soft and brave and full of truths I understood now and maybe even felt myself. By the time I hit the last line, I felt like my lungs had forgotten how to expand. I exhaled slowly and ran a hand through my hair.

"It's good," I said. "Really good."

She looked at me then, as if trying to figure out if I meant it or if I was overwhelmed. Honestly, I still couldn't quite believe it. I—we had a daughter out there.

"I just..." I hesitated, pressing my palms to the floor like I needed grounding. "I don't know if I can add anything to that. I just found out she existed. You've had thirteen years, and I'm still trying to catch up."

Mallie didn't flinch. She just nodded and opened a new blank document, the cursor blinking and expectant.

She said softly, "That's okay. But let's make it something from both of us."

I didn't know where to begin. "You want to start?" I asked softly, glancing over at her.

She nodded, just barely, the glow of the screen lighting up her face. She seemed to stare at the blinking cursor, just as lost as I was. Then, slowly, she began to type:

* * *

Dear Abigail,

We know this letter might feel like a lot. It's a lot for us, too. But we wanted to write to you together—to say hello, and to say something we've both been carrying in our hearts for you.

We're Mallory and Jameson, your birth parents. The truth is, we loved you since before you were born.

A lot of hard things happened when we were your age—things we didn't get to choose. But loving you and wanting what was best for you? Those were never the hard things. Those parts were easy.

She glanced at me, "So… what do you think?"

I smiled. Her words tugged at my chest a little. "I like it."

"You sure?" she asked, without looking at me.

I swallowed the lump in my throat.

"Yeah." I tilted my head, thinking. "What if we say something like… 'We want to get to know you when you're ready.' Or is that too much?"

She barely shook her head and softly said, "No, that's not too much. But should we add there's no pressure?"

I nodded. "Yeah, let's let her know this can go at her pace."

She typed it out:

There's no pressure. No expectations. We want to get to know you, on your timeline and when you're ready.

(This part is from Mallory.)

I wanted to tell you a little about myself. I am the youngest and have a big brother. I am a writer, and I love to paint. And I hope one day we can meet.

* * *

She turned toward me. "Do you want to write your own part? Or we can keep going together."

I nodded. "No, I'll do it." Then, I reached for the laptop.

My fingers hovered for a moment before I started typing, each word pulled straight from the center of my chest. Slowly, deliberately, I added:

(This part is from Jameson.)

I just found out about you a few days ago. I'm a musician in a band, and I play the guitar. I've written songs since I was a teenager. And even though this is all new, a part of me feels like I've missed you all along.

I paused, heart thudding a little too loudly in my ears. When I glanced at Mallie, her hand was pressed over her mouth, eyes shining.

"Too much?" I asked, quieter than before.

She shook her head, blinking fast. "No," she whispered. "It's… perfect."

We kept going. Slowly. Carefully. Pausing to talk. Mallie wrote the final lines, quietly speaking as she typed:

We would love to hear from you. But only when you're ready, and only as much as you're comfortable sharing. We'll be here, whenever that is.

She let out a breath, looking back at me with hopeful uncertainty. I smiled faintly, my heart aching but somehow full. We read all of it together once more. Slowly. Carefully.

And then we signed our names.

With all our hearts,
Mallory & Jameson

* * *

We sat in the quiet for a moment, the glow of the laptop screen soft against her face. Her fingers still hovered over the keyboard, trembling, just barely, but I saw it. Felt it like a pulse under my skin.

She'd carried this for years. Alone. And she hadn't wanted it that way. She needed me back then. And I wasn't there. Not because I didn't love her, but because no one let me.

My chest tightened as I thought of everything she'd endured—the way her mom lied. How I believed, even for a second, that Mallie might have hated me. She didn't. She loved me. Just as much as I loved her. And I still did… so much.

I reached out and closed the laptop and set it aside, and reached for her hand, lacing our fingers together like it was second nature. Like it had always been this way.

Her lips parted like she might say something, but I didn't wait. I came close enough to breathe her in, then kissed her, lingering. The kind of kiss that felt like an answer to something unspoken. Her hand found the side of my neck, anchoring herself to me.

"Jace… I…"

My voice came out rough. "All those years, Mallie… you were never alone. I didn't stop thinking about you. Not once." I paused, my thumb brushing across her knuckles.

She breathed in sharply, then melted into me like she'd been waiting for this moment longer than she knew. Her hand slid up tangling in my hair as she shifted into my lap, her thighs sliding over mine until she was straddling me. My hands instinctively found her hips, and then her waist, pulling her closer like I couldn't stand even an inch between us.

Her mouth was warm and open against mine, all

urgency and years of what-ifs melting into the space between us. My shirt was gone before I realized I'd pulled it over my head. Hers followed, and muscle memory took over like we'd done this a thousand times.

When I unhooked her bra, she let it fall like shedding the last piece of hesitation. My hands moved reverently—like a prayer I hadn't known I'd been saying for years. I kissed her neck, her collarbone, and let my lips trace down to her peaked nipple, sucking it into my mouth. She arched her back, and I felt her shudder under me.

My hands palmed her breasts gently, reverently, as my lips trailed between them, back up to her throat, tasting her skin, feeling her heartbeat race under my mouth. She tilted her head back and sighed—soft, aching, utterly unguarded. Every part of her was pressed against me, warm and wanting, and I didn't want to be anywhere else.

But the floor was hard.

I slipped my hands down to her thighs and tugged her legs around my waist. "Hold on, baby."

She tightened her arms around my neck on instinct, letting out a startled giggle. "What are you doing?"

"First," I said, lifting her off the ground like she weighed nothing, "I'm taking you somewhere softer."

Her laughter followed us as I crossed the room. I tossed her onto the bed with a gentle bounce, her hair spilling across the pillows, her eyes wide and shining.

"And two..." I said as I reached for my belt, unbuckling it slow and deliberate, letting my jeans hit the floor. I crawled onto the bed after her, voice low, teasing. "I want to do... you."

She let out a breathless laugh, biting her lip as I reached for the button of her jeans.

"You're ridiculous," she whispered, smiling up at me like I was both the wildest idea she'd ever had—and the one thing she never wanted to lose.

I grinned, tugging her jeans down. "And you love it."

She blushed as she giggled and I settled over her, my arms caging her in. I leaned down, capturing her lips, nipping her bottom one.

And then, there was only skin and heat and the sound of us, falling back into each other like we were made for this. Whatever was waiting for us on the other side of that email, of this moment... we could face it later.

Right now, we just had each other. And after all these years away from her, that felt like everything.

CHAPTER TWENTY-SIX

Mallie

Present Day

I don't think either of us slept, not that I regretted a single second of it. After we finished the letter, the weight of everything I'd been holding onto lifted, like the knot in my belly had finally been untangled. And once it slipped free, something in me shifted — quietly, profoundly. Like the shape of my heart had changed. Like somehow I'd always wished and hoped he'd been there waiting. And now that I knew if he'd had the chance, he would have stayed by my side through all of it. That just made me want to choose him all over again.

We made love like we were trying to rewrite time. Like we could stitch back together everything we'd lost over the years. It was slow, then desperate. Sweet, then tangled. I needed his touch, the feel of his skin against mine, and without it, I couldn't bear it. By the time I started to drift off to sleep, we were curled up in each other in a knot of limbs and breath and heartbeats.

This wasn't about forgetting. It was about finally

letting myself feel it all. Letting myself believe that maybe… I was allowed to have this. Him. Us. A second chance. And when I fell asleep in his arms, tangled and bare beneath the motel sheets, it was the first time in years I'd felt free.

But morning came. And reality with it. We went to breakfast with the rest of the band at the diner in the motel parking lot. As we walked in, Jake looked up from his pancake tower and smirked.

Eddie held up a coffee cup like he was toasting us. "Dude, you're smiling like you saw boobs for the first time."

I couldn't stop my smile as I burrowed deeper into Jace's hoodie, the fabric soft and safe as my face went up in flames.

Dean didn't even look up from his eggs. "Can't believe you let her steal your hoodie, man. Rookie move."

Jace just grinned and dropped into the booth beside me, brushing his knee against mine. "Nah, worth it."

Afterward, we stood at the back of the van while the guys loaded up. Jace opened his duffel and grabbed a sweatshirt, pulling it over his still-damp curls from the shower where we'd kissed under the hot water like we were afraid to say goodbye.

"Just a couple more shows," he said, eyes locked on mine. "Come with me."

I wanted to say yes. I wanted to so bad it hurt. But the thought of coming with him with no plan, no reason, just because I couldn't stand to be away from him? That made my stomach twist. What would my brother think? Skipping town with Jace would only confirm what I was afraid he still believed about me, that I was impulsive. Reckless. The same kid who looked like she just ran away instead of growing up.

I worried the edge of my sleeve, the seam rough under my thumb. "If I stay, it's just… another thing that I just let happen to me. I want this— I mean, you—I want you, Jace. I really do, but I also want it to be something I choose."

He didn't argue. Didn't tug me closer. His mouth stayed steady, but something in his eyes flickered, like he was bracing. He let the quiet sit between us instead of filling it.

Then he leaned in until our foreheads touched. "If it helps," he murmured, breath warm against my lips, "I'm choosing you. Every day. Until you say it back."

Dean rolled down the window. "Jay, let's move. Traffic's already starting."

Jace leaned in and pressed his lips to my temple— gentle, brief, not enough—and the reckless part of me read it like a promise while the careful part filed it under "goodbyes."

He opened my door, and I slid into the driver's seat. After he shut the door, he bent to the glass, eyes on mine, with that half-smile that always felt like ours. He mouthed a sentence, and halfway through, I swear I saw *I love you.*

The urge to yank the handle and make him say it out loud—make it real—hit hard. But I just touched the glass, and with a small, almost helpless smile, he blew me a kiss. Then, I gave him a nod I hoped looked brave as I grabbed the seatbelt like it could hold me together.

The van rattled as Dean revved the engine and leaned out to say something. Jace nodded, already stepping back, and my chest did that hollow drop, like when you missed a step on the stairs. I told myself this was normal for him—tour and come back. Still, the worry slid in. What if I were just a soft place to land between cities? What if I were the one feeling everything?

He gave me one last look, longer this time, like he used to look at me at the end of every summer, like he was memorizing me, and I told myself I was making a big deal out of nothing. Then the door slammed, and they pulled out of the parking lot and merged into traffic. I watched the taillights until they blurred.

The ghost of his mouth was still warm on my skin, and I was still trying to decide if that was a beginning—or if I'd just watched the ending drive away. For a brief moment, I told myself that if I stayed right there in that parking lot, maybe I could trick myself into believing the last twelve hours weren't already behind us. But eventually I had to, or I'd miss my flight.

The drive to the airport felt like I was being dragged away from the man I couldn't get out of my head—the one I thought I might be falling back in love with, or maybe I'd never stopped. The silence was too loud. I kept glancing at the passenger seat, half-expecting to see him there, cracking a joke, singing under his breath, reaching for my hand.

This was so new. Yet, we'd just parted, and I missed him terribly already. Maybe I should have thrown caution to the wind and just gone with him.

But then the questions came creeping back in. The ones I'd been trying to outrun since the second we found each other again. What if this was just a rebound? What if I was chasing a feeling because I've been lost for so long? What if I didn't know how to be okay without someone else anchoring me?

The airport was its usual blur of motion—rolling suitcases   clattering   over   tile,   snippets   of conversation in half a dozen languages. I bought a cup of burnt coffee, wrapping my hands around the cardboard sleeve as if the heat might work its way into the ache in my chest.

At the gate, I found a seat against the wall and pulled my legs up, curling into myself. Across from me, a young couple leaned together, laughing over something on a phone screen. Their shoulders bumped, their fingers threaded, and every so often they looked up at each other like no one else in the world existed.

I should have looked away. Instead, I cataloged them. Every brush of skin, every shared smile, like an anthropologist studying a language I used to know but had somehow forgotten. That had been Jace and me once. Bonfire nights, late-night walks on the beach, whispered promises we were too young to understand. And then... silence. More than a decade of pretending none of it had mattered, only to have it come roaring back in a single night that left me feeling both lighter and more undone than I'd ever been.

My boarding group was called. I shuffled forward with the herd, clutching my bag and trying not to think about how empty my hands felt without his.

On the plane, I slid into the window seat and buckled in. A toddler in the row ahead of me kicked the seat back in erratic rhythm, singing to himself. Across the aisle, a man in a suit had his laptop open before we'd even left the ground, already lost in graphs and spreadsheets. Everyone seemed to know exactly where they were going, exactly what they were returning to—everyone but me.

While everyone was still boarding, I pulled out my phone, thumb hovering over his name. Every part of me screamed to call. To say screw it, walk off the flight, and find him. But I didn't. Instead, I opened my notes app and stared at the blank page. Words were easier when I couldn't say them out loud.

I typed: **I want to choose this. I want to choose you.**

Then I deleted it before I could overthink.

Moments later, the engines roared and the next thing I knew the plane tilted upward, and my stomach dropped. Through the window, I watched the desert peel away into cloud cover. Leaving Jace behind felt like ripping out a stitch before the wound had healed.

I tugged his hoodie tighter around me, burying my face in the collar. It still smelled faintly of his scent, clean and warm, and for a second it tricked me into believing he was close enough to touch. But my heart knew better.

The rest of the flight blurred into white noise. My row was empty. I stared out the window as the clouds passed. I wasn't crying. But the backs of my eyes burned, and my chest ached like I might if I let myself.

I'd decided to leave Thailand and Devon behind after everything, and I'd finally done something for myself. But now I was running headfirst into another relationship. Something familiar. Something I used to pray for. Was it real? Or just... convenient?

I let myself wallow and spiral into that for three hours, replaying every moment, every word. Convincing myself I was reading more into this than he was. Maybe this was just some ridiculous fling. He probably had a lot of... flings. After all, he was quickly becoming a freaking rock star. I saw the way women looked at him, the way they practically threw their underwear at him. The other guys ate it up, but was that Jace, too?

When the wheels hit the ground in Dallas, I waited until we were parked at the gate before turning my phone off airplane mode. And that's when I saw a string of texts from the last few hours, nearly since we'd said goodbye this morning. Jace's name. Over and over.

Jace: Still thinking about your mouth. And your hands. And the way you moaned my name.

Jace: We finally made it to Vegas. You home yet?

Jace: Did you take my favorite hoodie? I can't find it. It's okay if you did ;)

Jace: Eddie told me to stop smiling like that. I said I would... if I ever stop thinking about last night. Spoiler: I won't. ;)

Jace: Hope your flight was okay. God, I miss you... so much.

My stomach flipped as I clutched my phone to my chest and closed my eyes, biting back the stupid smile I couldn't stop. It wasn't just me. God, I wanted this. I wanted him. I should have stayed...

I sent him a text back:

Me: Home now. Yes, I stole your hoodie. Hoping I took your heart, too. I miss you more than I want to admit.

CHAPTER TWENTY-SEVEN

Jace

Present Day

I was still toweling off my hair, half-dressed and groggy from the nap I barely meant to take, when I grabbed my phone to check the time. A few new notifications blinked on the screen—one from Dean about load-in, one from the venue manager. And one from *her*.

Mallie: Home now. Yes, I stole your hoodie. Hoping I took your heart, too. I miss you more than I want to admit.

I sat down hard on the edge of the hotel bed, towel still around my shoulders, phone clutched like it might vanish if I blinked.

Jesus.

I read it again. Then again. My heart kicked like a drum in my chest, fast and full, because there it was—*Hoping I took your heart, too.* Proof that I wasn't alone in this. That she wasn't brushing it off as some nostalgia trip. She missed me—more than she wanted to admit.

Fuck, I missed her, so much. So many years. It was like coming home to a place I forgot I was missing, not that I ever forgot. How could I?

Back then, I didn't know the word for forever. I just knew at five years old I was going to marry the girl with the little dent in her cheek when she smiled. It just grew stronger year by year, sharing our freezer pops, sand between our toes, and promises whispered where the dunes kept our secrets. And then... we were done without ever getting to the end.

Between then and now, I tried. I dated. Some were kind, some were chaotic. But none of them were easy the way Mallie was, like breathing, like a song I could never forget. I kept chasing that click. Once, I thought I'd found it, but I never tried very hard to make time for her. I hated being the guy who wrote songs about a ghost and pretended they were about something else.

She would ask who the song was for, and I'd say "no one" and watch her go quiet. And even on the good days, I measured her against the girl from the beach I could never let go. That wasn't fair to anyone. I knew it. Eventually, I realized that until I could figure out how to get Mallie out of my system, being alone was just... easier. But now...

Now here we were again, finding our way back to each other. Thirteen years gone and still—the same pull, the same gravity. There were never any real comparisons. That was over. It was her. It had always been her. And I wasn't losing her this time.

I stared at the screen for a second, then stopped myself. I didn't want to send something dumb or rushed. I wanted her to feel it—how serious I was.

I leaned forward, elbows on my knees, and

whispered it into the empty room first, just to make sure I could say it. "I miss you, too, Mal. So much it hurts."

Then I started typing.

Me: I miss you too, Mal. Like I'm walking around half awake without you. Hoodie looks better on you anyway. And my heart's yours if you want it.

I stared at the screen for a beat, then hit send. No edits. No hesitations. Just the truth. Because she had it, my whole damn heart.

She'd taken it when she started calling me Jace that first day, like it was already a nickname only she got to use, and she helped me rebuild my sandcastle. When she sat next to me on that porch swing, the summer I got stitches and never once acted like she didn't want to be there or that she was missing out on the entire summer.

I'd loved her then. I loved her when we lost each other. I loved her in silence for thirteen years. And I loved her now. She had my heart. She had all of me. And I wasn't asking for any of it back.

The knock on the door came hard and fast, knocking me back to reality.

Dean, as always. "Time to go, lover boy. Sound check in thirty. Let's move."

"Yeah, yeah. I just need… a few minutes."

"Whatever, dude. Just be at the van in twenty."

I grabbed my bag and slung it over my shoulder, still thinking about her standing in the motel room in nothing but my hoodie. Still thinking about how soft her voice sounded last night and how badly I wanted her back in my arms.

I tossed my phone on the bed, still half-smiling at her text. Her hoodie confession. Her heart, too. I ran a hand through my hair, still damp from the shower, and let myself sink into the edge of the mattress.

A few minutes later, I was outside. The guys were already idling in the van.

Jake yanked the side door open, hanging half out with a shit-eating grin. "So nice of you to join us."

I matched it, grabbed the handle, and hauled in past a stack of cables. "Fuck you, too."

He barked a laugh and slid the door shut. Dean dropped us into gear as the van lurched, the city unspooling before us. I thumbed the star at my throat, phone heavy in my pocket, and let the road take us.

Dean glanced at me in the rearview. "Done with your nightly check-in?"

"Just shut up and drive, Dad." I said, but I was still smiling.

Eddie leaned over the third row. "Quick band meeting. Is this where a girl finally breaks us up? Because I had fifty bucks on Jake."

Jake thumped his chest. "Aw… thanks, man."

"We won't say break up," Dean said. "We'll say 'creative differences…'"

"Relax," I said. "No one's breaking anything. She even likes you idiots."

Jake snorted. "I bet that's what John said when Yoko showed up."

"Bite me," I said.

Dean merged into traffic. "So… if Jay elopes, who sings 'Real You?'"

I rolled my eyes. "Set stays the same. Show stays the same," I said. "I'm not going anywhere."

Eddie eyed my phone. "But you… you're definitely not the same."

I looked out at the highway lights dragging past.

"Yeah..."

"Ground rules then," Jake said, ticking fingers. "No quitting, no acoustic-only phase, no girlfriends producing from the couch..."

Dean offered, "And no ghosting the group chat."

"Deal," I said as I slid on my headphones and opened up a playlist to get myself ready for tonight.

The rest of the way, I let my mind wander as I listened to the music. Usually at the end of tour I would ask myself, "Then what?" But this time, I just didn't care about the usual blur of tour life. My mind was already somewhere else. Somewhere warmer. Quieter. Somewhere with her.

The beach house.

The thought came out of nowhere and hit like a wave, sharp, cold, right in the chest. I hadn't been there in years. Not since... that last summer when I was a teenager. The following summer, I had refused to go.

But suddenly I could see it all again, those weathered steps, the screen door that always squeaked and slammed too hard, the stretch of sand where we used to chase the tide like we had all the time in the world. It had been ours. In the way only childhood summers and first kisses could be.

I grabbed my phone again, opened my calendar, and counted days. Yeah. we could make it work after the tour, after her brother's wedding. I'd already be in Dallas, and we could rent a car and drive down. No tour. No pressure. Just us.

I didn't want to text her about it. It felt like something I wanted to give her—no, share with her. Not because I had something to prove, but because I wanted to show her there was still a piece of the world where we fit. Where we always had. Where maybe we always would.

After the show, I lay on my back on the ratty couch in the green room, my phone balanced on my chest as I scrolled aimlessly through old listings. I typed the address slowly, like it might summon a piece of my childhood from thin air. Nothing official came up. Maybe it had been sold. Flattened and turned into one of those sterile beachfront condos with security gates and no soul.

Still, I couldn't shake the thought. I opened my texts and sent a message.

Me: Hey, you up?

My mom replied immediately.

Mom: Yeah, what's up?

I didn't hesitate and just hit call.

She answered right away. "Jameson? Everything okay?"

"Yeah, all good," I said, rubbing my eyes with the heel of my hand. "We're about to leave and drive straight through to L.A."

We made small talk—how the Vegas show went, how Dean almost wiped out tripping over his own amp cable in the middle of the show, how Jake lost his wallet again. She laughed the way she always did when she was trying not to worry.

Then I cleared my throat and went for it. "Hey, random question, but... do you remember that beach house we used to go to when I was a kid?"

She paused. "The one on the Gulf? Of course I do. Why on earth are you thinking about that place now?"

I hesitated, then said, "Just... nostalgic, I guess. Was wondering if it's still around. If someone's still renting it out."

She made a noise somewhere between a scoff and a sigh. "It was falling apart when you were a teenager. I doubt it's even standing now."

I nodded, even though she couldn't see me. "Yeah. Makes sense."

There was a pause. Then her voice changed, curious, a little sharp. "Why the sudden interest? What's really going on?"

I swallowed hard. "Mallie and I have been talking again."

Silence.

I could hear her breathing on the other end—tight, shallow like she was holding something back or bracing for impact. I waited. One second. Two. Three.

"Mallory Wright?" she asked.

"Yeah. Her."

The line went quiet again, but not empty. I could almost hear the memories turning over in her head —sharpening like old glass. The accusation. The threats. The way everything between our families had collapsed like it was rigged to fall.

When she spoke, her voice was thinner than before. "Are you sure that's a good idea? After what happened? Her mother—she said some terrible things. Your dad and I were terrified. We thought—"

"I know. But none of it was true."

"What? What do you mean?"

I rubbed the back of my neck, trying to find the words. "Mallie told me everything. Her mom lied. She said I'd hurt her to keep anyone from asking questions. The truth is... Mallie was pregnant. And the baby was mine."

There was a stunned beat of silence.

"You're a..." she said, before her voice dropped to

a whisper and asked, "...a baby?" as if the words physically winded her.

"Yeah." I nodded even though she couldn't see me. "One of the last nights at the beach house... we were together. We wanted it to be each other. Our first time."

"Oh, Jameson," she breathed. "But... what happened to the baby?"

"I know it was a girl. Mallie gave her up for adoption. Her mom forced her."

My mom sucked in a breath like she'd been slapped. "That's what this was all about?"

"I think so," I said. "Mallie's parents didn't want anyone to find out. Her dad's political campaign was taking off. Her mom told you I—" My voice caught.

"I can't believe this," she whispered. "We lost touch with almost everyone from Texas after the move. And I just... I was so afraid for you. And part of me thought—if something had changed, someone would've told us."

I rubbed at my eyes again. "I know," I said quietly. "But I think they kept it hidden, and it wasn't Mallie."

Silence again. Not the stunned kind this time— just heavy. She didn't speak for a long moment. I could picture her sitting at the kitchen island, hands curled around her tea mug, eyes full of concern.

She asked softly, "How... how did you even find each other again?"

I smiled before I could stop myself, the memory hitting me square in the chest.

"After a show," I said. "I was manning the merch table, and I looked up and... there she was. Just... standing there. Like no time had passed at all."

I paused, remembering the way her eyes locked

with mine across the table, how nervous she was, but as soon as she spoke, the noise around us faded, like the world had disappeared to give us a moment alone.

I chuckled and said, "Dean had to take over the table because I literally couldn't pull myself away from her."

"Oh, Jamie," my mom whispered.

"I convinced her to have dinner with me after the show. I took her to that diner in Deep Ellum," I said, smiling. "You know the one with the milkshakes that taste like heaven? We sat there for hours. One thing led to another... and we've been flying out to see each other while I've been on tour."

"You've been seeing her this whole time?"

"Yeah," I said. "She's... she's it for me, Mom. Always has been."

"Are you sure this is a good idea, sweetheart?"

"I've never been more sure of anything," I said. "I love her, Mom."

Her voice wobbled. "So... what do you want to do?"

I sat up, looking around the room. "I want to take her to the beach house. If it still exists. I want to go back there, just the two of us. I don't know why. It just... feels right."

Mom exhaled slowly. "I'll make a few calls. See if I can find anything out, if anyone still has ties to it."

"Thanks," I said, and meant it.

After we hung up, I sat on the edge of the bed for a long time. I felt cracked open, exposed, but lighter somehow. I didn't know what the beach house would look like now. But I knew exactly who I wanted to be standing beside me when I saw it again.

CHAPTER TWENTY-EIGHT

Mallie

Present Day

Walking through the terminal, it was like surfacing from a dream. The world felt too bright, too fast. My body ached from the flight and the exhaustion of everything. But I was lighter. I wasn't dragging that secret behind me anymore. It was still there, but different now because Jace was carrying it with me.

I followed the signs toward the exit, as I had only brought my carry-on. My feet moved on autopilot, my heart still somewhere back in that motel room, curled beside Jace.

Sonny had class and couldn't come pick me up. Neither could Claire. I'd told them a rideshare was fine—easy, no trouble—but Claire had insisted that Darci was off today and wanted to come. Darci had texted me a heart emoji with "I'm clearing my whole day just to pull up to Arrivals and pick you up dramatically... hair blowing, lip gloss shining, cue the slow-mo."

I laughed and graciously accepted, mostly because I didn't have the energy to argue. And maybe, a little, because I wanted to see her. Darci could pull a laugh out of me and set my worries aside for a while.

I'd been hesitant, but somehow, Darci and Claire had become my friends. It had sneaked up on me. I thought I'd be the outsider when I moved in with Sonny, like the kid sister crashing the adult table. But they never treated me like that. Not once. They included me in everything, even the stuff I tried to opt out of.

Claire would knock on the bedroom door with a mug of tea and a wedding planning question she probably didn't need help with. Darci texted me funny TikToks and sarcasm, dropped off treats, and made a point to invite me anywhere she was going. Surprisingly, I even took her up on it sometimes.

I was grateful for all of it. For them. For the chance to feel like I wasn't just surviving anymore, but maybe starting to live again and not just going through the motions.

Walking outside, the Texas heat hit me right in the face, and I blinked against the sun and scanned the pickup lane until I spotted Darci's navy SUV idling just beyond the No Parking Sign. You couldn't miss it with the slight dent on the bumper and the faded sticker in the back window that said "Built for chaos, dressed for a séance." The windows were already down, sunglasses up on her head with one arm slung over the wheel, and a smirk on her face like a woman who'd once hexed a man for ghosting her—and would do it again.

I didn't even have to wave. She saw me and grinned, then leaned over to shove the door open from the inside.

"You good?" she asked, glancing over. "You look like a Swiftie who's been cry-listening to *All Too Well* alone in a Chili's parking lot."

I barked out a laugh as I climbed in. The cool air inside hit me like a relief I hadn't realized I needed. I dropped my bag at my feet and buckled my seatbelt.

"I'm good. Just tired. Didn't sleep much."

Darci handed me a half-finished iced coffee from the cupholder. "Don't ask how old it is. Just trust me. It'll help."

I raised an eyebrow and stared at it. "I'm not drinking your mystery caffeine," I said, but took a sip anyway. It was perfect.

As she pulled away from the curb, she peeked at me over her sunglasses. "You do look... different."

I shrugged before turning to the window as my cheeks heated.

She glanced at me again. "Like someone who finally let go of something really heavy. Everything ok?"

I glanced at her before turning back to the window, watching the cars blur by. "Yeah... maybe."

"Wanna talk about it?"

I sighed and kept staring out the window, "Not yet..." giving her a small side-eye, bracing.

But she just gave a nod, like that was that. "Well... Claire's picking up dinner from The Green House, and if she doesn't show up with their lemon bars, I'm slashing tires. Lovingly, of course." She grinned.

I chuckled before saying, "Thanks for picking me up."

She handed me a slightly squished Twix bar from the console. "Bitch, please. I live for this shit. Now eat this sugar, and let's stop at Homegoods on the way back and go emotionally process at the candle aisle like the witches we are."

I grinned, resting my head against the headrest. I didn't know what would happen next—with Jace, with Abigail, with any of it. But I was no longer waiting or expecting for everything to fall apart. It felt like this time, things just might work out.

When I got home, Claire was in the kitchen in a tank top and leggings. She was unloading takeout boxes, her hair up in a clip. Bandit was asleep under the table.

Sonny had a late class, so it was just us girls tonight. Darci swooped in to help her, already digging through one of the bags like she had x-ray vision for those lemon bars.

I gave them both a smile and mumbled that I'd be right back, grabbing my bag and slipping down the hall to the guest room. I dropped my bag and sat on the edge of the bed, heart thudding as I pulled out my laptop. As soon as I turned it on, the letter was still there, the one Jace and I had written together, glowing softly on the screen like it had been waiting for me.

I read it one more time, mouthing the words. Then I took a breath, held it, and hit send. The whoosh of the email felt louder than it should've. I closed the laptop gently and stood up, the weight of all these years a little lighter on my shoulders, and headed back to the kitchen to find out if they'd already claimed all the lemon bars.

Maybe, I was ready for what came next.

Around eleven, the three of us were still in the living room, sprawled across the couches with takeout containers stacked on the coffee table, empty cocktail glasses pushed to the side, the end credits of our second true crime doc rolling, when Sonny walked in the door.

I stretched and stood. "Alright, I'm calling it and heading to bed before I fall asleep right here."

Claire reached out as I passed, her fingers trailing lightly down my hand. "Sweet dreams, Mallory," she said, then paused, a small smile tugging at her mouth. "I'm glad you're home."

I didn't know what to do with that. "Me too," I said quietly, before turning down the hallway and padding to the guest room.

I'd been asleep for a few awhile when my phone rang, the sound jolting me awake from a deep sleep. I almost didn't answer. An unknown number in the middle of the night? But something in my gut twisted like a cold, certain dread crawling up my spine. I didn't have a good feeling about this.

"I'm calling from Barstow Community Hospital," the woman said, her tone careful. "There's been... an accident. A van crash. Jameson Smith—he's stable, but we're arranging transfer to Las Vegas. You're listed as his emergency contact."

Emergency contact? The words snagged in my brain, mixing with the rest of what she'd said. And yet, in whatever form he'd filled out, whatever list he'd made, my name was now there. Not his bandmates. Not family. Me.

For a second, the rest of her sentence hung in the air, muffled by my own disbelief. Then the meaning started to sink in. Hospital. Accident. She'd said Jameson. My Jace.

Oh god. I couldn't go through this again. Please, let him be okay. Please. The thought flickered uninvited, fragile as glass.

The fog cleared all at once, leaving nothing but the hollow drop in my stomach.

I was already out of bed before the call ended, the

floor cold under my bare feet. I crossed the hall and pounded on Claire and Sonny's door. "Sonny!" My voice cracked in the middle, sharp and desperate.

The door swung open. Sonny stood there shirtless in gray sweatpants, blinking against the hallway light. Behind him, Claire was upright in bed, covers bunched in her fists, her face pale and tight.

"What's wrong?" Sonny's voice snapped awake instantly.

"They—" My throat seized. "Jace. His band. An accident. Somewhere in the desert. Barstow? And now… they're flying him to Vegas."

Claire pushed the covers back and swung her legs over the side of the bed. "How bad?"

"I don't—she just said stable and something about transferring him. I don't know what that means. I don't know if—" My voice broke, the words slipping out jagged, and I felt the hot tears coming.

Sonny was already moving, grabbing his phone from the nightstand. "We'll figure it out. I'll get you a flight, and we'll call the hospital and get more details. You need to pack."

"I can't just—" My hands were shaking so badly I could barely hold the phone. "What if I'm too late?"

"You won't be," Sonny said, already searching on his phone. Claire was on her feet now, pulling on a cardigan, her hair falling loose around her shoulders.

But the pounding in my ears wouldn't let up. All I could hear was that voice on the phone as I turned and stumbled back to the guest room. My suitcase was still half-unpacked from my last trip. I yanked it open and started throwing in clothes without looking—jeans, T-shirts, a sweater, my phone charger. My hands felt too slow, like they belonged to someone else.

Claire appeared in the doorway, her voice calm but quick. "The hospital says they've airlifted him to Vegas to UMC. He's in transport now."

I froze, sweater in hand. "Is he—"

She ran her hand down my arm and grabbed my hand. "They wouldn't say more. Just that he's alive."

Alive. God, that word didn't mean the same thing it used to. I zipped the suitcase, nearly catching my fingers in the teeth, and cursed.

Sonny's voice carried down the hall, low and sharp as he confirmed something with whoever was on the other end. Seconds later, he was in the doorway, keys in hand.

"Let's go. We can call for updates in the truck."

The house blurred around me as we moved— front door, porch, warm night air rushing against me. The driveway felt too long. Sonny tossed my bag in the truck bed and opened the passenger door for me. The slam of it shutting echoed too loudly in the stillness.

We pulled out onto the street, headlights cutting through the dark. My phone sat in my lap, screen lighting up with every call attempt to the hospital, every unanswered ring gnawing at my nerves.

At a red light, Sonny reached over and squeezed my knee, his voice steady even though I could see the tension in his jaw. "We'll get you there."

I stared out the window, the city lights blurring into streaks. My heart was pounding so hard it felt like my ribs were rattling. Every mile between me and Vegas was another chance for something to go wrong.

Please, let him be okay. Please. The words looped in my head with every highway sign we passed.

"Should I... should I call his parents? I don't know

if they know. They said I was his emergency contact…"

"Do you have their number?" Sonny glanced at me.

"No, but maybe I can find it or something."

I hadn't talked to them in years—not since before everything blew apart—but the hospital had called me, and if she didn't know—that just felt wrong.

I hit call. She answered on the third ring, voice rough with sleep. "Hello?"

"Hi… it's Mallie. Mallory Wright." My name felt strange in my mouth.

A pause. Then warmth, like she was reaching through the line. "Mallory? Oh, honey. It's been a long time. Is everything okay?"

"I'm sorry for calling in the middle of the night, but—" My throat tightened. "I wasn't sure if the hospital called you. About Jace."

Her voice sharpened instantly. "Hospital? No. What happened?"

The words came out fast, shaky. "There was an accident… the tour van. Out in the middle of the desert. They took him to some little community hospital, but they're moving him to a trauma center in Vegas. Um… UMC?"

"Oh god." I heard the rustle of drawers, the faint jangle of keys.

"They said he's stable," I added quickly, clinging to the only thing keeping me from falling apart. "I'm on my way to the airport now."

"I'm in San Bernardino," she said. "I can get to Vegas in a few hours. I'll meet you there."

Sonny's eyes flicked toward me, but he kept his foot pressed to the gas.

"Honey," Tessa said, her voice warm even through the static, "you're not alone in this."

It wasn't my mom's voice, but it felt close enough.

We pulled up under the harsh glare of the drop-off lights. The place was desolate. Sonny was out first, grabbing my duffel from the back.

"Come on," he said, ushering me toward the sliding doors. The blast of cold air hit us as we stepped inside, the space was quiet except for the occasional click of heels and a rolling suitcase. Even the coffee shop wasn't open yet.

"I booked you on the earliest flight to Vegas," he said as we made our way to the counter. "It boards in forty minutes, gate C10. I also got you a room at the Hampton—closest one to the hospital. You can check in whenever you get there."

The woman at the desk slid a boarding pass across to me. I clutched it like it might dissolve if I let go.

Sonny stepped in front of me, his hands warm on my shoulders. "If you need me—if you need anything—just say the word. I'll be there."

The hug was quick but tight, his chin brushing the top of my head before he pulled back to meet my eyes. I nodded, swallowing the lump in my throat.

Then I was moving toward security, the boarding pass warm in my palm, the world narrowing to one destination. *Jace.*

CHAPTER TWENTY-NINE

Jace

Present Day

The first thing I knew was the smell—sharp and chemical. Then the steady beeping. I cracked my eyes open, but the light stabbed straight through my skull. Something tugged at my arm—an IV line—and my ribs ached like I'd been used as a crash test dummy.

"...lucky he's breathing," a voice said somewhere to my left.

My throat felt raw, every word scraping its way out. "Dean... Eddie... Jake. Where—?"

A nurse appeared beside me, adjusting something on the monitor. "Your bandmates? From what I heard, only one other needed transport. Dillinger?"

"Jake?"

"I think so. He had a broken leg—he was airlifted to Los Angeles about half an hour ago. That's all I know."

"What about Eddie? Dean?"

She shrugged and shook her head and went back to the monitor.

The words *airlifted to Los Angeles* hit like a slow punch, and I realized our homecoming show —the one we'd been hyping for months—wasn't happening. Not any time soon. Probably not for weeks, at least. I hated the thought of fans who'd bought tickets, friends and family who'd taken time off, all waiting for a night that was no longer happening any time soon.

But worse? There was a part of me that wasn't thinking about the music at all, and if my bandmates knew, they might hate me for it. I was thinking about something—someone—else entirely. *Mallie.* Did she know yet? If she did, she'd be pacing, chewing her lip raw, probably already halfway to booking a ticket. I could almost see her, phone clutched in one hand, keys in the other. The thought tightened something in my chest. I wanted that picture to be real. I wanted to open my eyes in Vegas and find her there in my hospital room, because the truth was—lying here with that hospital smell in my nose and my ribs screaming every time I breathed—I didn't want to face this without her.

I shifted, trying to get my elbows under me, eyes scanning for my stuff. Pain ripped down my side— sharp enough to steal a breath. The cough came hard and sudden. Warm metal flooded my mouth, and I spit it out onto my hospital gown.

Red. Blood. For a second, everything went white noise.

"Hey—" My thumb mashed the call button. The beeps from the monitor ticked up, fast. I tried a shallow breath, held still. Don't move. Don't make it worse. Another swallow tasted like pennies, and my heart started doing rabbit kicks in my chest.

A shadow moved into my line of sight—a nurse, her hands gentle but sure as she eased me back.

"It's okay. You're okay. It happens if your ribs and lungs are injured. The x-ray showed you've got some bruising there, maybe a break," she murmured, like she'd said it a hundred times before. "We'll keep an eye on it until the transport team gets here."

I swallowed, my mouth dry enough to crack. "My… phone."

She hesitated. "It's probably in the bag that came with you in the ambulance. They'll get it once you're settled in Vegas."

Through the haze, I caught her voice again, talking to someone else. "His emergency contact… Should we update her?"

"She knows. She's meeting him there."

Mallie.

Even in the fog, I knew. A couple of weeks back, after those days we spent together—the ones that made us decide to give this thing between us a real shot—I'd been on the tour bus, killing time in the settings on my phone. The ICE contact field stared at me. My mom's name had been there for years, but my thumb hovered. Before I could overthink it, I erased it and typed Mallory Wright. Saved it without hesitation.

The beeping from the monitor never stopped, but underneath it came the squeak of rubber wheels against tile. Voices low and clipped. A gurney rattled into the room, the air shifting with the faint scent of diesel from outside.

The metal frame clanged as they locked it beside my bed. One of the paramedics gave me a quick once-over. "Alright, man, we're getting you to Vegas. Just hang in there."

When they leaned me to the side to slide the transfer sheet beneath me, pain tore through my ribs like someone had jammed a crowbar between them. I coughed again and groaned, the sound raw, and my fingers curled against the thin mattress.

"Easy there," the flight nurse said, leaning close. "You've got some rib damage—could be a break. We'll get you something for the pain once we're in the air."

The ceiling lights blurred past as they wheeled me out. The desert night hit me like a slap—cold, dry, and smelling of dust and fuel. The helicopter waited, blades churning the dark sky.

They slid me into the cabin, buckled straps across my chest and hips. The nurse's voice followed me in. "We'll be in Vegas in about forty minutes. You're in good hands."

A moment later, I felt something cool coursing through my veins in my arm. I tried to nod, but my eyelids were already pulling shut. The vibration of the helicopter sank into my bones, adding to the ache in my ribs. The last thing I knew was the pitch of the engines rising, the lift pressing me into the stretcher, and the thought, half-formed, but sure, that she'd be there when I opened my eyes.

The world tilted before I even opened my eyes. My stomach rolled at the drop in the engine's pitch, the thump of the rotors slowing. Cold air rushed in when the cabin door slid open, carrying the sting of jet fuel and something metallic—blood, maybe mine.

Hands were on me before I could focus—straps unbuckling, a voice calling out vitals over the din. The gurney jostled, metal grinding against metal, and I bit back a groan when my ribs flared in protest.

"Watch his side—it might be a fractured rib. He has a small volume of hemoptysis," the flight nurse shouted to someone I couldn't see.

The rotors roared again as they lifted me out into the open. Night air slapped my face, colder than I'd expected for Vegas, and my eyes watered against it. Shapes loomed at the edge of the helipad—three, four, maybe more—scrubs and surgical masks lit by the wash of the landing lights.

"He's stable, responsive," someone said at my head.

A different voice took over, crisp and fast: "Let's get him to trauma three."

The wheels hit the concrete, rattling up through my spine. I tried to turn my head, to catch a glimpse of… something, anything familiar, but the ceiling of the rooftop breezeway swallowed the night sky before I could.

Then the lights hit—blinding white that made my eyelids slam shut. The gurney kept moving. The change from night air to the warm, sterile breath of the hospital was almost dizzying.

They swung me into a room so bright it felt like stepping into the sun. Hands moved fast over me— peeling back blankets, sticking cold leads against my chest. The sharp tang of alcohol mixed with the chemical bite of antiseptic. Wires snaked out from me in every direction, feeding into monitors that hummed and beeped in quick bursts.

I caught a wrist mid-motion. "Is she here?" My voice came out rough, strained.

The nurse leaned over, her eyes above the mask sharp but not unkind. "Who?"

"My… my girlfriend? They said she was coming?" The word felt strange in my mouth— girlfriend—but right, too.

She shook her head slightly. "I don't know. We'll find out as soon as we can. First, we have to get you taken care of."

I let go, the fight draining as quickly as it had flared. The monitors kept up their steady chorus, but every sound seemed too loud, too close, and the only thing I wanted was her voice cutting through it.

The nurse's hands moved with practiced speed—a cuff tightening around my arm, something cool sliding into the IV line. My limbs felt heavier with every breath, the edges of the room softening, the glare from the overhead lights smearing into white haze.

I tried to hold onto one thought, one picture of her—hair loose around her shoulders, the twinkle in her eyes when she laughed—but the image kept slipping away.

The last thing I heard before the dark pulled me under was someone calling out numbers I didn't understand. But I had a quiet hope, buried somewhere deep, that when I woke up, she'd be here.

CHAPTER THIRTY

Mallie

Present Day

Five hours after the call, I finally pushed through the ER doors. The fluorescent lights hit me hard, all too bright after the endless stretch of highway as the sun rose just above the horizon. It was just after seven, and the waiting room buzzed with that strange, hushed chaos only hospitals have—phones ringing somewhere in the back, shoes squeaking on tile, a child crying in short, hiccuping bursts.

I went straight to the desk, my legs stiff and my hands aching from gripping the steering wheel. The woman behind the counter looked up, polite but unreadable, and I blurted out his name before she could even say hello.

"I'm here for Jace, uh... Jameson Smith. He was careflighted in. A car accident? They called me. I'm his..." The word snagged in my throat. *What was I?* "Um... his girlfriend?"

It came out like a question, small and unsure, like a word I hadn't earned—like I'd borrowed it from someone else's life.

Her fingers moved over the keyboard, the clack of each key pulling at my nerves. "Let me see…"

The doors behind me slid open with a rush of air. "Mallory?"

I turned, and there was Tessa—her hair now streaked with silver, the lines around her eyes deeper than I remembered, but somehow she still radiated that same warmth she had when we were kids and she'd sneak us extra popsicles on hot afternoons. The sight of her broke something in me.

She reached for me without hesitation, and I went straight into her arms, collapsing against her like I had a hundred times before when I was a kid. My face pressed into her shoulder, and the dam I'd been holding back since the phone call finally gave way.

"It's okay," she murmured, her voice low and steady as her fingers threaded through my hair. "We're here now."

I didn't have words—just the sound of my own shaking breath and the quiet rhythm of hers, like she could anchor me there in the middle of all this fear.

When I finally pulled back, swiping at my eyes, a nurse had appeared at the desk. I tried to stand straighter, pulling in a breath that only half-filled my lungs. Tessa gave me a small, reassuring smile and slid her hand into mine, squeezing once like we were about to face something together.

"This way," the nurse said softly, and we followed her down a large hallway, the scent of antiseptic hanging in the air, each step bringing us closer to Jace's room. My pulse thudded in my ears, but Tessa's hand stayed steady in mine.

The nurse pushed open the door, stepping aside so we could slip in.

The first thing I noticed was how quiet it was—

just the steady beep of the heart monitor and the soft hiss of the oxygen line. Jace lay on the bed, still as stone. His dark hair was a mess, flattened on one side, and there was a small cut near his temple, the skin around it bruised. The blankets were pulled up to his waist, the rest of him swallowed in a tangle of wires and leads.

I'd braced myself for something worse, but the sight of him—pale, lips parted in sleep—still hit me like a punch. He looked younger somehow, but also... fragile. And Jace had never been fragile.

I took a few steps closer, careful like I might wake him or break him just by breathing wrong. My chest tightened at the faint rise and fall beneath the thin hospital gown, at the way his hand rested open on the sheet, palm up, like he'd been waiting for someone to take it.

Beside me, Tessa stopped, her breath catching just barely, enough for me to hear it but not the nurse. She stepped closer to the bed, her hand brushing my arm as if to remind me I wasn't alone here. I glanced at her and caught the flicker in her expression— grief, relief, fear—all layered in one heartbeat.

Her eyes met mine, soft but steady, and she gave the smallest nod, like we were silently agreeing to be strong for him.

Only then did I move to the side of the bed, my fingers trembling as they hovered over his. I didn't take his hand—not yet—but I stayed close enough that I could feel the warmth radiating from his skin, proof that he was still here.

There was one chair next to the bed and another pushed against the wall. I didn't even think about it —I went straight for the one closest to him. Tessa set her purse in the other, her voice calm but clipped.

"I'm going to find a doctor, see if I can get some

answers."

I nodded, unable to tear my eyes away from him. Sliding my hand into his open palm, I rested my head against the cold metal of the bedside railing. His hand was warm—solid, grounding—like it could anchor me here if I just held on tight enough.

"Oh, Jace…" The whisper left me with a soft breath, my eyes falling shut. I'm not sure if I drifted off, but the next thing I knew, the door clicked open, and his mom stepped back in.

She came right to the bed, her gaze sweeping over him before landing on me. "I talked to the nurse," she said, her voice low but steady. "They're concerned there are bruises on his ribs and lungs. Right now, they're waiting to get a CT scan of his chest. Based on that, they think he's most likely going upstairs and will probably be here another day so they can watch him—make sure there's no internal bleeding or collapsed lung."

The words internal bleeding slammed into me. I sucked in a sharp breath, my hand flying to my mouth. "Internal bleeding? Oh god…"

Tessa's hand settled briefly on my shoulder. "They're being careful. It doesn't mean it's happening—it means they want to be sure."

She sank into the chair by the wall, the weariness in her face catching up with her now that she'd stopped moving. For a moment, neither of us spoke, just listened to the quiet hum of the machines.

Finally, she glanced at me, her expression curious but gentle. "So… you and Jamie. What's the story there?"

My pulse gave a nervous little jump. I could've laughed it off or dodged the question, but she was looking at me the same way she used to when I was a kid—like she could tell if I was lying before I even opened my mouth. So I told her. Not everything, but enough. Enough that the truth felt like it was sitting between us, warm and real, while Jace slept inches away.

I sat with my hand curled into Jace's, tracing the faint callus along his palm with my thumb. The monitor kept its steady rhythm, like it was breathing for both of us.

"We ran into each other in Dallas," I said quietly. "At one of his concerts."

Tessa's brows lifted.

"I've been a nomad the past few years—traveling the world, working remotely as an editor..." I admitted, my voice thinning on the edges, "and then things went a little sideways and I ended up back here, staying with Sonny for a while."

Her expression softened.

"He's getting married, by the way," I added, a smile tugging at my mouth.

Tessa blinked, then grinned outright. "Sonny? Really?"

"Her name's Claire," I said. "She's perfect for him. She's a librarian. Their wedding is just a couple of weeks away. Lots of stuff to do... so I've been trying to stay out of their hair. That's why I was at the concert. I had no idea Jace was even in a band. And then..." I let out a small laugh, shaking my head. "There he was. Up on stage."

Tessa's gaze drifted to Jace, her expression somewhere between wistful and proud. She didn't say anything. She'd been there for all of it, long after I'd gone.

Her gaze lingered on him for a long moment, her lips curving into the smallest, knowing smile. "Some things," she murmured, "just have a way of finding their way back."

I didn't answer—couldn't, really. My throat felt too tight.

The door opened, and a woman in dark blue scrubs walked in, her badge reading Radiology. "We're going to take him down for his scan now," she said, checking the lines and unplugging the cords from the wall. "You can wait here—he should be back in about half an hour."

Tessa rose from her chair, stepping back so the tech could unlock the brakes on his bed. I stayed right where I was until the last possible second, my fingers still wrapped around his. When she gently pulled his bed toward the door, I let go, my hand lingering in the air for a beat before I lowered it to my lap.

The door swung shut behind them, and the room felt too big without him in it.

Tessa settled back into her chair, her expression calm but watchful, like she was reading my mind. "Half an hour," she said softly. "We'll be right here when he gets back."

I nodded, forcing a deep breath into my lungs— half an hour. I could do that.

The room felt strangely hollow without him, the steady beep replaced by the softer hum of air conditioning and the occasional shuffle of feet in the hallway.

Tessa crossed her legs, leaning forward just a little. "Can I ask you something?"

I glanced over. "Sure."

Her voice was careful, like she was handling glass, "Your parents... how are they—?"

I shook my head. "They... they died a few years ago."

Her eyes went wide. "What?!?"

I let out a breath, "Yeah. They were flying from

Austin up to Dallas to see Sonny—in my dad's plane. There was a freak storm. He tried to land on a road out in the country, but he hit a car." The words came out flat, almost rehearsed, like I'd told the story enough times for it to stop sounding real.

"Oh, Mallory..." Her face softened, and she reached over, resting her hand briefly on mine. "I'm so sorry."

I swallowed hard, managing a faint smile. "We weren't close after..." My voice dropped off as I looked away. "...after everything. But... it's still strange. Knowing they're just... gone."

She squeezed my fingers, then let go. Her eyes held mine for a beat longer than was comfortable. But it was in a gentle way that made it impossible to pull away.

"Jameson told me... um, about the baby. I wish things had been different for you," she said quietly.

I shrugged, looking toward the door where they'd wheeled Jace out. "Me, too. But... maybe if things had been different, I wouldn't be here right now."

A small smile curved her mouth. "Maybe."

A while later, the door opened again, and the same tech wheeled Jace back into the room. He looked pale under the hospital lights, eyes half-lidded, the corners of his mouth slack from whatever they'd given him.

His gaze drifted first to Tessa, and a faint, sleepy smile touched his lips. Then his eyes found me. For a second, the exhaustion seemed to clear just enough for something warm to flicker there, recognition or maybe relief, but then his lashes dipped again.

Tessa stepped forward as the tech hooked him back up to the monitors, brushing her hand over his hair. "They're done with your scan, sweetheart. Just rest now."

She glanced over at me, that same small, knowing smile returning. "I'm going to run down to the cafeteria and grab some coffee and maybe something to eat. Want me to bring you anything?"

I shook my head. "Not hungry."

She nodded. "I'll bring you something anyway. You'll need your strength." She picked up her purse and gave my arm a light squeeze before slipping out, the door closing softly behind her.

I turned back to Jace, the room suddenly quieter, his breathing the only steady sound. "Hey," I murmured, sliding my chair closer. "Welcome back."

His eyes fluttered open again, hazy but trying to focus. "Mallie?" His voice was rough, not quite a whisper.

"Yeah," I said softly. "I'm here."

A faint crease formed between his brows. "You... came."

"Of course I came." My hand found his where it rested on the blanket, fingers curling gently around his. "The hospital in Barstow... they called me."

For a moment, he just looked at me, like he was trying to piece something together through the fog of pain and medication.

"You okay?" he finally asked, the corner of his mouth tugging faintly upward despite everything.

I huffed a quiet, shaky laugh. "You're lying in a hospital bed and you're asking me if I'm okay?"

His eyelids drooped, but he managed, "Just... needed to know."

I swallowed past the tightness in my throat. "I'm fine. Better now." My thumb brushed along his knuckles, slow and careful. "They said it's your ribs. They're making sure they're not broken, and there's no internal bleeding. You're probably staying another day."

He made a low sound in his chest, something between a groan and a sigh. "Figures."

"You scared me," I admitted, the words slipping out before I could catch them.

His gaze softened, even through the haze. "Sorry."

I shook my head. "Just get better. That's all you have to do right now."

The quiet between us settled into something almost peaceful. His warm hand stayed in mine. He sighed, and his eyes had drifted shut again, but his fingers still curled faintly around mine, warm and comforting, like he wasn't letting go even in sleep.

I was starting to nod off in my chair when the door swung open with a soft creak, and Tessa stepped back in, two steaming paper cups in her hand, and a plastic carryout bag on her wrist. The rich scent of coffee filled the room instantly.

"Got the good stuff," she said, holding one out to me before setting her purse and the plastic bag down on the chair by the wall. "Or at least, the best the cafeteria can manage."

"Thanks." I took the cup, the heat sinking into my palms.

She glanced at Jace, her expression relaxing just a little. "Looks like he's resting. That's good."

I nodded, easing my hand from his so I could take a sip, even though part of me didn't want to break our connection.

Tessa lowered herself into the other chair, coffee in hand. "Alright," she murmured, her voice lighter now, "here's the plan—we'll keep him comfortable and caffeinate ourselves while we munch on some donuts."

We'd barely had a chance to settle back and drink

our coffee when the door opened again. This time, it was a man in a white coat accompanied by someone in black scrubs, pushing a rolling cart with a laptop behind him.

"Morning," he said, glancing between us before stepping closer to the bed. "I'm Dr. Patel. I've just reviewed Jameson's CT results."

My spine went rigid, coffee forgotten on the rolling table beside me. "Okay?"

He gave a slight nod, his tone calm but deliberate. "Good news—there's no sign of internal bleeding, and his lungs look clear. No pneumothorax."

I let out a breath I hadn't realized I'd been holding, my shoulders sagging. "So he's going to be okay?"

"Yes. But he has a contusion on his left lung and some bruising on his ribs on both sides. Both can be quite painful and take time to heal, but neither requires surgery. We'll keep him here another day to manage his pain and monitor him, but barring any complications, he can recover at home."

Tessa reached over, giving my knee a gentle squeeze. "That's good," she said softly.

I nodded, still watching Jace as if I needed to see him breathing to believe it.

Dr. Patel offered a reassuring smile. "Let him rest. The best thing you can do for him right now is be here and make sure he takes it easy when he's discharged."

"We can do that," Tessa said, looking at me, her voice firm in that way that left no room for argument.

The doctor left, and I turned back to Jace, my chest loosening for the first time since that phone call.

CHAPTER THIRTY-ONE

Jace

Present Day

The first thing I saw when I opened my eyes was my mom, asleep in one of those plastic hospital chairs, her head tilted back at an angle that was definitely going to make her regret it later. Mallie was in the other chair, knees pulled up, chin tucked against her shoulder. She had a hospital blanket wrapped around her shoulders. They both looked uncomfortable as hell, but they were here.

I shifted, and Mallie's eyes blinked open. She leaned forward, her voice soft. "You're awake."

Mom stirred at the sounds, straightening in her chair. "Morning, honey. How're you feeling?"

"Like I lost a fight with a grizzly bear," I muttered.

A few minutes later, the door swung open, and a woman in light blue scrubs with a badge that said R.N. B.S.N. stepped in, walking towards the computer at my bedside. "Morning, Mr. Smith. The doctor went over your scans yesterday. Your ribs are bruised, not broken like they originally thought.

You do have a contusion on your lung, which is probably why you were coughing up blood." She turned towards me, "Are you still coughing up blood?"

I shifted, trying to catch Mallie's eye and not freak her the fuck out. But, I hissed when I felt an ache course through me. "Not since the other hospital."

"Good." The nurse went back to typing. "There were no signs of internal bleeding or lung collapse. So... he thinks you're stable enough to go home today, as long as you have someone with you for the next few days. No lifting, no driving, and no being a hero."

Her eyes slid from me to my mom and then to Mallie.

Before Mom could even open her mouth, Mallie piped up, "I've got him. I'll stay with him."

The nurse smiled faintly, typed something in my chart, and told us she'd be back with the discharge papers and a list of my prescription medicines to pick up at the pharmacy.

My phone buzzed on the tray table, Dean's name lighting the screen. I swiped to answer, and his voice came through on speaker.

"You alive, man?" Dean asked.

"Barely," I said. "What's going on? Where are you? Hospital, too?"

"No, dude. Eddie needed stitches on his forehead, but he and I walked it off with just a few cuts and bruises. We're already back home."

I chuckled, "Lucky."

"Jake's at Loma Linda. His parents are with him now. Busted ankle and needed surgery. He's already in a cast, but he's got a concussion, too. They're keeping him another day or so to watch for swelling."

"Damn," I said. "He gonna be okay?"

"I think so," Dean said. "He's pissed about playing. That left ankle's out for a couple months. No hi-hat—everything's definitely going to feel off. What about you? You home yet?"

"No. Got sent to Vegas. But they're releasing me today. They thought I might have broken ribs, but they're just bruised."

"Geez, man. That's rough."

I glanced over at Mallie and tried to smile. "Yeah… We're going to have to push the L.A. show for a few weeks. At least."

"No shit," Dean said, "Just get better. People'll understand."

We kicked around ideas for dates and possible backup plans until the tech came in for vitals. Afterwards, Mallie helped me ease upright, untangle wires, and shuffle to the shower. It was lukewarm with more drizzle than water, and my IV pole was a pain in the ass, but when the water hit my skin, the grit and adrenaline finally slid away. I felt human again.

At lunchtime, the nurse came in with the stack of discharge papers and went over all the rules—no heavy lifting over 15 pounds, take the pain meds for at least a couple of days around the clock, and call if I suddenly get dizzy or short of breath.

Mom was already in logistics mode. "I think you should fly back to L.A. from here," she said. "Four hours in a car will wreck your ribs."

Mallie nodded immediately. "I'll go with him, stay a couple of weeks, and get him settled."

Mom gave her a look. "You sure? I can take some days off work and come down once I clear my schedule."

"I've got it," Mallie said, like it wasn't even a

question. "He won't lift a finger."

I grumbled, "You two do realize I'm sitting right here?" but neither of them looked at me.

After I signed the discharge papers, Mallie helped me dress while Mom handled our plane tickets. She even made multiple trips to the car with my things. Before we drove away, Mom pulled Mallie into a hug and told her to call if we needed anything.

Mom drove me to the airport since Mallie had a rental and needed to turn it in. When it was time to say goodbye, she gave me a careful hug at the curb near our gate, mindful of my ribs.

"Call me when you're settled," she said before climbing back in her car for the long drive home.

I headed inside and shuffled toward security to wait for Mallie. She jogged up a little while later, slid her hand into mine, and we walked through together. By the time we found our seats, she'd gotten a pillow from a flight attendant and tucked it against my ribs and squeezed my knee. The flight to L.A. was short—barely enough time for a sip of water—but every shudder of turbulence pressed against my ribs like a finger digging into my side.

When we landed, I moved slowly, keeping one hand braced to my side as we walked off the plane. The whole terminal blurred. I edged the wall, and Mallie stayed close, carrying both our bags as she matched her steps to mine without saying a word.

Outside, the air smelled faintly of warm asphalt. She scanned the curb until she spotted the rideshare, then touched my elbow like I was something breakable.

"This one's ours," she murmured.

The ride was quiet. Mallie's hand rested lightly on my arm whenever the driver hit a bump. By the time we got to my apartment in Silver Lake, I was ready to collapse. Mallie unlocked the door, set our bags inside, and eased me onto the couch with a blanket and some pain meds.

Later that night, after a dinner she cobbled together from whatever was in my freezer, my phone buzzed. Mom's name lit the screen.

"You settled?" she asked, her voice a mix of worry and relief.

"Yeah, we're good," I told her, leaning back against the cushions.

From the kitchen, Mallie called, "He's set up and behaving."

Mom laughed softly through the receiver. "Good. I'll check in tomorrow. Try not to give her a hard time, okay?"

I smirked. "No promises."

After two weeks, I was finally feeling like myself again. One morning, Mallie walked into the living room with her phone in hand, a crease between her brows. She didn't look at me right away.

"I have to go back. My flight's tomorrow," she said softly, eyes on the blanket she was folding like it mattered.

The words landed heavier than they should have. I sat forward on the couch, my ribs no longer protesting as severely as they had been, and gave a single nod as I set the remote on the coffee table.

"What time?"

"Early." Her fingers played on the edge of the knit. "I have to get back. The bridal shower with Darci..."

I nodded because I felt like saying 'stay' would make me seem selfish. Too needy. Still... I saw it in her eyes. She didn't want to go either.

"Okay." I slid my hand over hers, light. "I hate

this part," I said, softer than I meant to.

"Me, too." She looked up then, brave about it and not at all. "It's just a few days."

I squeezed her hand, slowly. "Text me from security. From the gate. From… everything." I tried for a smile. "And tonight, can we just… hold each other?"

She edged closer on the couch until her knee touched mine. "As long as you want."

"That's the problem," I said, and leaned in to kiss her temple—a place that always made me feel like we were already home.

She glanced up at me. "You're still coming, right? To the wedding?"

I met her eyes. "Wouldn't miss it for the world."

Her phone kept lighting up, but she ignored it. Her knee angled toward me. She lowered herself onto the couch beside me, close enough that her hip pressed into mine. Her fingers brushed my hair back from my forehead, lingering just a second too long.

"Promise you won't do anything stupid while I'm gone," she murmured.

I reached for her wrist. A light touch, a question. She answered by flipping her palm and threading our fingers. My ribs pulled when I shifted, and she gave me the look. But I shook my head. I was fine. I wasn't, but I was fine.

"Hey," she said.

I tugged, and she came closer. We met in the middle like we'd been practicing this all along. Unhurried, like we were just inevitable. Like we had all the time in the world,

"You sure?" she whispered, thumb skimming the tender spot under my ribs.

"Come here," I murmured against her mouth,

reaching for her, sliding a hand around her waist and pulling her into my lap. My ribs twinged again in protest, but I didn't let go. She gasped at the sudden movement, then melted into me, her knees bracketing my hips.

The kiss started slow, like she was afraid she might hurt me, but it deepened when her fingers threaded into my hair. It said all the things we couldn't—stay, I don't wanna go, please, I love you.

She tasted like coffee and something sweeter that was all her. I kept one arm locked around her, ignoring the ache in my side, my other hand splayed across her back, trying to memorize the feel of her body against mine.

We kissed until the need to breathe was the only thing that could pull us apart. She stayed pressed against me, chest heaving, forehead resting against mine, and our breaths tangling. My thumb ran up and down her spine, stalling for another second, another heartbeat, another anything that would keep tomorrow from coming.

My hand found the edge of her blouse, sliding upward. Every brush of my fingers was a dare.

She leaned back just enough to search my face. "Are you sure?"

"Yes..." I swallowed, pain humming under my skin, but nowhere near enough to stop me. "I'm sure. I'd take ten times worse for this."

That made her smile—that wicked, knowing smirk that had lived in my head since we were kids.

She stood, stepping back from me with a slowness that could've been cruelty if I didn't want it so badly. I reached for her, but she shook her head.

First, her shirt came off in one smooth pull. Then her bra, and my mouth went dry.

She turned away, glancing over her shoulder like

she was checking to see if I'd break first. Then she bent just enough to catch my attention, and the ache in my ribs was nothing compared to the one that surged when she hooked her thumbs in her waistband and took her sweet time sliding her jeans and panties down inch by inch, her hips swaying, her bare skin glowing in the early sunlight.

"Mallie..." It came out like a warning, maybe a plea. Hell, I didn't even know which.

She laughed softly. That was it. I pushed through the sting in my side, lunging forward to grab her before she could finish her little striptease. My hands closed around her hips, and I hauled her back against me like I'd been starving for years. Because I had been, without her, all this time.

She was still laughing when I pulled her back to me, settling her across my thighs. Heat. Skin. The kind of closeness that short-circuited a man. She rocked once. Twice. My head tipped back against the couch. A sound tore out of me.

She kicked her pants completely off and turned around, her fingers finding the drawstring at my waist. A tug. Another. The knot slipped. I swallowed the grunt that wanted out, forcing my breath smooth. Commando had never felt smarter. These sweats had been the only thing I could stand to put on. No layers. No shirt. Nothing that hurt too much to put on.

"Careful," I breathed, more out of habit than fear. There was a low throb in my ribs. I tried to ignore it when she moved—slow, testing, learning me again.

Her mouth curved as she slid her hand under the waistband. I flattened a palm to the couch, tipped my hips to help, and kept my core still like the PT had drilled into me. She felt the give and worked the fabric down, slow and sure, knuckles grazing my stomach. I lifted just enough for her to clear my hips, and the relief that there wasn't another layer to fight made my head thump back against the cushion. Just her, warm, wet, and wicked, settling back over me like we'd never learned how to be anything but this.

She stilled and asked, "Are you okay?"

"Not pain," I managed, voice rough. "You just—" Words failed. I tightened my hands at her waist. "I just can't stop thinking about being inside you."

Something in her went molten at that, and she slowly slid down on me. We both groaned as she set the rhythm, measured, devastating. Every shift of her hips wound a wire tight in me. Two weeks of being careful, of sleeping on my back, of pretending I wasn't counting the minutes until I could breathe without wincing—gone, burned off by the way she moved over me.

"Mallie," I breathed out.

She answered with a roll of her hips that knocked thought clean out of my head. I gripped a little harder, guiding her, letting her take what she wanted and giving it right back to her. My breath hitched.

She searched my face as she slowed, teasing, a wicked little smile curving her mouth.

"Too much?" she asked.

"Not enough," I said, honest and starving. "Fuck, you feel so good." I swallowed, heat prickling behind my eyes for no good reason except that it had been too long. "Don't stop."

She didn't. The room narrowed to the sound of us, the soft catch of her breath, the rough edges of mine. I tried to hold on—God, I tried—but she knew exactly how to tip me past sense, and I was already there, my lips against her shoulder as the coil finally snapped. Everything blurred—her rhythm, my name on her lips, the world narrowed to pulse and breath until the only thing left was the way we fit and the way it undid us both.

Later, when the world slid back into focus, she was wrapped around me on the couch, my palm warm over her heartbeat. My side complained now that the rush had faded, a low, familiar ache. It was worth it, every second.

"You sure you're okay?" she murmured, turning enough to study me.

I kissed her temple, pulling her closer, but careful of my side. I wasn't ready to let her go yet, maybe I never would be.

"I'm okay," I said, and meant it. "Better than okay."

Her smile was soft and a little sad, as she knew she would be leaving in the morning.

"We'll be together again in just a few days."

"I know," she murmured, her fingers rubbing over the star pendant on my chest.

"Yeah. I'll even wear a tie if it means I get to dance with you."

That earned me a laugh, small but real—a sound I'd been chasing our whole lives. She raised her head to look at me, eyes shining.

"You better be healed enough to dance."

"I'll be ready." I slid my fingers through hers, locking them tight. "We promised, remember? Nothing comes between us. Always."

For a beat, she just breathed, her eyes searching mine. And I saw it—the shadow of everything that could break us. Distance. Family. Doubt. But then she pressed her palm over my heart, steady and warm.

"Always," she said, like she was sealing it all over

again.

Relief broke through me as I bent to kiss her, slow and sure, like I could hold her to that vow. Morning would take her. Distance would test us. Life would try to wedge itself in the cracks we'd only just started to mend. But with her body against mine, her word fresh, I believed we were stronger than all of it.

CHAPTER THIRTY-TWO

Mallie

Present Day

I hadn't expected the email. I'd told myself it would take longer or that she might not write back at all. But just a couple of days later, I was checking my email in the late morning, and there it was. The notification popped up on my phone, and my hands went cold.

**Subject: RE: Letter from Mallory and Jameson
From: Janis Mitchell**

Hello,

Please see attached response from Abigail Tompkins, sent with permission.

I sat down on the edge of my bed, heart pounding as I opened the attachment. I didn't wait to read it. The font was simple—the words, anything but.

Hi,

I wasn't sure I was going to write back, and I wasn't sure how I felt about any of this. It kind of feels overwhelming. But then I read your letter. Twice. I may have cried the second time.

I know I'm only twelve, but I've spent a lot of my life wondering where I came from. Who I looked like. Why I loved music more than anyone else in my family. Why I make up stories in my head all the time. I used to think maybe I was just weird. But your letter made me feel less weird.

I don't know what happens next. I don't think I'm ready for everything. But I am ready for something. I'd like to ask you questions if that's okay. I'd like to hear more. Maybe we could do a video chat.

Thanks for writing me back,

—Abigail

I pressed the phone to my chest, blinking back tears as the words sank in. She wrote back. She wanted to know us. My fingers shook as I typed out a message to Jace.

Me: She wrote back. She wants to talk to us.

The dots started dancing instantly.

Jace: Where are you? At home? I'm coming.

I tried to talk him out of it, to give his ribs a few more days to heal. But after dinner, I was sitting on the edge of my bed when I heard the knock at the front door. Bandit started barking. But I didn't move for a second, and then I flew down the hall.

Sonny and Claire were both in the kitchen, looking up as I passed, but I didn't stop to explain. I yanked the door open and there he was—duffel bag over his shoulder, eyes wide and red-rimmed.

"Hey," I said quietly. "You should have told me about your flight. I would have picked you up."

Jace didn't say a word. He just stepped inside and pulled me into his arms, holding me so tightly I forgot how to breathe.

"It's okay," he said into my hair. "I knew you were busy doing wedding stuff. And I just wanted... I needed to be with you when we answered her."

I nodded against his chest, tears already gathering again.

Claire popped out of the kitchen with a dish towel over her shoulder. "Jace! You want anything? I've got sweet tea, water, leftover meatloaf, and half a dozen strawberry cupcakes that need someone to eat them."

He shook his head with a grin. "Thanks, I'm okay. Just... needed to see Mallie."

"Well... if you change your mind," she said, warmly with a grin, "help yourself to whatever you want. Our house is yours."

Just before I was about to drag Jace to my room, Sonny walked into the living room from the kitchen, already arching an eyebrow with a smirk. "Jameson." He broke out in a grin as he clapped him into a quick hug and said, "You look like you lost a fight with a time zone."

"Felt like it," Jace chuckled as he said.

Sonny glanced at me, then back to Jace. "It's getting better?"

Jace grinned and said, "Yeah... the pain is slowly going away."

"Good." Then, Sonny smirked, "Now, house rules —you're welcome, shoes off, and do whatever Claire says." Then he deadpanned, "But… if you make my sister cry, I will make you play 'Wonderwall' at every family gathering for the rest of your natural life."

Claire rolled her eyes and flicked the towel at him. "Be nice."

"I am being nice," Sonny said, a grin breaking. He pointed two fingers from his eyes to Jace's, mock-serious. "I'm kidding. Mostly."

I caught Jace by the sleeve and started steering him toward the bedroom.

"Thank you, Head of Security," I called over my shoulder. "And 'Wonderwall' is never happening."

We sat on the floor in the guest room that had become my safe haven for weeks. I was cross-legged, and Jace was leaning back against the bed beside me, staring at the phone between us where Abigail's words waited.

I reached for his hand. "She wants a video chat to ask us questions."

"Then we'll do it and give her answers," he said, lacing our fingers together.

We stayed like that for a long time—talking through what we would say. Jace had never seen her or held her as a baby, but the way he spoke about her made my heart ache in the best way.

"I don't want to be a stranger to her," he said quietly.

"You won't be," I answered.

When we finally opened the laptop and drafted our reply, we kept it simple.

Abigail,

We're honored you wrote back. We're happy to answer your questions—whenever and however you want. You let us know when you want to do the video chat.

With love,
   Mallory & Jameson

This time, we didn't hesitate. I immediately hit send. And then we crawled into my bed in the quiet together, holding on to each other, holding on to hope. From the moment I walked out of that hospital without my baby, everything felt... lost. Even now, my arms still ache to remember holding her. But tonight? Tonight felt like a way forward.

When I woke up, the sun was already pushing through the curtains, and I felt Jace stir beneath me. His chest lifted with a deep inhale, but he pressed his free hand to his side, letting it back out slowly. Then, his other arm tightened around my back like he wasn't quite ready to let the morning in.

I stayed where I was, curled against him, my cheek over his heart, just breathing in his warmth and that unmistakable male scent of him. His fingers drifted lightly across my back like he wasn't even fully awake yet. But then I felt the press of his lips in my hair.

I let out a long breath and stretched, my legs pushing deeper into the sheets. I tipped my head back to look up at him.

"Morning," I said, grinning at the scruff along his jaw and the sleepy crinkle in his eyes.

"So I wanna ask you something," His voice came out rough and warm. "Are you... busy for the next few days?"

I raised an eyebrow, resting my chin on his chest. "Next weekend is the wedding, but right now..." I trailed off, waiting.

He looked suddenly boyish, a little shy as he

brushed some of my hair away from my face. "What would you think about going down to the Gulf? Seeing if we can find the old beach house?"

My heart stuttered, like it had been waiting to be asked that exact question. "The beach house?"

He nodded. "Just you and me. Couple days. We'll be back in time."

I propped myself up on my elbow, searching his face. "Are you serious?"

He nodded again, slower this time. "I just thought… maybe we could… go back to where it all started."

"I think that sounds like the best idea you've ever had."

I smiled, soft and slow, and leaned up to kiss him. He grinned into the kiss, one hand sliding up to cup my cheek, his thumb brushing under my eye like he couldn't believe we were real.

"You sure?" he murmured.

I nodded, letting my forehead rest against his. "Yeah. Let's do it."

He exhaled like he'd been holding his breath all morning. "Good. Cause I already rented a car."

I laughed, swatting his bare chest. "You did not."

"I did," he said, grinning like a kid who just got away with something. "Rented it last night. After you fell asleep. You were drooling, by the way."

I gasped, swatting him again. "Liar."

He shrugged, totally unapologetic. "I took a picture."

"Jace!"

He rolled me onto my back, bracing himself on his elbows, wincing a little as he hovered above me—still a smirk playing at his lips. "You can punish me later. For now, I vote plotting our escape to the beach."

I grinned up at him, heart light in a way it hadn't felt in a long, long time. "Only if we stop in West on the way down."

His eyes lit up. "That's non-negotiable."

We lay there for another minute, not rushing the day, just grinning at each other like two idiots. It felt like I could stop asking if it was right and just let it be ours. With him. Again.

Anyone who drove I-35 down south from Dallas knew The Czech Mate in West was a roadside paradox—half beloved bakery, half vaguely gross gas station with flickering fluorescent lights and a bathroom that smelled like mildew and mop water. The linoleum floors were always a little too sticky, and the place was a little dingy. But none of that mattered the second you caught the scent of warm pastry dough and smoked sausage.

The line for kolaches snaked past racks of stale beef jerky and dust-covered snow globes, but we all knew the same truth—this place might look like a gas station off a lost highway, but it had the best damn kolaches in the state. And it was part of the ritual—stretch your legs, grab a box of kolaches, and try not to get powdered sugar on the steering wheel as you got back on the road.

Jace stood beside me, arms crossed, sunglasses pushed up in his hair as he read the menu. His phone buzzed in his pocket, and he pulled it out, glancing at the screen.

"It's my mom," he said, brows lifting. "Gimme a sec."

I gave him a nod and stepped forward with the line, already eyeing the apricot and cream cheese ones in the case. Behind me, his voice dropped as he answered.

"Hey, Mom… Yeah, we're on the road…. No, I'm not driving. We just stopped at The Czech Mate. Mallie's ordering kolaches. Priorities, you know?"

A pause. I glanced over at him, and something in his posture shifted—his grin dropped a little and he stood up straighter, eyes flicking away toward the parking lot.

"Wait, seriously? You found them?" His voice pitched up, excited now. "They're willing to rent it out? That's amazing."

I tried not to listen, but it was hard not to catch the warmth in his tone as he jotted something down on his phone. "Yeah, I'll call right now. Thanks, Mom. Love you."

He hung up just as it was my turn at the register. I ordered way too many for just the two of us—four sausages, two apricots, two poppyseeds (for nostalgia), two peaches and cream, and a cinnamon roll the size of my face. By the time I turned around with the white box in hand, Jace was nowhere in sight.

Standing in line to pay, I spotted him just outside the entrance, pacing near a picnic table, phone to his ear again. His free hand was in his pocket, but he looked so much like the boy I used to know— nervous energy and that half-cocked grin. My heart squeezed.

He came back a few minutes later, brushing windblown curls from his eyes.

I raised an eyebrow. "Everything okay?"

He smiled, the kind that made his whole face light up. "We got it."

"The kolaches?" I teased, holding up the box.

He shook his head, eyes gleaming. "The beach house. It's ours for the whole week."

I blinked. "Wait. Seriously?"

"Just finished some renovations, apparently. The owners were super chill. My mom tracked them down and gave me the number. I called, and…" He shrugged like it was no big deal, but his grin said otherwise. "We're booked."

I laughed, bumping his shoulder as we walked back to the car. "You're dangerous with a to-do list, huh?"

"When it comes to you?" he said, opening the passenger door for me, "I don't want to waste any time."

I blushed, turning toward the window as I tried to hide my smile—and failed miserably.

We pulled onto the highway, the sun warming the dashboard, the scents of sweet rolls and sausage filling the car. Everything felt like it was falling into place. Me and him, the road, and the sea waiting at the end of it.

CHAPTER THIRTY-THREE

Jace

Present Day

The sun was setting when we pulled into the sandy driveway. The smell I remembered so well from childhood hit me as soon as we got out of the car—the salty breeze, sand, and… summer.

The house hadn't changed much. A few coats of paint, a new swing on the porch, but I swear it was the same old screen door with the same sighing creak when we opened it.

I dropped our bags just inside the door, the sound of them hitting the old wood floor echoing louder than expected in the quiet. Inside, it smelled like fresh paint and sunshine baked into cedar—almost exactly how I remembered it. My chest tightened.

Mallie stood next to me, eyes wide, sweeping across the living room. A patchy quilt was tossed over the back of the saggy couch like someone had just gotten up. A seashell windchime danced in the breeze on the back patio.

Every memory I had with Mallie seemed to live here. The first time I held her hand. The first time I kissed her. The sound of her laughter echoing off the patio. I could almost see us as kids, barefoot and sunburned, still thinking the world was ours.

"It's strange how it feels the same," she said softly.

I turned to her, lacing our fingers together, grounding myself with the feel of her skin. I pulled her into me until her cheek brushed my shoulder, and I bent close, breathing her in.

"I know," I murmured into her hair. "It's like time's stood still here."

We walked through every room together, laughing at the creaky floorboards that still complained in the same places. Racing each other up the stairs to the third floor, where we used to sneak out of our rooms at night to walk the beach, trading whispered promises back when forever felt like something we could touch.

Neither of us had to say it. We both knew where we wanted to go as we headed across the way toward the beach. The tide was out, and the wet sand reflected the sky like a mirror—pink and gold and bruised blue. We didn't talk much as we made our way down towards the dunes.

Mallie walked ahead of me, her sundress fluttering around her knees, her braid swaying gently with each step. Her bare feet left soft impressions I couldn't help but follow.

Every few steps, her fingers brushed mine. Not quite holding. Not quite pulling away either. When I finally reached for her hand, she let me take it.

We ducked under the old sea grass path, climbing through a narrow cut in the dunes until we reached the edge of the bluff. From there, we scrambled down, and her gasp echoed off the rocks when I slipped and nearly fell, holding my side. Then we rounded the last dune, and I stopped.

"I'll be damned," I whispered.

Hollowbone was still there.

The cave was still hidden by sea grass and time, tucked beneath a sandstone ridge, but I'd have known it anywhere. The curve of the entrance, the cluster of smoothed driftwood for seating we'd dragged in as kids. We pushed aside a curtain of vines, and there it was—carved initials still faded but legible on the wall. *MW + JS.*

Mallie knelt and ran her fingers over them, like she couldn't believe they were real.

And then she gasped. "Is that…?"

I followed her gaze to the back corner, where something soft and crumpled was wedged between stones. Our old blanket. Faded, weather-stained, but unmistakably ours.

She looked back at me with wide, gleaming eyes. "How is this even possible?"

I didn't have an answer. But I went for it, shook it out, and laid it out on the floor, just like we used to do when we were kids. Then, I reached for her again, pulling her against me. There was something electric in the air—old memories humming like static, charged and waiting. The cave sheltered us from the wind, and the sound of waves muffled like a heartbeat in the distance.

I kissed her as our bodies sank onto the blanket like muscle memory. There was no rush. She climbed into my lap, sundress bunching around her thighs, skin warm where it met mine. My hand found the soft hair just above the nape of her neck. I pulled the hair tie off her braid, sliding it on my wrist, and threaded my fingers through the strands as I eased her hair over her shoulder.

I was strung out on her scent as I leaned in,

tracing the curve of her neck with my mouth. My hands ran down her back, skimming up under the soft cotton, taking two handfuls of her ass and squeezing.

She whispered, "Here? Really?"

Against her throat, I said, "Say no, and I'll stop. But don't think for one second I don't want to worship you right here, like we were always meant to."

Her breath hitched, and she leaned back, searching my eyes, as a seductive smirk spread across her face. She grabbed the hem of her sundress and pulled it off, tossing it aside. She cupped my face and kissed me like she'd been craving this her whole life.

I lay her back gently on the blanket, her dark hair now framing her. I took my time, savoring her as my mouth found one nipple, then the other, licking slow, sucking deep, letting her arch beneath me as I worshiped every soft, perfect inch. She trembled beneath me, her breath faltering as she dug her fingers into my shoulders when I switched sides, tongue circling, lips tugging until she whimpered. Only then did I start to kiss lower, teasing my way down her ribs, over her stomach, licking her navel as I chased every shiver all the way to her belly.

I sat up, yanking my t-shirt over my head and tossing it aside. Her eyes darkened, tracing every line of my body as she reached for me, fingertips brushing across my chest, urging me closer. I hooked my fingers under her panties and dragged them slowly down her thighs, letting them join my discarded shirt.

Sliding my hands beneath her legs, I settled them gently over my shoulders and sank lower, pressing my mouth against her heat. The first slow lick up to her clit drew a shuddering gasp from her lips.

She tasted heavenly—warm and sweet, addictively all her—and I groaned softly as I sucked, licked, and nibbled, slow and deep. Her hips rocked, chasing every stroke of my tongue. Her fingers threaded into my hair, gripping tight, holding me exactly where she needed me.

"Fuck, Jace," she moaned, arching into my mouth as I circled that perfect, swollen bundle of nerves, losing myself in the way she trembled beneath me.

She whimpered, her breath quickening as she ran her fingers through my hair, grinding against me as I lapped at her. I slipped a finger into her, slowly pumping in and out, continuing to nibble and suck. Her hips flexed against me as I pumped faster, deeper, harder.

"Oh god, oh fuck, oh god," she whimpered, and then screamed my name as she clenched against me.

I traced slow circles with my tongue while she came down, catching her breath. Her hands reached for me, tugging me up, her fingers gripping my shoulders as she pulled me toward her. I sat back on my knees with a smirk, savoring the sight of her flushed cheeks and heavy-lidded eyes, then pushed my shorts and boxers down, kicking them aside.

I fumbled briefly for my pocket, grabbing the condom I'd slipped in earlier, tearing the wrapper. Her eyes followed every movement as I rolled it on, anticipation shimmering between us.

Caging her beneath me, I leaned in, brushing my lips against her ear. "I want to fuck you until you forget everything but my name," I whispered roughly, feeling her shiver beneath me.

Her hands slid down my chest, fingertips tracing a heated path across my stomach, then wrapping firmly around me. A sharp breath hissed between my teeth, the heat of her palm nearly undoing me before we'd even started.

She guided me to her entrance, and I pressed forward, slow and steady, burying myself inch by aching inch. A moan slipped from her lips as she arched beneath me, her body tightening around mine.

"Mallie," I groaned, voice ragged against her neck. "So fucking good."

I held perfectly still, just feeling her heat wrapped around me. She was fire, and I didn't realize how badly I needed to be burned until she touched me like that. Because I was hers, body and soul. Always had been.

She kissed me, hard and deep, flexing her hips and whispering against my lips, "More..."

She wrapped her legs around my hips, urging me deeper, every thrust slow and deep, matching the rhythm of waves crashing somewhere beyond us. Her fingers trailed down my back, digging in as she held me tight, pulling me impossibly closer. I braced myself on my elbows, forehead pressed to hers, our breaths mingling as her body rose to meet mine. Each thrust drew a quiet, desperate moan from her lips, spurring me on.

She whispered my name, a soft plea that sent that fire racing along my skin. My hips moved faster, each stroke more urgent, my heart slamming against my ribs as tension built, coiling tighter and tighter until she cried out softly beneath me.

Her body shuddered, her nails biting into my shoulders, the sweet rush of her release dragging me closer as she clenched so tightly around me. The world narrowed down to nothing but her—her breath, her warmth, the way she whispered my name again, gasping it like a prayer.

"Jace," she breathed, shivering, trembling beneath me, her pleasure pulling mine from somewhere deep in my chest.

Her name broke from my throat in a rough whisper as my hips snapped once, twice, before I came undone inside her, losing myself in waves of pleasure that left me breathless, helpless, and completely at her mercy.

For a moment, we just stayed like that, my body braced above hers, both of us breathing heavily in the hush of the cave. Then, slowly, I eased myself from her, rolling carefully onto my side, pulling her into my chest. My heartbeat thundered against her back as I held her close, my lips brushing softly against her shoulder.

We didn't speak. We just lay there, letting the world outside Hollowbone fade away, wrapped up only in each other.

"You ever think we'd end up here again?" she asked quietly.

I admitted, "I think I hoped that one day...," but I didn't finish the thought.

I felt her relax against me. For a while, neither of us moved. My fingers traced her hip, and when she finally pulled away and turned, her gaze caught on my arm.

"Your tattoo..." Mallie's voice was hesitant, like she wasn't sure if she had permission to ask. "That bone—what is it?"

I glanced down at the ink, the narrow bird bone nestled in the poppies, etched with lines of dots and dashes running inside it. "It's a bird bone," I said, flexing my bicep, "a hollow bone. A reminder of this place with you."

The air shifted, as if Hollowbone itself exhaled around us, carrying the salt and the memory of summers past.

Her gaze lifted to the ink, then met my gaze—wide, shining. She bit her lower lip, blinking hard before her brows drew together, curious. "What about the marks?"

I huffed a laugh. "It's just a dumb code I got when I was younger. You'd laugh if you knew."

Before she could press, I caught her mouth with mine, stealing the question right off her lips. When I pulled back—just an inch, just enough to breathe— she stared at me like the tide had shifted.

"I... I don't know how to do this," she said after a beat, her words trembling like they belonged to the wind more than her.

"Be in love with me?" I asked.

She laughed—really laughed—and Hollowbone caught the sound, echoing it back to us the way it always had when we were kids, like it wanted to keep her joy safe inside its ribs.

"No," she said. "That part I remember."

I leaned back, looking down at her, brushing a piece of hair from her cheek. "Then let's start with that."

She stretched up, and her lips were soft when they met mine. Like coming home to something I never really left.

When she curled against me and the surf crashed in a slow rhythm outside, she traced my jaw with a fingertip and whispered, "I love you. I never stopped loving you."

I pressed a kiss to her temple, breathing her in. My voice came out low, barely more than a breath. "I love you, too. I don't think I ever knew how to stop."

She curled closer, and I wrapped my arms around her tighter, like holding her could anchor the both of us.

My voice was rough when I said, "I gave you my heart when I was five, Mallie. I never asked for it back."

And I meant every word. I didn't want to go back. I just wanted us to claim the place that had always belonged to us. Making something new in the bones of what we left behind.

CHAPTER THIRTY-FOUR

Mallie

Present Day

I'd been staring at the screen for ten minutes before I could bring myself to hit "Join." My palms were sweating. I kept smoothing the patchy quilt across my lap, then folding it back, then smoothing it again. Jace was seated next to me on the couch, his legs bouncing with nervous energy that mirrored mine. He'd said maybe five words all morning. I hadn't said much more.

We'd been at the beach house for a few days when Abigail replied to our letter yesterday, asking if we could set up a video call. Just a quick conversation, her mom had written, a few minutes. Her parents were supportive, wanting her to take the lead, and she was curious and nervous. Her mom had made it clear that Abigail didn't know what she wanted this to be, but she wanted to talk to us.

I read her message at least a dozen times. I cried the first few times, and Jace just held me. Now, the Zoom link sat there in my inbox like a doorway I wasn't sure I dared to walk through.

"You don't have to be perfect," Jace said softly beside me.

"I know."

"Just be yourself. She just wants to get to know us."

"I know that, too."

He reached over, took my hand. "We'll do it together. Just like everything else."

I gave a shaky nod, my stomach twisting. And then... I took a breath and clicked the link. The screen shifted, buffering for a second, and then there she was.

Abigail.

My breath caught in my throat. She was beautiful and reminded me of myself when I was her age. Everything about her was me and Jace. Long dark ringlets pulled back in a loose pony, hazel eyes like mine behind wire-rimmed glasses, and a hesitant smile that looked so much like Jace's, I had to blink back tears.

"Hi," she said, her voice higher than I imagined, still soft with girlhood but edged with the confidence of someone figuring out who she was.

"Hi," I managed, my voice too thick.

Jace cleared his throat. "Hey, Abigail..."

"Hi." She looked at him shyly and shrugged. "Is it okay that I call you Mallory and... Jameson?"

"Of course," I said, thrilled she was even speaking to us at all. I never in my wildest dreams thought this day would come.

There was an awkward pause, long enough that I worried we were already messing it up.

"I like your room," Jace offered.

She smiled, glancing at the wall behind her, where posters of bands I didn't recognize hung beside a bookshelf full of books, and a window full of tiny succulents. "Thanks. I cleaned it before this. Kind of like a first date."

We all laughed—relief, bright and sudden. The tension loosened, just a little.

She asked the easy things—where we lived, what we did, what we loved. I said I write and paint. Jace talked about the band, grinning as he offered to save seats if she and her parents wanted to catch a show on the next tour. Then his voice went softer. He said he loves writing songs more than performing them.

"Used to make up songs about a girl on a beach," he said, tossing me that crooked smile.

After a while, she asked, "What happens now?"

I glanced at Jace. He nodded at me, like it should come from me first.

"Whatever you want to happen," I said gently. "We're here. However much or little you need us to be."

She looked down, like she was holding something back. Then she said, "I think I'd like to meet. In person. Someday."

Tears sprang to my eyes. "I would love that, too," I whispered.

She smiled again. Brighter. A little braver.

She looked off-screen. "I have to go soon," she said before her voice dropped, almost shy. "But… thank you."

I blinked, my throat tightening all over again. Thank us? I wanted to tell her she had no reason to, that if anyone should be saying thank you, it was us. For giving me a chance I'd never thought I'd get.

I looked at Jace, and he squeezed my hand, warm and comforting, like he could feel it too—how impossible and sacred this all was.

"Thank you," I said softly, because I didn't know what else to say. "For… this."

Jace's voice was low and thick. "Yeah. For real… thanks for meeting with us."

She smiled again, just barely, but it was enough to undo me. And then the screen went dark, but I couldn't look away. I just sat there, frozen, as if staring long enough, it might flicker back to life.

Jace's hand was still loosely holding mine. I tucked my knees to my chest, resting my chin on top. I could feel the warmth of him beside me, steady, grounding. But inside, I was somewhere else entirely.

We'd seen her. We'd heard her laugh. Watched her tuck a loose curl behind her ear. Listened to her voice. I kept replaying it, every little moment. The nervous way she'd said hi. The flash of her smile when Jace complimented her room. The exact breath I took when she said, "I think I'd like to meet."

I pressed my forehead to my knees, blinking fast as I wrapped my arms around myself.

"She's really something," Jace said, voice low and rough.

"She is," I murmured. My throat tightened. "She really is."

He was quiet for a beat, then added, softer, "She has your eyes."

A smile tugged at my lips. I looked up and turned toward him, my cheeks heating. "And your smile."

His hand found mine and drew it into his lap, our fingers lacing slow and sure, like he needed to hold on to something solid. I needed it, too.

He turned to look at me, eyes searching. "You okay?"

I didn't answer right away. Just unfolded myself and leaned over to lay my head on his shoulder, nestling against his neck. I breathed him in and let it all settle. And finally, there was nothing clawing at my chest, no weight pressing down. Just light. Air. Her.

"Yeah," I said finally. "I think I am."

Later, we were barefoot in the kitchen, the worn wooden floor was cool beneath my feet as we moved around each other like we'd been doing it for years. I was chopping bell peppers while Jace worked the skillet, flipping shrimp with the kind of concentration that made me grin. Some mellow indie band hummed through an old Bluetooth speaker we found in one of the drawers, and the smell of garlic and butter filled the air.

He said something—some dumb joke—and I laughed without meaning to, tossing my head back, a little tipsy on wine and sunshine and him. I caught his eyes on me then, soft and warm, and something unspoken passed between us.

For a second, I saw something else. Not the past. Not the pain. Just... what could've been. A life not lost, but paused. And now, maybe, finally pressing play.

After dinner, the dishes stayed where they were. We opened the windows wide, letting the breeze off the water come in as we tangled together in bed. The sound of the waves against the shore was a rhythm we already knew, and I lost myself in him — slow, sweet, steadfast like a new story, written in the language of us.

Afterwards, my cheek rested against his chest, the rise and fall of his breath as steady as the tide outside. Moonlight spilled across the sheets, catching the curve of his shoulder and the edge of my knee, which was draped over his thigh. His fingers absently moved up and down my back, soft enough to make me shiver.

I closed my eyes and listened to his heartbeat, so

comforting, and tried to memorize the sound. It hadn't been long. Just weeks. But it already felt impossible to imagine a world without this—him. Us. Every day.

I thought about after the wedding, about L.A. calling him back, and it pulled something tight in my chest. I pictured no wrap-me-up hugs that tell the world to be still, the bed without that warm dip where he sleeps, my phone lighting up where his face should be. I didn't want to go back to being brave and surviving on my own. I wanted mornings, grocery runs, his hoodie on the chair in the bedroom, the soft landing of his mouth at my temple at night. I wanted the ordinary—with him in it.

He pressed a kiss to the top of my head and whispered, "What do you think about inviting Abigail to visit… here? At the beach house?"

I froze, not out of fear, but because the hope in his voice cracked something open in me.

I smiled against his skin. "I'd love that."

And just like that, the place that I used to think of as the end of something now felt like a beginning.

On Wednesday morning, the sun was not even above the horizon as I curled into the corner of the worn couch, one leg tucked beneath me. The beach house was quiet except for the distant rhythm of waves and the occasional seagull cry drifting through the open window.

Jace stood in the kitchen pouring coffee, wearing nothing but sweatpants and sleep-tousled curls. He looked so effortlessly at home here, like he was made to belong to mornings like this. He brought me a mug, then slid onto the couch beside me, one arm draped across the back, fingers brushing my shoulder.

"We doing this today?" he asked softly.

I nodded, exhaling slowly. "Yeah, why not?"

We hadn't rushed it. After the video call, we gave Abigail space. We sent a quick thank-you message. Told her she could reach out at any time. And then we waited. But now... now we were ready to offer her something a little more—an invitation.

I grabbed my laptop off the coffee table and opened a blank email. Jace leaned in beside me, his knee pressed against mine.

"What should we say?" I asked, fingers hovering over the keys.

He was quiet for a moment and shrugged. "That we've been thinking about her. That we're here and wanted to offer something."

I typed:

Hi Abigail,

We've been thinking about you a lot these past few days since our video call. We're writing because we want to offer something. No expectations. Just an invitation.

There's a place we used to go—a beach house that's full of memories and quiet mornings and the kind of peace that only happens near the ocean. It's special to us. It's where we met. Where we first became something. And we were wondering... if you'd ever want to visit with us?

I paused, looking at him. "Too much?"

He shook his head. "It's perfect."

Then, Jace leaned in and gently added:

No pressure. No big plans. Just take a step forward if you'd like. Just a weekend. You and us. Your parents are more than welcome, or it can just be you, whatever you want.

You can say no. You can say not yet. You can say maybe.

Whatever you choose, we're with you. And we're grateful for you. Always.

With love,
* Mallory & Jace*

I sat back, staring at the screen.

Jace squeezed my shoulder. "Well? What do you think?"

I let out a long sigh. "I think... it's good."

Jace tucked a lock of hair behind my ear and asked, "You ready for this? If she says... yes?"

I nodded. "I think so. Are you?"

"Me, too, probably since the moment she smiled on that call."

I clicked Send, and then slowly closed the laptop.

Jace laced his fingers through mine. "You know what?"

"What?"

He kissed the top of my head. "No matter what happens, I'm proud of us."

I leaned into him. "Me, too."

Jace gave my hand a gentle squeeze, then tugged me off the couch. "Come on," he said, a spark in his voice. "Let's watch the sunrise one last time before we head home."

I followed him barefoot through the house and out to the beach. It was quiet, and the morning air was cool against my skin. The sky was soft and streaked with pink as we stepped onto the sand, the waves whispering a welcome.

Together, we stood at the edge of it all, watching the sun lift itself a little higher over the ocean—not knowing exactly what came next, but ready for it anyway. And the silence between us felt full of hope and possibilities.

* * *

Sonny had ordered Januzzi's pizza, and it had just arrived when we walked in the door after our hours-long road trip back home. We'd only stopped once for lunch, and now we were starving and exhausted. The boxes were stacked on the counter, the smell of pepperoni and garlic hitting us like a warm hug from an old friend.

We tiredly greeted Claire and Sonny, but we didn't even pretend to be normal about it. Jace grabbed one of the pizzas, and we slipped down the hall like brooding teenagers instead of the fully functional late-twentysomethings we were supposed to be.

Sonny yelled something about paper plates, but Jace just held the box like a sacred offering, and I trailed behind him, grinning.

The door clicked shut behind us, muffling the noises of the house. My room was dim with early evening light, the ceiling fan spinning slow circles overhead. Jace dropped the box onto the bed and flopped down beside it, looking entirely too smug for someone who'd just stolen dinner.

"Rebels," I said, curling up beside him.

He handed me a slice like a peace treaty. "Star-crossed pizza thieves."

After we ate, I sat cross-legged on my bed, nervously twisting the fringe of the blanket between my fingers. Outside, twilight brushed soft hues of purple and gold over Denton. Jace's duffel was still packed from the beach house, waiting in the backseat of the rental car like an unspoken reminder that tonight had arrived too fast. He had a red eye to catch tonight.

Tomorrow, Claire and I would leave early for the library—officially because I was tagging along to do some "work" with some imaginary copywriting gig. In actuality, I was helping Darci with Claire's surprise bridal shower. But right now, though, the only thing I could think about was the growing ache in my chest, knowing Jace was leaving.

"You sure you can't miss your flight?" I asked, trying to keep my voice light, though it caught a little in my throat.

Jace turned from the window, his eyes warm, softening as he crossed the room toward me. "Trust me, if I could, I would. But I need to be with the guys for the studio time."

"I know it's only a couple of days," I murmured.

"Hey," he said gently, sitting beside me and tucking a strand of hair behind my ear. "We'll be together in Vegas for the wedding before you know it. You can't get rid of me that easily."

"I don't want to get rid of you at all," I said softly, the words slipping out before I could second-guess them.

His smile turned tender. He cupped my face, tilting my chin up so I'd meet his gaze. "Three days, Mal. Then it's you, me, and whatever cheesy love songs Sonny and Claire make us dance to."

I laughed softly, feeling the ache ease slightly. "I'll hold you to it."

He leaned in, brushing his lips against mine, slow and deep, savoring every second. When he pulled away, he stood reluctantly, pausing at the doorway, fingers lingering on the frame.

"I'll text you from the gate," he promised quietly.

"Okay," I whispered.

He hesitated for another heartbeat, eyes searching mine in the soft evening shadows. "I love you, Mallie."

"I love you, too," I said softly.

He smiled once more, gentle and sure, before the door closed quietly behind him, leaving me counting the hours until I'd see him again.

CHAPTER THIRTY-FIVE

Abigail

I read the email again. And again. And again.

Then I shut my laptop fast and went to the bathroom. My face looked back at me in the mirror —messy ponytail, freckles, thick glasses, eyes too wide. I went back and opened it again, slower this time, holding my breath.

Yep. Still there. I'd seen it two days ago but didn't open it till today.

The words felt warm, like a sweatshirt from the dryer. But also heavy, like holding my breath too long and finally coming up for air. Could I do this?

My heart bounced weirdly in my chest. I didn't feel like crying, but I wasn't smiling either. I just spun a little in my desk chair while this new feeling pressed in from all sides.

A beach house. Where they met. Where everything—maybe even me—started. Ew. I did not need that mental picture.

Mom always said big decisions need quiet. So I sat really still. And thought about what I wanted and how I felt. I felt... noticed. Like somebody scooted over on a couch I hadn't seen before and patted the spot next to them and said, "Come sit by me."

I grabbed my phone. My wallpaper was the ocean, wide and blue. I picked it ages ago because it made me feel calm. Now it felt different, like destiny. Like, I finally knew why.

They both gave me their numbers after the video call, but texting Jameson still felt a little weird. Mallory felt easier. Safer. My thumbs hovered, then I typed fast before I chickened out:

Me: I want to come. When were you thinking?

I stared at the screen, took a shaky breath, and hit Send. My heart did a little leap. Something was changing—quiet and big. And I was ready.

CHAPTER THIRTY-SIX

Jace

Present Day

Mallie had said Sonny and Claire were like a fairytale come to life, and being there and seeing it, I felt it. The wedding had gone off without a hitch. The weather during the ceremony had been perfect. Their vows were exchanged beneath a sky that looked hand-painted and cloudless, bluer than memory, like someone had ordered up perfection just for them.

But when Mallie walked down that aisle and stood up at the front, all I could see was her, and the picture in my head wouldn't let go—one day it would be our turn. Without a doubt, I knew that one day, she would be the one walking toward me.

And then, during the reception, I finally met people who were important to Mallie, shaking hands and smiling, hoping I measured up.

Long before Mallie had moved in with Sonny, Darci had offered to watch Bandit while they were in Greece for their honeymoon. So... we slipped away, back down the coast, back to our favorite house at the edge of the sea.

When we got there, I found myself smiling every time I heard the screen door creak—like this old house recognized us, welcoming us back to the place where everything began. Mallie loved it, too, her face brightening whenever the rusty hinges sighed their familiar greeting.

Now we were waiting. Because in just a few days, Abigail would step through that screen door. I still couldn't quite wrap my head around it—our daughter. I had a daughter, and she was nearly a teenager, and... She was coming here, to this place that felt like ours, where we fell in love. Where we made her. The words still felt impossible, but in these quiet, hopeful moments, they were becoming real.

I found Mallie standing in one of the upstairs bedrooms, a stack of folded sheets heavy in her hands, wondering if Abigail preferred the softness of blues or the warmth of yellows. Since the first one, we'd had more video conversations with her, and we'd gathered precious fragments of her life— her quiet passion for music, her careful words, her shy smile, her confessed hatred of broccoli, and her devotion to blueberry pancakes. But there was still so much we didn't know, so much we'd missed—an entire childhood's worth of memories that we'd never witnessed.

"Do you think she'll like it?" Mallie asked, turning towards me in the doorway.

I leaned against the frame, watching her, a vase filled with freshly picked wildflowers in my hands. Sunlight caught her dark hair, tied loosely up, tendrils framing her face. She looked beautiful. Anxious, but beautifully hopeful.

"She'll love it," I said, and I hoped she knew I

meant more than just the room.

I stepped closer, setting the flowers on the dresser. She hesitated, turning to look at me. "I keep overthinking everything. Should we buy her a welcome gift? Should we give her space, or try to talk about things right away?"

"We'll figure it out together," I said gently as she set down the sheets. I pulled her toward me. "We'll prepare, we'll give her room to breathe, and we'll let her decide what she needs from us."

Mallie pressed her forehead against my chest, sighing softly. "What if she comes here and decides it's too much? What if she never wants to see us again?"

I kissed the top of her head, breathing her in. "Then we love her anyway. And we let her go, knowing we did everything we could."

She nodded slowly, her body relaxing into mine.

Later, we made dinner barefoot in the kitchen, music playing softly as twilight settled over the ocean. Mallie teased me about my terrible chopping skills, bumping my hip with hers, stealing tastes from the pan, and laughing when I pretended to scowl.

I couldn't stop watching her, marveling at the way the world outside this kitchen faded into the background. Something about this house loosened her—less tension in her shoulders, a laugh that came quicker, like the salt air took the cautiousness right out of her. And the girl I remembered peeked through. Seeing her like this felt like we'd never lost those years, as if this had always been ours.

After we ate, we snuggled on the couch in the living room. The house was still, filled only with the distant, steady rhythm of the ocean. I brushed my fingers lightly along her shoulder, whispering what

I'd been thinking all night.

"This feels like the life we were always meant to have."

Mallie shifted in my arms, raising her head to look at me. Her eyes were soft and full of quiet certainty as she said, "It's ours now. That's all I care about."

It was everything. Yet somehow, my heart begged for more.

Hours later, as moonlight painted the walls and the salt breeze drifted gently through the window, I ran my fingers along her hip, whispering into the peaceful silence, "What if this became a tradition? Coming back here—every year, the three of us?"

She turned toward me, half-asleep, a gentle smile curving her lips. "That sounds like home."

I held her tighter, pressing one last kiss against her forehead, letting the rhythm of the waves carry us toward sleep.

In three days, Abigail would arrive, but the waiting was the hardest part—three days of second-guessing the pillows, the snacks, all of it.

When the day finally arrived, I'd been watching the clock for the last hour, pacing the kitchen, pretending I wasn't. Mallie was just as bad, folding and moving the same throw blanket at least six times. My stomach felt like it had been holding its breath all morning.

And then we heard it, the tires crunching on the gravel before we saw their car pull up. A moment later, she stepped out of the backseat, backpack slung over one shoulder, and I would have sworn it was Mallie back when we met here every summer. Then, her mom stepped out of the passenger seat, while her dad stayed in the driver's seat. Abigail and her mother exchanged a few words and hugged before they turned toward the house.

Abigail seemed tinier than she had appeared on the video call. She wore a faded sweatshirt, denim shorts, and a pair of old red Converse. Her hair was in a braid tossed over one shoulder, and her hands fidgeted nervously at her sides.

I opened the door before they got to the porch. "Hey," I said, grinning.

Her mom, Rebecca, smiled warmly at me as they made their way from the car. Mallie walked up next to me, and we both just stood there, silent, still, watching her walk toward us like a living piece of our hearts had finally come home.

Abigail stopped at the bottom of the porch steps, her mom a few feet behind her.

"Hi," she said, her voice small but steady.

"Hi," Mallie breathed, every part of her shaking. I wrapped my arm around her shoulders and squeezed her, just to let her know I was here.

I gave a soft smile. "We're really glad you're here."

Abigail looked down and scuffed the toe of her shoe against the step. "I almost changed my mind this morning."

"That's okay," Mallie said gently. "We would've understood."

"But I didn't," she added, eyes lifting to first Mallie and then me. "I wanted to see the ocean."

I looked over at Mallie as she took a breath and blinked back tears. She said, "You will. It's right across the way, waiting for you."

I extended a hand. Not pushing. Just offering. Abigail hesitated, then climbed the last few steps and slipped her fingers into mine. Her other hand reached for Mallie. And suddenly we were standing there, the three of us, holding on in the doorway like we were anchoring each other through time.

"Want to come inside?" Mallie asked.

She nodded. "Yeah. I do."

I stepped back, holding the door open wide. And together, we walked into the place where everything started—where something entirely new was about to begin.

We weren't sure if her parents would stay. None of us really knew how this was supposed to go.

But her mom held back and said, "Abigail wanted it to be just the three of you."

She told us they thought it was important to let her choose, so they were staying at a hotel a few miles down, right on the beach. Close, but not hovering. Before she left, she asked Abigail if it was still okay to go, and Abigail nodded before hugging her mom one last time.

As their car pulled away, Mallie glanced over at Abigail—this girl who looked so much like both of us—and said softly, "Ready to see your room?"

Abigail looked up with surprise, "My room?"

Mallie nodded. "Yep, we made it just for you."

I slipped my hand into Mallie's without thinking, just needing to feel that tether. Her fingers closed around mine. Abigail didn't say anything else—just gave the smallest nod. But her eyes were glassy as she turned to look around the house.

We showed her the room we'd set up. It was on the second floor, peaceful, a breeze drifting in from the ocean through the open window. We'd stacked a few books on the shelf, left a journal on the nightstand, and folded a soft quilt in shades of blue at the foot of the bed.

"I like it," she said quietly.

The way she stood in the doorway, like she didn't want to mess it up by stepping inside too fast, said more than words could.

We followed her as she wandered through the beach house, as if she were walking through a museum of our history together. Her fingers skimmed the banister, the edge of the kitchen table, some old paint flaking off a windowsill. She didn't say much—just looked around with wide eyes full of questions she wasn't ready to ask.

When she asked if she could see the ocean, we walked down to the beach. She kicked her shoes off at the edge of the dunes, and when we got to the shore, she immediately sank her toes into the wet sand.

The water in the bay was calm, so I taught her how to skip stones. She was terrible at first—kept throwing them straight into the water like little cannonballs—but then she got one to bounce twice and her whole face lit up. Arms in the air like she'd just landed a gold medal.

I laughed. I couldn't help it. It bubbled up and out of me before I even knew it was coming. And then she looked over at me, and I swear, something shifted, and the corners of her mouth tugged up, like maybe she hadn't expected that sound from me.

Mallie followed behind us, watching quietly as we walked the shoreline. Eventually, we all started collecting shells and bits of sea glass worn smooth by time. Abigail found a sand dollar, mostly intact, and held it up in the sunlight as if it were delicate and precious.

"Do you remember the first time you saw the ocean?" she asked me, voice soft.

I nodded. "I was three. It was here, actually. My parents started renting the beach house back then. And... at first, I hated the way the sand stuck to my toes."

She glanced at me, cheeks flushed. "So... I guess

that's genetic."

I laughed, and my heart caught in my throat for a second. It was the first time she'd admitted what we were—without hesitation.

We stayed out there a long time, but when the sky turned gold, we headed back to the house. I was in the middle of grilling steak out on the deck and had come in to grab some foil when I found her standing in the kitchen, slicing strawberries and watermelon with Mallie for a fruit salad. Her braid was a little messy from the wind, and her cheeks were still flushed from the sun. She looked like she belonged here, and like maybe she felt it, too.

"Were you good at school?" she asked suddenly, still cutting fruit.

Mallie looked at me and blinked, caught off guard. "Um. Kind of? I loved English and art. Math and I had a deeply unhealthy relationship."

Abigail snorted, "Same."

After dinner, we sat out on the front porch steps with Abigail between us and bowls of ice cream balanced on our knees. For one breathless second, Abigail leaned her head against Mallie's shoulder. No big gesture. Just a moment. But I saw the way Mallie froze, how she didn't move or even breathe. She just let it happen, let Abigail choose closeness on her own terms.

Then she suddenly turned to me. "What was the first song you ever wrote?"

I groaned. "It was terrible."

"Do you still remember it?"

"Unfortunately."

"Will you play it for me sometime?"

I chuckled. "Only if you promise not to tell anyone."

She stuck out her pinky, and I grabbed it with

mine. "Deal."

As the stars blinked to life, I ducked inside, dropping our bowls in the sink and grabbing my guitar. I sat down on the porch swing, strumming low, and Abigail came and sat next to me, humming along like we'd been doing this forever.

Mallie leaned against the railing, watching us with that soft, stunned look she got sometimes—like the weight of it all was almost too much and somehow not enough.

We weren't some perfect family. This was all completely new and messy, maybe even a little heartbreaking. But we were together and figuring out how to hold all this without dropping it.

In the morning, the house had a hush to it when I woke up—the kind of calm that you feel near the ocean—peaceful but full of movement. I lay there just listening and heard the faint rustle of wind, the hush of waves just beyond, a soft creak from upstairs.

Mallory was still asleep, curled beneath the quilt, one hand tucked under her cheek. I slipped out of bed quietly and padded barefoot down the hallway, pulling on a T-shirt as I moved.

The kitchen smelled like coffee and something warm. And then I saw her—Abigail. Sitting at the table with her knees pulled up, a mug between her hands. Sleep-mess hair, the oversized sweatshirt she'd arrived in. She looked up when she saw me.

"Morning," I said, careful not to make it too cheerful.

"Hey." She sipped. "I made coffee. Pretty sure it's terrible."

I smiled and walked over to pour a mug. "Let's test that theory."

She watched me taste it, bracing like she actually

wanted a review.

I made a face. "Okay, it's not terrible. But it's... bold. Very confident."

She laughed—quick, surprised. "That's a nice way to say I have no idea what I'm doing."

"Please. That's pretty much all of adulthood. We're all just confidently winging it with caffeine." I tipped my mug toward hers. "Question, though— you're still pretty young. Are you even allowed coffee at home?"

She rolled one shoulder. "Technically, yes. One cup. Mostly milk and a little sugar. Cream and chocolate syrup, if Mom's feeling really wild."

"So... a supervised latte situation," I said, nodding.

"I guess." She lowered her voice like we were plotting. "But when I'm with my friends, we get real coffee. I like it strong, with a little sweet. Don't tell."

"Your secret's safe with me," I said. "Tell you what—let me make you a not-terrible cup, and we'll call it educational."

She slid her mug across the table, grinning. "Deal."

I brewed a fresh pot and poured two cups. She drowned hers in sugar—more than I'd ever take— and we let the quiet sit with us. It wasn't tense. It was just full of things we didn't quite know how to say yet.

She shifted in her seat. "So... you play guitar every day?"

"Almost every day. Gotta practice, and... it keeps me sane."

She nodded slowly. "Do you think I got my love of music from you?"

It hit me harder than I expected—that little question, so casual and colossal at the same time.

"I don't know," I said honestly. "But I like thinking that you did."

She looked down into her mug. "I used to wonder where it came from. Nobody else in my family really plays an instrument. But I... I feel it. You know?"

"I do." I paused, choosing my words carefully. "Music and writing songs were how I survived some hard teenage years."

She looked up at me and nodded. Her eyes were so much like Mallie's that it was almost unbearable. She was quiet for a long time. Then she set her mug down, stood up, and walked around the table.

I didn't move. She sat beside me, not looking at me directly, just close enough for her shoulder to brush mine. She pulled her sleeves over her hands and looked down at her knees.

"I'm still figuring out how this all fits in my life," she whispered. "How y'all fit."

I gave a slight nod. "That makes sense. I've been trying to figure that out, too."

"Were you scared?" She glanced at me then, just briefly, "When you found out? About me?"

I let out a breath as I arched an eyebrow. "Terrified. Still am. But... I'm here for the long haul, not going anywhere, if that's what you want."

Something flickered across her face like understanding or relief, maybe. She didn't say anything else. Just leaned the tiniest bit into me, shoulder to shoulder, like a question she wasn't quite ready to ask, and I stayed still, steady, answering it anyway. And we sat there, staring out the window at the vast blue sky, the quiet between us finally beginning to feel like something shared.

Eventually, she tilted her head a little. "So what was that first song you ever learned to play?"

I grinned. "Like, learned properly? Or butchered with dramatic flair?"

She smirked. "Both."

"'Wonderwall,'" I admitted.

She pinched her eyebrows together, "Never heard of it."

I glanced at her. "You're kidding."

She laughed and shook her head, "I'm only twelve, you know."

I couldn't help but chuckle, which made her burst, and then I couldn't stop myself. She had Mallie's laugh, lighter but the same cadence, and it nailed me.

When we finally calmed down, she was quiet for a moment before she asked hesitantly, "Would you... show me something? On the guitar? I mean. But... only if you want to."

I blinked. "Yeah. Yeah, of course."

We walked into the living room, and I grabbed the old acoustic I'd brought with me—weathered and familiar—and sat down on the couch as she settled beside me. She hugged her knees to her chest, her chin resting on top, watching with wide, curious eyes.

I strummed something soft. Slow. Just a few quiet chords, nothing flashy. Something I'd written years ago, back when music was all I had. She watched my fingers carefully, not with awe, but with intent. Studying. Absorbing.

"You want to try?" I asked gently.

She hesitated.

"Only if you want to."

She nodded slowly. "Okay."

I passed the guitar to her, adjusting it in her arms, her posture instinctively good. She strummed a bit, tentative at first, then more confidently, fingering the chords. Not perfect—but there was rhythm. There was soul.

"You've got a good ear," I said.

She handed me the guitar back and said, "Music's the only thing that ever really makes sense in my head."

God. That was me as a kid, too. I looked at her and saw it—this bright, brilliant thread of something that lived in her, something she probably didn't even know had a name. And then, I played a few chords, and she hummed along. And without meaning to, slowly, we started building the chorus to a song neither of us knew yet. Something simple. Something ours.

Mallie walked in a little later, pausing in the doorway as she took us in. Abigail, singing and humming with me beside her, strumming along, both of us deep in the kind of moment you don't try to explain.

Mallie didn't say anything, just smiled and left us to it, and went to the kitchen. And that's when I looked over at Abigail and saw a flicker of something new in her face, that maybe this wasn't just a one-time visit but a beginning.

CHAPTER THIRTY-SEVEN

Mallie

Present Day

The screen door creaked open behind me, that soft, familiar squeak like the house clearing its throat. I didn't turn. Just pulled the blanket tighter around my shoulders and kept my eyes on the horizon. The stars were so bright, scattered across the dark like spilled salt on velvet. The ocean moved below, steady and soft.

The door clicked shut again. Then footsteps—light ones, almost hesitant, but she sat down beside me. I held up the corner of the blanket without a word. She just took it and tucked it around her knees. Our shoulders barely brushed. For a while, we listened to the surf, the wind, the hush between us.

"He told me about things," she said eventually. Her voice was so quiet, I almost couldn't hear her. "Jameson. Not the whole story. Just… what it felt like. Not knowing about me until just recently."

I swallowed, the ache blooming sharp in my throat. I let out a long sigh. "Yeah… I wanted him to know, to be there, but it just didn't… work out that way." The words drifted off into the dark.

She nodded, eyes on the waves. "You got to hold me, though, right? Before they took me away?"

The smile came anyway—soft, but it stung. "Yeah, for just a few minutes."

"Oh…" she murmured, realizing how little time we'd had together.

"It's okay," I said. "I spent those fleeting moments just memorizing you. I can still remember your sweet baby smell."

She smiled, small and faraway, clearly imagining it.

"I thought I'd be angry," she said. "That you gave me up. That no one told me sooner. But I'm not. I just… needed to know it wasn't because you didn't want me."

I turned toward her, fully this time. My heart broke apart from the guilt and the longing, and I let it.

"I wanted you so much, but I also wanted everything for you," I said. "Everything I couldn't give you because I was so young. Not because I didn't love you, because I did. I do. So much."

She looked down at her lap, fingering a loose thread at the hem of her sweatshirt. "They're good parents, you know," she said. "My mom cried when we left for this trip. My dad packed me, like, three kinds of snacks."

A laugh bubbled up, warm but aching. "They definitely sound like the good ones."

"They are." She hesitated, then added, "But I think there's room for you, too."

That broke something open inside me, and if I'd been alone, I would have sobbed. But I took in a shaky breath and held it together and reached for her hand, and she didn't flinch or pull away. She just let me have it.

"You know, you don't owe me anything," I said. "You get to choose how this goes. When it goes."

"I know," she said. "But I thought I'd leave with answers. And I think I'm leaving with… something more… like more family."

I didn't respond. I wasn't sure what to say to that. I just sat with her, wrapped together in the same blanket, our fingers laced beneath the stars.

"Can I tell you something?" Abigail leaned in like we were co-conspirators, eyes bright with a secret she'd been keeping. "It's not a big deal—well, it feels big to me, but it's silly, probably."

"Tell me," I said, hoping she couldn't hear the way my heart stalled.

She lifted her hand like she was cupping words. "I've never liked my name," she whispered. "Abigail never felt like… me."

"Okay. So is there a name that feels like you?"

"I don't know." Her smile twisted as she rolled her eyes. "It's fine. It's a perfectly good name. I just… whenever I picture myself—like, when I'm journaling or talking to myself in my head—it's never Abigail. It's always… Violet."

Internally, I gasped so hard that everything went white around the edges. How had she known? She had just been a newborn. But… *Violet.* I tasted the syllables like salt on my tongue.

I kept my face neutral and my voice steady. "Violet," I echoed, testing it like fabric between my fingers. "It feels more like you?"

Her shoulders dropped, probably relieved when she half expected me to laugh, and I didn't. "It does. I don't even know why. It just always has." Her laugh shivered. "God, that's weird, right? I shouldn't have said anything. Forget I—"

"No," I said, and my voice came out threaded with something like conviction. "Don't take it back."

Abigail looked up at me as my hands found each other on my knees. I stared at them for a heartbeat, then lifted my eyes back to her. "Can I tell you something, too?"

She nodded, suddenly looking unsure.

"From the very beginning, I knew you were a girl." I looked out at the horizon, the memories of that time coming fast, "I don't know why, but I just knew. And... when you were still in my belly, I swore you told me your name... in a dream."

I looked back at her, and our eyes locked.

"I did?"

I nodded. "When you were born," I said, "I held you for a few minutes. It wasn't long. You were so small, so tiny that your whole body could fit in the crook of my arm." I smiled at the memory, looking down at my arm as if she were still there, and it hurt and glowed all at the same time. "You had this tiny crease here." I touched the bridge of my own nose. "Like you were already trying to think very hard."

She smiled.

"It wasn't... it wasn't my place to give you a name." My voice thinned but didn't break. "But when I held you, I... I whispered the one you had told me, anyway. And it was... Violet."

Everything went absolutely quiet. I could have sworn even the waves stopped to listen for a beat or two. I watched her face change—like sunlight moving across a room, shadows sliding, everything coming into focus.

Her breath hitched. "No."

I nodded, barely.

Her eyes filled, and she scrubbed at one with the

heel of her hand, a shocked laugh breaking out on a tear. "No way. There's no way that's true." She leaned forward, hands gripping mine. "You're messing with me."

I shook my head and said, "I would never."

She let out a strangled sound that was half laugh, half sob. "This is crazy. That's, oh my god, that's the name I write on the backs of my sketches. It's what I put on the stories I write only for myself. It's the name I... I call myself when I need to be brave."

She made an incredulous, breathless noise and pressed her palms to her mouth, shaking, laughing again. "This is crazy!" She looked around like the world might explain itself, then back to me, eyes huge, wild with wonder. "Okay, I'm freaking out."

"It's okay." I squeezed her fingers, not saying the thousand apologies bottled up in my chest. "We can freak out together."

And I didn't mean to cry, but there it was, tears dripping down my face, quiet and unstoppable. "Would you... want me... us... to call you that? Violet?"

She dropped her hands, cheeks wet, smile breaking wide open like a tide releasing. She inhaled, steadying, and then the words tumbled out of her, fierce and certain, as if she'd been waiting her whole life to hear herself say them, "Okay..." she breathed out. "I think I do want you to call me Violet."

I nodded. "Then that's what we'll do."

The tide rolled on, carrying my guilt with it and somehow bringing back the child I thought I'd lost forever. For so long, I'd told myself that I had done the best I could, and when I felt for that constant ache I'd lived with for all these years, I realized that finally it was smaller and softer, and felt more like mercy now.

The next morning, Violet was already in the kitchen when I came down.

She stood at the stove in mismatched pajamas — flannel pants and an old school tee — carefully flipping pancakes with her hair pulled up in a messy knot. She looked over her shoulder and grinned like it was the most normal thing in the world.

"I found blueberries in the fridge," she said. "Hope that's okay."

"Okay?" I smiled. "It's perfect. And they smell amazing."

Jace wandered in a few minutes later, curls sticking up in all directions, blinking like he hadn't quite woken up yet.

"Smells like home," he mumbled, kissing the top of my head as he passed.

Violet rolled her eyes in mock horror before turning back to watch the pancakes. "You two are so sappy."

"Get used to it, *Violet*," he teased.

For a heartbeat, I forgot how to breathe. I watched her head lift, watched the way her whole face lit up at the sound of it. That grin — wide, unguarded — I hadn't seen before. She didn't answer, just held on to the word like it was a secret she'd been waiting her whole life to hear.

And I knew. She knew I had told him, and instead of pulling away, she let it bloom. My chest ached with joy, a little guilt, and relief, until it all blurred into one thing — gratitude. That he loved her enough to call her by the name she wanted and that I had whispered once, when she was minutes old. That she loved it enough to smile like that.

We ate on the back deck, the morning sun warm

on our shoulders. There was syrup on the table, sand between my toes, and laughter—real, unguarded laughter that filled the air and settled somewhere deep in my chest.

After breakfast, we spent the day without plans. We walked the beach again, all three of us barefoot, Jace showing off his wildly terrible cartwheels, Violet trying to bury his legs in the sand while he shouted dramatically for help. We built sandcastles like Jace and I used to do as kids and collected shells again. She found a broken one shaped like a heart and tucked it into her pocket, flicking her eyes at me without a word.

Later that night, we built a fire pit out of driftwood and made s'mores as the sky turned tangerine. Violet licked her fingers, sticky with marshmallow and chocolate, and I couldn't stop smiling. It wasn't perfect. Nothing ever was. But it was good. It was becoming easy. It was ours.

That night, after we cleaned up and the stars came to life overhead, Violet stood in the doorway of her room and looked at both of us.

"Tomorrow's gonna suck," she said, blunt as ever.

Jace nodded. "Yeah. It will."

"But," she said, glancing at me, "I'm really glad I came."

"So are we," I said, my voice catching.

She yawned and gave a little half-wave, then ducked inside, pulling the door mostly closed behind her. I stood there for a moment, staring at the place she'd just been, feeling the quiet settle around us.

Jace slipped his arms around my waist as we walked down the hall. "She's got your fire, you know."

"And your sarcasm," I said, smiling through memories from last night and today.

I turned in his arms. He looked at me like he always had—like I was something precious. Like he saw every version of me I'd ever been and wanted all of them. The teenage girl on the beach. The broken one who'd survived. The woman standing in front of him now, unsure what she was doing but open.

"Come on," I said softly, threading my fingers through his. "Let's go to bed."

We walked downstairs without saying much past the kitchen, where the sink still held the dishes from dinner. The lights were low, the house quiet.

In our room, I kicked off my shoes and pulled my sweater over my head, letting it fall to the floor. Jace leaned against the door frame and watched me for a beat longer before stepping inside and shutting the door behind him.

He reached for me, and I met him halfway.

"I love you," he said, real and honest.

"I know," I whispered. "I love you, too."

He cradled the back of my neck, threading his fingers through my hair as he pulled me in. His lips brushed mine once, twice, and then I opened for him. Our kiss was everything, and all I could think was how I wanted this with him every day.

His hands were warm against my skin as he lifted my t-shirt. I undid the buttons of his jeans. We undressed each other without hurry, like every piece of clothing was a small ritual.

The bed creaked as we sank into it. The sheets cool against our skin, the rhythm of the ocean drifting through the open window. His hands never left my skin—tracing, learning, needing—like he couldn't bear it unless he were touching me. And I felt it, too. The way my fingers clung to his back, the way my mouth kept finding his. It was less about hunger and more about survival. It ripped through my middle—the life I'd lived without him, all at once.

I kissed him again, and again, like the breath of life itself was hiding between his lips, like if I let go, I might lose him forever. We were heat and hands and the slow, aching drag of my skin against his. When he finally sank into me, we both groaned, and I ran my nails against his back as his body aligned with mine, with the certainty of a vow. Every thrust felt like a promise, like we were stitching what was torn from us so long ago—binding it tighter with every slide, every moan, every desperate pull of our mouths.

He kissed me like he needed to memorize the shape of every sound I made. I clung to him, arching up to meet each roll of his hips, my legs locked around him, holding him there—inside, against, within. I never wanted to let him go. The world narrowed to the point where our bodies became one, slick and relentless, chasing something holy.

I held his face in my hands as he moved above me, his forehead pressed to mine, sweat beading along his temple. When we came, both hard and gasping, it felt like the universe began again with light and sound rushing back in.

Afterward, we just lay together in the dark, the sheets twisted around us, the air thick with salt and something sweeter. His hand ran over my hip as I relaxed against him, falling towards sleep in the quiet.

"She'll come back," he murmured, his voice rough against my hair.

I nestled closer into him, pressing a kiss to the

hollow of his throat. "I hope so..."

But with his heartbeat steady against me, I knew I wasn't just hoping anymore. I believed it.

In the morning, I woke up early and padded barefoot into the kitchen to find Violet already there, curled on the window seat with a glass of orange juice, knees tucked into her chest. Her hair was still damp from her shower, her bag already zipped and leaning against the table.

She looked up when I entered, offering a sleepy smile. "Hey."

"Hey," I said, grabbing the coffee pot to fill it with water. "Sleep okay?"

"Yeah. I woke up a couple times." She shrugged. "Didn't want to oversleep today and miss the last morning."

I nodded, trying not to let my chest cave in at her words.

We didn't talk much as I made breakfast—just eggs and toast this time. Simple. Easy. When she came over to the table, I set a tiny glass jar of strawberry jam in front of her, the kind I'd bought on a whim at a roadside stand a few days before.

She looked at it, then at me. "You remembered I like strawberry."

"Of course I did."

After we ate, she slipped outside with Jace while I cleaned up the dishes. When I peeked out through the screen door, I saw them walking slowly along the sand, side by side, hands in their pockets, talking. It made something deep in me ache—but in the best possible way.

The screen door creaked as they came back in, sand still clinging to their ankles. Jace was grinning at something Violet had just said, and she looked lighter, brighter, than I'd seen her these past few days. For a second, I just stood there watching them, memorizing it.

Then I swallowed and forced the words out. "Your mom just called," I said softly. "They'll be here any minute."

Violet's smile faltered, but she only nodded, slipping her hands into the pocket of her hoodie.

Jace shifted closer to her, his voice low but sure. "You're always welcome to come back."

Her eyes flicked up at him, grateful, and then to me. It felt like the house was holding its breath when she pulled something small from her hoodie pocket—a folded envelope—and handed it to me.

"I wrote this last night," she said quickly. "You don't have to read it now. I just... wanted you to have it."

I nodded, heart already in my throat. "Thank you."

She looked at both of us. "I don't really know how to say goodbye."

"We don't have to," Jace said. "Just say, 'see you soon.'"

She smiled at that. "Okay. See you soon, then."

And then she did something I hadn't expected. She stepped forward and hugged me. Tight. No hesitation. I wrapped my arms around her and closed my eyes, breathing her in, trying to memorize the weight and warmth of her.

"I love you," I whispered. "No matter what. Always."

She didn't say it back. But she didn't let go right away either.

When she finally pulled away, she turned to Jace and hugged him, quick and awkward, like she wasn't sure where to put her arms. He looked at me and smiled through it, holding her like she was something precious.

Then, without saying a word, he stepped aside and picked up the weathered guitar case leaning against the wall. I recognized it instantly—the faded stickers, the scuffed latches. It was his first one. The one he used to play for me on the porch when we were kids. The one he'd written his first songs on.

He held it out to her.

Her mouth parted slightly. "Is this…?"

He nodded. "It's yours now."

She stared, like the weight of it hadn't fully hit her yet, then wrapped her arms around the case, holding it tight to her chest.

"You better practice," he said, softer now. "Next time we meet, we're writing a song together."

She smiled, just a little. "Deal."

Her parents pulled up a moment later. We walked her out to the car as her mom popped out and thanked me with a hug. Jace held the door for Violet as she slid into the backseat and helped load her bag and the guitar case. And then she was gone, just like that.

Jace and I stood on the porch for a long time after the car disappeared down the road, the salt breeze curling around us like the sea itself was trying to offer comfort. I felt it the moment the car vanished as if the world had tilted, closing and opening in the same breath. My arms still ached from holding her, and my heart ached in a deeper way, not with regret, but with a longing that finally had a shape.

"She'll be back," he said softly.

"I know," I whispered.

Jace slid his hand into mine and gave it a gentle squeeze.

"Come on," he said, voice low and warm. "Let me take care of you."

I let him lead me inside. He walked me down the hallway to our room. The door clicked softly behind us. Morning light spilled across the bed, and Jace turned to face me.

His hands slid to my waist as his eyes searched mine. "You okay?" he asked.

I nodded, not trusting my voice. My throat was tight.

"Come here," he whispered, pulling me closer, wrapping me in his arms.

I melted into him, my forehead pressed to his chest, hands fisting in the worn cotton of his t-shirt. He held me like he knew I'd try to stay strong, but I might shatter if he let go.

Then he tipped my chin up and kissed me. His lips moved with intention, kissing the silent tears that ran down my cheeks. His fingers traced the curve of my jaw, the slope of my spine down to my ass—just warmth, and closeness, and a love that had survived so much.

We undressed each other in soft, silent motions, shedding layers and emotions. By the time we sank into the sheets, wrapped in sunlight and nothing else, all the edges of me had softened. He kissed every part of me like he'd memorized it long ago and was just now rediscovering it, touching me with the kind of care that made my tears keep falling.

Our lovemaking was slow and deep and tender—like we had all the time in the world. Like his body knew every place I'd ever ached for all those years apart.

After, I lay with my head on his chest and our legs entwined beneath the covers. His breath was warm against my hair as he ran his fingers against my hip.

I felt whole, being with him like this, after

everything we'd lost and found. But wholeness wasn't enough if he was going to be hundreds of miles away soon. I didn't want distance. I wanted forever.

My fingers drifted down his arm, over the ink etched into his skin. I traced the hollow bone, the tiny dots and dashes inside it.

"Are you ever going to tell me what this code says?" I asked, tipping my head up to look at him, my voice quiet in the dim light.

For a moment, he stilled. Then his hand covered mine, holding it against the tattoo like he was afraid to let the truth loose. His eyes closed as he drew in a breath.

"It's your last text," he said finally, voice rough. "The one you sent before you were gone. 'I carry you with me now.' And back then… I had no idea what you were trying to say, but now…"

The words broke me instantly, my throat closing as tears slipped free before I could stop them. I buried my face in his chest.

"Hey," he whispered, lifting my head with his hand and brushing them away with his thumb, his touch unbearably tender. "Don't cry. You were never gone from me. Not really. I had you here," he pressed my hand against his chest—against the star, "always here."

I closed my eyes, letting the weight of his words settle into me, and I couldn't help the tears that fell harder. For so long I'd carried the ache of thinking he hadn't known, that I was alone in what I'd suffered, that my last piece of love had vanished into silence. But he had kept it, inked it into his skin, woven it into his very being.

When I opened my eyes again, he was watching me like I was the only thing in the world worth looking at.

"We're not losing us again," I whispered. "Not to time, not to distance, not to anything."

His mouth tightened in quiet conviction. "We won't. Whatever comes, we'll carry each other through it. Always."

I smiled through the blur of my tears and tightened my arms around his shoulders, holding on for dear life, and he held me back just as fiercely, as if we were daring the world to try and break us again. And I believed nothing could.

CHAPTER THIRTY-EIGHT

Jace

Present Day

The barn smelled like cedar and coffee, and fresh-cut grass, which seemed to always drift in, no matter how tightly the doors were shut. Sunlight streamed through the high windows, casting long stripes across the wooden floor where we sat in chairs in a loose circle, notebooks open, guitars leaning against knees, everyone tossing out lines and chords like we were fishing for something magical.

I should've been more focused. Usually, writing was my favorite thing. It had always been like breathing—easy, necessary. But today I couldn't stop checking my phone. Mallie had sent a photo of the sunrise from her morning walk with Bandit hours ago, with a quick note about the air smelling like honeysuckle. Sonny and Claire were still on their honeymoon, and she was home alone.

I couldn't stop myself from looking at it over and over again. I stared at that message for too long, rereading it like it might bloom into something more.

It had only been a week since we'd left the beach house. We'd driven back to Denton, and then I'd caught a flight back home to L.A., immediately coming on this road trip with the guys for a writing session here in Napa. It had been a week since I kissed her goodbye outside the airport, both of us pretending it wasn't ripping us in two. And now I was here in northern California with the guys, technically working, but mostly wishing I'd been watching the sky shift from pink to gold beside her back at the beach.

"Jace?" Eddie said, snapping his fingers. "You with us, man?"

"Yeah," I said automatically, but I was already shaking my head. "Actually, can we take five?"

Nobody argued, but I could see the looks of disappointment. They were used to my ghosting lately. Half a heart wasn't the best writing companion.

I stepped out into the open air, the sky wide and blue over the hills. Found a shady spot under an old eucalyptus tree and dialed the number I hadn't used in a while.

"Hey, Sam," I said when my accountant picked up. "Quick question. Hypothetically—what would it take for me to buy a house?"

He asked me more—location, square footage—most things I had no idea about, but I told him what I could.

"A beach house?"

"Yeah. It's from my... childhood," I said. "I know it's crazy. But I want to surprise my girlfriend. I want to make it ours."

There was a pause. Then Sam laughed. "You've got the funds. And if the owners are interested in selling, I don't see why not."

We talked details as I took notes on my phone. Then, I called my mom, and she gave me the contact info for a friend back in Texas who was a realtor. I sent her the info I had about the house and the owners and headed back to the barn with my heart thudding steadily, the kind of thump that comes when something just feels right.

It wasn't just a plan now. It was happening. I was going to build a life with Mallie. I just hadn't figured out how to tell her yet.

"Look who finally decided to join us," Jake said as I walked back in, twirling a drumstick between his fingers like he'd been waiting all morning to use the line.

"What? I've been here all day," I said, setting my case down beside the amp. "At least I'm still prettier than you."

That got a groan from Eddie and a snort from Dean.

"Debatable," Jake said, spinning his stick. "The crowd's here for me and my tragic backstory now."

"Yeah, nothing says rock and roll like a guy with a medical boot," Eddie muttered, plucking at a string on his bass.

Dean leaned back on his stool, smirking. "You could bedazzle it for the encore."

Jake pointed a drumstick at him. "Don't tempt me."

Their laughter bounced off the walls, and for the first time since the accident, it felt easy again. The kind of noise you don't realize you've missed until it's back.

"All right, comedians," I said, slinging my guitar strap over my shoulder. "Let's run through the set before the label starts thinking we forgot how to play."

"Which one?" Dean asked, hands hovering over the keys. "The 'we survived a van crash and learned feelings' version or the one where we pretend we're fine?"

"The one that's gonna remind L.A. we're still here," I said, checking my tuning.

Eddie grinned. "Good. Feelings make me itch."

Jake tapped his sticks together. "One, two—"

The first hit of sound cracked through, sharp and alive. Every chord rattled through my chest, each note anchoring me back where I belonged.

For a few minutes, the world outside didn't exist. It was just the music. The noise. The pulse. All of it that somehow survived.

When the last note faded, Jake leaned forward on his snare, breathless. "Think we're ready?"

I wiped sweat from my forehead, grinning. "We'd better be."

A few days later, I was back home. Everything was finally clicking again. The band had found the momentum we'd lost after the accident. The trip up north had turned into real songs, rehearsals actually felt like shows, and for the first time in months, it all felt easy. We still had a couple more run-throughs before the L.A. show next Friday, but for once, I wasn't worried.

I'd just stepped out of a quick shower, still half-asleep from the week's marathon writing and rehearsal sessions, when I heard my apartment door open. It was Saturday morning, and I wasn't expecting anyone, barely past eight.

My heart kicked. I hadn't buzzed anyone in. I stepped into the hallway, hair damp, with a towel wrapped around my waist, when I saw her.

"Mallie?" I said, stunned.

Windblown and beautiful, her bag was still slung

over a shoulder. She was in jeans and a sweatshirt, and that expression she wore when she was trying not to smile too soon.

"Hi," she said softly. "Surprise."

For a second, I didn't move. Didn't breathe. I wondered if I was dreaming. Then I took three strides and reached for her, pulling her into my arms, breathing in her sweet scent of cocoa butter and warm sugar.

"You're here," I breathed, pressing my lips to her hair.

"I wanted to see you," she said against my chest. "They're back from their honeymoon, and I just couldn't stand being across the country from you one more day."

I kissed her, slow and grateful, and then—

She walked to the middle of my apartment, dropping her bag on the couch, and… froze.

I watched her eyes move—slow and wide—taking in the cluttered sprawl of the space. Boxes stacked like crooked towers. Everywhere. A few labeled, most not. Open ones with stacks of folded t-shirts, stacks of books, and another with coiled guitar cables. A dish towel was tossed over the edge of a half-packed kitchen box sitting on a barstool.

She didn't speak at first. Just slowly walked towards the kitchen island as her smile slipped. I followed her gaze to the counter—the contract. I hadn't bothered tucking it away. The beach house address stared back in bold type. And something shifted in her posture.

Shit.

I felt it, like a wire snapping taut between us. My stomach dropped.

"Mallie—wait. It's not… I didn't know you were coming."

She turned to look at me, eyes searching. Her voice was tight, "Are you... moving? When were you going to tell me?"

I opened my mouth. Nothing came out. The fridge hummed too loudly. There was the distant whine of a lawnmower outside. But between us, it was just complete silence.

She took a step closer. "Jace? Were you going to tell me?"

Her tone was even, but I heard it—the catch in the middle. The flicker of something like fear. Like she'd stumbled into a story that had already started without her. And I hated that I'd let her walk into it blind.

I let out a sigh as my stomach twisted tighter in that knot. I took her hands gently, my thumbs brushing over her knuckles.

I spluttered, "I was... going to tell you next weekend. In person. When I came to Dallas."

She held her breath when she asked, "Tell me what?"

I took a breath. "I bought the beach house." I stepped closer, careful. "I wanted to surprise you."

Her laugh was short and flat. "You didn't even ask me."

"I was going to." I ran a hand through my hair. "I had a plan. Dinner. A whole thing. I thought if I showed you what it could be—what we could be— you'd see it."

She stared at me.

"I couldn't stop thinking about it," I said, words tumbling now. "About our trips there. About you. About Violet. It's the place where everything began, and where it felt like we started over. I didn't want to leave it behind."

Her lips parted, stunned.

Softer now, I said, "I was going to ask you... I want you... to come with me. To move in. To make that place our home. Together."

Tears welled in her eyes. "You were going to do that? For us?"

"I already did."

She looked around again, this time with something like stunned wonder.

"Mallie," I said, stepping closer, cupping her face, "I don't want a life without you in it. Not part-time. Not long-distance. I want coffee with you in the mornings and to fall asleep with you on my chest at night. I want that goddamn squeaky screen door and a front porch swing that's always waiting. I want you. Always."

She let out a breath like she'd been holding it for weeks.

"I thought I was just surprising you," she whispered. "But you were already planning to change everything. Without me."

"With you, Mallie, with you." I smiled, "You are everything."

Her face changed. The wonder drained out of her eyes like the tide pulling back from shore. She took a step back, just enough that my hands slipped from her face.

"But you didn't even ask me," she said, her voice low and trembling. "You just made this... this huge decision all on your own. You didn't even ask me if I wanted that life."

I froze.

She shook her head slowly. "My whole fucking life, everyone's made decisions for me. My parents. Devin. Sonny. And I thought you were different." Her voice cracked on the last word. "I thought..."

She didn't finish. She turned, fast, grabbing her

bag as she headed for the door. I followed her, my heart in my throat.

"Mallie, please—wait. Don't go."

But she didn't stop. She yanked open the door and disappeared down the hallway. I caught up to her at the car, just as she was unlocking it.

"Mallie," I said again, softer now. "Please. Talk to me."

She turned, eyes blazing. "You don't get it, Jace. You made this big, sweeping romantic gesture, and yeah, it's beautiful. But you never stopped to ask if I was ready. If I wanted it. If I were even on the same page."

"I just want to build a life with you."

"But you didn't even give me the chance to say yes." Her voice caught. "You took away my choice."

Something hot and defensive burned through me. "Like I had a say with Violet?"

She went rigid. I knew instantly I'd said the wrong thing. The worst thing.

Her face crumpled. "You think I got a choice?" she whispered. "I was fifteen, Jace. I begged my mother to let me tell you, to let me keep her. And she flat out refused and kept me like a prisoner."

"I know." My voice broke. "God, Mallie. I don't blame you. That was stupid. I'm sorry. I shouldn't have said it. I didn't mean it like that."

But she was already stepping back.

"I need a minute," she said, motioning with her hands. "I need... to think about all of this."

"Okay..." I took a breath as I nodded. "Okay... just please—please don't fly home without telling me."

She got in the car and drove away, and I stood there with my hands on my hips, watching the taillights blur.

The moment the silence settled, I started to spiral. Of course, I'd screwed this up. Of course, I'd said the one thing that would hurt her most. I wanted to punch something, to take it all back. I wanted to chase her, but I knew better.

Instead… I called my mom.

She picked up on the second ring. "Jameson?"

I didn't say anything at first. Just let out a shaky breath.

"Oh no," she said gently. "What happened?"

I told her everything. How I thought surprising Mallie with the beach house would be sweet and romantic. How I hadn't asked. How I'd said something I shouldn't have.

She was quiet for a beat, then said, "Give her some time. You two always had something rare. I saw it even when you were kids. Mallory was always your person."

"I hope she still is," I whispered.

"She is," my mom said, like she already knew. "You just have to let her find her way back."

But would she? Or had I ruined everything?

CHAPTER THIRTY-NINE

Mallie

Present Day

I gripped the wheel so tight my knuckles ached, hot tears blurring the streetlights into streaks. God, I was furious. Furious at him for throwing Violet in my face—like I'd ever had a choice either. Like fifteen-year-old me hadn't begged and pleaded, like I hadn't been locked in my own house until it was too late. He knew better. He had to know better.

And the beach house. That fucking beach house. Who does that? Who drops a mortgage on forever like it's some grand romantic gesture, without even talking to me first? Like surprising me was supposed to erase the fear that had lived in my chest since I was old enough to lose everything, like I wouldn't look at those papers and feel the ground drop out from under me.

I knew what he wanted. He wanted it to be bold. Permanent. But to me, it felt like he'd packed up our future in neat little boxes and handed it to me fully built. No questions, no conversation. No space for me to decide a goddamn thing.

I swiped angrily at my cheeks, breath stuttering. Because the truth was, I'd walked in on his apartment already in pieces. His life stacked in boxes, like leaving it all behind was easy. Like it didn't scare me half to death to think of moving in together, to think of him being all-in when I wasn't even sure we had figured out us yet.

And beneath the fury, beneath the ache, was the smallest, sharpest fear of all—that maybe he didn't know me as well as I thought. I wasn't the same girl he'd remembered and grown up with. I wasn't her anymore, not after everything. What if she were who he wanted, and I couldn't be her anymore?

So I kept driving, angry tears burning tracks down my face, as if I drove fast enough, I could outrun the words we'd just hurled, the house he'd already bought, the years we'd already lost. But my chest still thudded with his voice, his hurt, the way he'd looked at me like I'd just ripped the ground out from under him, too.

The green highway sign flashed past—Beach Access—and before I could think better of it, I took the exit. I'd never been to a beach in Southern California. Rockport was the only beach I'd ever known, our beach, and the ache in my chest told me maybe I needed the ocean, even if it wasn't ours.

I followed the signs until they funneled me into a crowded public lot. The place was swarming with so many people—families with coolers, teenagers dragging surfboards, music blaring from someone's speaker. I shoved my hands in my pockets and walked down to the sand.

It wasn't like Rockport. Not even close. Too crowded, too loud, voices colliding with gulls and car horns and the endless hum of traffic behind me. But when I sat down in the damp sand, the waves still came. They didn't care about people, or parking lots, or my anger. They kept rolling, steady and relentless, and the sound curled through me in a way that felt so familiar.

The waves were him. *Jace.* Every summer. Every promise. Every piece of me that still wanted to believe we were meant to survive this. And I let the water's rhythm thrum against me until it felt like I could breathe again. Then I pushed myself up, brushing sand off my jeans, and crossed the street toward a strip of souvenir shops and boardwalk vendors.

The air smelled like fried dough and sunscreen, with tourists bustling past, carrying shopping bags and dripping ice cream cones. I ducked into a store and fingered the racks until I settled on something cheap—a bracelet strung with shells. Nothing special. It was just a tourist trinket, but on my wrist, it became a talisman—a little shield against the world and the fault lines running through me.

I tugged my sleeve down over it and walked back out, back to my car, not sure if I felt steadier or heavier. I didn't know how to feel, but that ridiculous bracelet made me feel calmer, like I had something to hold on to.

The beach and strip mall faded in the rearview, and I drove aimlessly until I found a coffee shop that looked inviting. It seemed like the perfect place to sit and think about everything. The bell over the door chimed as I walked in, and the scent of cinnamon hung in the air. A row of empty stools lined the counter. I took the third one and pulled my sweatshirt sleeves over my palms.

The barista hovered with a tired smile. "Latte?" he asked.

I nodded. I didn't need the caffeine—just the warmth. When he slid the mug over, I wrapped both hands around it and let the warmth climb back into my fingers as I tried to quiet the storm in my chest. The fight replayed again and again—his boxes stacked, the mortgage papers on the counter, the look on his face when I got in the car. I'd told myself I should just get on a plane, that maybe distance was safer. But the truth was, I didn't want safe. I didn't want to leave it like that.

I'd been sitting there a while, stirring sugar into the foam, when a man's voice broke through. "Seat taken?"

I shook my head without looking up. "No."

He settled onto the stool beside me, ordering black coffee. We didn't talk at first, just the clink of his spoon against the mug and the hiss of the espresso machine behind us. But somehow, the quiet gave way. First, he made a comment about the weather, and then I said something about the crowd at the beach, and suddenly, words spilled out of me.

Maybe it was the fact that he was a stranger I'd never see again, but one thing led to another, and before I knew it, I was telling him everything. About those summers, about Jace, about Violet. About the fight. About the beach house. About the way love terrified me because losing it once had already broken me.

He listened, quiet, elbows on the counter, watching me carefully until I trailed off. Then he set his mug down and said, "Sounds to me like you're fighting the wrong battle."

I blinked at him. "What do you mean?"

"You're mad because he didn't ask," he said gently, "but isn't that because you already knew your answer?"

The words settled in my chest, sharp and steady. My throat burned. Because he was right. I wasn't afraid of Jace. I was scared of choosing him, of us choosing each other, and watching it come apart in our hands. But I wanted Jace. God, I wanted him—more than anything.

The man drained the last of his coffee and set the mug down with a soft clink. Pushing back from the counter, he slid a few bills under the saucer and reached for his jacket.

"Love's a risk every time," he said, voice low. "No guarantees. But when it's been there from the start..." His eyes met mine, kind, knowing. "...that kind of thread doesn't snap easily."

Before I could find words, he gave me a slight nod and turned toward the door. The bell chimed as he stepped out, leaving me staring at my still untouched latte and the ache of his truth still ringing in my ears.

Before I knew what I was doing, I already had my phone in my hand, heart hammering. I stared down at Jace's name on the screen for a long second, then pressed call.

My voice cracked on the first words, "Can I... can I come back? I don't want to end it like that."

There was a long silence, the kind that could have been goodbye. My chest seized, but then he whispered my name, relief heavy in the sound, and said, "You never have to ask."

The drive twisted on for twenty minutes, following the blue line on my phone. By the time I got there, he was already opening the door. His hair was mussed from running his hands through it, his eyes wild with sleeplessness—and when I stepped inside and wrapped my arms around his waist, pressing my forehead against his chest, the world tilted back into place.

"I'm sorry," I whispered, voice muffled against

his shirt. "For storming out. For blowing up."

His arms locked tight around me, his chest rising hard with every breath. "I'm sorry I didn't ask you. It was shitty. I should've talked to you first."

I felt him swallow against my temple, his voice rough when it came. "I'll rip up the papers if you want. Or sell it. Whatever it takes."

The words caught me off guard, thick with sincerity, like he meant every bit of it. He'd bought a whole future without me, and now he was ready to burn it down if it wasn't ours.

My throat tightened as I lifted my face to his, searching his eyes as mine burned. "You really want to make a life there?"

His answer came without hesitation. "Only if it's with you."

I kissed him, slow and aching, and when I pulled back, I found myself smiling through the sting of tears. "Well," I breathed, "I guess we'd better finish packing."

For a second, he just stared, eyes wide, lips parted, like he was afraid to blink in case the moment disappeared. Then quietly he asked, "You're sure?"

I rested my forehead against him, the weight in my chest finally lifting. "I've never been more sure of anything in my life."

My gaze swept over the towers of half-packed boxes again—but this time without fear. I pushed up my sleeves, pulled my hair up in a ponytail with the hair tie on my wrist, and crouched beside the nearest one.

My fingers traced the cardboard edge before I looked up at him. "Packing tape?"

He blinked at me, like he'd forgotten what language was. "Hmm?"

I brushed past him with a smirk. "Because if we're doing this, we'd better hurry up before I decide the only thing I really want to unpack... is you."

His laugh broke the tension in the room, rough and relieved, and I thought it was the best sound I'd ever heard. He found the tape gun, handed it over, and our fingers lingered together a beat too long.

"We're okay?" he asked, voice low.

I sealed the box and met his eyes. "We're more than okay. And I think we were always headed there."

I didn't have to say where. We both knew. The beach house. The ocean. Our home. He kissed me once more, grateful and gentle, and then we started taping boxes shut together.

By Wednesday, we put the packing on hold. The Midnight Run's hometown show was finally here. The one that never got its moment before the crash.

Jace had been running on energy drinks and coffee, rehearsing late with the guys, and every night he came home with that same spark in his eyes, like the boy I used to know, the one who believed music could save him.

The club wasn't big, but it was full, a sold-out show, hot and buzzing with sound. The air smelled like beer, sweat, and electricity. Every light pulsed in time with the heartbeat of the crowd.

Jace's parents drove in from San Bernardino, and I stood with them near the side of the stage. Tessa wrapped me in a hug the second she saw me, her perfume soft and familiar.

"It's good to see you, sweetheart," she said, her voice thick with pride.

"You too," I murmured.

Fred gave me a quiet nod and a smile that said

everything. The band filtered out one by one, greeted by cheers. When Jace stepped into the lights, the noise nearly lifted the roof.

They tore through the first few songs, tight and alive. The band had their rhythm back—the kind that came from muscle memory and love.

Midway through, Jace slung his guitar low and grinned into the mic. "Before we keep going, we gotta thank a few people," he said, scanning the room as the noise settled. "Our families, our friends—everyone who kept believing in us when we couldn't even stand up straight. You're the reason we're here tonight."

The crowd cheered again, whistles echoing from the back. But then Jace set his guitar carefully on the stand, took the mic off, and started walking toward my side of the stage. My stomach flipped. Oh god… this was it.

"There's one more person," he said, voice warm, carrying over the room. "Even when we lost touch, she never really left me. Every song, every storm… I think I was just trying to find my way back to her."

The light followed him, and suddenly I was in it, too.

"This is Mallie," he said, eyes locked on mine. "My best friend. My girlfriend. My heart."

The crowd erupted, and before I could process what was happening, he reached for my hand and gently tugged me a few steps forward.

"Come on," he whispered, low and teasing. "Just give them a wave."

My cheeks burned as I did, laughter bubbling up as I felt hundreds of eyes on me. When I turned back to him, he was smiling, soft and full of something that made everything else disappear.

He leaned in close enough for only me to hear and

murmured, "Couldn't have done any of it without you."

He pressed a kiss to my cheek before I slipped back into the wings, heart pounding.

As he pressed the mic back into the stand, he said, "Now, let's get this place jumping."

The band launched into the next song, and he turned back to the crowd, energy snapping through the air like electricity. From where I stood, I could see it all—the music, the joy, the commitment they all had for each other.

Tessa wiped at her eyes beside me, whispering something about how proud she was. I just smiled, that shell bracelet cool against my wrist, and the future tugging at the edge of my mind.

In a few days, we'd be packing the last box into the truck and heading back to Texas. Back to Rockport. Back to the place where it all began. And as Jace's voice filled the room, I knew—this time, we were ready.

CHAPTER FORTY

Jace

Present Day

The U-Haul sounded like it might rattle apart before
we even cleared Los Angeles, but I didn't care. I had
both hands steady on the wheel and a grin I
couldn't wipe off. Every few minutes, I checked the
side mirror just to see Mallie in the Tacoma tucked
behind me. She looked so small in my truck, her hair
whipping in the wind with the windows down, her
arm resting on the door, sunglasses on, like she
didn't have a care in the world. And every time I
saw her there, following me, it hit me again—she
was here. With me.

She'd stayed two weeks past when she was
supposed to fly out, canceling her ticket like it was
nothing. We'd packed up my whole life together—
guitars, stacks of records, that wobbly college coffee
table, too many band shirts and hoodies, not nearly
enough dishes. She'd found the box of letters I'd
written her over the years and never sent. I hadn't
even tried to hide them. She hadn't brought them up
yet—but I knew her. She'd read every word once we

338

made it to the beach house.

It took us three days to make the drive to Texas. Three days of long highways, cheap motels, and gas station coffee that tasted like mud but kept us going.

The first night, somewhere in Arizona, we sat on the tailgate of the Tacoma eating greasy burgers under a sky full of stars. She leaned against me, her laughter brushing warm across my neck when I told her the U-Haul was giving me tinnitus. I pressed a fry against her lips just to make her roll her eyes, and when she opened her mouth, I kissed the salt from her smile. The desert felt endless around us, but I couldn't see past her.

At one of the rest stops, she laughed at the way I couldn't sit still, tapping my boot against the bumper, drumming out rhythms against my thigh.

"You're worse than David was when he was sugared up at the beach house," she teased.

I told her she'd just forgotten how restless I was without a guitar in my hands.

The second night, somewhere in New Mexico, we got stuck in a motel room with two twin beds because the place was overbooked. The broken AC rattled as bad as the U-Haul, and the walls were so thin we could hear someone's TV two doors down. She curled up on one bed, me on the other, but by midnight she crossed the room in her socks, slid under my scratchy motel blanket, and tucked herself against me.

We lay there in the dark, whispering. We talked about nothing and everything all night long as I held her. About Violet. About our summers. About the years we'd lost. It wasn't all easy, but it was honest. We didn't make love that night—not with the paper-thin walls and the weight of the road ahead—but we didn't need to. It was enough just to hold her, to fall asleep with her heartbeat under my hand.

By the time we crossed into Texas, the miles had started to blur, but every gas station stop felt like a snapshot I wanted to keep—her rolling her eyes when I bought a pack of bubblegum cigarettes, me catching her dancing along with the radio in the candy aisle when she thought I wasn't watching. I loved the way her smile came easier now, freer, like she was finally letting herself believe in things again.

Saturday afternoon, the sun was high when we turned down Sonny and Claire's street. Pulling into the driveway, I killed the engine and climbed out, wiping my palms on my jeans. She rolled up in the Tacoma a second later, cut the engine, and stepped out. For a second, we just looked at each other across the driveway, both of us knowing what this meant.

"You ready?" I asked, grinning despite the lump in my throat.

She nodded, swallowing hard. "I still can't believe you really bought it."

"*We bought it.* The beach house is ours now," I said, reaching for her hand when she came close enough.

That's when Claire stepped out onto the porch, a mug in hand and a smile that looked way too much like approval. She waved, coming down the steps to meet us. There was a dolly leaned against the porch rail, as if Sonny had been waiting all morning for this moment.

By the time we had loaded Mallie's things it hit me—she really didn't have much to move. Years of drifting around the world, of never staying long enough to unpack, had left her life trimmed down to a couple of duffels, three boxes, and a few keepsakes. Everything she owned fit into the Tacoma's bed with room to spare.

Claire disappeared into the garage and came back a few moments later. "I've still got some furniture from my old apartment," she said, almost sheepish. "A dresser, chest of drawers, a lamp. I'm never going to use them. You could."

Mallie froze for a second, her brow creasing like she wasn't sure if it was an offer or a pity gift. "Are you serious?"

Claire smiled in that no-nonsense way of hers. "They'll be happier in Rockport than gathering dust in the garage here."

I watched Mallie's throat tighten as she nodded, her voice quiet. "Thank you."

It was such a simple thing—secondhand furniture—but I could see what it meant to her. She'd been a nomad for so long. A dresser. A lamp. A chest of drawers. It was… roots.

By the time we had everything in the Tacoma's bed, Sonny was leaning on the tailgate, arms crossed like he'd already made up his mind. "Why don't we ride down with you? Claire and I can drive the truck. We can help you unload, and then you can drop us at the airport in Corpus."

Mallie's eyes flicked to mine, soft and grateful, and gave me a subtle nod, like she couldn't quite believe she wasn't in this alone anymore.

"Yeah," I said, cinching down the last strap. "That works."

A little later, the plan snapped into place. Mallie would ride with me in the U-Haul, and Sonny and Claire would follow in my truck, flying back home in a few days. The only loose end was Bandit.

Claire called Darci, and she showed up the next

morning in oversized shades, a tote bag that looked ninety percent snacks, and Alex in her wake. Bandit saw her and torpedoed—seventy-five pounds of joy slamming into her. She laughed, braced, let him cover her in kisses.

Then she saw Mallie as we were tightening the straps in the truck bed. Her laughter thinned to a soft hush, and she came over, setting her hands on Mallie's shoulders and whispered something I couldn't catch. Mallie's mouth trembled into a smile, and Darci pulled her in, hugging like gravity. Darci barely cleared Mallie's shoulder, but she held on like she meant to keep her.

Alex stood on the porch with Bandit, the leash looped loose in his hand. Darci stepped in front of me and took off her sunglasses, eyes all glitter and steel with a saccharin smile.

"Break her heart and I break your kneecaps. With love."

I let out a breath that wanted to be a laugh. "Understood," I said.

She studied me for a beat, then nodded like I'd passed a pop quiz I hadn't known I was taking. "Good boy." She jerked her chin toward Mallie. "Hydrate her. Feed her. Tell her she's the best thing that ever happened to you as often as you think you should."

I broke out in a wide grin. "I can do that."

"Do it loud," she said, sliding the sunglasses into her hair. "She pretends she doesn't need it. But... every girl does."

Behind us, Sonny slammed the Tacoma's tailgate, and Claire climbed in. He gave a wave to Alex, who lifted a hand and said, "We've got him. Go make waves."

Mallie slid into the U-Haul beside me, slipping

her flip flops off, knees up, her hand finding mine. I started the engine, checked the mirror, and pulled onto the road.

The drive south stretched over half the day. The U-Haul sounded like it was held together with duct tape, but every time I checked the side mirror, the Tacoma was steady behind me, Sonny at the wheel, Claire in the passenger seat. Mallie sat beside me in the cab, her legs tucked up, her elbow resting on the open window.

We made our first stop at a gas station outside Waco. Sonny grabbed an energy drink, and Claire bought a bag of peanut butter M&M's and passed them around as we stretched our legs. Mallie stuck her tongue out at me when I stole the last handful, and I laughed so hard my cheeks ached.

For lunch, we stopped in Austin and went to El Arroyo. Claire fussed over Mallie, making sure she ate more than a couple of spoonfuls of rice, and Sonny insisted on paying for our meal.

After Austin, we drove straight to Rockport with long, boring stretches of highway. The closer we got to the coast, the more Mallie leaned toward the window, like she could already smell the salt air.

By the time we turned onto the familiar stretch of road leading into Rockport, the air was thick with the promise of the ocean. My chest thudded hard, steady, like a drumbeat I'd been waiting for all my life.

The U-Haul groaned as I pulled it to a stop in the sandy driveway. In the mirror, Sonny parked the Tacoma behind us as dust plumed around the tires. I looked over at Mallie. Her eyes were shining, the light catching every shade of hope I'd ever dreamed of seeing on her face. We weren't just moving things. We were moving her life into mine. This was ours.

And now? We were home.

Claire was the first one out, stretching, her smile all warm approval. "Oh my God," she breathed, a grin breaking across her face. "It's perfect. We're totally coming back for Labor Day. BBQ, beach chairs, fireworks—you can't stop me."

Mallie laughed, her hand finding mine as she slid out of the cab. I swear I could feel the tremor of nerves running through her, but her smile was steady.

Sonny leaned against the hood of the Tacoma, hands in his pockets, giving the house a slow once-over. "Yep," he drawled, deadpan. "Same sad blue paint. Same crooked porch. Smells like the same dead fish in the air. Real dream house, Jameson."

I shot him a look as I walked up the steps to unlock the door. "Good thing you're not on the mortgage."

Mallie elbowed me lightly, but I saw the way her lips tugged upward. She knew Sonny's sarcasm was his version of affection.

We hauled boxes first, then my bed and frame, and finally Claire's hand-me-down dresser and chest of drawers. It took all four of us to muscle the heavier pieces through the narrow doorways, the wood scraping against the door frames worn by salt air and time. The house groaned as if it were getting used to us again.

Inside, Claire immediately started rearranging things in her head. "Dresser in the corner by the window," she said, pointing. "Lamp on the nightstand. You just need some curtains— something light and breezy. Oh, and don't forget to get some citronella candles for the porch and patio. Trust me."

Sonny pushed back the chest of drawers with a

grunt and wiped his hands on his jeans. "Or," he said, "you leave it the way it is, let the place rot a little more, and call it *authentic coastal charm.*"

Claire rolled her eyes, but Mallie was already running her hands over the smooth top of the dresser, her hair falling loose from her ponytail. She looked up at me, her smile small but certain.

"It feels real now."

And God, it did. Seeing her here, settled into a room that wasn't temporary, wasn't borrowed, wasn't just a stop along the way... this was ours. This was home.

When I wrapped my arms around her from behind, she leaned back into me, her head against my chest, and I thought, Sonny can make all the sarcastic cracks he wants, Claire can start planning holidays, but we were here. Together. Finally.

By the time we had most of the furniture inside and Claire had fussed over where to put a floor lamp, the sun was dropping low. We were all starving, too tired to drive into town, so we cobbled together something simple, a spaghetti dinner from ingredients Claire had insisted on bringing "just in case," complete with frozen garlic bread in the oven and a salad from a bag.

We ate standing up at the kitchen island, and it felt less like moving in and more like some half-improvised celebration.

Later, the four of us drifted onto the porch, beers in hand from a 12-pack Sonny bought at one of our gas station stops. He and Claire claimed the porch swing, its rusty chains creaking with every lazy sway, while Mallie and I took the steps. The wood was still warm from the sun, and when she leaned into me, her shoulder pressing into mine, I felt like the last piece of the day finally clicked into place.

Sonny stretched his long legs out in front of him, beer dangling from his fingers.

"We brought a blow-up mattress and a quilt," he said, nodding toward the Tacoma. "Couple of pillows, too. Figured we'll leave 'em here, stash 'em in a closet for the next time. That way, Claire and I don't have to sleep on the floor when we come mooch off your beach house."

"Like you used to mooch off Mom and Dad?" Mallie asked, grinning.

"Tradition," he said, winking as he lifted his beer in a toast.

"Future visits," Claire said firmly, her head on his shoulder. "Labor Day's first—like a housewarming for you guys. After that... Thanksgiving, maybe Christmas. And one day, all of us will be back here with kids in tow—babies napping inside, toddlers building sandcastles, bigger kids racing to the water." She turned her face toward Sonny then, and the look she gave him made it clear exactly whose babies she meant.

Mallie laughed softly, but her hand slipped into mine, fingers twining tight. When I glanced at her, I saw the way her gaze had gone distant, soft with memory. And I knew exactly what she was thinking.

Because I was thinking the same thing, of our own summers as kids on this very sand, barefoot and sunburned, with freezer pops in our hands, staying out until the stars came alive. Those weeks had shaped us, bound us. And now we were back, standing at the edge of something ready to make new summers of our own.

I didn't care that the house might need some work, the U-Haul still had a shit-ton of boxes, or that Claire and Sonny were inviting themselves over. This was exactly what I wanted—a home already full of laughter and love.

CHAPTER FORTY-ONE

Mallie

Present Day

The last box thudded onto the porch, Sonny grabbing it and carrying it upstairs. We'd done it — emptied the U-Haul until there was nothing left but the smell of dust and miles. Jace brushed the sweat off his forehead and grinned at me, the kind of grin that made me want to kiss him right there in front of Sonny and Claire. Instead, I picked up the lamp Claire had given me, carried it inside, and set it on the dresser like it had always belonged.

We left them at the house the next morning, and I followed in the Tacoma as Jace drove the U-Haul into town. He swung into the rental lot, the truck groaning as he cut the engine, and I pulled in behind, watching him climb down from the cab and hand over the keys. It felt like a small exhale. The moving part was done, and now the rest could begin.

We grabbed some food on the way back, and after a quick meal, it was time for them to fly back to Dallas. We stood in the driveway, the four of us shuffling around trying to stretch out the moment before it ended. Claire hugged me first, all warmth and certainty, whispering promises of Labor Day and long weekends that would stitch us together as a family. I held her tight, grateful for the way she already believed in both me and this place.

Sonny was next, his arms wrapping around me tight, almost lifting me off my feet, the kind of hug that pressed everything he couldn't put into words straight into my chest. He smelled like coffee and his familiar citrus scent that always grounded me.

He wasn't just saying goodbye—he was reminding me of every time he'd picked me up when I'd fallen, every time he'd stood between me and the world. When he finally pulled back, he pressed a kiss into my hair and whispered, "You've got this, sis."

I nodded, throat tight, though my voice wouldn't come.

He moved on to Jace, pulling him in close. Their heads bent together, voices low. I couldn't catch Sonny's words, just the weight of them, the way Jace's shoulders straightened as he listened.

Then Jace nodded once, firm. "Always," he said.

Sonny clapped him on the back, the moment over before I could ask what it meant.

Claire was already sliding into the cab of the truck, calling for Sonny to climb in. Jace gave me a quick kiss and hopped into the driver's side.

Sonny rolled down his window and gave me a smirk with a nod as he said, "We'll see you soon, Mal."

I grinned and watched as the Tacoma rolled down the drive, gravel spitting under the tires, until the taillights disappeared around the bend as they headed towards Corpus.

The silence afterward was different. The house was quiet in a way that felt alive. I walked through each room on the lower level slowly, touching the edges of boxes, dragging my fingers along a door frame, breathing in the weight of everything. This wasn't a borrowed place anymore. Not a dream. Not just summers that were long gone. It was ours.

I stood in the living room a moment before my feet carried me up the staircase. The boards creaked in all the same places they used to, the walls still painted the same shade of faded blue of a hundred summers. At the very top, I stopped outside the door at the end of the hall. Jace's old room. The one where he'd stayed every summer. The one where we stopped being kids. The night everything changed, when we first gave ourselves to each other—awkward, scared, wrecked in the best way.

My hand lingered on the knob before I pushed it open.

The room was empty now, stripped down to bare floorboards and some sun-bleached curtains that stirred in the breeze left by the previous owners. But it still had the same smell I remembered, still hummed with memories. I could still see him sprawled across that queen-size bed, guitar balanced on his chest. I could hear our laughter in the dark, the way we whispered secrets like they might never come true if anyone else ever heard them.

I stepped inside, running my hand over the windowsill, the wood worn smooth. So much had happened here—so much had ended, and so much had begun. And standing there, I felt the ache in my chest ease.

I whispered into the stillness, "We made it back." The words settled into the empty room, soft and sure, like they belonged here as much as we did.

And I knew it was going to be okay.

After Jace got back, we didn't finish unpacking. Not even close.

The mattress was still on the floor of our bedroom, the one with the window that faced the ocean. The one we'd stayed in every time we'd been here this year. The headboard and the frame still leaned against the wall, wrapped in a blanket, and the boxes were stacked in uneven towers like quiet sentinels, keeping watch while we tried to figure out where everything should go.

I flopped on the mattress, and my heart felt light.

Jace walked in behind me, his shirt damp with sweat, two glasses of water in hand, both sloshing with every step, and I could tell he'd forgotten which one he'd already drunk out of.

He grinned and said, "I'll get better at being domestic."

I sat up and accepted a glass, leaning into him and taking a sip. "What are you talking about? You hung string lights over the back patio and fixed the ceiling fan. You're already perfect."

He kissed me then like a promise.

Later, we ate tacos on the couch from the shop that was once the ice-cream parlor we used to sneak to as teenagers. I tore off a piece of tortilla and popped it into his mouth, just to see him smile.

We lit a candle in the bathroom because we couldn't remember which box the lightbulbs were in. We brushed our teeth standing side by side in the too-small bathroom, and Jace made faces in the mirror. I rolled my eyes and tried not to laugh with a mouth full of toothpaste.

We curled up on the mattress in our room with nothing but a single sheet and the sound of the waves outside. The ocean was louder than I remembered. But comforting. Like a lullaby that didn't need words.

He tucked me against him, and I traced patterns on his chest.

"This doesn't feel real," I whispered.

He kissed the top of my head. "It does to me."

We didn't talk about Violet. We didn't talk about the past, the years we lost, or what might come next. We just lay there in the dark, wrapped around each other like we were holding the whole fragile world between us.

Eventually, his breathing slowed. And sometime around midnight, just before I slipped under, I felt his hand find mine beneath the sheet and squeeze once, like a secret only the two of us knew.

Sometime in the night, he woke and curved in behind me, his palm tracing a slow line down my side, like he needed to remind himself I was real. His forehead pressed to the back of my head as he kissed my neck, and I felt his breath shiver out.

"We're home, Mallie," he said, softer this time.

I turned and pulled him closer, fisting the cotton of his shirt, until his mouth found mine. The kiss was unhurried, the kind that didn't need to prove anything. It just was—like us, like this house, like the tide rolling in.

He shifted, bracing on his elbows, lowering himself over me, the mattress groaning beneath us. A memory popped up, of us, our first time—the nervous laughter, the clumsy way we'd figured each other out. This wasn't that. This was steady, certain, a lifetime's worth of longing eased into the curve of his body against mine.

His hand slid beneath my t-shirt, and I arched to meet him. When he whispered my name against my throat, I felt it sink all the way through me, rooting deeper than anything ever had.

His mouth followed, kissing lower, finding the edge of my shirt. I gasped as he pushed it up, his knuckles skimming my ribs, the rough pad of his thumb circling my skin like he needed to memorize every inch.

"Jace..." I breathed, but it came out wrecked, more plea than warning.

"Tell me to stop," he rasped, his forehead pressing to mine.

I shook my head, tugging at his shirt until I got my hands on his bare skin. "Don't you dare."

His mouth crashed back to mine, hungrier this time. His palm cupped my breast, thumb brushing over my hard nipple, teasing until I whimpered into his kiss. He growled low in his chest, and I cried out, arching hard into him.

The mattress groaned as he shifted over me, his thigh wedging between mine. Instinct took over—I rocked against him, desperate, friction sparking sharp and sweet until I was trembling. He bit down gently on my bottom lip, breaking the kiss only to trail his mouth down my neck, across my collarbone, lower still.

I shoved at his shirt, and he tore it off in one motion. My t-shirt followed, tossed aside carelessly until it was just skin and heat between us. His mouth closed over my nipple, tongue flicking, sucking until I gasped and fisted his hair.

"Fuck, Mallie," he groaned, the sound vibrating against me. His hand slid down, skimming my stomach, dipping beneath the waistband of my panties.

I begged, "Please."

He shoved my underwear down as his fingers

slid through my wetness, circling slow, teasing until my body was trembling under his touch. Then one finger sank inside me, then another, curling just right, and my back arched off the mattress with a strangled cry.

He kissed me hard, swallowing my sounds, his thumb pressing against my clit as his fingers worked me open. I felt the coil pull taut as my body clenched around him, every nerve on edge as he coaxed me higher.

"Let go," he whispered against my mouth. "I've got you."

And I did. The orgasm tore through me, shaking me apart, leaving me gasping into his kiss. Before the aftershocks even faded, he was shoving his boxers down, his cock heavy and hard against my thigh. He braced himself above me, panting, his forehead pressed to mine.

"Where'd we put the condoms?" he rasped.

"Drawer," I managed, nodding toward the nightstand.

He fumbled for one, tore it open with shaking hands, and rolled it on. Then he was at my entrance, pushing inside, slow and steady. My gasp turned into a moan, the stretch burning and perfect.

"Jesus, Mallie..." His voice broke on my name.

He bottomed out, and for a moment, we just breathed—foreheads pressed together, bodies locked, the world narrowing to this. Him. Me. Us.

On a gasp, I breathed out, "Fuck... you feel so good..."

Then he started to move. Slow at first, every thrust deliberate, like he wanted me to feel how much he meant it. How much I meant to him. The friction built, sharp and sweet, until I was clinging to him, nails digging into his shoulders.

I met him thrust for thrust, gasping his name, begging for more, for harder. He gave it to me, hips snapping, the sound of skin on skin mixing with the rhythm of the waves crashing outside.

"Always you," he groaned against my mouth, his thrusts turning frantic. "It's always been you."

The world shattered with me, my body clenching hard around him as the orgasm tore through me. Tears spilled hot down my cheeks before I could stop them, my sob catching in my throat.

"It was always you, too," I gasped, my voice breaking. "It's always been you—I never stopped, I never could—Jace, I love you so much."

The words tumbled out raw and shaking, my face wet, my body trembling beneath his. His mouth crushed against mine, swallowing the sobs, his rhythm carrying me through the quake of it until I collapsed against him, spent and undone.

The waves outside beat steadily against the shore as our breathing slowed, both of us clinging like we were afraid the other might slip away. His weight eased over me, shifting to his side, but he didn't let me go. His arms wrapped around me, pulling me close, his chest damp with sweat against my back.

For a long moment, he just held me. Quiet. Steady. My tears dampened his arm where it curved beneath my cheek.

Then, in the hush of the room, his voice came—low, rough, but sure. "I love you, Mallie."

The words wrapped around me like a warm current, and I knew—this time, we weren't breaking.

CHAPTER FORTY-TWO

Mallie

Present Day - One month later

I'd been avoiding the last of the boxes. They sat stacked in the corner of the bedroom, half-opened, waiting for me to deal with them. Every time I walked past, I told myself I'd do it tomorrow.

But this morning, Jace had to go into town, and I stayed home. So I pulled one open.

The first couple of boxes were nothing but clutter —shirts, paperbacks, a picture frame swaddled in newsprint. Then I opened the next one and found a smaller box inside. I knew it immediately—the one I'd unearthed when we packed his apartment. Inside lay a bundle of envelopes, uneven and frayed at the edges, tied with twine. My name sprawled across each in Jace's hand.

My knees gave out, and I sank onto the bed. I'd meant to read them when I found them the first time, but the weight of it had felt like too much. Now, with the house quiet, there was no more running. I lifted the box into my lap and eased it open.

The first letter trembled in my hands as I slid it free.

Mallie,

I don't know how to write this without my hands shaking. My mom told me what your mom said that I forced myself on you. That I hurt you.

It's a lie. You know it. I know it. So why is she saying it? Why are you letting her make me look like a monster? Did you say it too? I keep trying to hear your voice in my head, and all I get is silence, and it makes me feel sick.

I'm so mad I can't think straight. Mad at your mom for making up lies. Mad at mine for looking at me like she's not sure who I am. Mad at you for disappearing and leaving me here with a story that isn't true.

I keep replaying that night—the way you looked at me, the way we kept whispering always like idiots who believed it. Was any of that real?

I can't eat. I can't sleep. I walk around school, and it's like I'm not even there. The star you made me is still on my neck, and I hate it. I've tried to take it off, and I can't. It's the only thing that says I didn't make us up.

I need to talk to you. Not through our moms or anyone else. You and me. If something happened, tell me the truth. If you regret it, just say it. If you wanted me gone, tell me to my face. But don't let this be our story. Don't let a lie be what's left of us.

Please. Say something.

Always,
Jace

By the second paragraph, I couldn't see for the blur in my eyes. I pressed the page to my chest, rocking once like I could fold his younger self into my arms, like I could stitch him back together. Anger flared hot and ugly at the memory of my mother—if I hadn't already hated her, I did now. She'd driven a wedge between us and left him standing there, wondering if I'd ever meant it at all.

He never took off the star necklace, even then. Somehow, he'd still believed in us, even when he was furious.

I grabbed another letter with shaking fingers.

Mallie,

I broke up with her tonight. She was kind and funny, someone I thought maybe could be the one. I wanted it to work. God, I wanted it to so badly.

But every time she laughed, I wanted it to be your laugh. Every time she reached for my hand, I remembered how you used to grab mine first. She looked at me like she was searching for something, and I realized she was searching for the part of me I gave away to you a long time ago.

It wasn't fair to her. It wasn't fair to me either. Because no matter how hard I tried, I couldn't stop comparing her to you. And she always lost. Everyone does.

So I ended it. And now I'm sitting here wondering if I'll spend the rest of my life alone, chasing shadows of you, or if one day you'll come back.

I'd give anything, Mallie. Anything. Just to see again. Just to hear you call me Jace, like you were the first and only person who ever really saw me.

Always,
Jace

My breath caught. He had tried to move on. He had wanted to. And still—even then—I was there, in every laugh, every touch, every corner of his mind. Guilt sliced through me. For her, for him, for all the years we lost.

He'd written *I'd give anything, Mallie. Anything.*

The words blurred again as I reached for the last envelope. It was thicker, the paper newer—the date just a month before we ran into each other again. We were finally here, finally us again, but fear clawed at me—what if this was the letter where he'd finally accepted we were no more? Where he said goodbye to me? My chest ached just thinking of it, like I could be reading the words of a world where we never found our way back.

My hands shook as I held it, every part of me wanting to turn away. But I couldn't—not now, not after everything. Even if it shattered me, I had to see this through.

Mallie,

I don't know why I never told you this when we were still kids at the beach house. Maybe it felt too strange to say out loud, maybe I thought it would scare you, or maybe I just thought I'd always have another summer to tell you everything. But since I don't have that anymore, since you're somewhere else in the world, and we haven't spoken in years, I need to put it somewhere. So I'm putting it here.

The night you gave me the star necklace at the ice cream shop, you said it wasn't much, but to me it felt like everything. I still remember the look you gave me when I slipped it on, and that night, lying in bed, I rubbed the charm through my shirt over and over like it could keep me close to you.

And then something happened.

The room changed, and we were downstairs. We weren't kids anymore. You were older, your hair darker. There were moving boxes everywhere. The room was filled with your laughter. Sonny was there, in the kitchen with a red-haired woman. Another couple nearby—a tiny woman with her hands dusted with flour and a man I'd never seen before leaning close to her.

And then—I'll never forget this—there was some teenage girl in the hallway. Dark hair, curls like mine. She wore glasses, but she looked kind of like you. When she laughed, it was your laugh, I swear. It was uncanny, but her smile looked like mine. And it sent a shiver straight through me.

She looked at me like she knew me. Like she'd been waiting.

Then it was gone. Just the dark walls of the bedroom, the surf outside, and the necklace warm against my skin. But it didn't feel like a dream. It felt like something more.

I should have told you then. I should have told you a hundred things. But I didn't. And now you and I don't talk anymore, and yet—I still feel like it's going to happen. Like the necklace was never just a gift but a thread tying me to you, through everything, no matter what.

I feel this certainty now, and it almost feels like a sense of peace. I don't know when we'll find our way back. I just know we will.

Always,
  Jace

I covered my mouth, sobbing into the paper. He had seen her. Our Violet. Long before she was real, he had carried her like a promise in his chest.

When I finally folded the letter closed, I cradled the stack in both hands. There had been hope written into every line. And it didn't feel like I was reading something from the past. It was like I was holding proof of the future we'd somehow found again.

A moment later, I heard the crunch of his boots on the porch steps and then the creak of the front door. My heart lurched. By the time he pushed the bedroom door open, I was already wiping at my cheeks, though the papers still shook in my hand.

"Mallie?" His voice was soft, questioning.

I looked up, throat tight. "I finally, um, read them." I cleared my throat.

For a second, he just stood there, framed in the doorway, his eyes falling to the stack now in my lap. Then he crossed the room in two strides. He sank beside me on the bed, close enough that our knees touched, but he didn't reach for the letters. He reached for me.

I let him, sliding into his arms, pressing the bundle of envelopes between us. He tucked me under his chin and held me like I was something precious and fragile.

"I never... had the nerve to send them. You weren't supposed to read those," he whispered, voice rough.

"You know I had to," I breathed. "I needed to know."

He pulled back just enough to look at me. His eyes were glassy, unguarded, every wall gone. "And now that you do?"

I swallowed, my fingers brushing an envelope. "Now I know you never stopped. Not even when I thought I'd lost you forever."

His hand cupped my cheek then, his thumb brushing away the wet streak there. And before I could breathe again, his mouth was on mine— hungry, desperate, years of silence and ache spilling into the kiss.

I clutched at his shirt, dragging him closer, the letters slipping to the bed. His other hand tangled in my hair, angling me to him, and I opened for him like I'd been waiting since the beginning of time. The mattress dipped beneath us as he leaned me back, the world narrowing to the heat of his mouth on mine and the weight of his body pressing into me.

When we broke apart, both gasping, his forehead pressed to mine. "Always," he murmured, the word like fire and prayer all at once. With his hands on me and his letters at our feet, I knew—always was real. Always was ours.

EPILOGUE

Present Day - One Year Later

Jace

We were sitting in the waiting room, the kind with vending machines that only take crumpled bills and chairs that creak every time you shift. The type of place where everything felt too quiet and too loud at the same time.

Mallie sat next to me, her hand on top of her bouncing knee. I reached over and slid my hand onto hers, stilling it. She looked over, her eyes soft, a smile tugging at the corners of her mouth.

Sonny had come out to share the news that Claire had just given birth to a little girl. He was supposed to come back out as soon as she was done feeding her.

I leaned in, my lips brushing her ear. "You ever think about doing this?"

She turned, her eyes searching mine. "Of course I do," she said quietly. "I want that. To be married, have a baby... a family."

My heart cracked open a little wider. "With me?"

She nodded, and God, the way she looked at me. "Yeah, of course, with you. I just didn't know if you wanted that, too…" Her voice trailed off softly, "… after everything."

I took a breath, the kind you take before jumping into something that's been calling your name for years.

"I want that, too. I've known that since we were fifteen."

Her eyes widened, blinking like she was trying to catch up to what I just said.

"Really?" she whispered.

I nodded and leaned in to press a kiss to her lips—soft, full of everything I hadn't said. When I pulled back, I shrugged a little. "So… let's do it."

She arched a brow. "Have another… baby?"

I laughed under my breath. "All of it. Let's get married, have babies, and live the kind of life we never thought we'd get."

She stared at me like she was trying to decide if I was serious.

"Wait," she said slowly. "Are you… Are you really asking me to marry you? Right here? In the middle of a hospital waiting room?"

I looked around at the cracked linoleum, the humming soda machine, the vending machine offering stale peanut butter crackers and potato chips. Then back at her.

"Yeah," I said, grinning. "Yes, I am.

Mallory Wright, I want to marry you."

Her eyes locked with mine, a thousand things flickering in their depths.

She broke out in a laugh so hard she nearly dropped her purse. "Are you kidding me right now?"

"Completely serious," I said. "Though I admit the ambiance could be better."

She looked at me like I'd just given her the entire universe.

And then she said, "Okay," voice catching.

I tilted my head. "That a yes?"

She let out a laugh that sounded like home. "Yes. Absolutely yes. I'd love to marry you."

The hospital doors slid shut behind us, and I felt like my chest was cracked wide open.

Mallie tucked her arm through mine, her smile soft and dazed—the way it always was when her heart was too full to hold. We'd just met the baby. All seven squishy pounds of her. Pink-cheeked and sleepy, wrapped in a floral blanket like she'd been swaddled in love from her very first breath. Her name was Amelia.

"She's perfect," Mallory whispered.

I nodded, tightening my arm around her shoulders. "She is."

And maybe it was the joy in the room.

Or maybe it was how Mallory had reached into the bassinet and whispered, "Welcome to the world, Sweetheart," with tears in her eyes. Or maybe I'd just waited long enough.

The drive back home was long. It was filled with golden light and music from the radio. Mallory sat sideways in her seat, barefoot, her hand in mine, humming under her breath.

She thought I was quiet because I was still caught in the moment. But really, I was planning something. Because her yes had never been a question in my mind. I'd carried that answer in my back pocket for years, along with the ring that had been burning a hole in it for months now.

And I was going to do it properly. One more time. Because in just over a week, I'd be leaving for the biggest tour of my life—opening in arenas, headline spots at smaller venues, a team bigger than anything I'd ever had before. She was coming with me for the first leg. Violet would meet up with us for a couple of shows. It was the life I'd dreamed of, but now with something better.

Someone better.

I pulled off the highway without saying a word, driving down a familiar road that curled past the dunes and opened to another part of the stretch of beach where we first kissed again. Where she'd told me she loved me. The same sand where she'd held my hand like it meant something.

"Jace?" she asked, brow furrowing. "Aren't we going home?"

"We're just making a quick stop. You'll see."

We parked, kicked off our shoes, and I took her hand again. I led her barefoot through the sand. The sky was soft pink above us, waves slipping close to our feet.

She turned to look at me, her smile puzzled but glowing. And that's when I dropped to one knee. Her breath caught.

"This," I said quietly, pulling the velvet box from my pocket, "is how I was always supposed to ask you."

Tears welled in her eyes as she covered her mouth.

"I know you already said yes. But I wanted you to have this moment. The one you deserve. With the ocean in the background. With your feet in the sand. With the whole world quiet enough to hear your heart."

I opened the box.

"Mallie, marry me. For real this time. Forever. For Always."

She didn't say a word. She just nodded, dropped to her knees in front of me, and kissed me until the ring was forgotten in the sand and the sky turned purple.

And just like that—our next chapter began.

THE END

Thank you so much for reading THE BEACH HOUSE, book 3 in The Enchanted Heart Series, a magical realism romance series.

I hope you enjoyed it! If you did...

1. Help other people find this book by writing a review.
2. Sign up for my email list so you can know when the next book is coming out.
3. Come follow me on Instagram, TikTok, or Facebook.
4. Use the QR code below to visit my website:

A Peek at The First Sin

You thought you understood love. You haven't met Luc. *The First Sin* is a dark romantasy where immortal devotion collides with fate, memory, and the weight of eternity. What you're about to read is only the prologue — the spark that set everything in motion. If it grips you, the full story is waiting.

PROLOGUE

Long before the Garden was planted or the stars were given names, this tale began elsewhere.

In the beginning, the First Light created the angels, beings of brilliance and beauty and order, flawless in form, without the burden of choice. They were not given souls. They were not meant to wonder. They were meant to serve. To worship. To protect.

But among them stood one unlike any other. He was the most precious to The First Light. He was the brightest of the hosts and created to illuminate. He was the most beautiful. He led the celestial choirs, his voice the golden thread that bound harmony to Heaven itself. When he moved, creation stirred. When he sang, the stars aligned.

Lucifer. The Morning Star. Lightbringer.

He was adored. Admired. Set apart. And yet, there was something in him that even the First Light did not see. He had something different. Not visible. Not named. Not known, even to him. But it flickered beneath his brilliance like a secret spark.

Where others obeyed, *he considered.* Where others worshipped, *he listened.* Where others stood still, *he wandered.* It was not pride. It was curiosity. And that difference would eventually change everything.

But a mere millennium after creating the angels, the First Light grew restless and bored. He longed for more than obedience. He longed for beauty. And so, He created a sacred few—the Heavenly Artisans. Beings of both soul and flame. Endowed with free will and gifted with the power to create not by command, but by *choice.*

To them, He gave the task of shaping Eden. They carved starlight into rivers. Painted dawn into the bones of the world. They strung the skies with constellations and taught the wind how to dance.

But among them was one unlike any other. One who radiated beauty in not just her own being, but in her creations.

Ediphiel. The Maker. The Singer. The Light Within.

Lucifer watched her from afar for centuries. In her, he saw not just beauty. Not just power. He saw freedom. She didn't serve. She *dreamed*. And when he saw her dreaming, *he dared to want.*

One day, he approached her and asked her to teach him. And she did.

Creation became conversation. Conversation became communion. And communion became love. Together, they were something new. Unexpected. Something unspoken. The stars shifted. Trees bloomed out of season. The sun rose too early, as if drawn by their song as time stilled.

The more they were together, the more Lucifer craved her. And on the night their bond was finally sealed, when Ediphiel finally gave her body to his, The First Light's radiance flickered. The raw, defiant spark inside Lucifer collided with the wild, endless wonder of her, and the world burned bright around them, a fierce, forbidden radiance that for one trembling instant outshone everything, including Heaven.

And it noticed. The First Light noticed and shook with rage.

Soon, they were summoned before the Throne. The Seraphim stood in judgment. The Judicars waited, silent, at the top of the Scala Animarum. And a sentence was passed.

The voice of the First Light rang out through the Heavens, not in sorrow, but in fury. It cracked across creation like lightning through crystal, rattled the bones of stars, and split galaxies in silence.

It was the voice that once sang the worlds into being and now turned to judgment. No angel dared lift their eyes. And even Lucifer, brightest of them all, felt his own light recoil.

"Lucifer. The Morning Star. Lightbringer. I made you the first. The brightest. The most beautiful of all My host. Yours was the voice that led the stars in song. I made you the reflection of My radiance to illuminate, not ignite."

But you have burned where you were meant to shine. Your pride has been a torch raised against My own light. And for that, you will fall."

You shall be cast down—not only as a warning, but as a wound in the fabric of creation. Crowned in ash. King of the Damned. The earth shall fear your shadow, and Hell shall kneel at your feet. For an age of ages, you will rule in the absence of grace. And you shall rule alone."

Lucifer said nothing. His wings dimmed. His light flickered low. And slowly, he lowered himself—first his head, then his knees—before the One who made him. Not in defiance. Not in worship. But in something older than both—Grief.

A pause. The hush between the thunder and aftershock.

And then another name was spoken.

But when the voice spoke again, it was different. Quieter. Not soft, but steady. Cold as stone shaped by time. There was no rage, only the sound of unchangeable truth, of laws older than love.

A sentence spoken not from wrath... but from the grief of knowing it must be spoken.

"Ediphiel."

Lucifer's head snapped up. His light flared once—wild, broken. His gaze found her across the span of eternity. She stood alone, no chains—only silence. Her hands were at her sides, her eyes bright, fixed on the throne.

And in that moment, horror carved itself into him. This was his punishment. He had chosen. He had loved. But she had only answered. She had given him beauty and a name for the ache he didn't understand. He had burned for her.

"Ediphiel, Artisan of Eden—your soul shall not die, for it is divine. But it shall be cast into mortality. Reborn again and again, into dust and flesh. Yours will be a name no longer spoken. A memory no longer permitted."

Your soul shall live a thousand lifetimes beneath the veil of forgetting... and it shall never remember why it aches."

Lucifer rose to his feet, but too late. He tried to speak, to reach, to defy. But before he could move, she was gone. Now she would live, but unremembered, unloved, aching for all time, never remembering what they had.

Their love was hidden, and something else rose. A force that would bring about the great unbalancing that twisted their story. And the truth was buried. Because it could not be known that something shaped like this could rival the Creator, that love could shine brighter than obedience. That Lucifer had not fallen out of pride... but for choosing to love someone.

He watched as Judicar Gravem tore a page from the Book of Names. And then... his memories started to fade, and he fell into the fire to forget her for an eternity.

So the story was changed. It was hidden. They said he had grown vain, desiring the throne. That he tried to become the same as The First Light. Because the lie was safer than the truth, because the world could never know the First Sin... was love.

But some lights do not go out. They flicker in memory, in skin, in dreams, in time. And one day, the Morning Star will look into a woman's eyes and see *her*. He will not remember her name. But he will feel it in his bones, in his blood, in the burning center of who he once was. He will remember what it cost him to love her. And this time, he will vow to burn Heaven down before he lets her go.

If you're not ready for obsession, stop now. *The First Sin* is live on Amazon and Kindle Unlimited. Read it before Book 2 makes everything worse.

About the Author

Stephanie Pass hails from a tiny Texas town where she lives with her husband, children, and a Boxer dog who talks more than she does. She writes contemporary romance with magical realism and romantasy. Soon, she will dip her toe into some sci-fi romance. She loves books about love, magic, and high fae. She had her own real-life romance story come true when a chance encounter led her to meet her now husband. When she's not writing romance stories, Stephanie is a mom blogger dancing to Taylor Swift at https://thetiptoefairy.com. But you can often find her at the roller skating rink or dancing at the goth nightclub.

To learn more join Stephanie's email list - https://thetiptoefairy.myflodesk.com/join-romance-list